THE EXECUTIVE MURDER

THE EXECUTIVE MURDER
THE WOODHEAD & BECKER MYSTERIES
BOOK IV

PAUL AUSTIN ARDOIN

THE EXECUTIVE MURDER

Published by Pax Ardsen Books

This book is a work of fiction. Names, characters, businesses, organizations, places, events and incidents either are the product of the author's imagination or are used fictitiously. Any resemblance to actual persons, living or dead, events, or locales is entirely coincidental.

ISBN 978-1-949082-55-5

For information please visit:

www.paulaustinardoin.com

Cover design by Ziad Ezzat of Feral Creative Colony: feralcreativecolony.com

Chapter One

❧

"I feel ridiculous," Bernadette Becker said.

Lieutenant Maura Stevenson, walking briskly alongside Bernadette, turned her head. Her eyes dipped to Bernadette's nondescript black flats and swept up to the oversized shoulders of her gray blazer. "You look fine."

Bernadette grunted. Of course, Maura, who always appeared as if she'd stepped off a fashion runway, would think Bernadette was concerned about her clothing choices. True, the blazer was too hot for a sweltering Independence Day morning. Her uncomfortable flats crunched on the gravel of the parking lot at the Taycheedah Correctional Facility. Her boss may have been trying to reassure her, but her target was off.

"I don't mean my outfit," Bernadette muttered. "It's the S.W.A.T. team."

Agents in helmets and tactical gear: three in front and three behind. Bernadette, though fit and strong, felt small next to them. They all towered over her. Their arms and legs, even under their black official engagement gear, were thick with muscle.

"They're not your entourage." Maura rolled her eyes. "They're here to keep you alive. You're not ending up like Marcie Fisk on my watch."

Bernadette blinked hard. Warden Fisk had been killed less than a month before. Prison riot, officially. Unofficially, both Bernadette and Maura—and nearly everyone else at the Controlled Substance Analysis Bureau—knew her death involved Annika Nakrivo. True, Nakrivo had been in the prison infirmary at the time, slashed across the face in a yard fight. But after evidence appeared of Nakrivo's missing sister in the Taycheedah area—well, as Bernadette often said, it was too coincidental to be coincidental.

Not how Bernadette wanted to spend her Fourth of July. But the front desk supervisor had made a few large purchases since the warden's death: a pair of jet skis and a huge white pickup truck. Suspicious, like he'd been bought off.

But because of the holiday, that front desk supervisor had requested the day off—and so had many of the regular staff. So Bernadette and Maura expected a fresh-out-of-training correctional officer named Matthew Vermeil, usually stationed at Calumet, to be behind the front counter. A stroke of luck. The chances were good that Vermeil wasn't compromised like they suspected the supervisor was.

They stepped from the gravel onto the shiny, wet asphalt of the parking lot, and the mad crunching of eight pairs of feet changed to an orderly marching cadence. The agents all walked in step, like soldiers in formation. Bernadette's feet, and Maura's too, soon fell into the same rhythm.

The rain had poured down on the way from Milwaukee to Fond du Lac, and steam rose from the hot ground. She glanced over her shoulder at the agent following slightly behind her left side. Taycheedah was still a state prison, and the Wisconsin Department of Adult Institutions Policy stated that even federal agents could not bring firearms onto the property. Maura had tried over the course of several days to find a federal judge to exempt CSAB for this one visit, but to no avail. Maura had a judge sign an order allowing Maura and Bernadette to be accompanied by the six agents, even though Taycheedah only allowed two visitors at a time per inmate.

Even with all their firearms in locked cases back in the SUV, the six agents could likely get Maura and Bernadette out of most situations. The agency had trained them to fight in close quarters. If another prison riot broke out, Maura and Bernadette would get out safely. Probably.

A bead of sweat started at the nape of Bernadette's neck and ran down her back. Could have been the heat, but maybe it was nerves. She shook her hands out and exhaled, cheeks puffed out. Were those pins and needles in her hands? Would it be like the last time she was at Taycheedah—or worse, the ambush in Wichita?

A pounding in her ears: her heart was racing. She took a deep, measured breath, then another, and her heart rate slowed after a moment. Still fast, but manageable. She could do this.

On both hands, she tapped her thumbs to the tips of each finger: index, middle, ring, pinkie. Full feeling; no pins and needles. That was a good sign.

Bernadette glanced around the parking lot. No one else. Still an hour before official visiting hours started, but as law enforcement representatives—and with a signed order from Judge Larchmont—they would be allowed to see Annika Nakrivo.

The agent at the front—at least six foot eight—held the door of the guard station open for the others. The formation of the agents subtly changed; one at the rear stepped forward just enough to maintain the three-in-front, three-in-back balance. They *were* trained well.

The guard standing next to the metal detector eyed them all warily. "Visiting hours aren't till noon," he said.

As if choreographed, all six agents, as well as Maura and Bernadette, pulled out their CSAB badges. "Federal agents," Maura said. "Here to speak to an inmate who is a material witness in an ongoing investigation."

"No more than two visitors per inmate," the guard said. "Even for law enforcement."

Maura pulled out the signed order from Judge Larchmont and held it out for the guard.

He leaned forward and glanced at it. "Might not get by the folks in charge of visitation, but as far as I'm concerned, you can go on through." He straightened up and held out a plastic basket. "Sign in on that sheet. Electronics in here. Purses?"

Bernadette shook her head. She and Maura just had their IDs. Only the agents had brought their service weapons, but they were stored in their locked gun cases in the back of the second SUV in the gravel section of the parking lot.

It took several minutes to get processed. The hulking agent who had held the door open signed in first; when Bernadette signed in, she noticed his name was Xavier Reese. A good federal agent name. The agents walked through the metal detector, then the guard passed a wand over all of them before he finally let them go on. Was he just buying time for the gatekeepers in visitation—And how would Matt Vermeil react? Would he stop Maura and Bernadette from interviewing Annika?

As they walked down the corridor between the guard station and the visitation room, Bernadette's breaths came shorter and faster. *Relax*, she told herself, but she couldn't. Maura was in front of Bernadette, so there was no way for Bernadette to read her boss's face. Had Maura wavered from her normal unflappable demeanor?

The corridor emptied into the visitation waiting room, with the same blue plastic chairs Bernadette remembered from her trip to Taycheedah three weeks before. The day of the prison riot, though she had left before it began. Maura stepped to the side and let Bernadette approach the screened counter.

"May I help you?"

Bernadette scrutinized the face of Matt Vermeil behind the Plexiglas screen. He looked much the same as the photo in his file, but somehow even younger than his twenty-five years. She smiled at him—no reason to get confrontational. "Good morning, officer," she said. "We're from the Controlled Substance Analysis Bureau. My name is Bernadette Becker, and I'm a case analyst. I've got Lieutenant Maura Stevenson with me. We're here to interview Annika Nakrivo, inmate number 13G-458."

Matt Vermeil's eyes darted from Bernadette to Maura and then to the other agents around the room. "I'm afraid I can only allow two visitors—"

Maura stepped forward, the signed order in her hand.

Vermeil took the form from Maura, his hand shaking slightly. He began to read it.

Bernadette was impressed. Vermeil didn't just glance at it or skim it; he furrowed his brow in concentration and read it, his lips moving in a few places. The seconds ticked by, and it felt like an hour before Vermeil handed it back.

"This is unusual," Vermeil said.

"It's an unusual situation," Maura replied.

The defining moment was here. Would Vermeil call the supervisor who had called in sick? Bernadette mentally crossed her fingers and realized she was holding her breath.

After another moment or two, Vermeil nodded. "Everything seems in order, but I'll need to report this to my supervisor."

Maura tapped the paper. "Immediate access, officer. We've had issues in the past with this facility."

Vermeil put his hands palms-out in front of him. "Hey, I'm just filling in today. I don't have any issues with the feds here. I'll get your prisoner. Uh, I think Visitation Room 3 should be big enough for all of you. But only three chairs. Most of you will have to stand."

"That's fine," said Agent Xavier Reese.

"Down the hall on your right." Vermeil picked up the phone. "We'll bring out the prisoner to you soon. Fifteen or twenty minutes."

Bernadette nodded stiffly. If Annika showed up in under forty-five minutes, it would be a miracle.

The eight of them walked down the hall. The beige linoleum floor, the light gray walls, and the blue-tinged fluorescents were far less than welcoming, and Bernadette caught the scent of lemon cleaner. A door on the right was marked *Visitation Room 3*, a metal door with a small window. Xavier Reese reached out and opened the door. Was he the designated doorman of the group?

Once everyone was inside, the six agents didn't sit, leaving the three chairs at the metal table for Bernadette,

Maura, and Annika Nakrivo. After a moment, Bernadette took a seat on the side of the table with two chairs. Maura paced around the room slowly.

Xavier Reese walked in front of the table and stretched his arms above his head, catching Bernadette's eye. She smiled.

"So," she said, "the exciting life of a CSAB agent."

He nodded. "Yeah. Been here about six months myself."

"What do you think so far?" Bernadette asked.

Reese smiled. "It's fine. Good to get out of D.C. every once in a while."

She couldn't think of anything else to say, and Reese crossed the room again.

This room was larger than the room she'd interviewed Annika back in March; that was on Bernadette's very first case with Kep. There was no way the eight of them could have crammed into the old room.

The awkward silence stretched out. Maura reached into the folder and pulled out an eight-by-ten photo of the man Bernadette knew as Darko Divjac, only that wasn't his name. Whoever he was, he'd followed her from Taycheedah to the Upper Peninsula of Michigan and almost killed her and her colleague.

Speaking of her colleague, she was glad Dr. Kep Woodhead wasn't on this trip with them. He'd have gagged on the smell of the lemon cleaner in the hallway, and his head would have spun with the cacophony of odors in this room. Plus, Xavier Reese wore a cologne that smelled faintly of cedar and vanilla. Kep might have gone apoplectic. She liked the scent, though. Agent Reese had been in the other SUV, so she hadn't even gotten his name until she spied it on the sign-in sheet.

Where was Annika? She looked at her watch.

Oh. Not even ten minutes.

It had been weird, arriving at the Milwaukee airport and *not* seeing Lamar Chesapeake. After Bernadette's last case, she knew the long-distance relationship with Lamar wasn't working. And it was her, not him. Maybe her separation from Barlow Finnegan was simply too fresh.

But she still had taken Lamar's advice and brought Sophie to Summerfest. When else would she and her daughter have an opportunity to go to the largest music festival in the world? Nine days over three weekends, so they had to pick carefully. But it wasn't tough for Sophie: her favorite artist—well, favorite artist this month, anyway—would start her set on one of Summerfest's eleven stages that very evening. Bernadette exhaled. She was glad Jenna had come. Sophie and Jenna had been best friends since elementary school, even though they'd probably go to different high schools starting in September. Bernadette was even more grateful that Jenna's mother had taken time off work to join them. Since each day started at noon, it was a godsend to have an adult to go to the early shows with the two almost-freshman girls while Bernadette made this trip to Taycheedah.

Jenna's mom, Rochelle, was a ball of energy, and often dressed in long, flowing skirts and lace-trimmed tank tops, with strappy sandals on her feet unless it was snowing. She laughed a lot; an almost-too-loud bray that sometimes made people in restaurants turn and look. But Rochelle was kind, and she set boundaries with Jenna. With Sophie too, fortunately.

Bernadette had kissed Sophie's forehead in the Plank-inton House Hotel lobby that morning as Bernadette's

FlashRide app pinged to say her driver was two minutes away. "Bye, kiddo. Have fun with Jenna."

"Why do you have to go?" Sophie had said. "I thought we were on vacation."

"I won't be long. Just meeting your Aunt Maura at the airport, and we just have to take care of a little business. I should be back in plenty of time for Laney the Great."

"Laney the *Rich*, Mom."

"Right." Her brain pinged with worry, but the hotel was only a fifteen-minute walk from the Summerfest grounds. Expensive, but hopefully worth it.

Sophie had absolutely *beamed* when Bernadette told her Laney the Rich was performing. That made the last few months of work hell worth it. Even though Bernadette felt guilty going to Summerfest without Lamar.

Coming back to the present, Bernadette tapped her fingers on the metal table, her fingernails clicking on the steel. The table was cold to the touch, quite a contrast to the hot mugginess outside on this early July day. She closed her eyes and ran through the questions she planned to ask.

Has Marguerite contacted you since we last spoke, Annika?

Do you recognize the man in this picture?

Who would want to kill Dr. Woodhead and me?

Do you have any former colleagues who have used C4 plastic explosives in the past?

Has anyone at your previous employer tried to contact you since you've been incarcerated?

She and Maura had done everything they could to ensure no surprises this time. They'd gone over the questions again and again.

And, since they'd both suspected Bernadette's CSAB-issued cellphone was how the bad guys had tracked Bernadette last time, the whole team got new phones.

These were ugly, heavy behemoths, but had innovative tech that threw location services into disarray. Untraceable —or so the higher-ups at CSAB had them believe. The phones were a little slow, but it was better than Parr Medical being able to track their every move.

Despite all the expense CSAB had gone through and the preparations they'd made, Bernadette was certain this would be a waste of time. Annika was skittish and stand-offish when it was just the two of them, and an interview room full of CSAB agents would be a surefire way to clamp Annika's mouth completely shut. There was no way Annika would answer even one question.

Unless.

Unless the hope of seeing her sister alive again would do it. Less than a month ago, someone had swiped Marguerite's expired debit card at a gas station about an hour away from Taycheedah, and while Bernadette doubted that Marguerite had been present for the card swipe, the possibility might give Annika just enough hope to let some information come spilling out.

Maybe the name of a Parr Medical employee who'd hired Annika to kill the medical researcher—and Curtis Janek, the CSAB technical specialist, too—who'd been romantically involved with Maura.

Bernadette glanced at Maura. She wasn't pacing so much as meandering, as if her thoughts were elsewhere. Bernadette set her mouth in a line. Beneath that calm exterior, was Maura seething with rage? Would she leap at the chance to attack Annika, to get her back for the pain of losing Curtis? Yes, Maura had played it cool with the much-younger Curtis, not even acknowledging their rela-tionship publicly, but she hadn't fooled Bernadette: it wasn't just a fling; Maura had had feelings for Curtis. And Annika had killed him.

Bernadette shook her head to clear the cobwebs out. Not a good headspace to get herself in before she had to interrogate a prisoner. Getting Annika to cooperate would be difficult in the best of situations. Thoughts about Curtis and Sophie would only distract Bernadette.

The back door of the interview room opened, and a woman entered wearing an orange jumpsuit. About five and a half feet tall, light brown hair, a little past shoulder length, and a wound—healing, but still ugly—across her left cheek. Annika had had a beauty mark, perfectly circular, above her thin upper lip on the left side. Now, the line of the wound ended where the beauty mark had been.

"Annika Nakrivo?" Maura asked.

"That's me," the woman said.

"Inmate number 13G-458," the guard said.

Bernadette stared at the cut across the woman's cheek—then replayed her "that's me" in her head. Her eyes darted to the woman's face.

The woman's eyes were a dusky blue—not an ice blue.

"That's not Annika Nakrivo," Bernadette said.

Chapter Two

"WHAT DO YOU MEAN?" Maura asked.

"Inmate number 13G-458," the guard repeated.

"There must be a mistake," Bernadette said, turning to the guard. "We wanted Annika Nakrivo."

"I am Annika Nakrivo," the woman said. "Perhaps you do not recognize me because of the cut on my face."

Bernadette looked closer.

No. Annika had ice blue eyes, not dusky blue. Annika's eyes were set further apart, and larger, too. Height was about the same, as were the lips, but not the eyes. And not the voice, either. This woman had a trace of central Europe in her accent. Annika had a perfect generic-American accent.

Several scenarios raced through Bernadette's head. Maybe Annika had died in the prison riot. Maybe she *had* known too much—and rather than risk her giving up the identities of the Parr Medical Employees who had hired her, the company had her killed, too. The shiv could have done it. Hell, the woman in front of her could have done it, then cut her own face to replace her.

Everyone had a price—maybe this woman had agreed to wound herself and spend a few years in jail for the right payday.

Whatever the scenario, at least some Taycheedah employees must have been involved in the cover-up. It was a good thing they'd waited until the new kid was at the front desk.

"I have news about your sister Mariska," Bernadette said.

"Where have they taken her? Have you found her?" The woman's questions were unprompted, but sounded wooden, almost rehearsed.

Bernadette shook her head. Pushing her chair back from the table, Bernadette motioned to Maura with her head. They walked to the other side of the room—not really out of earshot, but if they whispered, the woman pretending to be Annika wouldn't hear.

"That's not Annika," Bernadette murmured. "Annika's sister is Marguerite, not Mariska. And the eyes, the voice—all wrong."

"Obviously," Maura whispered back. "She's not fooling anyone. And she probably knows it, but I have an idea of how we're going to play it. And I'm glad you suggested coming here on the Fourth. None of the regular employees are here. So they won't know we've seen the fake Annika."

"I'm worried Annika's been killed."

"Or just escaped," Maura said. "Now follow my lead." She turned toward the prisoner.

"I tell you," the woman said from the table, "I am Annika Nakrivo. Inmate number 13G-458."

Maura turned toward the woman. "Correct," Maura said. "You're Annika Nakrivo. We believe you."

Bernadette blinked. What was Maura doing?

"Yes," Maura continued. "You're right. We didn't recognize you with the cut on your face."

The dots finally connected for Bernadette: this woman, whoever she was, would probably report back to Parr Medical somehow. If she knew CSAB didn't believe her, Bernadette might have a target on her back again.

Bernadette walked back to the table, Maura following. "I didn't expect to see you look so different."

Maura sat down. "Are you sure Marguerite hasn't tried contacting you? Maybe three weeks ago? The day after you went into the infirmary? The day before the prison riot?"

"I know nothing about the prison riot."

"No—of course not," Maura said, not unkindly. "We thought for sure you might know where Marguerite had gone."

The woman glanced up at Xavier Reese, but spoke to Bernadette. "Why did you bring all these people?"

"Because we wanted to track Marguerite." Bernadette followed the woman's eyes to Agent Reese. "And we would've needed the manpower to track her."

"My sister is tricky."

"We're getting that idea. Of course, so are you."

"Not tricky enough. I'm in prison, after all. And Marguerite is out there. Still free."

That didn't match with what the real Annika Nakrivo had told Bernadette. *They have my sister.*

"Okay," Maura said. "We can go."

"You have nothing else for me?" the prisoner asked.

Maura shook her head. "I'm sorry. If Marguerite hasn't contacted you, this trip has been for nothing."

In the parking lot, with three agents in front and three agents behind, Bernadette piped up. "So how do we—"

"Shh," Maura said.

Only when they were safely ensconced in the back of the SUV and they'd turned onto U.S. 151 South did Maura turn to Bernadette and speak. "Whoever that woman is, she'll be reporting back to Parr Medical."

"I get it." Bernadette felt her cheeks grow hot. She hoped she hadn't blown it. She was so emotionally involved with this case that she hadn't been able to think on her feet.

Maura ran a hand over her face. "But there's a saving grace."

"Which is?"

"Her fate lies in her ability to fool us. If she didn't fool us, Parr Medical could have her killed. She's a loose end."

"So even though she's probably aware that she didn't fool us—"

"Because we insisted she *was* Annika, she'll tell Parr Medical that her ruse was successful."

Bernadette's shoulders lowered, a little more relaxed. "So, what do we do now?"

"There's nothing *to* do. Just act like everything is normal. I'll return to D.C. Go back to the music festival with Sophie."

"You want to come? You can buy tickets at the gate."

Maura smiled sadly. "I'm too old for music festivals."

Bernadette shrugged. "I'm older than you."

Maura tilted her head from side to side and changed the subject. "I'm assigning Agent Xavier Reese to you." A touch of a smile on her mouth.

"Assigned to me? No—this entire case has disrupted my life enough as it is."

"Don't worry." Maura clicked her tongue. "He'll hang back, make sure he doesn't freak out Sophie's friend or her mom. But I'm not risking you getting kidnapped or killed."

"You said I was safe. CSAB and the FBI had gone through Joanna's files and found nothing that—"

"Yes," Maura interrupted, "but that was before we knew that the woman imprisoned at Taycheedah was *not* Annika Nakrivo. I'm confident our ruse worked, and that impostor will hopefully say she tricked us. But if Parr Medical finds that we know Nakrivo isn't still in prison, you could be in danger again."

Bernadette groaned inwardly. Danger again. Something else that Barlow could use against her in a custody case.

Maybe it would be better for Sophie to be with the parent who *wasn't* constantly in danger. If Sophie were full time with Barlow, Bernadette could visit on alternate weekends and every other Christmas. It wasn't what Bernadette wanted, but as long as she had this job, that was reality, for better or worse.

And lately, it had only seemed like worse.

❧

The SUV dropped off Bernadette at her hotel in the Deer District in Milwaukee by four o'clock. Still plenty of time to see some bands with Sophie. As she entered her hotel room, she checked the parking apps. Yikes. Forty bucks to park. And she checked the FlashRide app—surge pricing was in effect.

She wanted to get there quickly, but she hadn't gotten in much of a workout that morning, anyway. She looked at the map application on her phone. Only a mile.

"The best bad option," Bernadette muttered to herself.

She changed into a workout tank and shorts, kicked off her flats and laced up her running shoes. Walking out of the hotel, she turned left toward Lincoln Memorial Drive and Lake Michigan. At the corner of Wisconsin and Second, the Walk sign lit up, and she started the timer on her phone, slipped it back into her shoulder strap purse, and sprinted.

She crossed the Milwaukee River. The summer afternoon was hot and humid, and dozens of pedestrians lined the sidewalk. She threaded through them and turned right down River Walk.

The temperature was a few degrees cooler on the wooden walkway next to the Milwaukee River, and her running shoes thudded with each step, rattling the wooden planks. She passed the markers etched into the wood, then heard the dinging of a raising drawbridge to her right. Excellent—she wouldn't have to slow down crossing the next street to wait for cars to cross, because they'd all be stopped at the drawbridge.

She sprinted out into Michigan Street, parallel to the closed traffic arm, and raced past the bank building for the sweet shade of the I-794 overpass. Kayaks out on the water. The sound of the bands at Summerfest in the distance. Her breathing was slow, even. Her muscles were loosening up and she could feel the stress melt from her body.

Bernadette slowed slightly through the tables behind a taquería as she crossed behind the Buffalo Street dead end, but picked up speed as the wooden sidewalk dipped slightly. Then the wooden slats of River Walk ended, and she turned toward Water Street.

Another dinging on the river. The Water Street bridge

was opening. Not sure if she was still going the right way, she turned left at the confluence just past Erie Street, across Water Street, and raced loudly down a spiral staircase behind a sign for The Starling. Another wooden walkway, this one empty of pedestrians.

Her legs felt strong. She checked the timer—slower than her usual sprint because of the pedestrians and café tables she had to avoid, but a good workout nonetheless. Besides, if she had to sprint to get out of danger, she'd always have obstacles in her way. Good practice.

Boat slips on her right. Riverfront condo buildings on her left. The MIAD sign—that was the art school, right? Then, just as her lungs began to burn, Trestle Park. She turned left and saw a line of cars on Erie Street waiting to pay their forty bucks to park. Traffic cops. People in Summerfest jackets—really, in this heat?—taking credit cards.

She raced between cars to the other side of Erie Street and saw the street sign. *Summerfest Place*. She hadn't gotten lost.

But the pedestrian traffic was thick here, and Bernadette slowed to walk behind them. She checked her phone: one-point-zero miles. Eight minutes and thirty-one seconds. Not bad for a sprint littered with urban hurdles. Bernadette took deep breaths. Probably should have brought a bottle of water, but she'd get one once she was inside.

She'd always focused on strength building in her workouts—and had the delts, traps, and biceps to prove it. And since Kep had discovered the plastic explosive in her rental car a few weeks before, she'd added sprints to her workout. Fight or flight. She was confident in her ability to fight, but after her first set of sprints resulted in woefully slow times, she knew she'd have to get quicker. And she wasn't getting any younger. She'd never win any medals for her sprinting, but she knew she could get faster. And eight and a half minutes was pretty good.

With the mass of other pedestrians, she walked to the Summerfest grounds, showed her ticket on her phone after going through security, and spent six bucks on a bottle of water.

After killing a third of the bottle in one drink, she texted Sophie. Jenna and Rochelle were with Sophie at the Abber Jabber show at the Corpex Amphitheater—of the eleven venues, it was the one closest to the children's aquatic center, right at the south entrance of the festival grounds.

After threading her way through the masses of people milling about on the grounds, Bernadette turned into the area for Corpex and found the three of them about ten rows from the back. Sophie and Jenna stood on the metal benches, hopping and dancing in time to the music. Bernadette looked on the stage; the bass player was driving a funky, hard rhythm that Bernadette begrudgingly admitted was pretty cool.

After the show, they walked shoulder-to-shoulder with the other attendees into the main thoroughfare of the festival grounds, stepping their way forward slowly in the crush of people.

"What do you want to do next?" Sophie asked.

"I could go for a beer," Rochelle said. "What was that cream ale that I liked yesterday?"

"Spotted Cow," Bernadette said. She pointed to a stand advertising bratwurst and weisswurst. "They've got it there."

"I want a bratwurst," Jenna said.

"Me too," Sophie echoed.

Bernadette nodded. "You two run and get in line. We'll be there in a minute."

As the kids hurried off, Rochelle affectionately bumped Bernadette's shoulder with her own. "Thanks for the invite out here, Bern."

Oof, *Bern*. She might hate that even more than *Bernie*. Ah, well. She didn't have many female friends besides Maura. She could let it slide.

"Since the divorce, I've had trouble making friends," Rochelle continued, as if reading Bernadette's mind. "All my old friends are still married, and it's like they have no idea what to do with me."

Bernadette nodded. "I feel the same way. Barlow moved on with the woman he had an affair with, and just because I'm the single one, I'm no longer invited to anything." Though when they'd been married and she *had* been invited, she often declined because of her business travel.

Rochelle nodded. "And I can't figure out what the hell is going on with Jenna half the time."

"Sophie, too."

"So, anyway, thanks. This is the best I've gotten along with Jenna since Tom and I separated."

Bernadette smiled sadly. "I guess it's the same with me and Sophie."

Rochelle turned to watch the two girls, standing and giggling in the long line for bratwurst and beer. "What band did they want to see next?"

"Uh—Zilla Lude Tribe."

"That's a mouthful."

"Yeah." Bernadette cleared her throat. "The band name makes it sound like they sing about drugs and porn."

Rochelle shrugged. "That's assuming you can understand them." Then her eyes widened. "Oh no. I sound so *old*."

Bernadette chuckled. "Yeah, I can't tell you how many times I've caught myself sounding old since Barlow left." She stopped; they were almost close enough for the kids to hear, although neither Sophie nor Jenna were paying attention. "The other day, I went to bed at nine o'clock. The sun had barely set."

Rochelle took a step closer to Bernadette. "Want to hear something a little scandalous?"

"Sure."

Rochelle glanced up at the girls, who still paid no attention. "I got a message from a guy I used to date in college."

Bernadette raised her eyebrows.

"You heard of The Usurpers?"

"Yeah," Bernadette said. "They had that one song that was all over the radio—what, twenty years ago?"

"Eighteen," Rochelle said. "My ex-boyfriend is their guitarist. When they got signed, he dropped out of college, broke up with me, and went on tour."

"Are The Usurpers at Summerfest?"

Rochelle nodded. "They play in a half hour. And my ex-boyfriend gave me a backstage pass."

Bernadette cocked her head, a smile coming over her face. "Really?"

"Really." Rochelle furrowed her brow. "What should I do?"

"I'll go with the girls to Zilla Lude Tribe," Bernadette said. "You go see your ex. It'll make you feel good if he's hot and still carrying a torch for you. And it'll make you feel even better if he got ugly."

"Ugh," Rochelle said. "It'll make me feel ancient. But I guess if he's still hot, it'll make me think I have excellent taste."

"If he's ugly," Bernadette said over the increasing crowd noise, "it'll be because he dumped you."

"For a rock-and-roll life full of groupies and cocaine," Rochelle said, a touch of venom in her voice. "Plus, I look fantastic. My hair's a lot better than it was in college."

"Then go," Bernadette said.

After getting brats and beer, Rochelle left to go see her ex play guitar with his band. Bernadette and the two girls walked in the sweltering heat to the stage where Zilla Lude Tribe was scheduled to play. They found a few open seats together, and Bernadette sat on the bench, trying not to let the dread of her expectations drown her.

Then the music began, and Bernadette was shocked. Zilla Lude Tribe was more rhythmically complex than she'd expected, and their lyrics were surprisingly politically astute. Jenna and Sophie stood on the metal bench, and after hesitating for a moment, Bernadette clambered up too. She nodded along to the music, and during their third or fourth song, she looked up at the stage, the guitarist and bass player in a groove, feeling their way through the jazz-tinged solo, and she closed her eyes.

If I could let myself stop worrying, this would be the best feeling ever.

Bernadette let the music wash over her, the sound waves driving the fear and the pain and the anxiety from her shoulders and her forehead and between her shoulder blades. Banishing thoughts of Barlow and Lisa laughing with their old friends at a backyard barbecue. Sophie and Jenna, best friends throughout junior high, having the time of their young lives, seeing these cool bands that only the cool kids at their school knew about. Sophie and Jenna, not knowing if their friendship could survive going to different high schools in the fall, but living in the moment, dancing on the hot asphalt, the threat of thunderstorms in the air, thousands of people basking in the music.

The song ended.

A buzz from her phone.

She opened her eyes. Ugh. What a terrible time for work to interrupt her. She was supposed to be on vacation —the trip to Taycheedah was supposed to be a one-off this week. Or maybe it was Barlow, texting to ask her to bring Sophie home early. That would be annoying, but not entirely unexpected.

Whoever it was, it had better be important.

Maybe it was. Maybe something had happened with Annika's impostor, or Barlow had been in a car accident.

She pulled the phone out of her purse. But it wasn't a text from work—or from Barlow.

PIKE PLACE MUSIC

You have an urgent message from Alaska Afternoon. View the message in the Pike Place Music Forum app

Then a URL. Great. She'd visited Pike Place Music exactly once—that was to get back Annika Nakrivo's Balkan stringed instrument called a gusle, which had led to the discovery of an SD card hidden within. The SD card contained a list of names of dead people—probably homicide victims.

The music store had been crucial to the Parr Medical investigation. But now she was on their marketing list. And she'd be damned if she was going to download yet another app just to read this message.

Bernadette jumped slightly at the crash of the beginning of the next song, raising her eyes to the lead singer wailing the opening note. That was unexpected.

Alaska Afternoon. What a weird username.

Hang on a second.

This was the first message she'd ever gotten from Pike Place Music. If she'd gotten put on a marketing list, wouldn't she have gotten notifications before now?

She furrowed her brow and stepped off the bench onto the ground.

Was someone trying to tell her something?

She closed her eyes again, trying to shut out the music. Annika Nakrivo—that wasn't her real name. Her *real* name was Anja Kerovic—in fact, uncovering Annika's real name had been Bernadette's first step to finding that gusle.

Anja Kerovic: A.K.

And the postal abbreviation for *Alaska* was *AK*.

Bernadette opened her eyes and shook her head. It was a stretch at best. She felt like a ghost hunter staying the night in a run-down house, jumping to conclusions about the paranormal with every floorboard creak. Besides, there were a lot of other explanations: Seattle, the home of Pike Place Music, was tied culturally to Alaska: Alaska traditionally rooted for Seattle's sports teams, for example. And with how far north Alaska was, the solstices brought either a day full of darkness or a night full of daylight. Could be a reference to Alaska's unusual P.M. hours.

Oh.

P.M. was one way to abbreviate the afternoon hours. And P.M. also stood for Parr Medical.

Bernadette frowned. It was still a big stretch. Annika Nakrivo, after all, was no longer at Taycheedah. Whether she escaped or died, there'd be little reason for her to reach out to Bernadette.

But maybe it was worth downloading the app and finding out what the message was.

She sat on the bench, and Sophie gaped at her for a moment, then turned back to the music and swayed next to Jenna.

Bernadette tapped the URL and then clicked the side button when the app store asked her if she was sure she wanted to download. The download was slow; with tens of thousands of people here, texting each other and uploading videos of the performances to Photoxio, no wonder the network slowed to a crawl.

On stage, the song ended, and Sophie and Jenna screamed their approval.

Sophie hopped down from the bench. "Hi, Mom!"

"Having a good time?"

She wiggled her head, not quite a nod. "This is cool. None of the kids at school have been to Summerfest."

"You looking forward to Laney the Great?"

"Laney the *Rich*, Mom."

"Oh, right." Barlow probably would have gotten that correct.

"Can we get some ice cream after this?"

Bernadette had done her research; the vendor outside their stage officially sold *frozen custard*, not ice cream, but she didn't correct her daughter. "Sure. You want it now?"

"No, I'll wait till the end of the show." Sophie pointed to the phone in Bernadette's hand. "Is that work?"

"Nothing to worry about. Just give me a minute."

Sophie nodded, then she jumped back up next to Jenna as the next song started.

Bernadette glanced at her phone again; the message

had timed out. Bernadette tapped *Refresh*. A moment later, Rochelle appeared, craning her neck, then saw Bernadette waving her arms. She stepped over the benches and stood next to Bernadette.

"Did you talk to your ex-boyfriend?" Bernadette yelled over the music.

Rochelle raised one eyebrow. "Safe to say the thrill is gone." She crinkled her nose. "He smelled like vodka and Drakkar Noir."

Bernadette laughed out loud, then checked her phone. Still processing. She hoped it wouldn't time out again.

"Now come on, girl. You're on vacation. Can't your work leave you alone?"

"I got a weird message," Bernadette said, gears turning in her head. "I'll just be a minute."

"Probably a scammer. Or a catfish."

"I apparently have an 'urgent message' on an app."

Rochelle raised her eyebrows. "Don't let your work ruin Summerfest with your kid."

Bernadette smiled and nodded, but her mind was a million miles away. She looked back down at her phone and the app had finished downloading. Opening the Pike Place Music app—fortunately, she'd saved her login credentials the last time she'd visited the website—she saw the message from Alaska Afternoon in the forum and tapped it.

> Reply here when you get the next communication. You'll know what I'm referring to. Maybe I can help.

That was annoyingly vague. She wasn't even sure this was Annika's message.

Then three dots appeared. Oh—Alaska Afternoon was on the app right now.

After a moment, the next message appeared.

> And I'm not the one who took care of Leopold

Bernadette blinked. Took care of Leopold? Like—*killed* him?

Okay, *that* made her think Annika was on the other end of this thread.

She started to type back.

> Where are

Then she stopped. What would she ask Annika that wouldn't get her to close off? And she hadn't gotten any message—there was no "next communication," at least not that she knew of.

Then the last message disappeared from the chat.

Yikes. What was the name? Leopold, wasn't it?

She didn't recognize that name. Tapping her phone, she brought up a web search. The first results weren't promising. King Leopold II of Belgium—a video condemning his takeover of the Congo in the 1890s. A Leopold's Bookstore ninety miles west, in Madison. A Holy Roman Emperor also named Leopold II, just like the Belgian king.

Hmm. She typed in the window for a new search: *Leopold Parr Medical.*

And there it was: *Leopold Montclair.* Voting member of Parr Medical's Board of Directors. His résumé on ProfLinks.

And a news article from the day before on the *Cleveland Chronicle* website.

Leopold Montclair found dead in home

Bernadette tapped on the article, but the site didn't load right away—and then she noticed the bars on her phone had disappeared. Not surprising.

And then an error message. *Cannot connect to internet.*

"What is it?" Rochelle asked.

"My case," Bernadette replied. She didn't want to leave Summerfest, and she wanted more time with Sophie. But a leader of Parr Medical had just died. Was this the end of Bernadette's troubles? Maybe this Leopold Montclair person had been the one behind it all. Or maybe he hadn't been involved at first, then found out something he shouldn't have.

Whatever it was, Bernadette was distracted. And with Annika contacting her, she wouldn't be able to enjoy her time with Sophie until she had some answers.

Besides, Sophie was busy dancing on the bench next to Jenna.

She stood from the bench, still clutching her phone, and tapped Sophie.

"I'm sorry, Sophie—I need to head back to the hotel."

Sophie rolled her eyes. "This won't be one of those things where you say you'll be gone for twenty minutes and you're gone the rest of the day, is it?"

Ouch. "I hope not. I hope this is good news, in fact."

Sophie nodded. "Tell me when you're on your way back."

The elevator opened on the fourth floor of the Plankinton House Hotel and Bernadette hurried down the hall toward the suite they all shared.

Then she stopped. What was she doing? Once again, she was prioritizing work before everything else. Why didn't she just stay at Summerfest? Turn her phone off. Let everything go to voicemail. Let emails go unanswered. She was with Sophie, without Barlow, on a real vacation for the first time in... well, she didn't remember when she took her last real vacation.

She clicked her tongue, then unlocked the door to their suite and stepped inside. Five minutes, ten tops. Then she'd go back to Summerfest, she'd bob her head to Laney the Rich. Maybe she could even get some financial pointers from the lyrics.

Bernadette went into the bedroom she shared with Sophie and grabbed her laptop bag, bringing it out to the small coffee table in the suite's living room. She tapped the power button to wake up her PC from sleep and sat down on the floor next to the coffee table.

She took a deep breath—if Annika was right, Bernadette would receive a message of some sort—a communication that would make Bernadette want to contact Annika.

A chill ran down Bernadette's spine. She thought of Dr. Woodhead's son Jack, an investigative journalist who'd been murdered a few years before. How much money and time had Kep spent on trying to find Jack's killer?

She thought of the C4 plastic explosive underneath her rental car in Lost Dish. She knew in her heart that Parr Medical was behind the explosion that had almost killed her and Kep. And Parr Medical had hired Annika Nakrivo.

No doubt about it: she wasn't looking forward to this communication—whatever it would be.

She logged into the CSAB network, authenticating on her phone.

Nothing in her work email.

She checked the messages on her phone. Nothing there, either. She checked her spam and junk folders, just in case. No and no.

Her personal email was next. If someone were trying to get her a message without alerting CSAB, that might work.

Her personal email was full of marketing offers from restaurants she frequented. Everyone she talked to—Sophie, Barlow, Maura, Lesley—either texted her or sent messages through work.

Bernadette blinked.

A new email. And this one was from *Joanna Quimby*. The FBI agent who'd betrayed her. Who she'd had to kill in self-defense not three weeks before. A lump caught in her throat; Joanna had been, besides Maura, her closest friend. And it had been a lie.

An email from a dead FBI agent.

Oh, this wasn't good.

Chapter Three

HEART IN HER MOUTH, Bernadette clicked on the email from Joanna Quimby. It had been sent only two hours before.

The email may have come from Joanna's email, but Joanna hadn't written it. Obviously. And the message only took two lines.

Get Joanna's encryption key or Sophie dies
Send within 4 days

This had to be a joke. Someone had hacked their way into Joanna's personal email and had sent this as some kind of sick joke. Right?

She shifted positions on the carpet, tucking her legs under herself and pulling the laptop on the coffee table toward her another inch.

Two files at the bottom of the email. JPEG files: image-1.jpeg and image-2.jpeg.

She swallowed hard, then double-clicked on the first file.

Barlow dropping Sophie off at school.

With a shaking hand, Bernadette double-clicked on the second file.

Sophie in the mall. Jenna was behind her, out of focus. They both stood in line at a fast-food place. Sophie was laughing, and Jenna had a smile on her face, too.

Bernadette froze, her fingers over her laptop keyboard.

Sophie—she had to save Sophie.

She picked up the phone and called Sophie's phone. She and Barlow had fought whether Sophie was too young for her own phone, but now Bernadette was glad she'd lost that argument. But it went to voice mail. She called Rochelle.

"Bernadette?" Loud music in the background.

"Are the girls okay?" Bernadette said.

"They're having a great time!" Rochelle shouted over the roar of the music.

"Listen, I got a weird email," Bernadette said. "Probably nothing." Her mouth went dry with the lie. "But just the same, keep a close eye on Sophie, would you? Maybe come back to the hotel early."

"I can't hear you," Jenna said. "But don't worry. If you need to work—"

Bernadette closed her eyes. The email said she had four days. She was spinning with worry, but this was related to the Parr Medical case. And if they said they'd give her four days, they'd give her four days. "Just get them home safe," Bernadette said.

"We'll come back to the hotel right after this set," Rochelle shouted.

After Bernadette hung up, she felt nauseated. The room spun, and Bernadette's breaths were coming too short and too quickly. She pulled herself from the floor onto the sofa, forced herself to take deep, slow breaths, and she felt less light-headed after a moment.

She paced unsteadily around the small living room. Maura would know what to do. Yes, Maura might pull her off the Nakrivo case and force her into protective custody, along with Sophie—and maybe even Barlow—but that would keep her safe.

Bernadette grabbed her phone, tapped the screen, and selected Maura from her favorites. The call went directly to voice mail. Oh, of course. Maura was on her way back to D.C.— probably on a plane over Ohio right now. Bernadette tapped *End* without leaving a voicemail. She was spinning too hard right now to make much sense, anyway.

She sat down heavily on the sofa and stared at her laptop screen.

Get Joanna's encryption key.

This was a directive to Bernadette—not to CSAB. But Bernadette had no idea what the email referred to. Encryption key? How was she supposed to find it when she didn't even know what it was?

Encryption keys weren't Bernadette's thing. But Lesley Gill might have an idea of what to do. Her tech savviness had been crucial to the team's success. Plus, Lesley was one of the few people Bernadette trusted implicitly.

Lesley's line rang three times, then went to voicemail. This time, Bernadette left a message. "Lesley, it's Bernadette. Call me back. It's urgent."

She stood and paced around the living room area a little more.

Annika had told her to contact her once she got the communication. This had to be what Annika referred to. Leopold Montclair—she'd said she didn't kill him. She should finish her previously interrupted web search to find out more about Leopold Montclair—and if he had anything to do with this threat to Sophie's life.

She sat on the sofa, leaning forward to type into the search engine. His biography was the first hit.

Leopold Peter Montclair was a biotechnology innovator, businessman, television executive, and philanthropist.

Her eyes flicked over to his picture. Leopold's face was round with a prominent nose; though gray, a full head of hair, parted on the left, straight and professional. His brown eyes sparkled in the photograph; this was a man whose face showed a lust for life.

One younger brother—Ferdinand Ernest Montclair. Their father made his millions in the airline industry in the 1980s. She read further, scrolling past Leopold's education. Eschewing his father's push to go into airlines, Leopold majored in microbiology at Harvard and developed a test for genetic markers that made him a multi-millionaire by the age of thirty.

After which, according to the biography, he'd joined the board of directors of Parr Medical.

Bernadette ran her hand over her face. Montclair's death had been two days before Bernadette got the demand to get Joanna's encryption key. She searched her mind: was it an encryption key for one of Joanna's FBI files? Maybe a hired killer's file that someone wanted deleted?

She scrolled down further.

Two days before, on a Tuesday afternoon, Montclair's housekeeper found him unresponsive in his study. The cause of death was undetermined, although initial reports by the medical examiner suggested a massive heart attack. Montclair was sixty-one years old. Never married, no children. The article said Leopold had left his fortune to charity, the vast majority of which went to the Cleveland Arts Foundation.

She tapped her phone screen again and went back to the Pike Place Music app. There was her message from Alaska Afternoon. She replied to the last thing Annika had sent.

> I got the message

After only a moment, three dots, then a response.

> Who did it threaten?

Bernadette drew in a deep breath. Did Annika get a threatening message, too?

BB35901
> Sophie

ALASKA AFTERNOON
> For me, it was my sister
> At least I know she's still alive

BB35901
> What do you have to do?

ALASKA AFTERNOON
> I had an assignment emailed to me
> Had to complete it in 7 days

BB35901

I have to get an encryption key from a
dead FBI agent

ALASKA AFTERNOON

Joanna Quimby, right?

BB35901

How did you know?

ALASKA AFTERNOON

I heard about what happened in Lost Dish

Besides, you were closer to Joanna than
anyone else

Did you get 7 days too?

BB35901

4 days

What does Leopold Montclair have to do
with this?

Quite a long pause before the response.

ALASKA AFTERNOON

I was supposed to kill him on Tuesday

BB35901

Who hired you

ALASKA AFTERNOON

Never revealed their identity

But Leopold was dead when I got there

BB35901

Why are you telling me?

ALASKA AFTERNOON

Because I think the killer is the same person who wants Quimby's encryption key

BB35901

You said you could help me keep Sophie safe

ALASKA AFTERNOON

If you investigate Leopold Montclair's murder, I can help

This wasn't getting Bernadette anywhere.

BB35901

I don't want to investigate Montclair's death. I need to keep my daughter safe

ALASKA AFTERNOON

You think they're going to stop with Quimby's encryption key?

First you do that, then they'll ask you to destroy evidence

Then you'll belong to them

No

I did that and I've been doing their bidding for years with no way out

This ends now

Get the killer, get out of this

Bernadette took a deep breath. She was in over her head and she knew it, but she wasn't sure whether Annika was playing her or not. She had a point: just like blackmail, the threats would continue. If Bernadette got the encryption key—whatever it was—it would probably be the first in a long line of requests that would threaten Sophie. Bernadette would never feel safe again.

Not a position she wanted to be in, but she didn't really have a choice.

BB35901

What's your plan

Bernadette waited. No response.

After a moment, all the messages disappeared.

Well. No message trail. Bernadette supposed that way there wasn't a way for Parr Medical to track their conversation. And it didn't sound like Annika would have any additional help to give Bernadette today.

Bernadette leaned back on the sofa, her head on the top of the back cushion, staring at the ceiling.

What was she going to do?

She wouldn't give in to the demand, would she?

Deep, even breaths. The last thing she needed to do was panic, though it was the first thing she *wanted* to do.

No Maura. No Lesley.

She called Kep.

He sounded chipper when he answered the phone. "Good afternoon, Ms. Becker. How are you enjoying your music festival revelry?"

"It's—uh—listen, Kep, we have a problem. *I* have a problem."

Silence.

"Are you there?"

"The problems you and I have shared in the past few months have been of the lethal kind."

"Yeah."

"I hope this is different."

"Sophie is in danger."

Stunned silence from Kep. Then, softly: "*Your* Sophie?"

"Yeah. I don't know how else to describe it." And Bernadette relayed everything: the visit to Taycheedah with the woman who wasn't Annika, but then, only a few hours later, getting the messages from Annika Nakrivo along with the threat on Sophie's life.

"And you don't know what this encryption file refers to?" Kep asked.

"Not a clue. Maybe it has to do with the hit list on that SD card? But we already know what's on that list. I assume Parr Medical knows who they've hired people to kill, too. So that can't be it."

"And who is the deceased victim Annika denies killing?"

"His name is Leopold Montclair."

Silence.

"Do you recognize him?"

"It rings the proverbial bell. I know the name. I struggle to place where I know him from."

"Since he's on the Parr Medical board of directors, I bet you've seen his name before."

"Ah, yes, of course," Kep said. "Mr. Montclair."

A moment of silence.

"I found Montclair's biography online, Kep. That's why I'm calling you. He died of a heart attack—I guess the cause of the heart attack is unknown. But Annika says she was hired to kill him. And when I found out he's on Parr Medical's board..." She tailed off.

"I don't know what to say."

"You don't know what to say? How about saying you'll help me save Sophie?"

"Unless you believe I can detect the scent of Ms. Quimby's encryption key—"

"No, Kep! I'm not giving in to that. Annika said Leopold Montclair's killer is the same person threatening Sophie."

"And how does she know that?"

"Well—I guess because she's been in bed with these people a long time."

"And yet she doesn't know who hired her?"

"Look—are you going to help me solve the murder of Leopold Montclair or not?"

A hesitating breath on the other end of the line, then Kep's voice, tentative. "You don't know that Mr. Montclair's death resulted from foul play. I'm looking at the same *Cleveland Chronicle* article you mentioned. The medical examiner hasn't ruled it a homicide."

"Why else would Annika contact me for this?" Bernadette demanded.

"Because," Kep said carefully, "she knows Sophie is—how did you put it a few weeks ago? Your 'Achilles heel.' She is someone for whom you would go to extraordinary lengths to protect."

"What mother wouldn't?"

"Particularly," Kep said, "a mother whose ex-husband is threatening a complex and emotionally demanding custody battle should she not acquiesce to his demands."

It was Bernadette's turn to be silent, although the rage built inside her stomach.

"Having experienced the loss of a child," Kep said—did his voice crack on *child?*—"I understand the desire to act without regard to my own safety or those around me. When one faces a situation where one's child is endangered, one rarely sees the ways in which emotional manipulation can happen."

Bernadette pursed her lips. Kep's phrasing was careful, not blaming her. Yet she felt empty and angry and terrified. Someone would take Sophie away—whether it was Parr Medical, or Annika Nakrivo, or her soon-to-be-ex-husband. She wanted to scream.

"You know I'd do anything to save Sophie," Bernadette said.

"As, in all likelihood, does Annika. She may have been the one to break into Ms. Quimby's email."

"To what end?"

"Aha. That, unfortunately, I am not sure of. But Annika Nakrivo hides much about herself. Her goal may not be immediately visible."

"Then help me, Kep. Even if I'm being manipulated, you know Leopold Montclair was murdered."

"I don't—"

"I'm not talking about evidence, Kep. You know in your brain, in that big smell-o-tastic noggin of yours, that if the M.E. runs the right tox screen, they're going to find some weird poison we haven't dealt with yet."

"I'm all for bringing killers to justice, but how will catching the killer of Mr. Montclair keep your daughter safe? Do you believe Annika that Montclair's killer is the same person threatening Sophie?"

"It's all I have to go on," Bernadette said quietly.

Kep said nothing for a moment. Bernadette could almost hear the gears spinning in his head. No one had ever talked to him about helping keep Jack safe. No one had stepped up to help Kep solve Jack's murder. He'd lost his job on the television show, his wife had left him—and for what? For a private investigator who fired him after taking his money for two years?

The seconds ticked by, each one like an hour.

Finally, Kep spoke. "It would be most prudent to let me make the initial contact with Lieutenant Stevenson on this matter."

Bernadette let out a breath.

"The lieutenant would attempt to talk you out of solving the Montclair case, as she might believe you are acting from a place of pure emotion. I can shield you from that."

"Thank you, Kep. That means a lot."

"Where was Mr. Montclair found dead?"

"In his home."

"Pardon; let me rephrase. In what city?"

"Oh, sorry." Bernadette clicked onto the web page of the biography. "Cleveland. A suburb, actually—Huntsman's Park."

"Ah, yes," Kep said. "A high median income. And it's fortunate I know the medical examiner in Cuyahoga County."

Bernadette wasn't sure if that was a good thing or not. Kep rubbed a lot of people the wrong way.

Her phone beeped. She took the phone away from her ear and stared at the screen. Lesley Gill.

"I gotta take this, Kep."

"Call me back," he said. "*Speak to me as to thy thinkings, As thou dost ruminate, and give thy worst of thoughts the worst of words.*"

As he clicked off, Bernadette grimaced. These surely were the worst of thoughts.

"Lesley?"

"You okay?"

"I—" She stopped. "No, I'm not okay. Sophie's in danger."

A low grumble. Was that a growl from Lesley's throat? "Parr Medical?"

"I think so, but it's not like they signed their threat. A demand. I need to get Joanna's encryption key or they'll kill Sophie."

"*What?*"

"I know." And Bernadette related the story: the impostor at Taycheedah, Annika's messages in the music store forum, the dead Parr Medical board member, and Annika believing the killer was the same person threatening Sophie. "And I don't know what encryption key they're talking about."

Lesley grimaced. "I can't believe this. What are you going to do?"

"I don't think I have a choice. I have to find Montclair's killer. Otherwise, I'll never get away from these threats."

"But—I mean, what are you going to do to protect Sophie?"

Bernadette was silent. "I don't know. Catch the killer in the next week."

Lesley clicked her tongue. "Protective custody. They can't kill Sophie if they can't find her."

Bernadette was quiet for a moment. "Yeah. I can talk to Maura. Kep's going to talk to her about getting us assigned to the Montclair case, anyway."

"Didn't you say the M.E. hasn't declared it a homicide? You know if this guy is involved with Parr Medical, they didn't use cyanide or arsenic. You know they used some untraceable nanobot technology or something. And that might make it hard for CSAB to step in."

"Yeah. But we've got Kep. I bet he can smell evil nanobots a mile away."

Lesley stifled a laugh, then cleared her throat. "I can try to figure out what the encryption key is for. And maybe why they think *you* can find it."

"I must have access to something they don't."

"Okay, let's start there. Did Joanna ever give you access to something private? Something only you knew about?"

Bernadette thought for a moment. "Not that I can think of. Hasn't anything in Joanna's files jumped out at you?"

"Not much. We found something curious about an FDA inspector. James Chester. His name appeared on the list of dead people on the spreadsheet on that SD card."

"Maybe Chester was about to decline a medication for Parr Medical."

Lesley exhaled loudly. "Looks like the opposite. He recommended approval for five different Parr Medical medications. Soralate, fenezamil, worparenamib—"

"Now you're just showing off your pronunciation skills. I bet you screwed those all up and just thought I wouldn't notice."

"My point is, Chester didn't seem to be on Parr Medical's bad side."

"Maybe he tried to blackmail them after the fact."

"I'll dig into it. Chester died in a car accident three years ago. One of the first names on the list. I'll see what else I can find."

"As far as the investigation we're supposed to be working on," Bernadette said, "can you dig up any useful info on Leopold Montclair? And maybe see if you can find where Annika is."

"You know as well as anyone how good she is at

covering her tracks." Then a finger snap. "Oh—I didn't tell you this earlier. We're all having a hell of a time making sense of Joanna Quimby's finances, but we *did* discover a regular series of payments—all under ten thousand dollars, so they're not triggering auto-reporting to the feds."

"Who paid her? Maybe it's the same person who wants her encryption key."

"Possibly. It's some fake company name. But I would bet it all came from Parr Medical."

"Have any evidence to back that up?"

"The bank," Lesley said. "Caskill & Dunleavy Bank of Huntsman's Park. That's a neighborhood—"

"Near Cleveland," Bernadette finished. "And Leopold Montclair's body was found in his home in Huntsman's Park."

Chapter Four

"Look, Barlow," Bernadette said into the phone, "I don't know how long this is going to be."

"I thought I was away from all this bullshit when I—"

"Yeah, yeah," Bernadette said. "I get it."

"Your job puts our daughter in danger. I told you what I'd do about custody if this continued."

Bernadette bristled. "You think you and Sophie would be safe if Sophie simply didn't live with me at all? That's not how this works."

"However your job *works*, Bernadette, this isn't *working* for me. I can't teach my classes. How am I supposed to get paid?"

"You don't go back to your classes until mid-August."

"That's not the point."

"Despite your cheating on me, I don't want you to die, Barlow," Bernadette snapped.

"That's not fair—"

"You know," Bernadette interrupted, "I could just go into protective custody with Sophie. Leave you out of it. Maybe the bad guys would threaten *you* instead of Sophie.

How do you think I'd deal with choosing between national security and *your* life? You think you'd win that one?"

Bernadette could feel his anger, even through the phone, even through his silence.

"So maybe consider yourself lucky that I care enough to get you into protective custody, too."

"And Lisa?"

"Lisa is probably safe."

"Why is she safe and I'm not?"

"Because," Bernadette said, trying to keep the panic out of her voice, "you are the father of my child. Even if I can't stand you, the impact your death would have on Sophie would be immeasurable. It's in my interest to keep you alive."

"But not Lisa?"

"If you were the bad guys," Bernadette said, "would you kidnap the mistress of the ex-husband of your target? Would you think you'd have any leverage at all? Or would you think there's a chance I'd *want* her dead?"

He was silent for a moment. "You're not like that, Bernadette."

"The bad guys don't know I'm not like that."

Another pause, this one longer.

"Tomorrow morning," Bernadette said, "you're getting picked up by two CSAB agents. You can bring two suitcases. Bring some clothes for Sophie."

"But what about—"

"Sophie's flying out with a CSAB agent. You and Sophie will meet at an airport somewhere, and agents will accompany you to—to where you're going."

"Where *are* we going?"

"I don't know."

"What do you mean, you don't know?"

"Don't you get that you're in danger? And you and Sophie will be in *more* danger if I know where you are. So we're planning for a bunch of different scenarios. There are probably three people in all of CSAB who will know where you are, and none of them will give your location up. If Maura gets taken, and I have to disclose your location to the bad guys or they kill her, I don't want to know. Do you get it?"

"I wish I'd never—" Then Barlow stopped.

"Yeah, yeah," Bernadette said. "I'm sure Sophie will be delighted to hear that you wish you'd never met me. She's pretty pissed off at me too, because Laney the Rich is at the Pavilion stage tonight, and we had sixth-row tickets. You two can commiserate about what a terrible mother I am when you meet up tomorrow."

"What about Jenna and *her* mother?"

"They've got another two days here. And they're not in danger."

"Says you."

"Yeah, says me. Look, I'm telling you what you need to know."

Barlow said nothing, but Bernadette could picture steam coming out of his ears. Part of her felt sorry for him; he didn't ask for any of this.

"I hope we can get what we need—fast. Maybe this will all be behind us by Monday. Maybe life can go back to normal."

"I wanted you to quit, Bernadette."

"And I wanted you to keep it in your pants," Bernadette said, then sucked in a breath. "Sorry, sorry. That slipped out. Look, the thought of quitting? Yes, it's crossed my mind, but quitting now won't make Sophie safe. We've got to catch these bad guys." Bernadette paused. "And right now, I'm more inclined to do the opposite of what you want if you speak to me like that."

"You have grown increasingly difficult in the last few years."

"And—" Bernadette stopped. How was she going to finish that sentence? A snarky stab at Lisa? Petty one-upsmanship? She closed her eyes. "And yet I'm still doing all I can to keep you alive."

In the main terminal of the General Mitchell International Airport, Bernadette hugged Sophie, but Sophie pulled away almost immediately.

"It's not fair," Sophie said.

"I know."

"But I mean, Jenna and Rochelle are going to see Laney the Rich, and I have to go—I don't even know where."

Bernadette shot a glance at Agent Xavier Reese. Reese was stoic, especially behind his sunglasses. Six eight, all muscle: no one would mess with Sophie if Reese was with her. Bernadette cleared her throat and stepped forward to Agent Reese.

"Hi, Agent Reese. We didn't really get a chance to talk yesterday. I want to thank you for making sure we were safe."

Reese took off his sunglasses. "It was an honor to do it. Your reputation precedes you."

Bernadette's face fell.

Agent Reese furrowed his brow. "That's a good thing. At least, for most of us. I have to tell you, I was shocked to find out Joanna Quimby was working for the bad guys. I've been on my fair share of assignments with her. Suppose it just goes to show you that you never really know someone."

"No," Bernadette agreed, tightness in her throat. "I thought I could trust her."

Reese nodded. "I know how important your family is to you, Agent Becker."

"I'm not an agent anymore."

Reese paused. "After all you've done in the last few months? You'll be back to agent status soon enough." He looked down at his feet. "At any rate, I assure you, your husband and daughter will be in good hands."

"Oh—uh, ex-husband. Well, the divorce isn't final yet, but..." She trailed off, then shook her head. "Anyway, he's important to Sophie, so he needs to be kept safe, too." Bernadette smiled slightly.

"I understand."

Bernadette nodded and took a few steps back toward Sophie.

"I hate your job," Sophie said, crossing her arms.

"I hate it too."

"Then why do you have it?" Sophie said. "Why can't you be a normal mom, with a normal job? You're always gone. And even when we *finally* do something cool together, you have to screw it up?"

Bernadette looked her daughter in the face. Sophie was angry, but her words—as much as she intended to wound Bernadette—were purely from a place of confusion. Sophie *didn't* understand what was going on. Hell, Bernadette didn't even understand what was going on.

She looked at Agent Reese, but he'd put his sunglasses back on and hadn't reacted at all.

"Promise me you'll find something else," Sophie said.

"Like a different job?" Bernadette cocked her head. "Did Dad ask you to say that?"

Sophie looked down at the floor. "Doesn't mean I don't think it too."

"Yeah, fair enough." Bernadette frowned. "This sucks. I didn't think this would happen, Sophie. I thought after—after what happened a few weeks ago, we'd go back to normal. This case analyst position was supposed to be way less dangerous than me being an agent."

Sophie looked up again. "I don't even know when I'm going to see my friends again. And I'll lose my place on the softball team."

"I know."

"I don't even know when I'll be able to see *you* again."

Bernadette felt like pulling Sophie into a hug again, but Sophie obviously didn't want that. "I love you. I'm sorry about all this."

"Sorry enough to do something about it?"

"I know what I have to do to keep you safe."

"For what? Another two weeks?"

Bernadette frowned, her lip trembling. She wouldn't cry in front of Sophie, not at the airport in front of all these people.

"I'm really mad," Sophie said, and a tear welled up in her eye and chased down her cheek.

"Yeah, me too."

They stood in silence for a moment.

Agent Xavier Reese cleared his throat. "I apologize, but we need to get to our gate."

"Okay, kid," Bernadette said. "I'll see you. Have a good flight. Tell your dad I feel truly shitty about everything."

"He's scared," Sophie said.

"Yeah, well, I am too," Bernadette said. "And that's why you're going where you're going."

Sophie nodded, then turned toward the TSA line. Agent Reese followed just a step behind.

Bernadette watched as her daughter went through security, her backpack on the conveyor belt into the scanner, Agent Reese walking through the entrance for air marshals and pilots. A few people looked at him strangely. When he got to the other side, he waited for Sophie, then they turned toward the D gates and disappeared down the wide corridor.

Bernadette took a deep breath, then pulled the paper ticket out of her purse.

She had about two hours before boarding her flight to Cleveland. Kep had left Boston Logan about fifteen minutes ago; he'd be waiting for her at Hopkins International.

❦

The Elderkin Lounge, just before the exit of Cleveland's Terminal B into the main terminal, was brightly lit, its interior polished steel and lush upholstery in earthtones. Kep sat at a booth near the window, looking out over the runways. A glass of iced tea sat on the table in front of him. His glasses had slipped down his nose, and he rested his bearded chin in his hand as he stared vacantly at the airplanes parked on the tarmac.

Bernadette, pulling her roll-aboard behind her, gave her name to the lounge concierge, and he checked the list, then smiled at Bernadette. "Welcome, Ms. Becker. Can I get you anything?"

"Gin and tonic."

"Coming right up. Have you decided where to sit?"

"With the bearded gentleman by the window."

"Very good."

She walked over to Kep, rolling her suitcase behind her. He didn't take his eyes off the runway. "Greetings, Ms. Becker."

"Hey, Kep."

"Have you seen the medical examiner's preliminary report?"

"Not yet."

Kep took his phone out, tapping then scrolling. "Obviously, there was a coronary event. The medical examiner has yet to determine the cause." He held the phone out toward Bernadette. "A red discoloration in the fingertips which also appeared"—Kep flicked the picture of red fingertips to one of red feet—"in the victim's heels and toes."

"It's not that unusual for someone to have discolored toes and fingers."

"This particular shade of red, however, has an orange tint to it. The cellphone screen fails to do it justice."

"I see." Bernadette pushed down the handle of her roll-aboard. "So, what does that mean?"

"Certain chemical compounds can create this type of discoloration, but only some of them are lethal." Kep clicked the phone screen off and placed the phone on the table. "I spent much of yesterday evening researching the new medications Parr Medical has in development. They have a promising erectile dysfunction medication currently in clinical trials."

"I know a doctor if you're looking for a referral." Bernadette forced a grin onto her face and took a seat across the table from Kep.

Kep took a sip of his iced tea and ignored her comment. "One of the waste products from the production of this medication is a clear liquid called bromeladine."

Bernadette straightened in her seat and cleared her throat. "Aha. I bet that's toxic."

"Your assertion is correct. Roughly half a milliliter injected into the bloodstream is more than enough to kill an adult male who weighs up to three hundred pounds. Our victim was roughly two hundred ten."

"And is there a tox screen for bromeladine?"

Kep blinked rapidly and pushed the glasses up on his nose. "I have difficulty answering the question."

"Why?"

"The short answer is no, but there is a two-step process that can detect bromeladine's presence by testing for the two components of its state after the affected blood interacts with oxygen."

"So 'yes.'"

"Practically speaking, yes. However, several websites assert that the CIA and FBI have been using bromeladine to assassinate problematic world leaders and suspected domestic terrorists for years—specifically because a single test for its presence does not exist."

The concierge came to the table and set down the gin and tonic in front of Bernadette.

"Thank you," Bernadette said absently, taking a sip of the drink. She set it back on the table and raised her eyes to Kep. "After the preliminary tox screen, did the medical examiner run this two-step test?"

"After I had a conversation with him, yes."

"What were the results?"

"I expect the Cuyahoga County medical examiner will have them to us tomorrow morning."

"Is there any other way to get bromeladine besides when you make this ED pill?"

"It was previously used in the manufacture of suede goods, but its use has been discontinued in the United States." He stroked his beard. "One of those suede manufacturers contracted with a company called Northern States Waste Solutions to dispose of the bromeladine. However, the company does not seem to exist."

"Oh, no," Bernadette deadpanned. "Must be the government killing people. And bromeladine is probably how we faked the moon landing, too."

Kep inclined his head. "When bromeladine is a waste product, such as what we see with Parr Medical, companies must dispose of it as hazardous medical waste. The government needs to track and certify the disposal company. Otherwise, the company could dump the waste into rivers or groundwater."

Bernadette nodded soberly. "You're right. Sorry for making light of it. How many companies have access to Parr Medical's hazardous medical waste?"

"That," Kep said, "is something I am certain Parr Medical keeps under lock and key."

"The bromeladine?"

"I was referring to the names of the people who have access."

"Oh, right." Bernadette leaned back in the booth. "Easy enough to get a syringe full of it?"

"Assuming one has access to the medical waste and a pair of chemical gloves, obtaining a syringe filled with bromeladine would be quite easy, yes."

"Or if you're a rogue government agent." Bernadette chuckled.

"So," Kep continued, "one could transport several small syringes in a glass container with minimal issues."

"I guess we need to talk to the technicians at Parr Medical."

Kep raised his eyebrows. "We suspect that Parr Medical had hired people to kill both of us. While we may currently not be on their 'hit list,' as it were, is it wise for us to dangle ourselves in front of Parr Medical's employees like chunks of raw meat in front of wolves?"

Bernadette furrowed her brow. "If we need to track the source of bromeladine, we'll need to ask, but you're probably right. And it can wait until we've gathered more data."

Kep leaned back in the booth and stroked his salt-and-pepper beard. "When is Detective Herrera picking us up?"

"He said about thirty minutes."

"Do we need to go to baggage claim?"

"No."

"You didn't pack your service weapon on this trip?"

"Not when I went to Taycheedah. They wouldn't have let me take it into the prison anyway. Besides, I was supposed to be on vacation the rest of the time I was in Wisconsin."

"We are journeying into the proverbial belly of the beast unarmed?"

"I can stop by the local CSAB office and check out a firearm for my time here."

Kep blinked. "Am I to understand our employer has a gun library?"

Bernadette grinned. "Not exactly—well, I guess. Pretty close."

"Will wonders never cease?" Kep said absently. "I don't mind telling you, Ms. Becker, that I fear for my life."

"Yeah, since Parr Medical has put a target on our backs, I feel the same way."

"And," Kep continued, picking up his iced tea, "I feel more emotional about this investigation than ever before." Was his hand shaking?

"Why?" Bernadette asked, stirring her gin and tonic.

"There is no need to play coy. Lieutenant Stevenson informed me that my son's name was on the hit list on the SD card you found in that gusle in the Seattle music store, and Marguerite Kerovic had traveled to Cleveland before she departed for Boston in the days preceding my son's murder. Evidence would suggest she was, in fact, hired to..." Then his voice trailed off.

Bernadette nodded. "Sorry I didn't tell you, Kep. I wasn't sure if Maura wanted to give you that information."

"Understandable, of course," Kep said, setting his iced tea down on the table without taking a drink. "I had hoped that discovering the identity of the responsible party would have given me some closure."

"We still don't know who hired her," Bernadette said. "I mean, yeah, we know it was someone at Parr Medical. But we don't know who's pulling the strings."

"Or even why they killed him." Kep woke his phone up. "Mr. Montclair was a member of the board of directors," he said. "When attempting to find the most likely suspects, I look for reasons why another member of Parr's leadership team would want Mr. Montclair dead."

"Makes sense."

"Now," Kep continued, "my first thought was Montclair had threatened to turn in others who were involved in their criminal enterprise."

"Ah."

"However, I have yet to uncover evidence that Mr. Montclair had a change of heart."

"Maybe we should eliminate other motives. Money, jealousy, that kind of thing. Though I don't think anyone would kill him to get rich. Didn't he leave all his money to charity?"

"That's correct. He has a brother who is an accountant, Ferdinand Montclair. My understanding is that he prefers the diminutive 'Fred' as a moniker. Fred had a daughter who passed away a few years ago. No other living relatives of whom I'm aware."

Bernadette nodded. "So we should look at Parr Medical. Leopold still could have been a whistleblower, even if we haven't seen evidence of it yet."

"That's correct," Kep said. "Once we obtain Mr. Montclair's phone records or emails, we can see whom he recently contacted: the FDA, healthcare oversight organizations, or simply a flurry of calls to others at Parr Medical, perhaps arguing with them."

"It's a good place to start," Bernadette said.

Kep scrolled on his phone. "When Mr. Montclair was the CEO of his own firm, he was friends with a television producer named Yates Raphael."

"I've seen that name before," Bernadette said.

"I'm not surprised. Mr. Raphael was a producer for *Cases That Won't Die*."

"So—you know him?"

"A colorful and problematic history at the network," Kep said. "And yet, he kept getting better jobs." He sniffed. "As much as I loathe the unholy union of hard news and reality television, I must admit that Mr. Raphael had his finger on the proverbial pulse of mainstream audiences."

"What's Yates Raphael doing now?"

"He has several irons in the fire. One of which is a supposedly hard-hitting news and opinion show."

"Why are you bringing this up?" Bernadette rubbed her forehead. "Are they still in touch?"

"Mr. Raphael and I became professional acquaintances at the network," Kep said. "And after you discussed Mr. Montclair's death with me, I called his office in New York. One of my former assistants now works for him, and he confirmed that Mr. Montclair asked to make an appointment to see Yates Raphael at his New York office."

"Was he a whistleblower? Maybe we should contact Raphael, see what he had to say."

Kep shook his head. "Alas, Mr. Montclair did not speak with him. Yates Raphael was scouting locations for a show that is filming at the Rock and Roll Hall of Fame—here in this very city. Raphael asked Montclair to wait until this week, when he would be in Cleveland for business."

"And now they can't meet because Montclair is dead."

"Mr. Raphael's assistant told me that Montclair said the meeting was of an urgent nature. He had a name written in the notes he took: *Andy Belgrade*."

Bernadette scratched her scalp. "I don't think I've heard that name before."

"Nor have I. A cursory web search revealed no people with that name."

"So—Annika said she didn't kill Leopold Montclair." Bernadette steepled her fingers. "Should we be looking for this Andrew Belgrade?"

"As Montclair mentioned Belgrade in his message, we would be remiss if we didn't try to identify him. But Belgrade may have nothing to do with Montclair's death."

Kep thought for a moment. "It could also be a person named Andy who lives in Belgrade."

"The capital of Serbia?"

"Or small towns in Montana or Minnesota. The possibilities are varied."

The name seemed important, but with no further clues, Bernadette tapped the screen on her phone, swiped, and held the phone out to show Kep.

"Did you intend to show me the Parr Medical leadership team web page?"

Bernadette nodded. "Whoever is pulling the strings with Annika—and whoever hired the guy I know as Darko Divjac to kill us—it's most likely to be a leader at Parr Medical. Someone invested in Parr Medical's success. For all these management leaders, we're talking hundreds of millions of dollars if Parr Medical corners the market on just *one* of the drugs where they have significant competitors. And they've done it a few times now."

"Do you believe a single one of these leaders could coordinate all these killings?" Kep asked, shifting in his seat. "It seems to me that a project such as this—with so many dead bodies littering the landscape—would require multiple people."

Bernadette nodded. "Multiple hired killers, certainly. And yes—many members of Parr Medical's leadership are making a lot of money. But whoever knows about the scheme to literally kill off the competition has to keep it secret. I know there are people out there who have taken pains to minimize their digital footprint. Maybe *Andy Belgrade* is one of them. And maybe there's a reason for that. Could it be a secret identity?"

"'To keep your secret is wisdom; but to expect others to keep it is folly.'"

Bernadette screwed up her mouth. "This is the first time we've seen a Parr Medical stakeholder killed. And a member of the leadership team."

Kep nodded, pushing the glasses up on his nose. "Perhaps we should examine the possibility that Leopold Montclair helped coordinate these evil deeds. Perhaps a misstep led to his demise, and if we can find that misstep, perhaps we'll discover the identity of his killer."

"So—who at Parr Medical had the resources to do all this?"

Kep looked at the screen. "The chief executive officer —Jeremy Niehaus." A balding man with thick glasses in small square frames whose long nose was nearly as prominent as his chin. "According to the biographical information on the page, he spent his career in the pharmaceutical industry."

"Biology major at Yale, M.B.A. from Columbia a few years later. Went right into management." Bernadette tapped the screen and went to a notes page labeled *Jeremy Niehaus*. "I looked into his personal life, too. Divorced, no kids."

Kep swiped back on Bernadette's phone and moved to the next bio. They went through several of the leaders of Parr Medical, from the vice president of sales to the head of research and development, from the chief technical officer to the chief legal counsel. All were experienced in the industry. She didn't recognize any names; neither did Kep. No one named Andy. No one with any mention of Belgrade or Serbia in their biographies.

"Anyone else?"

They scrolled through several more photos. A few of the board members lived far away from Cleveland, as did the chief operating officer and the vice president of product development. "I don't want to take these people off the suspect list," Bernadette said, "but whoever hired Annika coordinated her plastic surgery at a hospital in Cleveland. I think we should focus on the people who live locally."

The phone in Bernadette's purse dinged. She pulled it out and glanced at the screen. "Detective Herrera just got off the freeway."

"Are you ready to leave?" Kep motioned to her drink sitting on the table.

Bernadette stirred the gin and tonic. "I don't know why I ordered this. I need to be sharp for meeting with the detective."

"Yes, we need to be on our toes, as they say." Kep picked up his iced tea again, this time taking a sip. "However, these last few weeks have been stressful, and you have had minimal time to process the stress. Self-medication is a natural coping mechanism." He sniffed. "I would suggest, however, that the next time you choose to self-medicate, you opt for a higher-quality salve." He sniffed again and his lips turned down into a frown. "Their gin is Parker's, which uses low-quality juniper berries. I expect better from an airport lounge that charges fifty dollars for a single visit."

"I'll take it up with management next time." Bernadette rose to her feet. "Come on—the sooner we meet the detective, the sooner we can get the investigation started."

Chapter Five

THE SILVER BUICK in the pickup lane had its flashers on.
A short man with a black mustache, wearing a tailored tan
suit and horn-rimmed glasses, got out of the driver's side.

It was cooler here than it had been in Milwaukee by
about ten degrees.

The driver walked behind the car and reached his hand
out to Kep. "Bobby Herrera. You're Dr. Woodhead?"

Kep nodded and motioned to Bernadette. "My
colleague, case analyst Bernadette Becker."

Herrera leaned over into the car, and a second later, the
trunk popped open. Bernadette and Kep both put their
suitcases into the Buick's empty trunk.

"You're well-known around these parts," Herrera said.
"We used to have watch parties for *Cases That Won't Die.*
The only TV show that ever got the details right." He
smirked. "But I gotta tell you, no one believes you could
actually detect all those smells. I saw that one episode
where you couldn't get a good sniff because you were
allergic to eucalyptus."

"Not eucalyptus. A fungus that infected—"

Herrera chortled. "I bet you fool a lot of people. Makes for a good story, though."

Kep's nostrils flared, then he leaned forward toward Detective Herrera. "If you don't want your spouse to know about your affair, I suggest you don't shower with Vittori's Waterfall Crystals body wash after your dalliances. Your spouse likely expects the scent of Aspen Forest soap, which I suspect is in your shower at home. Even without consciously picking up on it, your spouse, I assure you, will soon suspect your infidelity."

Herrera straightened up. "What the hell?"

"I cannot speculate as to the nature of your relationship with your spouse," Kep continued softly. "Perhaps the two of you have an arrangement. Perhaps your spouse chooses to look the other way. Perhaps you think you've gotten away with it. I am simply informing you that your attempts to obfuscate evidence of your affair are not perhaps as effective as you think."

Herrera paled.

"Your affair partner lives close to the airport," Kep said. "The Waterfall Crystals scent is powerful but has a lower permanence than the average body wash. You got out of the shower—what, twenty minutes ago?"

"I don't let people talk to me like that," Herrera said, clenching his fists.

Bernadette stepped forward, glaring at Kep before turning to Detective Herrera. "He's doing you a favor, Bobby. Wouldn't you rather let Dr. Woodhead—how did you phrase it?—tell you a good story? Or would you prefer your wife try to figure out on her own why you smell like a soap you don't have in your house?"

Herrera closed the trunk a little harder than necessary. "You two can ride in back."

Kep shrugged and walked toward the back door on the passenger side. Bernadette walked around to the left side of the car.

Herrera grunted as he got in behind the wheel, then he turned on the radio to an R&B station, turned the volume up, and drove out of the pick-up lane. Deep bass and electronic drums filled the car, too loud.

Bernadette turned to Kep. "You just couldn't keep your mouth shut, could you?"

Kep blinked, pushing his glasses up on his nose. "He doubted my olfactory abilities."

"And now I doubt our ability to get the Cleveland P.D. to help us." The thumping kick drum made her head hurt. Bernadette learned forward. "Detective Herrera, would you mind turning the music down?"

Herrera tapped the steering wheel in time to the music, and his lips moved, half-singing along. He didn't touch the volume. Bernadette sat back in her seat.

Kep leaned toward Bernadette, his mouth close to her ear. "We should use this to our advantage," he said.

"Our advantage?"

"We don't know yet if we can trust Detective Herrera."

"Your insult made it more difficult for *him* to trust *us.*"

"Since he cannot hear our conversation," Kep said, pulling out his phone, "I wanted to share some information I received about my—my..." Kep took a deep breath, pressed his lips together, and looked out the window for a moment.

Bernadette nodded. About his son's murder. "Yes, I understand, Kep." She wanted to comfort him, but in the back of Herrera's police car, he probably just wanted to regain control of himself and act like nothing had happened.

"You also haven't seen anything beyond Parr Medical's public filing reports," Bernadette said. "They could easily use a foreign bank account or play fast and loose with a crypto account."

Kep breathed out through his mouth and turned back to Bernadette. "You are aware that I have had a private investigator attempting to gather information."

"And you believe your investigator was thorough?"

"I know he found evidence that convinced me Jack's murder was planned."

Bernadette was silent, the unspoken question on the tip of her tongue. But she waited.

"The evidence was a voice-activated recorder. Found in his apartment behind his television. Looked like part of the equipment. Had six months of standby time. Whatever he found and talked about in his apartment, someone was listening in. But that has nothing to do with financial payments."

"If I were behind all this," Bernadette said, "I would funnel money from Parr Medical into payments to a holding company with an offshore account. A fake company. That way, whoever's doing it could hide the true purpose of the payment from everyone—even people inside the company. So that way, when the company released their financial reports, everything looks on the up-and-up. Whoever is doing this doesn't even have to fake numbers or lie."

"Ah," Kep said. "Look at this." He tapped his phone, scrolled, tapped again. A financial records file popped up. "A large amount of Parr Medical stock transferred to what I assume is another financial institution. This stock matches a bonus payment that Jeremy Niehaus received." Kep swiped up, and another financial record displayed.

"And this one matches a stock award for Leopold Montclair."

"How did you get these?"

Kep cleared his throat. "We would be unable to use these documents in a court case," he said.

"That doesn't answer my question."

"Perhaps it's better that I leave it unanswered."

Bernadette tried to give Kep a stern look, but she was too surprised—and impressed—for her look to be anything other than amused. "Where did these payments go?"

"Ah—well, that is another kettle of fish. I wondered if perhaps Miss Gill could assist with that. I have routing and account numbers that match nothing I can find."

"And how would you get this to Lesley without her knowing you obtained this information illegally?"

Kep's ears reddened slightly. "Perhaps you could assist?"

Bernadette crossed her arms and tried to frown.

Kep cleared his throat. "I am an expert in olfactory recognition, not forensic accounting. But I suspect if I deliver this information to Miss Gill, she will discover the true nature of these payments."

"But you believe, given the information you've got, that either Jeremy Niehaus or Leopold Montclair could have personally financed the corporate espionage, the hired killers—all of it."

Kep pressed his lips together. "I believe we would be remiss if we did not further research the possibility."

"Anyone who hired Annika, Marguerite—and who knows who else—would have to cover their tracks." Bernadette shifted in the seat. The Buick's faux leather upholstery was worn thin, and the back of her arm stuck to the seat. "I don't know enough about how private pharmaceutical companies work to be sure about how well those tracks have to be covered."

The song ended on the radio and a commercial came on. Herrera lowered the volume. "Hey, I just thought of something."

"Yeah?" Bernadette said.

"So I heard you got an anonymous tip, about this Montclair guy dying? You're thinking it was murder?"

"Correct," Bernadette said.

"Want to see his house before we go to the precinct?"

"I'd actually like to get settled—" Bernadette started.

But Kep lightly touched her arm. "Detective Herrera, are you offering to take us to where the police discovered Mr. Montclair's body?"

"Absolutely," Herrera said. "Maybe I'll get enough stink of dead bodies on me to make sure my wife ignores the body wash."

"As much as I would love to see the crime scene," Bernadette said, "don't we need to check in at the precinct?"

"And do what?" Herrera said. "Shake hands with Captain Markham? Check your email? Get a cup of terrible coffee?"

"I was on vacation," Bernadette said. "I don't have my usual items—not even gloves, if we're going to look at the crime scene."

"There's a whole kit in my trunk," Herrera said. "Gloves might be a little big for you, little lady, but they'll work. So whaddaya say?"

Little lady? Bernadette could easily kick Herrera's ass in arm wrestling. But he was offering an olive branch. "I could go for a cup of coffee before we hit the crime scene," Bernadette said.

"I could too." Herrera chuckled. "Huntsman's Park is a good thirty miles from here. And I know a great place to get coffee on the way." Another song came on the radio and Herrera turned the volume up. "You like donuts?"

❧

Old Man Winter Donuts was a small, square white brick building on Pearl Road, close to the exit from Interstate 480. "Best donuts in the state—oh, what the hell, the whole nation," Herrera said, driving the Buick into the bumpy parking lot. He took up two spaces in the small lot and nearly jumped out of the car.

"He's certainly enthusiastic," Bernadette said. "Come on."

Bernadette and Kep followed behind Detective Herrera, who walked across the parking lot at a rapid pace. He was in line when they opened the red-rimmed glass door, humming under his breath and swinging his arms like a little kid.

"'Every batch from scratch,'" Bernadette read from the sign above the counter. And the display was filled with unexpected pastries: not the normal cake and glazed donuts, but a "Jacked-Up Peanut Butter" donut. Other options: a "Bizarro Cruller," cinnamon and crumbled bacon. "Hula Iced"—that one looked like it had candied pineapple on it. Bernadette's jaw dropped open.

Kep, with a forced grin, turned to Herrera. "Detective, which of these culinary delights is your favorite?"

Wow. Kep making small talk. Bernadette nearly pinched herself to make sure she wasn't dreaming.

"Lemon Dream Cheesecake, no question," Herrera said. "In fact, Larissa—that's the woman I was seeing just before picking you up—works here. Not today, but that's how we met. She kept recommending stuff."

"I don't need—" Kep protested. Bernadette covered her mouth to hide a grin.

"It's not like I was looking for this," Herrera continued. "But you know how these things are. Connie and I, we love each other. But there's no spark anymore. Not for either of us. I think you were right. This works for her. I've wondered if Connie has something on the side herself. Still a good-looking woman after twenty-eight years. But, you know, after raising four kids…"

Herrera droned on, barely stopping to order three Lemon Dream Cheesecake donuts—and almost not letting Bernadette order her large coffee. So animated was his diatribe that he was in the way while Bernadette tried to step around him to pay. While they waited, Herrera talked about the cruise he and his wife had taken around the Great Lakes a decade before. Kep squirmed every time Herrera discussed a detail of their intimate marital life. Bernadette was both horrified at Herrera's lack of boundaries and giddily amused.

"Bobby!" the woman behind the counter called.

"That's us!" Herrera squealed—and Bernadette almost laughed at him. He rushed forward, snatching the white bag out of the woman's hand. "Okay, let's go."

"My coffee," Bernadette said.

"Right, right," Herrera said. "You know, that's what's always getting under Larissa's skin. Me not waiting for her when we go anywhere. Movies, restaurants, whatever. 'Bobby, slow down, Bobby, wait for me, Bobby, it's my turn.' But what can I say? That's the way my mind works. Always moving. Always going. Love me at my worst, deserve me at my best, am I right?" He pulled a donut out of the bag with one hand and offered it to Kep. With visible effort, Kep forced a smile onto his face, took the donut with a slight bow, and bit into it.

Fascinating: Kep's face transformed from irritated skepticism to blissful delight. He chewed carefully, then swallowed, a dab of yellow icing on his mustache. "I must say," he said carefully, "that is remarkably tasty."

"Best donuts in the nation," Herrera repeated, taking a large bite out of his donut.

Bernadette noticed Herrera hadn't offered her a donut, and as good as it probably was, she wasn't hungry. She hadn't slept well the night before—thinking about the threat on Sophie's life—and needed the coffee more than anything.

The woman appeared behind the counter with a large coffee cup with an *Old Man Winter Donuts* logo and a white lid. Bernadette stepped behind Herrera and took it gratefully from the woman.

"Okay," she said. "Next stop, Huntsman's Park."

"Yep," Herrera said. "I've always wanted to analyze a crime scene with the famous Dr. Kep Woodhead." He grinned; the lemon curd was stuck to his front teeth.

⚜

Leopold Montclair's house sat at the top of a gently sloping hill of a cul-de-sac called The Grasslands. Dark red brick, a four-car garage, and a circular driveway. Bernadette wasn't sure why a single man would need—or even want— a six-thousand square foot house. Herrera opened the trunk, and they all gloved up. The gloves fit Bernadette's hands well for a *little lady*.

No police tape was strung across the double doors. Bernadette blinked. "Where's the crime scene tape?"

Detective Herrera gritted his teeth. "CSI has already been here. Maybe they removed it when they left."

Inside, the house had stark, white walls, with modern art in reds and purples, slashing lines and roughly rendered geometric shapes. The furniture was in varied shades of gray, from the sofa and coffee table in the living room to the kitchen table and chairs. Light maple floors throughout. Not a houseplant in sight. Definitely the house of an unattached bachelor.

Numbered tents on the floor next to the kitchen table.

"That's where the housekeeper found him," Herrera said, pointing to the floor where "7," "8," "12," and "13" were displayed. Yes, the house should *definitely* still have police tape across the doors.

Bernadette crouched; the other numbers were underneath the chairs.

A buzzing noise. Kep reached into the inside pocket of his tweed sportcoat and pulled out his phone. He glanced at the screen, then clicked the side button and slid the phone back into his pocket.

Bernadette raised her eyebrows at Kep, and Kep nodded in response. So Kep's theory had been correct: the medical examiner had found bromeladine in Leopold Montclair's system. That narrowed the field of suspects considerably.

"Has the crime scene unit cleaned this area?" Kep asked.

"Nothing's been touched," Herrera replied. "We dusted for fingerprints everywhere, though."

"If you don't mind," Bernadette said, "Dr. Woodhead requires an area without competing scents."

Herrera furrowed his brow.

"The, uh, body wash," Bernadette said. "Competing scent. Can you step out of the kitchen?"

"Oh—sure, no problem. Might as well search the back rooms. No telling what CSI missed the first time." He walked through the archway between the kitchen and the hall, his footsteps receding toward the back of the house.

Kep stepped over to the kitchen table, then crouched and took in a long, dramatic inhale. He stood, walked into the kitchen, and performed the same inhale with his face next to the kitchen counters: first near the sink, then next to the high-end refrigerator, then next to the six-burner stove that looked brand new, although Bernadette knew the model was at least five years old.

He straightened up.

"Anything?" Bernadette asked.

"Bromeladine, very faint, under the table."

"What exactly does it smell like?"

"I find it hard to explain chemical scents. The best I can do is tell you that bromeladine smells like daffodils without the floral scent, mixed with ammonia without the sharpness."

To Bernadette—and, she expected, to everyone else with the nose of a mere mortal—daffodils smelled only like a floral scent and ammonia only smelled sharp. She nodded as if she understood.

"Did the medical examiner find an injection site?"

"Yes," Kep said. "The small of the back."

Bernadette arched an eyebrow.

"He was wearing a T-shirt," Kep said. "So someone

could have simply put a friendly hand on his back and injected him."

"How quick would it have been?"

"Death? I suspect, if it were a half-milliliter syringe, his heart would have stopped within fifteen or twenty seconds."

Bernadette tapped her fingers on the kitchen counter.

"What are you postulating?" Kep asked.

"Mr. Montclair was a single man of sixty-one."

"Correct."

"It's not out of the realm of possibility for him to pay for, um, companionship."

Kep tilted his head. "You believe the murderer posed as an escort?"

Bernadette frowned. "Annika Nakrivo escaped from Taycheedah three weeks ago. And she has a history of posing as an escort. She killed—or, uh, I guess, supposedly killed—someone else the same way."

"With an injection of bromeladine?"

"No—by posing as an escort," Bernadette said.

"You told me that Annika did not commit this murder."

"Annika *told me* she didn't do it. Not exactly the same thing."

"So you believe she's the killer?"

Bernadette opened her mouth, then ran a hand over her face. "No. I know I shouldn't jump to conclusions, but I don't believe Annika killed Leopold Montclair."

Kep blinked, then took another long inhale.

"What is it?"

"This kitchen is clean to the point of being nearly ster-ile," he said. "It's clear Mr. Montclair did very little cooking. His housekeepers must have been fastidious. And yet."

"And yet?"

Kep sniffed again. "Cayenne."

"Cayenne pepper?"

"Cayenne *powder*, to be precise. Often, cayenne powder is made from bird's-eye peppers, but this is"—he dipped his nose to the counter next to the refrigerator again—"Egyptian cayenne peppers, mixed in a roughly half-and-half ratio with Numex Las Cruces cayenne peppers."

"Let me guess: those are expensive."

"More expensive than powder made from bird's-eye peppers; perhaps ten or fifteen dollars for a shaker rather than five."

"I see. And—why is this important?"

"I expect many smells in a kitchen, particularly dried spices. However, the scent of cayenne powder is particularly dominant. I would like to determine the cause."

Bernadette walked over to the cabinet above the counter Kep was just smelling. She reached out her gloved hand and opened the door. If there was cayenne in this cabinet, she couldn't smell it.

"Spice rack," she said. "But no spilled cayenne."

"The scent of cayenne is much stronger now," Kep said. "Perhaps the spilled cayenne powder is simply not visible at first glance."

Bernadette slid the nearest vertical rack out on its smooth track. She pulled her phone out, turned the flashlight on, and shined it into the cabinet. "Yep, there's a pile of dark red powder back here. Looks like it could be cayenne."

"Is there a container labeled *Cayenne Pepper*?" Kep asked.

Bernadette glanced through the twenty or so spices in the first sliding rack. "Marjoram, allspice, garam masala..." For someone who didn't cook, Montclair had a bunch of pricey spices.

"Try the middle spice rack."

Bernadette pulled the second spice rack out, and there, in the bottom row, about two-thirds of the way back, was a spice container labeled *Cayenne Pepper*.

"There's the culprit," she said.

Bernadette grabbed the five-inch-tall jar, lifting it above the edge of the spice rack before taking it out.

"Is it empty?" Kep asked.

"Feels like it," Bernadette said. Then a click of metal rattling against the plastic. Bernadette blinked and brought it closer to her face.

A key sat inside the empty cayenne pepper jar.

Chapter Six

BERNADETTE RAISED the spice container and showed it to Kep, rattling the key around inside.

"Annika Nakrivo is playing with us," he murmured.

"But why?" Bernadette said. "Leopold Montclair's death has all the hallmarks of those unsolved murders in the spreadsheet on that SD card hidden in the gusle I bought in Seattle. A sixty-one-year-old executive dies of a heart attack in his kitchen. Unexpected, maybe, but not that unusual. The medical examiner might not have even ordered an autopsy, since nothing would suggest foul play."

"Unless one knew exactly what to look for."

"And Annika's the one who's given us all the clues so far," Bernadette said. "No one would've realized this was a murder if Annika hadn't contacted me through that music forum app."

Kep furrowed his brow. "She certainly possesses a flair for the dramatic. How could she possibly have known—"

"Easy," Bernadette said. "We've opened inquiries for that long list of dead people on the SD card. We already know the FBI—and maybe even CSAB—have moles for

Parr Medical. That's how those inquiries got back to Annika, and as soon as she heard about that, she puts two and two together, and figures out I got the gusle she'd hidden the SD card in. From there, a couple of web searches and phone calls, and she figures out I bought it from Pike Place Music."

"So she uses the music store's online forum to warn you that your daughter is in danger? For what purpose?"

"Maybe she's grateful that I'm the only one taking her seriously about finding her sister. Returning the favor, perhaps."

Kep looked skeptical.

"Or," Bernadette said, "preying on my weaknesses so I'll do what she wants."

"That is a possibility," Kep said. "I am reminded of the fable of the scorpion and the frog."

"Right now," Bernadette said, "I don't see another way across the river."

Kep folded his arms.

"Look, Kep," Bernadette said, "Annika told us that Leopold Montclair was dead when she arrived. And obviously, Annika hid the key in the empty cayenne pepper jar. She's the one who pointed us to this crime scene, and she knew about your supershnozz. No one else would have been able to locate that key but you, and no one else knew you were coming here—and she only knew because she arranged it. So why would she leave us this key if *she's* the killer?"

Kep nodded. "I suppose there's no other reasonable conclusion." He took a step back and leaned on the counter. "But why would she want *me* to find the key?"

"Someone hired her to kill Leopold Montclair, but someone else committed the murder."

Kep furrowed his brow. "A simple case of miscommuni-cation, where the left hand doesn't know what the right hand is doing? Or is there perhaps a fissure developing at Parr Medical, where those involved are starting to turn on each other?"

Bernadette couldn't keep the corner of her mouth from curling into a half-grin. "Sounds like you're jumping to conclusions, Kep."

He frowned.

"In either case," Bernadette said, "Annika is worried. She's either leading us to the person who hired her—or she's leading us to her sister. Maybe both." Bernadette picked up the spice jar, examining it. "Looks like the key is the only thing in here."

"Shall we remove it?"

"Seems like the prudent thing to do." She straightened up as she heard footsteps in the hallway outside the kitchen.

Herrera stuck his head in the kitchen. "How's it going in here?"

Bernadette thought quickly—she didn't want to tell Herrera about the key. Not yet, anyway. "Kep and I were just thinking that Mr. Montclair had a home office. Can you look to see if he has bank statements, financial records, anything that might hint at a motive for who'll get his money?"

"Sure thing." Herrera turned and went back down the hall, his footsteps echoing on the hardwood floors, until he was out of hearing.

Kep lowered his voice. "Parr Medical is probably already theorizing how a seemingly innocuous heart attack has resulted in our getting involved."

"Do you think they suspect Annika told us about Montclair's death?"

Kep frowned. "She left no digital footprint, no record of phone calls. I don't believe Parr Medical is even aware of Pike Place Music, so there's no reason for them to suspect their music forum as a mode of communication."

Bernadette nodded thoughtfully. "But Parr Medical doesn't need proof of Annika contacting us in order to suspect she did. They don't need to prove her guilt in a court of law. If they thought Annika would go rogue, they could just kill her."

Kep stroked his beard. "Then Annika may believe her only chance to get out from under the thumb of Parr Medical is to have us solve this murder."

Bernadette raised the cayenne pepper container holding the key. "What do we do with this, then? We *don't* hand it over to Cleveland Police for fingerprinting?"

Kep hesitated.

"Look at you," Bernadette said, a smile creeping onto the corners of her mouth. "I thought you were such a rule-follower—"

"Not when there's a good chance that following the rules will lead to danger," Kep said, a touch of color rising to his cheeks. "Besides, I believe Annika left no fingerprints."

"What do we do with the key?"

Kep paused for a moment, then set his mouth in a line. "Open the container."

Bernadette unscrewed the top of the container, then shook the key out onto the counter. The silver key was flat with small key bows, its head shaped like a three-leaf clover.

"Doesn't look like it goes to a door lock," Bernadette

said, lowered her face closer to the counter. Then she pointed to the head. "A number." She pulled her phone out and took a picture of the key.

Stamped into the metal in small numerals: *6299 63621*.

"An ABA bank routing number," Kep said.

"It's for a safe-deposit box," Bernadette whispered.

Bernadette and Kep looked at each other.

"We need to take the key with us," Bernadette said. "And not tell Detective Herrera."

"You will, however, inform Lieutenant Stevenson."

"Of course." Bernadette picked up the key with a gloved hand and slipped it into the side pocket of her purse.

"Now return the spice container to its previous location, so Detective Herrera will not know we made a discovery."

Bernadette put the container back, pushed in the vertical spice drawers, and closed the cabinet.

Kep pulled out his phone and began furiously tapping on the screen.

"What are you doing?" Bernadette whispered.

"Concocting a cover story."

After a moment, they heard Detective Herrera's footsteps in the hallway, coming closer. "Good news and bad news, guys," he said.

"Let's hear the bad news first," Bernadette said.

"No paper trail. I mean, there are a couple of locked filing cabinets, but without a warrant, I'm not going to break a rich guy's lock. Even if he's dead."

"Understood, Detective," Kep said.

"Now the good news," Herrera said, holding up a paper —it looked like a bill or an invoice. "Docking fees."

Bernadette snapped her head up. "Montclair owned a boat?"

Herrera flipped the paper around and scanned it. "Slip 23 at the St. Clair Yacht Club." His eyes darted back and forth, then he let out a low whistle. "Ten grand for membership, another ten grand for docking fees, and another six grand for electricity and fuel."

"Six thousand dollars in electricity and fuel," Kep mused. "That suggests Montclair used the boat regularly. I assume Mr. Montclair's keys to his boat are here in the house. If we find little to go on here, we should search the watercraft as well."

"Of course." Herrera lowered the invoice. "What'd you find?"

Bernadette's mind raced. They hadn't mentioned the bromeladine in front of the detective, had they?

"Common kitchen cleaners," Kep said. "I smell no signs of recreational drug use. If Mr. Montclair was murdered, the scents in this room are giving me no signs."

"Kitchen doesn't even look used," Herrera said. "I bet the guy lived on expensive restaurant food. You know, even at good restaurants, there's a ton of sodium and partially hydrogenated fats in there. Eat enough of that, and no wonder you drop dead of a heart attack at sixty-one."

As opposed to your diet of Lemon Dream Cheesecake donuts? Bernadette cleared her throat, glancing at Kep. "It's made us wonder about the veracity of our anonymous tip."

"This is not the first time an anonymous tip has turned out to be erroneous," Kep said.

Herrera nodded. "Hey, you remember in Season One of *Crimes That Won't Die*, how you went with the cops on that anonymous tip to that factory in Nebraska, and it turned out a disgruntled employee was just trying to mess with his boss?"

"Of course," Kep said, "because we discovered they had disposed of their hazardous waste improperly."

"No murder, though," Herrera said, clicking his tongue.

Kep opened his mouth, then closed it. Bernadette had to avert her face so Herrera wouldn't see her laugh.

"Hello?" a nasally voice called from the front door.

Bernadette blinked and tensed. No police tape across the door.

Herrera stepped into the hall. "Can I help you?"

Bernadette walked toward the hall, stepping through the archway. The front door was open, sunlight streaming in. Backlit were two figures: a tall man in a dark business suit and a second man of medium height in blue jeans and a yellow polo shirt.

"Can you help *us?*" said the man in the suit. "You better tell us who you are before we call the police."

Chapter Seven

HERRERA PULLED HIS BADGE OUT. "Looks like the police are already here," he said. "This is an active crime scene. Please state your business."

The man in the suit stepped into the foyer. Now, out of the silhouette, Bernadette could see him clearly. Pale skin, slightly pink, with a full head of dark brown, lush hair, long enough to reveal a slight wave to it. He was reedy, with a pointed nose and chin. His eyes were steel gray and bright, seeming to suck all the information from the scene in front of him. He looked familiar to Bernadette, but she couldn't place him immediately.

"Officer—" he began.

"Detective," Herrera corrected.

The man in the suit blinked. "Detective? What's going on?"

"I'm asking the questions, sir," Herrera said. "Now, as I said, state your business."

The man in the suit motioned to the man in the polo shirt. "This house belongs to Leo Montclair. Ferdinand Montclair—"

"Call me Fred," the man in the yellow polo shirt inter-rupted. His face was round, with a thinning salt-and-pepper hair with a cowlick sticking out behind his right ear. He had a prominent nose, much like his deceased brother, but his eyes, though the same brown color, were tired and moody as opposed to the bright keenness of Leopold's.

"Ferdinand," the man in the suit said, "is the executor of Leopold's estate. And he requested the house be released from crime scene status when the CSI team was finished."

Bernadette remembered the mention of a brother from Leopold's bio. "And who are you?" she asked the man in the suit.

The man blinked. "Jeremy," he said. "I'm a colleague of Leo's."

"A colleague?" Bernadette asked. Then it clicked—oh, of course—Jeremy Niehaus. She'd seen his biography in the airport lounge with Kep.

"Leo was a member of the board of directors of Parr Medical," Niehaus said. "I'm the CEO."

Bernadette pressed her lips together. She couldn't let on that she and Kep both suspected Niehaus of hiring the killers due to the financial information Kep had dug up.

She hadn't recognized Niehaus right away, but the headshot of Jeremy Niehaus she'd seen on the Parr Medical website had been significantly different. For one, he'd had a receding hairline that was far closer to Fred's male-pattern baldness than Niehaus's current hairstyle. For another, he was missing the square glasses in his bio photo that had given him a more professorial look. She looked in his face, but she saw no recognition there of her. "So you two didn't work together daily?"

"And who are you?" Niehaus asked in a nasal, grating tone, dripping with disdain.

"Consultants with the Cleveland Police," Bernadette said.

Herrera looked at Bernadette out of the corner of his eye. Did he think it was odd for her not to disclose that she and Kep worked for CSAB? But of course if he was in Parr Medical's pocket, he'd know that Bernadette and Kep would be wary around any of Parr Medical's leadership. Did he recognize them?

Bernadette set her mouth in a line. It was a delicate dance: did they know that she knew that they knew that she knew? She felt a headache coming on.

"Consultants for what?" Niehaus's tone was guarded, trying not to be demanding.

Bernadette tilted her head. "I'm sorry; I don't believe I'm at liberty to disclose that."

Niehaus lifted his eyebrows, then turned to Herrera. "Exactly what are you looking for, Detective?"

Herrera shrugged. "We're following up on some information we received."

"What kind of information?"

"I'm afraid I can't tell you any more than that."

Niehaus opened his mouth as if he wanted to say something—Bernadette wondered if it would be some variant of *Do you know who I am?* But then he closed his mouth.

"You have my word we'll be out of your hair as soon as we wrap things up," Herrera said.

Niehaus leaned toward Fred and murmured into his ear.

"Have you removed anything from the house?" Fred asked, his voice cracking on the first syllable.

Herrera shook his head. "Everything is just the way we

found it. You'd have to ask the paramedics if they removed anything—that should be in their report."

Bernadette thought of the key in her purse but kept her mouth shut.

Niehaus took a step back, pulling Fred with him, and leaned close to his ear, whispering. Fred shook his head, murmured something in response, and Niehaus's hand gripped Fred's shoulder as he said something else. Bernadette caught the words "executor" and "warrant." She frowned and her skin prickled.

How much did Niehaus know—and how much was he responsible for? She looked at Niehaus again and caught his eye.

Nope. Nothing. No flash of recognition, no grimace of anticipated conflict. Was it possible Niehaus gave the directives without even seeing pictures of Bernadette and Kep?

"As executor of my brother's estate," Fred began haltingly, "I request—"

A withering look from Niehaus.

"—I demand," Fred continued, "that you remove yourselves from these premises, as you have no warrant and have not entered on—on..."

Niehaus whispered something.

"Good faith," Fred finished.

Bernadette nodded. "Understood." She motioned toward the front door with her head. "Gentlemen, let's go. You heard the man."

Herrera's forehead wrinkled in confusion. "This isn't—"

Bernadette raised her eyebrows. Herrera closed his mouth and followed Bernadette out the front door, Kep at his heels. Bernadette reached out to the handle to pull the front door closed—and a shiny black dress shoe stopped it.

Bernadette looked up into the smiling face of Jeremy Niehaus.

"Truly sorry about all this," he said. "Freddy hasn't been the same since he lost his daughter two years ago. And now his brother. Tragic, really." Niehaus clicked his tongue. "Makes him downright unpredictable. Never know what he's going to do next, that one."

Bernadette set her mouth in a line. So obviously a ruse to disguise his interest in following the case while blaming it on Fred Montclair's emotional state. She wanted to call Niehaus on his bullshit, but this wasn't the time. Or the place. "Please give Fred our sincere condolences."

"Next time, show up with a warrant." With a quick flick of his wrist, Jeremy Niehaus slammed the door in Bernadette's face.

She turned slowly and walked down the porch steps.

"You mind telling me what's going on?" Herrera asked.

"What do you mean?" Bernadette focused on the concrete path in front of her.

"Listen, I'm the federal liaison for Cleveland Metro," he said. "No federal investigator has ever gotten the 'who are you' question from a civilian and *not* pulled out their federal badges."

"Neither of us are agents, Detective," Kep said. "I am a paid consultant, and Ms. Becker is a case analyst—some of my more gauche colleagues refer to her as my 'handler.'" Kep motioned toward the house with his chin. "Mr. Niehaus is a powerful business leader, not just in Cleveland, but one of the most powerful executives in the United States. I don't wish for us to be on his radar until it's absolutely necessary."

"I agree," Bernadette said.

Herrera shook his head. "I don't buy that."

Kep blinked and rose to his full height.

"Look, I get it," Herrera said, holding his hands up in front of him. "You've probably been in pissing contests with local PDs before. Especially if you pulled that 'I-can-smell-you-had-an-affair' shit with anyone else. Or territory squabbles—either some hotshot detective wants to keep the big case instead of giving it to the feds, or no one wants the responsibility and everyone plays hot potato with the case that no one can solve."

They arrived at Herrera's car, and he walked to the driver's-side door.

"Maybe you don't want to trust me," Herrera said, "but this'll be a hell of a lot easier if we share information." He unlocked the car and looked at Kep out of the corner of his eye. "Even if you *did* sniff out my affair, that doesn't make you a better detective than me."

They all got in the car, Kep and Bernadette sliding into the back seat, and Herrera didn't speak again for several minutes. Bernadette stared out the window.

This wasn't the way they'd come. Her pulse raced, then —of course, they'd come from the airport and they were likely traveling back to the police station downtown. Sure enough, after a few miles, they turned left onto U.S. 322, following an arrow that clearly said *To Cleveland*.

Herrera pulled his phone out and made a call. She couldn't hear the conversation from the back seat over the engine noise, but caught a chuckle every so often.

They passed low-roofed shopping centers, then a large cemetery—one of the largest Bernadette had ever seen. A sign for the James A. Garfield Memorial. A glimmer of recognition of a long-ago trivia night with Joanna Quimby, back before Bernadette had been betrayed. To Bernadette, Garfield was the name of an orange cat from the comics, but to Joanna, Garfield was the answer to the question, "Who was America's first left-handed president?" She'd been right, and they'd won twenty bucks off their tab that night.

Then a laugh from the front seat. "Half an hour?" Herrera said. "Sure, I can meet you there."

She craned her neck and saw the buildings of downtown; the homicide division was housed only a couple of blocks away from the Public Square. Herrera ended the call and dropped the phone onto the seat. Then, suddenly, they turned right at the Cleveland Art Museum, away from downtown. Bernadette's sense of direction was muddled; she looked at Kep.

"Are we headed toward the lake?" Kep asked.

"Sure we are," Herrera said. "You want to check out Slip 23 before Mr. Important CEO drags the brother to Leopold's boat, too, right?"

Bernadette leaned forward. "Even if the boat's owner is deceased, we still need a warrant. And that'll take hours— maybe days."

"Not everyone needs a warrant to search a boat," Herrera said, a note in his voice reveling in his own cleverness.

Kep sat back and turned his head to Bernadette. "Aha. Coast Guard."

⚜

The St. Clair Yacht Club sat on the shore of Lake Erie, and the white clubhouse was a long, low-slung, square-roofed building parallel to the shore. As they walked from the car toward the clubhouse, sounds of splashing and children's laughter: a large pool sat about fifty feet from the side of the clubhouse, full of kids on this hot, humid early July morning. Behind the clubhouse, the masts of sailboats stuck up above the maple trees dotting the shoreline.

Herrera led the way up the flagstone walkway to the front door of the building, then held the door open for Kep and Bernadette.

As unassuming as the façade of the yacht club looked, the inside was luxurious. Nautical themes in off-white with royal blue and a dusky red accents. To the left, a large dining room with white tablecloths. Several families were inside at the round tables, and Bernadette caught a few people sitting at the bar, the ash and maple giving the room a light, airy feeling, belying its opulence. Ahead of her, a host station, about ten feet wide, a man of about twenty wearing a white golf shirt with the St. Clair logo.

"May I help you?" the young man said, pleasantly enough, but with a trace of warning in his tone. He likely didn't recognize them and knew they weren't members of the club.

Herrera stepped forward in front of Bernadette, holding his badge out. "Hi there," he said easily. "I'm Detective Bobby Herrera, Cleveland P.D. And you are?"

"Uh—I'm Marco."

"Hi, Marco. Listen." Herrera went to the host station, rested his hands on it, and leaned forward. He glanced over his shoulder at Kep and Bernadette, then made a slight motion of his head.

Bernadette took a few steps forward until she was directly over Herrera's right shoulder. Kep appeared over his left shoulder.

Like the proverbial angel and devil. Bernadette cleared her throat.

"These two are federal agents," Herrera said, "and I'm the department liaison. I'm going to tell you a few things here, Marco, and I need you to keep your voice down."

Marco gulped. "Uh—sure."

"One of your members was murdered earlier in the week."

Marco hesitated, then nodded solemnly.

"He's renting a slip here. Number 23."

Marco paled. "Mr. Montclair?"

"Did you know him, Marco?"

"Always treated me well," Marco said. "Helped him with his electricity and fuel. Last year, he asked me if I wanted to help out on deck while he was entertaining some clients. Paid me fifty bucks an hour."

"Entertaining a client?" Bernadette said.

"Sure. He did that a lot. He and that other guy."

Kep blinked, then pulled out his phone, tapped the screen, and turned it to Marco. It was still on the Parr Medical leadership web page.

"Recognize anyone else here?"

Marco pointed to Jeremy Niehaus. "Him. They were always together when they had clients."

"Jeremy Niehaus," Herrera said. "Anyone else from these photos?"

Marco looked as Kep scrolled, then he shook his head. "No one else looks familiar."

"So Mr. Montclair was always here with Niehaus?"

Marco shook his head. "Sometimes Mr. Montclair was by himself, or with a, uh, lady friend. Everyone who wasn't a member needed to sign in as a guest of the club, and he'd always let us know when he had clients. That way we could give them the white-glove service, go all out. We made sure to get our best people on maintenance and house-keeping. His boat was always in top shape."

"We'll need the names of the staff members who worked on his boat," Herrera said.

With a lady friend. Bernadette had a thought. She pulled her phone out and searched for a photo of Annika Nakrivo. There it was, from back in March. She turned the screen to Marco. "Is this one of Montclair's guests?"

Marco squinted. "I think so. But not on the boat. I think they had dinner together, after the end of the season, if I remember correctly. I didn't think she was one of Montclair's usual companions."

"Why not?"

"She wasn't all dolled up. Sweats, no makeup. Didn't really fit our dress code, but Mr. Montclair spends so much money with us, and we aren't very busy after the boats get winterized. I wasn't going to complain. He tipped me a hundred that night."

"When was this?"

"Like I said, end of the season. November or December." He shifted uncomfortably. "I got the feeling she was in some trouble. Seemed a little out of it."

Bernadette pressed her lips together. That would fit the timeline of Anya Kerovic having plastic surgery in Cleveland and transforming into Annika Nakrivo for her undercover corporate espionage operation at Kilbourn Tech. She'd landed in Cleveland on a Parr Medical private plane in late October and appeared with a slightly different face in Milwaukee in January. And the hotel she stayed in was right around the corner from the Parr Medical headquarters.

Montclair had dinner with her when she was recovering from plastic surgery. And a little over six months later, Annika got orders to kill him. A shudder went down Bernadette's spine.

☙❧

The wind whipped in off the lake, cooling off the late morning. Bernadette followed Marco out to the boat slips, Detective Herrera in front of her and Kep a step behind.

A Latino man, about five foot nine, stood on the dock next to a sign reading *Slip 23*. He wore a Guardians baseball cap, jeans, an aloha shirt, and leather boat shoes.

"Guillermo," Herrera said, "these are the feds I told you about."

Guillermo stuck out his hand. "Gui Herrera," he said to Kep. "U.S. Coast Guard, Great Lakes Region."

Kep shook his hand. "Dr. Kep Woodhead from the Controlled Substance Analysis Bureau. My colleague, Bernadette Becker."

Gui shook Bernadette's hand, too. Bobby and Gui must be brothers; they both had the same boyish smile and stocky build. Wedding band on Gui's ring finger. For a moment, Bernadette wondered if Kep smelled any evidence of Gui's affair partners too, then admonished herself for making terrible assumptions. They hung back, just out of Marco's earshot.

"Bobby says you're here investigating a murder," Gui said.

"And the deceased is the owner of this boat," Bernadette said.

"We didn't want to wait for a warrant," Bobby said. "Besides, the dead guy's brother is getting strong-armed by the CEO of the dead guy's company, and we want to take a look before the CEO or the brother figure out we might want to take a look at his boat. I don't think either of them knew the police were getting involved, much less the feds."

"Got it," Gui said. "Well, then, let's get started."

Marco had to wait for them for a moment, then he stepped forward and handed a key to Gui, glancing at Detective Herrera. "He wanted the boat kept in perfect shape in case a client came in at the last minute," Marco said. "We've had a copy of his key for years."

They walked out onto the slip. Bernadette could only describe the boat as an overgrown speedboat; shaped like the fast cigarette boats she'd seen in movies, but with wraparound windows in the lower deck, a large seating area in the fore.

"Isn't she gorgeous?" Marco said, envy dripping from his voice. "If I had a spare two million bucks, this would be mine. Fifty-two foot Croix-au-Vie."

"Overpriced and unreliable," Gui muttered under his breath. He stepped onto the boat, then reached out for Bernadette's hand. She hesitated for a moment before taking it and getting onboard.

With the four of them, the standing area behind the enclosed cockpit was cramped, but Gui soon unlocked the upper cockpit area.

"Glove up, everyone," he said, producing four pairs of latex gloves. "And a couple of evidence bags."

Marco balked. "I'll just be on the slip if you need anything."

After putting their gloves on and taking two clear evidence bags each, the four of them entered the cockpit area. It was larger than Bernadette originally thought. On the right, a ladder descended below. The two seats and the controls were at the front, while the rear of the area housed a square wooden table, three leather benches, and a small kitchen on the left, complete with refrigerator, oven, and a two-burner stove. Bernadette knotted her brow. Two million bucks only got you a two-burner stove?

"What are we looking for?" Gui asked.

"A motive," Herrera said. "Montclair was a rich guy, and Marco there says he entertained clients frequently. He ends up dead, and the feds think it was some kind of almost-untraceable poison. So you know what we know."

"You don't think he kept a file cabinet here that'll reach out and bite you, do you?" Gui asked. "Any kind of physical evidence—"

Detective Herrera put up his hands. "Yeah, yeah, I know, but like I said, I wanted to search the boat before the dead guy's brother stops it from being an option. Maybe take lots of pictures. If we don't know what we're looking for, we might miss it. We take pictures, we can always look to see what we might have missed."

Kep's mouth turned down, but he was the first on the ladder to go to the lower cabin. Bernadette followed.

The lower deck had a ceiling low enough that Kep had to duck his head. Here, a leather sofa and armchair dominated the space, with a flat-screen television mounted on the wall just on the other side of the ladder. A sliding door behind the sofa; probably the bedroom or the bathroom. The Croix-au-Vie would be advertised as sleeping six or eight, but probably only two people could sleep out here comfortably.

Bernadette began opening the cabinet doors that lined the room, but it was mostly pantry and cooking items, held in place by bands or mats. Blankets and pillows in the first one. Another was an empty drawer, probably for the clothes of guests who stayed the night.

Kep stared at the television for a long time.

"Any scents in here we should be aware of?"

"The cleaning staff uses Queen of Clean," Kep said distractedly. "From the lack of other scents, they do a thorough job." He took a step toward the television, then reached out and pulled it on its swinging arm mount away from the wall, turning his phone's flashlight on.

"What are you doing?"

Kep craned his head around the back of the television, then held his phone out to Bernadette. "Would you mind holding this?"

"Sure." Bernadette took the phone from Kep, its flashlight still on, then shone it on the back of the television. Bernadette saw nothing but cords and the black plastic molding of the back of the television.

Kep grimaced, reached up, and took hold of a piece of molding.

"Careful, you'll—"

A piece of the molding, about seven inches long and an inch high, with a rounded back, pulled off in Kep's hand. A light on the end of the molding glowed red.

That wasn't a piece of molding at all.

Chapter Eight

Kep turned the piece of molding over in hand. "I suspected as much." He ran his fingers along the back of the molding, popped a plastic cover off, then shook a flat silver battery into his hand.

Bernadette almost dropped the phone. "Is that—"

"This is a similar voice-activated recorder to the one found in Jack's apartment," Kep said. "I believe this is a newer model, but the execution is the same."

"How did you know?"

"The same people who are behind Jack's murder"—Kep closed his eyes and cleared his throat—"are likely behind Montclair's as well."

Bernadette blinked, then whispered, "Should we be talking? There could be other recording devices in here."

Kep shrugged. "These don't transmit. Neither did the one in Jack's apartment. Much less taxing on the battery."

"Then how do they get the recordings?"

"Someone must come in here every so often, perhaps once a week, remove the recording cards or download to USB sticks, maybe replace the batteries. I suspect someone at the cleaning service or the boat maintenance team. It could be a security guard."

"Think we can get fingerprints from it?"

"There were no fingerprints on the one from Jack's apartment. I doubt there are fingerprints to be found here."

Bernadette handed the phone back to Kep. "May I see it?"

Kep handed the recording device to Bernadette. She took it out from behind the television into the light of the large room. She held it up to the light and squinted. "Serial number. Maybe we can find out who made the purchase."

"My investigator attempted to find the order information from the serial number on Jack's device, as well. He came up empty."

"Lesley has access to databases your P.I. might not," Bernadette said, pulling her phone out and texting Lesley. "You know the make and model of this?"

"Broman Security Systems," Kep said. "The model my investigator found was the VA-2300A. As I said, I believe this is a newer model."

Bernadette typed the message out and hit *Send*. "Okay. Lesley will look for a newer model with this serial number. Come on, Kep, let's see if there are any other clues."

They searched the rest of the living room, including all the drawers, but found nothing suspicious. As Kep continued to sniff around the perimeter of the living room, Bernadette went through the pocket door and into the bedroom. A smaller television in here, solidly attached to the wall. She shined her flashlight on the mount, but there wasn't enough space for a recording device. She searched the room, including the drawers of the nightstand, then got on the floor, rolled onto her back, and looked up at the bottom of the bedframe.

There it was, attached to the inside of the bedrail. She pulled it off into her hand.

Kep entered the room, closed his eyes, and took a deep breath through his nose.

"Anything?" Bernadette asked.

"Shh," Kep said. He spread his arms wide, took another deep breath through his nose, then exhaled, opening his eyes.

Bernadette looked at him expectantly.

"I wish my house cleaners did as thorough of a job as they did here," he said.

"So nothing?"

"Not that I can smell."

Bernadette held up the recording device. "Another one. This one attached to the underside of the bed frame."

"Perhaps there's another device above deck."

"Maybe." Bernadette tapped her temple. "Same model as the other one. So this doesn't transmit either."

"Allowing them to operate for a longer time."

"So who's swapping them out without Montclair's knowledge?"

"I suspect someone from the cleaning staff, but anyone with access to the boat could do it."

Bernadette paused. "Do you want to tell Herrera about the recording devices we found?"

"I don't see how we can keep our discovery from him."

"I can put these in my purse. He'll never know."

Kep shook his head. "We need to enter these into evidence."

"How are these different from the key?"

"Because I suspect no one else knows about the key.

But someone will notice these recording devices have gone missing."

"You think we can trust Detective Herrera? Or the evidence room? Or do you think someone might tip off Parr Medical that we found recording devices?"

Kep folded his arms. "Parr Medical will discover we found recording devices soon enough."

Bernadette screwed up her mouth in thought. "We'll ask Maura."

Kep pursed his lips.

"Once we remove all the batteries, the devices can go in the evidence bags," Bernadette said. "That'll preserve chain of custody. We can talk to Maura when we get back to the police station."

Kep frowned but said nothing. Bernadette put the devices in an evidence bag, sealed them, and put them in her purse.

They found nothing else in the bedroom or in the small head. They climbed up the ladder just as the Herrera brothers were opening the door to the outside again.

"Find anything?" Bernadette said.

"This place is clean," Detective Herrera said. "It's like a showcase boat at the dealer. I can't even tell that people stayed here. Except for the champagne bottle in the fridge." He thrust his chin at Gui. "Now my brother, on the other hand..."

Gui stepped forward, a small piece of paper in one gloved hand. "Found this in a drawer underneath that center table on the top deck."

Bernadette took the paper. *From the Desk of Leopold Montclair* at the top. Obviously from a notepad, the five-by-eight sheet was covered in light pencil strokes, as if Gui had used the side of a sharpened pencil to cover the center section.

"A real Sherlock Holmes here," Detective Herrera said gruffly. "He probably saw it on one of those cop shows he's always watching. Wants to be a real cop, you know."

"Shut the hell up, Bobby," Gui said, though he was grinning.

Bernadette looked closer. In the sea of gray pencil, thin white letters. *Andy Belgrade — Orion's Wolfpack.*

"That mean anything to you?" Detective Herrera asked.

"Yes," Kep said. "Mr. Montclair called a television producer last week. The producer's assistant wrote the name *Andy Belgrade*. As for the *Orion's Wolfpack*, that I have not heard of."

"Me neither," Detective Herrera said. "Maybe it's the name of a spy show he wrote a screenplay for." He chuckled. "Everyone thinks they've got what it takes to make it in Hollywood."

"I don't know where the top sheet is," Gui Herrera said. "But it's not in the trash. I expect Montclair got a phone call while on the deck, wrote that on the top sheet of the notepad, tore it off, and took it with him or threw it away."

"It's something, anyway." Bernadette said. Another reference to Andy Belgrade.

"How about you?"

Kep stole a quick glance at Bernadette. "Besides the scent of Queen of Clean?" he asked.

For a moment, she thought about telling the detective about the recording devices. But if Herrera had been compromised, they couldn't let him know what they'd found.

"Like you mentioned," Bernadette said, "it's like a showcase boat at the dealer. You could bounce a quarter off the bed down there."

"Sorry to drag you out here for nothing," Detective Herrera said to Gui.

"Not nothing," Gui said, indicating the piece of paper still in Bernadette's hand.

"Oh, yeah," Detective Herrera said. "We'll let you know as soon as the first episode of *Orion's Wolfpack* is available on Flixtune."

◈

Kep and Bernadette were quiet in the back of the car on the ride to the police station.

The homicide unit was housed in the Civic Center District in downtown Cleveland, a block from the Cuyahoga County courthouse, and across from two high-rise hotels. Bernadette craned her neck to try to see the top of one of the hotel towers, but Herrera steered them into an underground garage before she was successful.

Herrera took Bernadette and Kep to the front desk to sign them in, scan their IDs, and get their visitor badges. The badges were marked with a "U," meaning they didn't need to be accompanied by an employee or officer. That mildly surprised Bernadette.

They went up to the third floor in the elevator. As soon as the doors opened, Herrera strode out into the hall, pushed through a set of double glass doors, then showed them a cramped conference room with a small round table, four chairs, and two file boxes on the floor in the corner.

"We appreciate the space, Detective," Kep said.

"I'll email you the instructions to get on the wi-fi," Herrera said. "You should be able to get the email on your phones." He closed the conference room door before either of them could respond.

"At least his brother was helpful," Bernadette said, putting her purse on the table and sitting down.

Kep shrugged as he pulled another chair out from the table. "If he has been compromised by Parr Medical, then it's appropriate. If he hasn't, then he will simply perceive us as rude."

Bernadette nodded.

Kep sat, took his phone out, and tapped the screen a few times. "No wi-fi instructions as of yet."

"He just left," Bernadette pointed out.

"My phone has service," Kep said. "Would you allow me to examine the key you took from the Montclair house?"

Bernadette pulled the key out of the side pocket of her purse and placed it gently on the table in front of him. Bernadette leaned forward, reading the number stamped onto it.

Kep tapped on his phone several times. After a moment, he grunted. "Would you be so kind as to read me the number on the key?"

"Six two nine nine," Bernadette said.

Kep tapped. "Yes?"

"Six three six two one."

Kep tapped, then with a flourish, gave a final tap and straightened in his seat.

"What is it?" Bernadette asked.

"Caskill & Dunleavy Bank."

Bernadette's eyes widened. "That's the same bank that's listed on the payments to Joanna Quimby. An office in Hunstman's Park, too—where we just came from."

Kep nodded.

"Is there anything else on the key?"

Kep turned the key over, and Bernadette leaned over. In even smaller characters than the ABA routing number: *D40387GH*.

"Is the penultimate letter a C?" Kep asked, adjusting his glasses.

"It's a G."

Kep tapped on his phone again, and after a moment, he looked up. "Parr Medical's main office is approximately three blocks southeast of here."

"Yeah—and the local FBI office is about five blocks northeast. We've got to keep our eyes out for them, too, since I'd expect at least one person there to be compromised, too."

"Caskill & Dunleavy is a rather small bank. I assume it caters to high-end customers. One location in Huntsman's Park and one downtown. Across the street from the Parr Medical headquarters. However, I'm unsure in which location the safe-deposit box is located."

Bernadette tapped the table next to the "D" on the key. "I bet the D stands for downtown."

"Not necessarily."

"We have nothing else to go on," Bernadette said. "Besides, we don't have a car. The Caskill & Dunleavy office is, what, a ten-minute walk? And I'm sure Herrera will love it if we ask him for a ride back to Huntsman's Park after we just got here."

Kep nodded. "And we should keep the detective on a need-to-know basis as much as possible."

Bernadette took out her phone and called Maura. It

rang four times before going to voicemail. "Checking in," Bernadette said after the beep. "Give us a call. We've got some questions for you." She hung up; that was probably too vague, but she didn't want to leave any details.

They studied the map on Kep's phone for a moment, then, leaving their laptops, exited the conference room, took the elevator down, and signed out at the front desk, confirming they could come back in.

"Surprised to see you leaving so soon," the desk clerk said in a Tennessee drawl. "Y'all just got here."

"Long day," Bernadette said. "Heading out for some coffee."

"Oh, sure. The coffee here is awful. There's a Spicy Siren Coffee in the next building over, but you should walk down past the Public Square and the visitor's center and go to the Firebird. Much better."

"Sounds great," Bernadette said.

Outside, the July afternoon was stifling. A light breeze was coming from the lake, but Bernadette broke out into a sweat almost immediately. She took off her blazer, which helped a little.

"Whose idea was it to walk through downtown at noon in the middle of the summer?"

"Perhaps we should rent a car," Kep suggested. Bernadette looked at him for a moment; he didn't seem bothered by the heat in the slightest.

Bernadette hadn't been to the Cleveland Public Square before. A seated statue faced the center of the plaza; she'd never seen something like that. Visitors crowded the square on this summer day. Families with strollers, small groups of teenagers, a few older tourists in T-shirts and sun hats. Bernadette and Kep, in their blazers and professional trousers, stood out among all the visitors.

They crossed through the plaza, across Superior Avenue, toward the eastern corner of the Public Square, then crossed the street and walked down Euclid. The buildings on this street were shorter, the restaurants all fast-casual national chains: a mediocre sandwich shop, a run of the mill Mexican fast-food place. A block further, a blues club with alternating flashing neon lights, barely visible in the middle of the day.

"Two more blocks?" Bernadette asked. She hadn't had time for a workout this morning before saying her good-byes to Sophie at the airport—and getting on the plane herself. Despite the heat, the outside air felt welcoming. She couldn't call it fresh air, exactly, as there was an undercurrent of stale cigarettes. In the last block, a light but pungent odor of dog feces was evident. She glanced over at Kep. His glasses had slipped down his nose, and he seemed to breathe through his mouth.

"Four," Kep said. He wasn't sweating, but the odors had put him in obvious discomfort.

On the left, a steak house. On the right, a Cajun restaurant. Bernadette looked up, but saw no sign for Caskill & Dunleavy Bank.

Two blocks later, they stepped around construction on the sidewalk, then a half a block under scaffolding. A large mid-century building, about five stories high and in beige concrete, sat next to the sidewalk. Double glass doors. Bernadette looked up and down the building. This was where she remembered it on the map. Kep set his jaw.

"Is this the place?"

"I believe it is." He turned and pointed across the side street. "That's the Parr Medical headquarters."

"Usually businesses like to advertise where they are."

"Perhaps the business model is different for financial institutions with wealthy clients."

Bernadette nodded. "We'll need a warrant to search the box."

"Yes," Kep said, "but no judge will grant us access to the box without knowing of its location."

Bernadette nodded.

They entered through the double glass doors. The lobby was small, and a counter at waist height sat between the entrance and the elevators.

"Good afternoon," the security guard behind the counter said brightly. "How can I help you?"

"Caskill & Dunleavy," Bernadette said.

"Certainly," the guard said. "They're by appointment only. Can I get your name?"

Bernadette pulled her identification out of her pocket. "Federal investigator. We don't need an appointment."

The security guard's eyes went wide, then he nodded. "Go right ahead."

They walked past the guard to the elevator and stood in wait.

"Kep," Bernadette whispered, "do you know what floor they're on?"

"No," Kep said. "But I believe there are only five floors, and they're not on the ground floor. Four floors shouldn't be that much room to cover."

A ding above them, then the elevator doors opened.

"Have a pleasant day," the guard said. Bernadette turned and nodded, then stepped inside with Kep.

No buttons in the elevator. Oh—Bernadette had been in a few hotels where the keypad in front of the elevator chose the floor. Maybe the security desk had the elevator controls with them. Interesting—it would make them hard to trick. Or maybe just a different kind of challenge.

The doors slid closed, and the elevator went up. Could have been three floors, or maybe all the way to the top. Bernadette opened her purse and took the key between her index finger and her thumb. Her palms were sweating.

The elevator gently stopped, and the doors slid apart.

This area of the floor had no cubicle walls; like a consumer bank, but small. Perhaps offices were behind the wall in front of them. Five L-shaped desks were arranged in the room, all equidistant from each other, in the same orientation. The monitors on each desk were in the same position on each desk, the keyboard and mouse at the same location.

Each desk was empty, except for the man at the desk closest to the door, who stood as soon as they stepped out of the elevator. He wore a white dress shirt under his gray suit jacket with a navy blue tie. His short hair was dark brown, and he looked young. He wore no glasses, and his brown eyes darted from Kep to Bernadette.

"Holding down the fort?" Bernadette asked, plastering a friendly smile on her face. Usually lunch time was a busy time of day for banks—but as Kep said, maybe this wasn't a normal bank.

"I'm sorry," he said, "but we're by appointment only. There must be some mistake."

"We're here for a safe-deposit box," Bernadette said, holding up the key.

"Oh—well, perhaps I missed the communication," he said. He squinted at the key in Bernadette's hand. "That's one of ours?"

Bernadette nodded. The man stepped forward.

Bernadette handed him the key, and after examining it quickly, gave it back to her. "Just a moment."

He hurried back to his desk, clicked onto another screen on his computer, typed in a few keystrokes, then watched as the screen changed. He brightened, stood, and walked to them.

"Yes—just checking that it was at this location. Ms. Synskey"—he nodded at Bernadette, then addressed Kep—"and Mr. Montclair, I'll just need to see some identification."

Bernadette shook her head. This would be tough—and it probably wouldn't work. But the bank employee was obviously new—and by himself. It might work. "Mr. Montclair is deceased. Dr. Woodhead and I are federal investigators looking into his death, and we need to get into the safe-deposit box." She held up her identification.

The young man's face changed from an expression of helpful service to impassive. "Do you have a warrant?"

"Not necessary," Bernadette said. "The renter is dead, and we suspect—"

"Our banking policy is quite clear for access to our safe-deposit boxes, I'm sorry to say," the young man said, though he didn't appear sorry at all. "You'll need the parties to consent to open the safe-deposit box." He folded his arms. "Of course, we support cooperation with law enforcement, but we have our clients' privacy interests at heart. I'm sure you understand."

"We have probable cause," Bernadette said. "The law is quite clear on this."

The young man tilted his head. "If the law is clear on this, you won't mind getting a court order."

Bernadette opened her mouth to speak again. She knew the law was on her side, but Caskill & Dunleavy was obviously used to catering to rich people who got their way and had enough money to get around the law. And she could get a court order, but that could take days. And it would definitely reveal that Kep and Bernadette had a safe-deposit box key in their possession.

An idea, half-formed, popped into her head.

So she said simply, "Thank you for your time."

Kep hesitated a moment—was he surprised by their sudden departure, or did he smell something?—but then he turned and faced the elevator. There was a single button here—the only exit from the floor was back to the ground floor. Bernadette reached out and pressed it, and an immediate ding signaled the doors opening in front of her.

They got in, and Bernadette pulled her phone out as soon as the elevator began moving. The wireless signal was a little weak, but after a moment, the search screen for LinkProfs came up.

"What are you doing?" asked Kep. "The Supreme Court ruled in favor of the police when this very same situation came before them last year."

"Yes," Bernadette said, "but going through the proper channels will take too much time. And the information will be out there that we hold the safe-deposit box key."

"So what do you suggest?" Kep asked. "Abandon the safe-deposit box entirely?"

"No," Bernadette said. "Looks like there were two people who were authorized to access this safe-deposit box. Montclair is dead. Let's see how Ms. Synskey is connected to him."

Kep glanced at Bernadette's screen. "Why are you choosing a professional networking website?"

"Because this is across the street from Parr Medical,

not in Huntsman's Park, where all the rich people live," Bernadette replied.

Kep stroked his beard and nodded.

The elevator arrived at the ground floor, and they got out. As soon as they walked past the guard station—the security guard giving them a withering glare on their way out—Bernadette's phone jumped in connectivity and the screen refreshed, showing all of Leopold Montclair's professional connections—over five hundred of them.

Bernadette sorted by relevancy, and there on the first page, just below Yates Raphael and Jeremy Niehaus, was another name: Marnie Synskey.

Clicking on her name brought up a professional resume.

"Head of Executive Services at Parr Medical," Bernadette read. "She must either be the admin for Niehaus or Montclair—or maybe both. Which means she might have information that's relevant to this investigation."

Kep pursed his lips. "I fail to see how we can convince Ms. Synskey to allow us access to Montclair's safe-deposit box."

Bernadette nodded. "Let me think for a moment." The idea was just out of her grasp.

Her phone buzzed in her hand. A text from Lesley.

Got an error on the two serial numbers you gave me from those recording devices

I dug into it a little more and a government agency bought the devices

I logged into a different system and found it

> The FBI purchased both

> Requestor's name is Joanna Quimby

> Got copies of the form—sending now

Bernadette blinked for a moment. "What the hell?" she murmured under her breath.

"What is it?"

"Those recording devices—they were purchased by the FBI. And Joanna was the requestor."

Kep blinked rapidly. "I thought—I thought the FBI simply had employees taking money to cover up evidence against Parr Medical."

"Apparently Joanna also got them government-quality spy devices. Lesley's sending me a copy of the forms."

Her phone dinged and she tapped the screen.

The form came up, a PDF file. She used two fingers to zoom in. Yes, there was Joanna Quimby's name and digital signature under the requestor area.

And the approver's name.

Andy Belgrade.

Chapter Nine

BERNADETTE STARED at the approver's name for a
moment, unblinking, then tapped the screen and called
Lesley.

"Hey, Bernadette. Did that come through?"

"Yes—and on the PDF you sent me, do me a favor and
go to the approver's name."

"Andy Belgrade." Lesley sucked in a breath through her
teeth. "That's not Joanna Quimby's boss. Do you think
Quimby let Belgrade know who this was for? Or do you
think she was investigating Leopold Montclair on her own
and Belgrade just signed what was put in front of him?"

"Not the first time his name has come up in our investigation. Leopold mentioned the name to a TV news
producer friend before he was killed. Can you find out
who he is?"

"It's going on my list right now."

"I hope Andrew Belgrade is an unsuspecting bureau-
crat, but he could be the liaison between law enforcement
and Parr Medical, making sure everything gets covered up.
Be careful. Make sure they can't track you tracking him."

Lesley exhaled loudly. "I'm not sure I can do that with the current equipment I've got," she said. "I'll talk to Maura and see if I can get some additional anonymizing software."

"Whatever you have to do."

❧

Back in the police station's conference room, a lunch of cheap Mexican fast food sitting uncomfortably in her stomach, Bernadette opened her laptop. Kep had opted for a sandwich at an equally mediocre eatery next door, and as he watched her screen over her shoulder, she could smell the pastrami on his breath. Maybe he'd chosen it specifically to block out the offensive smells of the Euclid Street neighborhood.

"So," Kep said, "this is the Pike Place Music website. You believe this is how we can contact Miss Nakrivo?"

"Honestly, Kep, I think this is our only move right now." She typed in the Pike Place Music URL, then clicked on the *Marketplace* link, then on the *Buy & Sell Forum*.

"I appreciate you informing me of your strategy." Kep shifted his weight from foot to foot uncomfortably. "However, I don't believe this is the best way forward."

"I don't expect you to. You're not a fan of morally gray areas." Bernadette clicked on *World Music Instruments*. "But keeping my daughter out of danger is pretty black and white to me."

"I understand your motivation, but gaining access to the safe-deposit box through fraudulent means—"

"Not fraudulent means," Bernadette said. "We have every legal right to access that box. The bank just won't let us. And if we simply convince them we're following the bank's policy, as long as everything we do is technically legal, we'll be fine."

"Any fruit of the poisonous tree—" Kep began.

"If it's fully legal, there *is* no poisonous tree." Bernadette gritted her teeth. "And you've made your objection clear. And I've stated that I *will* try to make this work. So either help me out or stay out of my way."

Kep was silent for a moment. Bernadette could almost hear the gears turning in his head. The plan wasn't just about keeping Sophie safe, either—as morally gray as it was, her strategy could help Kep get justice for his son's murder, too.

Bernadette stared at the blank entry on the Pike Place Music chat box, then opened her previous conversation with Alaska Afternoon and began typing.

BB35901:

Got your message. Need to discuss other information. Arrived in 216.

"Arrived in 216?" Then Kep's brow relaxed. "Oh, of course, Cleveland's area code." Kep frowned. "How did you know this was her?"

Bernadette scrolled up and clicked, scrolled again, and found what she was looking for. "There." She pointed to the screen. "User profile created two weeks ago."

Kep pushed his glasses up his nose and squinted. "That's her username? *Alaska Afternoon?*"

"Her real name—Anya Kerovic. AK. That's the two-letter postal abbreviation for the state of Alaska. And afternoon—"

"Aha. *Post meridium*—P.M. Those are the same initials as Parr Medical."

Bernadette touched the tip of her nose.

Kep furrowed his brow. "Not especially obvious. Frankly, I'm surprised you've made that connection."

"She reached out to me. Wasn't that hard since I knew what I was looking for."

"Your username isn't nearly as clever."

"I used up all my cleverness trying to solve *her* username."

Kep was silent for a moment.

"What is it?"

"One might consider your plan to be a felony, you know."

"You'd think so, wouldn't you?" Bernadette grinned. "But no. Safe deposit boxes aren't federally regulated, and Ohio law isn't clear about unauthorized access to them." Bernadette interlaced her fingers. "And there's precedent. Ohio allows the bank to turn over the contents of the box to the government when the holder of the account is deceased."

"You know as well as I that there are two account holders, and one of them is still alive."

"A situation that courts in Ohio have not dealt with. So the only precedent is on the side of giving us access to that box."

"You haven't explored legal ways to get the bank to provide access to you."

"Which will only send up a warning shot to Parr Medical." Bernadette refreshed the browser window. Nothing yet.

"What shall we do while we wait for Annika to respond?" Kep asked.

"If I'm right about this," Bernadette said, "Annika's probably got an alert set up on the Open Marketplace.

That means as soon as I made the post, she got an alert, which means—"

The strum of a harp sounded from the laptop's speakers, and a message appeared on the screen.

Bernadette scrolled and clicked on the Open Marketplace message.

ALASKA AFTERNOON:

Let's discuss the additional information.

2 PM Peace-Makers

Bernadette turned her head to Kep. "She must be in Cleveland. Peace-Makers—is that a bar?"

Kep shook his head. "We passed it this morning on our way to the bank building. It's in the Public Square."

"What—the statue of that guy sitting down on the circular dais? That's Peace-Makers?"

"No, no, that's Mayor Tom Johnson. And Peace-Makers isn't a statue. Across from that statue, there's a monument with a tall tower."

Bernadette nodded. "The tower is Peace-Makers?"

Kep ignored her interruption. "The tower is part of a Civil War Monument called the Soldiers & Sailors Monument, and each section of the monument has a different name. Several statue groupings, memorial tablets, stained glass windows, and bronze panels."

"Where do you learn all this stuff, Kep?"

"I'm surprised you don't know it. It's one of the few examples of late nineteenth century architecture that combines an obelisk with an interior room. The city government nearly destroyed it three times to make way for subway stations that have yet to materialize."

"All that knowledge about obelisks and interior rooms,

and a supershnozz, too." Bernadette smiled, then cleared her throat. "Where are we going?"

"A bronze panel on the north face of the monument depicts Abraham Lincoln holding a meeting with several Ohio historical figures who fought for emancipation. The panel is called *The Peace-Makers at City Point*."

Bernadette took a deep breath; that had been like pulling teeth. "So we need to meet at the bronze panel called *The Peace-Makers at Cleveland Point*."

"*City Point*. But otherwise correct."

She checked the clock in the corner of her screen. "It's just after one thirty."

"We only have about twenty minutes to get there." Kep pulled up his sleeve to look at his watch. "Annika must know we're at the homicide division."

"She wanted us to investigate a homicide in Cleveland. Where else would we be?" Bernadette stood. "Come on."

"While we can walk to the Public Square, I believe we shouldn't be relying on the detective for our transportation until we determine if we can trust him. I assume our investigation will not be confined to walking distance from the police precinct."

"True."

"Similarly problematic is FlashRide," continued Kep. "It requires long wait times and often employs drivers who are less than familiar with the city."

Bernadette opened a new browser window and typed into the search bar. "Okay—there are a couple of rental car places within a few blocks of the Public Square. Let's get a car after we meet with Annika."

Kep looked at Bernadette out of the corner of his eye. "You'll be able to rent a car? After what happened a few weeks ago in Lost Dish?"

"CSAB has excellent insurance." Bernadette grinned. "And one little exploded sedan won't affect CSAB's account."

Kep stood up to his full height and straightened his sportcoat. "If twenty minutes is all we have, I propose we leave now. I could use a liberal application of breath mints or chewing gum."

"That garlic pastrami is bugging you, too?"

Kep cleared his throat and his cheeks reddened slightly. "That's a bit mortifying. I assumed I was the only one who could smell it."

Bernadette stood from her chair and grabbed her purse. "Actually, it's nice to see you joining the ranks of the mere mortals every once in a while."

Kep opened the conference room door. "I appreciate your attempts to assuage my embarrassment."

Bernadette pulled out a pack of mint gum from her purse and held out a piece for Kep. "This should assuage it a little more."

❧

The sunny morning had given way to clouds, though the temperature had only dropped a few degrees as Kep and Bernadette walked out of the homicide division building.

"Did you check the forecast?"

Kep sniffed. "It does not smell like rain is forthcoming."

They crossed Rockwell Avenue and walked along the sidewalk next to the Public Square. Only a few tourists were taking pictures—probably because of the skies looking so dark. Bernadette looked up; the tall granite obelisk of the Soldiers and Sailors Monument was striking against the gray sky. She slowed her pace, beginning to look less and less purposeful with each stride.

"Are we not attempting to keep to a schedule?" Kep hissed under his breath.

"We're out for a pleasant mid-afternoon stroll," Bernadette murmured. "Maybe we should look for a bench to relax and take in the sights." She hooked her arm around Kep's elbow as professionally as she could, forcing him to slow his pace, too. "If Annika sees us making a beeline for our rendezvous point, she might think we're being too obvious and others will follow—maybe a few of the people from Parr Medical. We don't want to spook her, do we?"

"I see."

"Besides, we're ten minutes early, and we need to talk about what we're going to say to Annika when we meet her."

The northern face of the monument was about twenty feet in front of them, behind the plinth of a statue. They walked up a set of ten stone steps and turned toward the rear of the statue. The bronze panel came into view: a tall man in a top hat—probably Abraham Lincoln—stood in the center of a scene, surrounded by other men.

"Kep?"

Bernadette looked up. A man in a tweed jacket with elbow patches over a Union Jack tee shirt with stylishly ripped blue jeans was waving to them across the plaza.

Beside her, Kep sucked in a breath.

The man grinned broadly and hurried over to them. "Dr. Woodhead, my good man," the man said, tufts of his combed-over gray hair sticking up in the wind. "Fancy meeting you here."

"I could say the same," Kep said. Bernadette could tell

he was making a Herculean effort to keep the frost out of his voice. "I assumed you'd rarely leave the hustle and bustle of New York City."

Bernadette shot a look at Kep, but he didn't seem to notice. Of course, Kep wouldn't think to introduce her.

The man leaned forward conspiratorially. "New reality show about the music business. We're shooting a segment at the Rock and Roll Hall of Fame and I'm scouting other locations."

Was this the producer who Leopold Montclair had attempted to contact? The one who was supposed to travel from New York to Cleveland this week? His name slipped through Bernadette's mind—it was something like a famous poet or a famous artist.

The man clapped his hands together. "I'm sorry I can't stay and chat, but they expect me back in fifteen minutes." He furrowed his brow. "How have you been, Kep? Okay?"

"Keeping busy," Kep said. "Working, actually."

The man leaned back, hands at his sides, and looked Kep up and down, then Bernadette. Bernadette stared back at him.

Yates Raphael. That was his name. Both a poet *and* an artist. And a ninja turtle.

"Yes, well, I see." He reached up and clapped Kep on the shoulder. "You need anything, my good man, call me. Dreadful how they treated you upon your exit."

"The pitfalls of a life in show business," Kep said. "I may have been upset when it occurred, but I know you all did what the situation demanded."

Ah, so Kep was much closer to Yates Raphael than he'd originally let on.

"Doesn't mean I don't feel awful about it, Doctor,"

Raphael said, dropping his hand from Kep's shoulder. "I mean it. Anything you need."

Kep nodded and smiled through his salt-and-pepper beard. "Take care, Yates."

Her guess had been correct. Yates Raphael, the executive producer of not only *Cases That Won't Die,* but the producer who was supposed to meet with the murder victim.

With a flourish of his blazer, Raphael was off, back across the square, then across Superior Avenue.

Kep exhaled in relief. "My apologies," he said. "He tends to be quite long-winded."

"I noticed you didn't introduce us."

"He would have spent the next fifteen minutes flirting with you and endangering our meeting with Miss Nakrivo."

Bernadette nodded. She supposed she'd make the same choice.

She looked around. Nowhere to sit, really, except the edge of the planter around the statue's plinth. She unhooked her arm from Kep's, brushed off an area of the planter's edge, and sat. The stone walkway, about ten feet wide, sat between her and the bronze panel. Kep stroked his beard, then, chomping on his gum, took a seat on Bernadette's left.

A dark-haired woman with shoulder-length hair in a black cardigan immediately sat about two feet away from Bernadette's right hip. She took a sandwich out of a paper bag.

Bernadette looked at the woman out of the corner of her eye. She was in her forties, wearing round spectacles, with dark smile lines around her eyes and mouth. She wore a black cardigan with *Voramo Hotel* on the lapel—the five-star monstrosity across the street from the Justice Center.

"I see you got my message," the woman said in a perfect Midwestern accent.

Bernadette blinked and turned her head ever so slightly. The woman was too old—but no, those ice-blue eyes of Annika's were behind those glasses.

"We did," Bernadette said. "And we found your key."

Kep stiffened next to her. He wasn't used to this—hopefully he wouldn't ruin this rendezvous.

"Not my key," Annika said. "That was *his* key." The way Annika said "his" made it clear she was talking about Leopold Montclair. She narrowed her eyes. "So what was in that safe-deposit box?"

"What?"

Annika shook her head. "Don't play dumb with me, Bernadette. I saw the ABA number on that key. It's obviously for a safe-deposit box. I want to know what was in it." She paused. "If it'll get me any closer to finding my sister." She cast her eyes down. "Or what happened to her."

Bernadette shifted uncomfortably on the stone seat. "It's not that easy."

Annika frowned. "You can't fool me. I know government protocol. When the owner of a safe-deposit box is deceased, a federal law enforcement agency can—"

"That's if *all* the owners are deceased," Bernadette interrupted.

An elbow from Kep—*keep your voice down.*

Bernadette cleared her throat and looked straight ahead at the bronze carving of Lincoln. "Two names on the safe-deposit box."

Annika's brow furrowed behind the round glasses. "*Two* names?"

Ah. No wonder Annika hadn't tried to get into the safe-deposit box herself—she must have only been aware of the Leopold Montclair's name on the box, not Marnie Synskey's. Perhaps disguising herself as Leopold seemed like a bridge too far.

Bernadette unzipped the top of her purse, and Annika stiffened.

"I'm just getting my cell phone," Bernadette said. She pulled out the phone, unlocked it, and tapped the screen. A woman's picture on the screen; Bernadette turned the phone so Annika could see it. Light brown hair in a bob, a long, narrow face, small eyes set far apart.

"Marnie," Annika muttered.

"You know her."

"Professionally, she's the Head of Executive Services for Parr Medical. Real close with the CEO and the board. But I always thought she knew a lot more than she let on." Annika smiled. "You know the joke about how there's a woman at every Fortune 100 company named Pamela, who has a title like Administrative Assistant II, and the company would go under if she wasn't there? Well, I always got the feeling that Marnie is the Pamela of Parr Medical."

"Do you know why Marnie Synskey's name is on Leopold Montclair's safe-deposit box account?" asked Kep.

"I'm not in the inner circle for that kind of information," Annika replied.

Bernadette leaned forward slightly. "Was she the one who told you to take care of Montclair?"

"If only it were that simple." Annika gave Bernadette a tight-lipped smile. "Orders came to me on a burner phone. The phone would get delivered to my hotel or wherever I was staying. I'd get a phone call or a text telling me who the target was, and any other info I needed. Sometimes there'd be a bunch of background information on my target—but sometimes it was just a name."

"What about for Leopold Montclair?"

Annika's smile stayed on her face, frozen. "I got his name on a burner handed to me when the guards pulled me out of Taycheedah."

Bernadette paused, then turned her head and looked at Annika. "How exactly did that happen?"

"The prison escape?" Annika chuckled. "Water under the bridge. Let's focus on the future."

Bernadette didn't like it, but she'd take what Annika gave. "What do you think is in the safe-deposit box? Why do you want us to get it?"

Annika set her jaw. "I'm hoping there'll be proof of who's been giving the orders. If you can catch him—or her, or them—I'll get out from under their control."

"And yet," Kep said, "you're a convicted killer."

Annika smiled. "Annika Nakrivo, it's true, is a convicted killer. But once you have the people who are responsible for all the deaths, Annika Nakrivo will cease to exist."

"Anja Kerovic, too?"

Annika's smile faltered for a moment, but then came back. "She's already gone."

"And Marguerite?"

"If you take down Parr Medical, I'll find her." Annika swallowed hard. "If she's still alive." She straightened up into a rigid sitting position. "Can you help me?"

Bernadette tapped her chin. "I can't promise anything, but we can get into the bank's safe-deposit box."

"We?" Annika blinked and turned toward Bernadette. "Are you talking about you and Dr. Woodhead?"

"I'm talking," Bernadette said, "about all three of us."

A smile crept across Annika's face. "No way. You want me to pretend to be Marnie Synskey? I would need to steal her identification, and I can't take the risk that she knows who I am."

"You won't be the one to steal her ID," Bernadette said. "Leave that to Dr. Woodhead and me. We just need to know her movements. And once we get her ID—"

Annika nodded. "I can look more like Marnie Synskey than she does."

Kep pushed his glasses up onto the bridge of his nose. "And you believe we can get Ms. Synskey's ID back before she is aware of its disappearance?"

Annika cocked her head. "That depends. Are you sure you can do this? Parr Medical is looking for you. They know you're in Cleveland. The people who hired me must know by now that you're investigating Leopold's death. You interview the wrong people at the wrong time, you'll end up dead."

Bernadette grinned. "Hiding in plain sight."

Annika looked Bernadette up and down. "Given what I know of your skill set, I think that's the only hiding you can do."

۞

Bernadette pushed the heavy hotel room door open and dumped her laptop bag off her shoulder onto the bed. All the sneaking around and deceit—Annika, Detective Herrera—had been exhausting. Even though the sun was barely dipping behind the horizon, it was nine o'clock.

Bernadette just wanted to crawl into bed, especially since she needed to be at the top of her game in the morning.

But she wasn't done tonight.

She pulled out a flat black plastic bug detector from her purse. It wasn't as fancy as the voice-activated recorders they'd pulled off Montclair's boat, but it would do. It was just large enough to be unwieldy, but it would get the job done. Just like she'd done in Kep's room five minutes before, she scanned the room with the detector, especially by the electrical outlets, phone, and television. Under the bed, too. And just like in Kep's room, no beeps. No bugs or cameras.

She pulled her phone out of her purse and tapped the screen, then opened her phone app and called Maura.

The other end of the phone rang three times. Then a rustle of fabric for a moment before Maura's voice came on. "Bernadette?"

"Hey, Maura. I've got an update for you."

"Yes—right, sorry I didn't call you back. It's been a crazy day."

"Kep and I have uncovered some evidence."

"Good."

"We haven't yet shared it with the Cleveland Police Department. Frankly, we don't know who we can trust."

"What evidence is this?"

Bernadette told Maura about the key, about the recording devices, and about the purchase requisition made by Joanna and signed by Andy Belgrade. "Lesley's looking into this Andy Belgrade person," she told Maura. "But I'm afraid this goes way over our heads."

Maura clicked her tongue in thought. "For now, hang on to the evidence. I'll see what I can find out about the people in charge of evidence in Cleveland."

"And Detective Herrera, too."

"He's clean, as far as I can tell."

Bernadette's throat caught, and she swallowed hard. "You heard anything from Sophie or Barlow?"

"They're not letting me know where they are, if that's what you're asking. But I got a report that they reached their destination and they're safe."

"Yeah, okay." Bernadette thought finding out Sophie was safe would loosen the tightness in her shoulders, but no such luck. "Uh... if you don't know where they are, does that mean I can't call Sophie?"

"Correct. We've taken away their phones, anyway. Too likely that someone could track them. Plus, we don't trust a pre-teen girl with a phone."

"You'd probably have more trouble with my ex-husband, anyway." Bernadette sighed. "Are you sure there's no way for me to get in touch with Sophie?"

"I don't believe so," Maura said. "I'll see what I can do —but you know I won't do anything that will compromise them. Or you."

"I know."

Maura paused. "You be careful, Bernadette."

"Gotcha."

Bernadette ended the call and flopped back on the hotel bed. Now less than three days to get the encryption key before they came after Sophie—and she still didn't have a clue where to look.

❧

Five people stood in line at Firebird Coffee when the woman with the long, narrow face and brown bob in the gray business suit came in off the street. The morning was already growing warm at a quarter after seven. Bernadette had been worried; Marnie Synskey, according to Annika, usually arrived in the office between seven fifteen and seven thirty. She was running late a few minutes today, but maybe that was because of Leopold Montclair's untimely death.

Synskey let the door close behind her and gaped at the coffee line, twisting the toe of her black flat into the floor nervously. Bernadette saw the gears turn in Synskey's head. She was measuring whether she had enough time to stay.

Marnie Synskey had to stay. Otherwise, their plan wouldn't work.

Annika had said that the few times she had been to the Parr Medical offices—mostly after her plastic surgery to transform her from Anja Kerovic to Annika Nakrivo— Marnie Synskey had always had a to-go cup from Firebird Coffee in her hand when she got to the office in the morning. Even when running a few minutes late, old habits were difficult to break.

Synskey crossed her arms and tapped her foot for a moment, then she switched her purse to her opposite shoulder and strode forward to the end of the line. Bernadette breathed a sigh of relief.

A woman in a tank top and shorts came up to their table. "Are you using this chair?"

Bernadette nodded. "Yes—our friend is just in line there."

The woman frowned but stepped away.

Bernadette glanced at Kep's face.

Uh oh. His forehead had a light sheen of sweat. If the two of them were going to pull this off, he needed to get it together. It would never work if Synskey got suspicious.

"You okay?"

Kep straightened his sportcoat, sat up in the seat, and nodded.

"You had the commanding voice down really well last night. You can do this."

"I am aware." Kep pushed his glasses up his nose. "However, if Ms. Synskey doesn't recognize my name—"

"She knows who you are," Bernadette said. "Be as theatrical as you can be."

"My theatrics, as you so inelegantly put it, are part of my process." He frowned. "There are far too many competing smells in this coffee shop for me to assess any kind of leftover bromeladine scent from three or four days ago."

"But like I said yesterday," Bernadette said, "Marnie doesn't know that."

Kep leaned forward and put his hands on the table. "If she watched *Cases That Won't Die,* she might. I discussed the limitations of my process in several episodes."

Bernadette waved her hand. "All part of the Hollywood drama. Tell her you had to downplay your superschnozz for the cameras. What fun would it be if the viewers thought you'd easily solve all the crimes?"

Kep hesitated a moment, then nodded.

Three more people entered the coffee shop and got in line behind Synskey. Good—the more crowded, the better. The person at the front of the line finished ordering and stepped to the side, between the small, round table where Bernadette and Kep sat and the pick-up counter next to the espresso machine.

The seconds dragged like hours, but Synskey finally got to the front of the line and placed her order. Nothing too fancy, just a large iced latte. Bernadette craned her neck.

Synskey opened her purse—a snap, not a zip—and

took out a brown leather wallet, slightly wider than a dollar bill, unfolded it, and took out a card from the right-hand pocket. On the left side, under a plastic window, was an Ohio driver's license.

After paying, Synskey put her wallet in her purse, put the purse over her right shoulder, and joined the queue of people waiting for their drink orders. She stood back from the counter far enough where she was only a couple of feet away from Bernadette's chair.

Bernadette nodded to Kep. He took a deep breath then stood, a bit uncertainly.

"Remember, be confident," Bernadette whispered.

Kep drew himself up to his full height and took a step forward. "Marnie Synskey?"

Bernadette nodded slightly. Good. Deep, commanding. If she were Marnie, she'd have taken notice.

Synskey flinched at the sound of her name and turned to Kep. Recognition flickered in her eyes.

"My name is Dr. Kep Woodhead with the Controlled Substance Analysis Bureau," he said, keeping his voice deep and controlled. "My colleague and I are here investigating the death of Leopold Montclair—"

"Keep your voice down," Synskey said. "We're in a public place."

Kep blinked. He hadn't expected Synskey to interrupt him, but he continued, if at a slightly lower volume. "You were Mr. Montclair's administrative assistant."

A vertical line formed between Synskey's eyebrows. "My official title is Head of Executive Services."

"Please have a seat," Kep said.

Synskey glanced at Bernadette, then at Kep. Her eyes narrowed. "What's going on?"

"We've been called in because of an anomaly in Mr.

Montclair's blood work," Kep said. "I'm not sure if you're familiar with my history."

Synskey opened her mouth, then snapped it shut. Yes, she knew who Kep was, but not saying anything was a smart move.

"If you are, you may be aware that I have the ability to detect a large array of scents, even those that are days or weeks old," Kep continued. "I've been asked to assess those who worked closely with Montclair to determine whether they were exposed to the anomalous toxin as well."

Synskey flinched again. "You're—you're saying it was foul play?"

Kep blinked.

"Not necessarily," Bernadette said. "It may have been accidental exposure to a toxic substance in his house or at his workplace. We don't want others to be in danger." She smiled warmly at Synskey. "This won't take a minute. We'll be done by the time your coffee is ready." Bernadette pulled out the chair next to her. Kep began to sit in the chair on the other side, but Bernadette shot him a warning glance and he hovered over the chair for a moment.

"This is most unusual," Synskey muttered.

"Dr. Woodhead has a most unusual skill set," Bernadette said. "I promise we'll be out of your hair in just a couple of minutes."

Synskey sat down, her purse still over her shoulder, and the bag part of the purse resting on her lap.

"How do you want her arranged, Dr. Woodhead?" Bernadette asked.

"Arranged?" Synskey asked, eyes darting between Bernadette and Kep.

"Dr. Woodhead just needs to get a good—" Bernadette began.

"Bill W.," the barista called.

A burly man shoved past the seat where Synskey sat.

At the same time, Kep, in a sudden, jerky movement, thrust himself forward, putting his face less than a foot from Synskey's face, and took a long, slow sniff— Bernadette had never seen, not even on their first case together, such a theatrical inhalation from Kep before. Bernadette recoiled slightly in her seat in surprise—

But Synskey squeaked and pushed her chair back into Bernadette, who caught the back of the chair with her left hand. Synskey's purse strap fell off her shoulder and the whole purse fell off her lap onto the floor. Had Kep knocked it down on purpose?

Kudos to him if he had.

Bernadette didn't hesitate—she crouched under the table. She pounced on the purse, and in one fluid movement unsnapped the top. Her fingers found the wallet, traced the opening to unfold it, and her index finger slipped under the plastic window. Just a little more—

The driver's license slipped out into Bernadette's right hand, and she came up from under the table, clutching the purse in her left hand.

"Dr. Woodhead, perhaps a fair bit of warning next time," Bernadette said, putting as much schoolteacher admonishment into her voice as she could.

Synskey's eyes were wide. She probably wasn't sure what had just happened.

"My apologies," Kep said, leaning back in his chair. "I simply thought it best to perform this unseemly task as quickly as possible. I didn't realize that man would push past us—"

"He's not the one who startled me," Synskey grumbled.

Bernadette looped the shoulder strap of the purse over the back of Synskey's chair as she slipped the driver's license into her inside blazer pocket. Synskey stared at Kep—had she even noticed she dropped her purse?

"Did you detect anything, Dr. Woodhead?" Bernadette asked.

Kep shook his head. "Nothing anomalous."

"See?" Bernadette said. "We're done before your coffee is ready."

Synskey grabbed her purse off the back of her chair and put the strap over her shoulder. "How long will this investigation take?"

"Hopefully not too much longer," Bernadette said. "But you know how it is when your management sends you on a wild goose chase."

"Marnie!" the barista called.

Synskey stood and glared at Kep. "Maybe you need to switch careers instead of freaking people out by invading their personal space." She turned her back on them, grabbed her iced coffee drink from the counter, then stomped out of the coffee shop.

Kep slumped in his seat and exhaled loudly. "That was exhausting. I'm glad Annika agreed to return the identification to Marnie when we're through with it."

Bernadette took her phone out and tapped on the web browser, then navigated to the Pike Place Music website, then clicked on the Buy & Sell Forum. She scrolled until she saw the message from Alaska Afternoon, then clicked on the message and typed out a response.

> Ready for the transaction

"And now," Bernadette said, "we return to Caskill & Dunleavy."

⁜

A warm breeze blew south from Lake Erie down Euclid Avenue.

"Didn't we rent a car so we wouldn't have to suffer through the humidity?" Kep grumbled.

"It'd take us longer to find a parking space than to walk directly there." Bernadette looked up; the steakhouse on the left had a pointed archway but no signs of life. She turned her head forward again; the sidewalk was made of bricks here, in alternating six-foot-wide stripes of terra cotta orange and chocolate brown. An elegant touch that only slightly offset the heavy smell of smoked meat. "We still have ten minutes."

Bernadette's phone buzzed in her purse.

She took it out and looked at the screen. An area code from Northern Virginia. Maybe a call from CSAB or the FBI. She tapped *Answer.* "This is Bernadette Becker."

A woman's voice. "Ms. Becker, this is a call from the communications office at CSAB. Are you able to speak freely?"

"Uh—yes."

"One moment." The line clicked, then a low electronic clicking, then a deep voice. "Agent Becker, this is Xavier Reese."

"Reese?"

"This will be a quick call, but your lieutenant pulled some strings. We're on a secure line, and I can put your daughter on for one minute."

Bernadette stopped in her tracks on the sidewalk and waved her hand to stop Kep. "Yes, please—put her on."

"I will monitor the conversation," Agent Xavier Reese said. "No discussion of *anything* that could reveal a location. No time zones, weather, environment, food, nothing like that. Are we clear?"

"No talk about food?"

"Someone could mention eating something that's only available locally here."

"Right. Of course, of course I agree."

"Hold a moment." A rustling, then a bump of the phone.

"Mom?"

"Sophie!" Bernadette's shoulders loosened slightly. "It's so good to hear your voice!"

"Hi," Sophie said quietly.

"Agent Reese treating you okay?"

"Yeah, he's pretty nice. I guess I complained a lot on the plane. But then I heard Dad complaining more, and I thought it was kind of annoying, so I stopped." She paused. "I still wish I was with my friends and not stuck here."

"I know. I'm doing the best I can and working as fast as I can."

"We can't even get Flixtune here. No streaming services at all. Just a bunch of old movies on DVD."

"I'm sorry about all this."

Sophie was quiet, but Bernadette felt the sting of admonishment in her silence. Apologies wouldn't cut it anymore. This was significantly affecting Sophie, not just minor inconveniences. Bernadette could tell Sophie was angry, but trying to be civil—and maybe only because Agent Reese was listening in.

"The important thing is that you and Dad are safe."

A sigh. "Yeah, I know. I just—I just don't like being stuck here."

A rush of words flooded Bernadette's head: promises to make it up to Sophie, promises that it would all be over soon—but it all felt hollow. "I love you," she said instead.

A long hesitation, then: "I love you, too."

"I'm sorry, ladies, but our time is up," Agent Reese said.

"Thank you, Xavier," Bernadette said.

"Don't thank me," Reese said. "Thank your lieutenant."

The call ended, and Bernadette hung her head.

"Are you all right?" Kep asked.

"Yeah," Bernadette replied, raising her chin. "Got to talk to my kid. Wasn't expecting to do that for a few more days at least."

"I hesitate to ask," Kep said, "but do you need a few minutes to, as they say, get your head back in the game?"

Bernadette took a deep breath, then exhaled long and slow. "I'll be fine."

"You're certain?"

Bernadette gave Kep a determined smile. "Absolutely."

They crossed East Ninth Street and, in front of the hotel's awning on the next block, a woman stood. She had a brown bob and thin lips, and wore a gray business suit with black heels and cat's eye sunglasses.

Kep hesitated. "Did we not give Ms. Synskey enough time to get to work?"

"Relax," Bernadette said. "The Marnie Synskey we just saw in the coffee shop was wearing flats. This woman has heels on. Annika's about five foot six—Marnie Synskey has about two inches on her, so she needs the height."

Kep stared for a moment as he walked with

Bernadette, then nodded. "Excellent powers of observation. I did not think Miss Nakrivo would be ready so quickly." He squinted. "Annika's jawline isn't that square."

"That's why she's the one who's good at disguises. Some sort of theater putty, I guess."

They passed the hotel awning, and Annika, disguised as Marnie Synskey, fell into step with Kep and Bernadette. Bernadette reached into her blazer pocket and pulled out Synskey's driver's license. Annika took it from her hand without breaking stride.

Then the three of them were at the Caskill & Dunleavy building. Bernadette stopped to gather herself for a moment, but Annika strode between her and Kep and opened the glass door. Kep and Bernadette hurried in after her.

The same security guard stood behind the waist-high counter in the small lobby between the entrance and the elevators.

"Two days in a row," the security guard said. "I was given instructions not to let you in without an appointment."

"*I* have the appointment with Caskill & Dunleavy," Annika said—and her voice was nearly a spot-on mimic of Synskey. "I'm complying with a subpoena, and I've made an appointment to get this over as soon as possible."

The guard bent to a workstation on the counter. "Name?"

Annika pushed her sunglasses up on her nose. "Marnie Synskey. My appointment is with Claude Tristan."

The guard reached out with a finger and tapped the screen. "Ah, yes, here you are, Ms. Synskey." He glanced at Bernadette and Kep. "And these folks are with you?"

"As I said, I'm complying with a subpoena. It's not the most pleasant thing I've done this week."

"I'm afraid I have to ask you for identification."

"Of course." Annika held out Marnie Synskey's driver's license.

The guard took the identification from Annika, then glanced from the license to Annika's face and back again. He looked for a moment as if he wanted to ask her to remove her sunglasses, but then handed the identification back to her and nodded. "You know the way, I take it."

Bernadette nodded. "Same as yesterday."

They walked past the security guard. The elevator was open, and the three of them walked inside. The doors closed, and they went up.

"You have evidence bags, yes?" Annika murmured.

"Of course." Bernadette put her hand on her purse. She didn't trust Annika, although they needed her to get in. Bernadette fully expected Annika to make a play to take whatever was in the safe-deposit box—whether Annika was explicit or sneaky. And Bernadette didn't think she could prevent Annika from taking it, either—but what other choice did she have?

"I'll need the key," Annika said.

Bernadette blinked. "*We* have the key."

"Yes," Annika said, "but Marnie is supposed to have her own key. Why would you use the key you took from Montclair if you were supposed to subpoena me for access to the safe-deposit box?"

Bernadette frowned. Annika had a point—and if she held the key, it would be one step closer for her to clear out the contents of the box without Kep or Bernadette knowing what it was. But she didn't have a choice.

Bernadette dug the key out of her purse and handed it to Annika, who palmed it just as the elevator doors opened.

A man greeted them, different from yesterday. He had deeply tanned skin and a full head of wavy salt-and-pepper hair. His black suit fitted snugly to his trim, lanky body; a custom tailoring job.

"Welcome, Ms. Synskey," the man said. "I'm Claude Tristan. I apologize that Mr. Renscrift is not available."

"It's not a problem, Claude," Annika said. "As I stated on the phone, the sooner we can get this over with, the better."

"May I see the subpoena?" Claude Tristan said.

"I didn't bring it with me." Annika folded her arms. "Am I to understand that I need to show you a subpoena if I want to examine the contents of my own safe-deposit box?"

"Well—no—"

Annika cleared her throat. "I appreciate you looking out for my best interests, Claude. I'll put in a good word for you with Mr. Renscrift. Now, if you would be so kind, please lead us to the safe-deposit box so I can get on with my day."

"Certainly, madam." Claude Tristan turned and walked between the desks to the archway of a hallway. Annika followed closely behind him, with Kep and Bernadette bringing up the rear.

The hallway was narrow but opened into a wide hexagonal room, with a door or another hallway on all six sides. The floor here was black-and-gray marble, the walls a light gray. Claude Tristan turned right, stood in front of the second door, tapped a keypad on his left, then turned the door handle.

The long, narrow room was lit by fluorescents, with an off-white tile floor and a drop ceiling. On both sides of the room were hundreds of safe-deposit boxes, small doors with two keyholes each. A small table sat in the middle of the room.

"The number of your box, please?" Claude Tristan asked.

"D forty thirty-eight J-G-H," Annika said.

Claude Tristan took six steps forward and stopped in front of a column of smaller boxes. "Forty thirty-eight," he murmured.

Bernadette took a pair of latex gloves from her purse and put them on. Kep took a step back, giving Bernadette space.

Annika glanced over at her. "I thought you said you'd just *look* in the box."

"And as with all evidence uncovered via subpoena, if the contents are of interest to our investigation, we'll be taking possession of it."

"That wasn't part of our agreement," Annika said.

"That's the beauty of subpoenas," Bernadette said. "You don't actually have to agree to what it says to be forced to comply."

Annika turned to the safe-deposit box, the key in her hand. Claude Tristan held a key in his hand as well, and together they slipped their respective keys into the slots of D4038JGH. They both turned their keys clockwise and pulled the drawer out.

Claude Tristan carried the box to the table in the middle of the room and delicately set it down. "I'll leave you to it," he said stiffly, then exited the room.

Bernadette looked at Kep, then at Annika, and stepped

forward. She pulled up on the hinged top, and Kep and Annika both pushed forward to look inside.

A clamshell cellphone. A burner, from the looks of it.

And nothing else.

Chapter Ten

BERNADETTE GRABBED the evidence bag out of her purse and quickly reached her gloved hand out for the phone.

Annika bit her lip but said nothing.

"I think that's all," Bernadette said, slipping the bag back into her purse.

Kep reached out and closed the lid of the box.

Bernadette stepped back and rapped on the closed door.

Claude Tristan opened the door. "Have you finished already?"

"We have," Bernadette said.

"Thank you, Claude," Annika said. "I appreciate you being available for this service on such short notice."

"You'll have to sign a form if you'll be removing something from the box," Claude Tristan said.

"Not if the contents are being removed with the owner's permission," Annika said. "I appreciate your willingness to follow the rules for me, but I assure you, it's quite all right."

Claude Tristan inclined his head in a shallow bow. "Of course, ma'am."

Bernadette kept her hand on the evidence bag inside her purse.

Five minutes later, they were on the sidewalk, blinking in the bright sunshine.

"A cell phone," Bernadette said, still with her hand in her purse on the evidence bag.

"With only our murder victim and Marnie Synskey able to retrieve it," Kep said. "What do you suppose it means?"

"It's how they communicate with—whoever's giving the orders," Annika said.

"Does the person who gets the phone wait for a call, or do they make a phone call?"

Annika shrugged. "It depends if there's a number already programmed into the phone." She thought for a moment. "Whenever I got a burner phone, if there was a number in there, I was supposed to call it to get the name of—" She paused. "To get instructions."

Bernadette nodded. "All right. Let's go somewhere where we can look at the phone." She turned to Kep. "Conference room at the police station?"

Kep nodded. "That seems reasonable."

Annika balked. "You're not getting me in there."

"Why not?" Bernadette said. "You're not Annika Nakrivo, you're Marnie Synskey."

"Absolutely not."

Bernadette stopped. Instead of off-white concrete, the sidewalk under her feet was brickwork, interlocking reds and oranges and browns. "Look, Annika, you can probably tell by my death grip on the burner phone that I don't trust you not to grab the phone and vanish. And then my investigation will be dead in the water."

"Why would I take the phone when I led you to it? I already told you, I hoped that whatever was in the safe-deposit box would help you catch the people who've hired me. And get me out from under their thumb."

"And lead you to your sister."

"A girl can dream, right?" Annika clenched her jaw. "So why would I want to take the phone away from you? Then you wouldn't be able to trace it."

"It's a burner."

"It had to be bought somewhere, right? You can trace it to a store, or to an online marketplace. Get an address. Or if there's a number in there, track it."

Bernadette smiled. "I think you overestimate the power of federal agencies. Someone paid cash for this at a store where they don't have cameras and where the clerks don't notice who their customers are."

Annika pressed her lips together. "I'm still not going to the police station." She glared at Bernadette. "And you need me. If there's a phone number stored in the phone, do you think *you're* going to call the number? When they expect someone like me to call instead?"

"Then come with us to our hotel," Kep said. "We'll go up to Ms. Becker's room. She'll guard the door, and you and I will examine the phone together."

Annika nodded, then turned and continued to walk toward the Public Square.

"Where are you going?"

"You're at the Botticelli," Annika said. "It's on the corner of Huron and West Sixth. Now let's hurry. The sooner we find out what's on that phone, the better it'll be for me."

She walked a few steps forward, Kep and Bernadette frozen in their tracks. Then she turned. "Oh, come on.

Yes, it's a pricey hotel, but CSAB has a discount rate, and it's only three blocks from the Homicide Division." Annika raised her eyebrows. "But that thirty-dollar overnight parking fee adds up. You're probably wondering how to justify the car rental to your boss."

"You know a lot," Bernadette said.

"And if I wanted to take the phone," Annika said, "I'd already have it. You might have had your hand on it this whole time, but I could have gotten it. You'd open up the evidence bag and find a deck of cards instead of a burner phone."

Bernadette squeezed the bag—it sure felt like a phone, not like a deck of cards. "So you're saying I can trust you?"

"Of course."

"Only when our interests align," Kep said.

Annika's smile widened.

Bernadette tightened her grip on the bag. "I want my daughter to stay safe."

"And that means," Annika said, "that you and Dr. Woodhead need to find—" Then she stopped and looked around.

"...the person who killed Leopold Montclair," Kep finished. "Or, rather, the person who ordered Montclair's death."

"How about we talk somewhere more private?" Annika said.

"If I learned anything from our adventure in the Upper Peninsula a few weeks ago," Kep said, "it's that pay-as-you-go phones can be tracked as soon as they're switched on." He flicked his eyes to Annika. "Do you really want Parr Medical to determine that the cellphone is at the Botticelli Hotel? Or would you prefer them to see that it's at the Homicide Division of the police department, where they won't know who has it?"

"They certainly won't think you've gotten ahold of it," Bernadette said. "Especially since you've refused to go to the police station. They'll think the police got access to that safe-deposit box. But not you."

Annika bit her lip. "I don't like this."

"And I don't like my daughter being threatened," Bernadette replied. "Especially when I have no idea how to get the person threatening her what they want."

Annika stared at Bernadette for a moment. "You really don't know where the encryption key is?"

"I wouldn't even know where to start."

Annika looked at Bernadette for a moment, studying her face, then gave a brief nod.

They walked toward the police station, Kep and Bernadette flanking Annika, matching her long strides.

At the corner, a vendor was selling T-shirts. Some featured the Rock & Roll Hall of Fame, some featured "The CLE"; one hooded sweatshirt on display featured an illustration of the Cuyahoga River on fire. Sitting on top of the display were three teddy bears, one in each uniform of the professional football, baseball, and basketball teams.

Bernadette blinked. The teddy bear.

Maybe there was something Joanna had hidden in the teddy bear Joanna had given Sophie last year.

But she couldn't call Sophie or Barlow. They were in hiding, and she had no way of contacting them. But there was *someone*. Ugh—a slight taste of bile in Bernadette's mouth. But to save Sophie, she'd do it.

"You two go ahead," Bernadette said.

Kep looked over at Bernadette and pushed his glasses up on his nose.

"I need to make a phone call."

A smile quirked at the corner of Annika's mouth. "You thought of where that encryption key might be?"

"Maybe. It's a long shot." Bernadette took her phone out of her purse, stopping in the middle of the sidewalk as Kep and Annika kept walking toward the police station.

Bernadette closed her eyes, took a deep breath, and scrolled through her contacts until she found it: *Lisa Rothchild.*

The phone rang. Two times. Three times. Shit. Lisa was probably at work. Bernadette would have to wait until this afternoon—

"Hello?"

"Lisa." Bernadette said it flatly, not as a greeting, more like a statement.

"Oh—Bernadette!"

Fake surprise in Lisa's voice: Bernadette had called her cellphone, and Lisa would have seen Bernadette's name flash up onscreen before accepting the call. But she let it slide. Bernadette hadn't called Lisa since discovering her affair with Barlow—except in the rare cases when Barlow hadn't been able to pick Sophie up.

And Bernadette and Lisa had never talked about *why*. Why the affair? How did it start? Why decide to break up a family?

But those topics would need to wait for another day. Besides, Bernadette wasn't sure she wanted to hear those answers.

A thick layer of worry in Lisa's voice. "Have—have you heard from Barlow? And Sophie?"

"I spoke to Sophie this morning," Bernadette said, and her voice caught. She took a deep breath. "I don't know where they're keeping them, though. Better for everyone that I don't know."

"Oh. How is she?"

"Good enough, I guess. Pissed off at me for this whole situation." And now, the moment Bernadette had been dreading. "I need you to do me a favor, Lisa."

Silence.

"This is for Sophie. If you do me this favor and it works, she and Barlow will be home much sooner."

No hesitation on Lisa's end. "Okay."

"Are you at the office?"

"No, I'm working from home today."

"Good." Bernadette closed her eyes and tried to picture the teddy bear. "All right—there's a stuffed teddy bear of Sophie's. She didn't like it much, but I think it got packed for Barlow's—for your place."

"What does it look like?"

"It's about twelve inches long, maybe a little more. Dark brown, wearing a T-shirt with the Washington Monument on it. The bear's paws have the American flag design on the pads."

"Oh—yes, I think I've seen that. It's in a drawer or closet. Hold on." A rustling sound as Lisa walked through the house. "Are you—are you okay, Bernadette? I mean, besides all this."

"This is pretty much overwhelming everything else," Bernadette said, hearing the ice in her voice. She caught herself. "It's hard," she said. "I'm doing my best to make sure they get home safely."

"Right." More rustling. "I think it's in the bottom of this—" The sound of a drawer sliding open. "No, not there." Another drawer slid open. "There it is. The Washington Monument bear."

"There might be something hidden inside," Bernadette said.

"Hidden inside? In this teddy bear?"

"Yes. Someone—someone gave it to Sophie. And might have hidden something inside. If so, it's important. Can you check?"

"What do you mean, can I check? What sort of thing would someone hide inside?"

"Hang on," Bernadette said. "Let's switch this to a video call."

A moment later and a tap of the phone screen, and Lisa's face was visible on Bernadette's phone.

"How's that?" Lisa asked.

"I just see your face." And Lisa looked tired. Bags under her eyes, no makeup, a slight cast of acne over her forehead, her blonde hair a mess. She was just as worried about Barlow and Sophie as Bernadette was. And at least Bernadette could do something about it. Lisa had to sit at home and worry.

"Oh—hang on." A finger reaching out, then the screen shifted to a brown teddy bear wearing a T-shirt with the Washington Monument.

"That's it," Bernadette said. "Do you have a sturdy pair of scissors? Or a box cutter?"

"You want me to destroy Sophie's bear?"

Like you destroyed our marriage leapt into Bernadette's brain, but she pushed that thought aside. "Yes." She closed her eyes and pinched the bridge of her nose. Slow, even breaths. Panic wouldn't help. "This could save their lives."

"Then I'll do it." The sound of the drawer sliding closed, then footsteps, another lighter drawer opening.

Bernadette pulled the phone away from her face, then

took a few steps into the shade of the building next to her. That was better.

The Washington Monument bear was sitting on the kitchen counter, surrounded by a few dirty dishes and two empty wine bottles.

No, Lisa wasn't taking this well either.

"What do I need to do?" Lisa said.

"You have scissors?"

"Heavy duty kitchen shears. I figure if it can cut a chicken in half, it should work for a bear."

"First," Bernadette said, "feel around. Squeeze the bear's head, limbs, torso. See if there's anything solid inside. A USB stick, a SIM card, something like that."

The phone moved, then Bernadette saw nothing but the ceiling. Beige, with a can light, probably above the sink.

"I don't feel anything."

"Then," Bernadette instructed, "make a cut down the bear's back. From the nape of the neck all the way down to the butt."

Silence for a moment, then a muted sound of tearing fabric.

"What am I looking for?" Lisa asked.

"Anything that looks like a storage device. There's a—" Bernadette almost said *encryption key*, but stopped herself. "There's a file I need to locate, and I think it's on a thumb drive or something."

"Inside the bear."

"That's right."

Bernadette heard an exhalation of breath—Lisa thought this was weird, but probably was going along because she didn't have another choice.

"This isn't too likely," Bernadette said, "but it's the only thing I can think of."

"Okay," Lisa said. "I'm pulling the stuffing out now." The phone was still on the counter, staring at the ceiling, and Bernadette couldn't see what Lisa was doing. But Lisa probably needed both hands, so Bernadette wasn't going to complain.

"Nothing yet," Lisa murmured. "Oh—here." She grabbed the phone, and it jostled as a deflated bear sat listlessly on the counter, surrounded by white fluff. "I can prop this up…"

The camera stayed still, and Lisa's hands came into view, pulling more stuffing out of the bear.

But there was nothing inside. No USB stick, no SIM card, nothing.

Lisa pulled the last clump of stuffing out of the bear. "There's nothing in here."

Bernadette gritted her teeth. "It was a worth a try. Thanks for doing this."

"Yeah," Lisa said, and now it was her turn for her voice to crack. "Bernadette? It's going to be okay, right? They'll come back safe. Right?"

A slight hesitation. Bernadette didn't know. She had no idea what Parr Medical wanted. And if she couldn't capture whoever had threatened Sophie—

"Yes," she said, her voice sounding hollow. "Yes, Lisa. Everything will be all right."

Chapter Eleven

BERNADETTE CAUGHT up with Kep and Annika in the lobby of the police station. They signed in at the front desk of the Homicide Division, putting Marnie Synskey's name on the visitors' sheet. She and Kep flanked Annika as they walked through the halls to the conference room.

Detective Herrera stepped out of the break room and stared at the three of them. "This is what you've been up to?"

"Have you met Marnie Synskey, Detective?" Kep asked. "She worked closely with Leopold Montclair."

Herrera pulled Bernadette a few steps away. "What's she doing here?"

"Answering some questions," Bernadette said.

Herrera frowned. "Can I speak to you for a moment?"

"We're about to interview—"

"I'm sorry, but this can't wait." Herrera stepped forward and grabbed Bernadette by the elbow.

"Hey—"

Herrera led Bernadette into the break room.

"Take your hands off me, Detective."

He held his hands up in front of him. "Sorry. But—do you know how involved Synskey is with Parr Medical?"

"She's the head of executive services. Worked closely with our murder victim. So I'd expect—"

"Just be careful what you say. She's got more power in that organization than you think." He shook his head, as if clearing his thoughts. "But we've got another issue."

Bernadette took a step back. "Which is?"

"The victim's brother, Freddy Montclair. He's here, and he's demanding to know where we are in the investigation of Leopold Montclair's death."

Seemed odd for him—along with Niehaus—to block the investigation of the crime scene, yet demand answers on the murder. Maybe Niehaus was working to figure out how effective his obstructions were and wanted Freddy to ask. "You told him we can't comment on ongoing investigations?"

Herrera smoothed his mustache before answering. "He won't take 'no comment' as an answer. And I think he's doing the bidding of Jeremy Niehaus."

Bernadette studied Herrera's face: the worry lines of his forehead, the sheen just below his hairline. He feared Niehaus. She folded her arms. "And you want me to talk to him?"

"You're the federal investigator."

Bernadette sighed, nodded, and took a step out of the break room. "Kep, can you take Ms. Synskey to an interview room? I need to take care of something."

"They can wait right here," Herrera said. "I'll keep an eye on them."

Bernadette turned to look at Herrera again. Ah— Herrera didn't trust Kep to ask questions that wouldn't anger Marnie Synskey. Too bad Herrera didn't know this was an impostor.

It'd be five minutes, tops.

"Fine," Bernadette said. "Where is Mr. Montclair now?"

"Fred's in the small conference room." Herrera pointed down a wide hallway. "Second door on the left."

Bernadette strode down the hall, stopped in front of the closed conference room door, hesitated, then rapped on the door three times. "Mr. Montclair?"

Fred's timid voice on the other side. "Come in."

Bernadette opened the door. Fred stood behind the small round table in the middle of the room, his hands resting on the back of the chair. Instead of a yellow polo shirt, he wore a teal polo shirt. His cowlick stuck up at the same angle as it had the day before.

"I'm sorry," Fred stammered, "but I just want answers. I thought Leo died of a heart attack, and now I hear there are federal homicide investigators on the case?"

Bernadette thought for a moment.

"Look—I'm just an accountant." Fred spread his arms in front of him, as if pleading. "I took two days off, and I've got to get back to Columbus by tomorrow, or my clients will have my head. I'm trying to close out my brother's affairs as fast as I can—"

Bernadette held up her hand. "I'm not sure what your brother told you," she said, "but he was involved with some, uh, complicated issues."

"Complicated issues? What does that mean?"

"It means, unfortunately, that this will take some time to sort out. I'm sorry, Mr. Montclair. I know his death must have been sudden, and that this must come as a shock—"

His mouth turned down in disgust. "So I'll have to take additional time off once you sort this all out?"

"Well—I suppose so. But I hope you agree that we're prioritizing what happened to your brother. And who's responsible."

He looked down at the table. "I thought it was a heart attack," he mumbled.

"And I hate to say this," Bernadette said, "but I can't give you more information than that. This is an ongoing investigation."

"So that's it?"

Bernadette blinked. "Well—since you're here, I suppose I should ask you some routine questions."

His head snapped up. "Routine questions? Like what?"

"Please understand—we're asking these questions of everyone."

Fred licked his lips. "Uh—okay. I'll do whatever I can to help."

"Where were you between Monday evening and Tuesday afternoon?"

"Are you asking me for an alibi?"

"Like I said, Mr. Montclair, we're asking these questions of everyone."

Fred exhaled loudly, his cheeks puffing out. "At home in Columbus."

"Can anyone confirm that?"

"I stopped working at five-thirty."

"Anyone see you leave?"

"No idea. I run my own business, and my receptionist had already left. A woman was walking her dog when I got home. I waved to her."

"A neighbor."

"I think so. She walks that dog everywhere. I don't

remember her name, but her dog is Skippy. Little gray Schnauzer."

"Do you know what your brother does?"

"I know he made his money on pharmaceuticals. We weren't that close. Christmas cards and a call on birthdays, mostly."

Bernadette nodded. "Do you know who gets his money?"

"He trusted me enough to be the executor of his estate, but instead of being his beneficiary, he left his money to all kinds of arts organization." He scowled. "The guy had his money in a hundred different places, I have to sort it all out, and I don't even get enough to buy myself dinner."

"And the house?"

"Mortgaged up to his eyeballs."

She nodded. "As soon as we're able to give you more information, you'll be my first call."

Fred tilted his head. "Do you have my number?"

"You've left it with the detective, right?"

Fred nodded.

"I'm sorry for your loss," Bernadette said.

Fred mumbled his thanks, his hands still on the back of the chair, and leaned forward, bowing his head.

"I'll have someone walk you out."

"Thank you."

Bernadette left the room, closed the door behind her, and stepped out into the hall. "Guess he had to hear it from the federal investigator's mouth."

"He seem okay to you?" Herrera asked.

"Either he didn't like his brother much, or he's not processing the death very well. Or both."

"Did he say where he was the day his brother died?"

"He says he was home."

"Not a great alibi."

"Easy enough to check," Bernadette said. "Besides, he didn't benefit financially from his brother's death. So what's the motive?"

"True enough," Herrera said. "But we always look at family members."

"Of course. Anyway, I told him someone would walk him out." She smiled at the detective, joining Kep and Annika-as-Marnie, and left him in front of the break room.

They turned the corner, out of Detective Herrera's sight, and made a beeline for the conference room—no one-way mirrors in there. Bernadette opened the door.

Annika pushed past her, holding out a small gray wand in front of her—smaller than a TV remote, but larger than a pen.

"What the—"

Annika whirled around and put a finger to her lips.

Oh, Annika had a bug detector, too. Of course it would be more compact and more elegant, rather than Bernadette's device resembling a twenty-year-old hard drive.

Annika held the gray metallic wand in front of her. Tiny green LEDs flickered on the top of the wand. She crept around the room, taking extra time around the television and the coffeemaker. The seconds ticked by into minutes, and finally Annika clicked something on the wand and the green lights turned off. She motioned to Kep, who closed the door with a furrowed brow.

"We're clear," Annika said. "No bugs, cameras, nothing like that."

"You think—"

"Do I think Parr Medical has people at the Cleveland Police? They most certainly do. That's how they've been able to keep out of trouble for the last few years. But no listening devices or cameras in here."

Bernadette crossed the room in front of the flat-screen mounted on the wall and put her purse on the conference table. "Before we get started, I need you to tell me what exactly you know about my daughter being in danger."

Annika paused. "I intercepted a message, that's all."

"So who sent it?"

A smile touched the corner of Annika's mouth. "Well, it wasn't Joanna Quimby. Word is, she's dead."

Bernadette frowned. "But you don't know who broke into a dead FBI agent's email account and sent an email that threatened my daughter?"

Annika sat back in her seat. "I'm willing to bet whoever killed Leopold Montclair is the same person who threatened your daughter."

"How did you come to that conclusion?"

Annika tapped her fingers on the table, took a deep breath, and exhaled through her mouth.

Bernadette crossed her arms.

Annika leaned forward. "Okay. I must have arrived right after the killer left."

"Why?"

"Laptop on Montclair's dining room table. The lid was closed, but the machine was still warm. Could have been an hour before it went to sleep, could have been two minutes. I don't think it was an hour, because the battery was still almost full."

"You opened the laptop?"

"Sure."

"Wasn't there a login screen?"

Annika was silent for a moment, then Bernadette let out a small grunt. "Fingerprint scanner?"

"Right."

"So—something on the laptop made you think the killer threatened my daughter?"

"The screen just showed the desktop. Like the last user had quit everything."

Bernadette cocked an eyebrow.

"I launched a browser, went to the history page, and there it was. Joanna Quimby's personal email. Someone had visited her email on that PC that day, because it didn't even ask me for a username and password, just let me right in. I read a couple of emails, then clicked on *Sent Items,* and there it was: an email sent to you, threatening Sophie."

Bernadette flinched. She didn't want Annika knowing her daughter's name. "And you determined the person who sent the email was the same as the killer?"

"Of course. They didn't find what they were looking for at Montclair's house, so they figured they'd get you to do it for them. And they didn't want to use their own computer to send you the information, so they used Montclair's, after he died." Annika wiggled her fingers. "Same fingerprint I used."

"What were they looking for? The safe-deposit box key?"

Annika shook her head. "The key is how I think we'll find the killer, not what the killer was looking for. They didn't take the safe-deposit box key because they didn't think it was important."

Bernadette clenched her fists. "So you don't know how to find Joanna Quimby's encryption key?"

"Nope. I didn't even realize Joanna was that closely involved. I just figured she was paid to make sure the FBI stayed out of Parr Medical's business. Didn't realize she'd have some encryption key."

Bernadette grunted.

"Didn't think she'd try to kill you either," Annika said, more softly. "Sorry about that."

And now Sophie was under threat. Whoever was behind this was right: Bernadette would do anything to save Sophie. If Bernadette knew where that encryption key was, she'd have given it up in a second, even if the next threatening request was right around the corner.

"Do you know what this encryption key does?"

"I bet it's the key to a file that proves Parr Medical is guilty of something." Annika lifted her head and stared at the ceiling. "You know, they've got a medication in clinical trials right now."

"The new erectile dysfunction medication? Kep told me."

Annika chuckled. "No. It's called vezuflozin."

"Vezuflozin?"

"Yeah, not the easiest to say, but it's a medication for several types of—oh, what's it called..." Annika rubbed her temple with her left hand, then opened her eyes and snapped. "Chronic kidney disease, heart disease, that kind of thing. Broad applications, promising results."

"I sense a *but* coming."

"Unacceptable side effects. Triggers autoimmune disease in a bunch of the study participants. All that research money down the drain. We're talking losses in the mid seven or eight figures of R&D. And millions in post market profit." Annika sat down heavily in a chair on the other side of the conference table.

"What would this file do?"

"If I had to guess? Fake results, maybe. Or a file of real

results. The file would be encrypted, of course—private patient data and all that. You'd need an encryption key to read it, and maybe that's what they want. If Parr Medical didn't want the file to see the light of day," Annika continued, "they'd want to digitally shred the encryption key."

Bernadette nodded. Deleting or overwriting an encryption key—*shredding* in cybersecurity parlance— would render the file unreadable. She briefly wondered if someone had shredded Joanna's encryption key.

"You are speculating now," Kep said to Annika.

"That's true," Annika said. "Maybe after trying to kill the two of you, they decided they're done with all this and they're escaping with their money to the Caribbean. So I guess the encryption key could be to a Swiss bank account or something."

Kep opened his mouth, and Annika raised her hand.

"Yes, yes, speculation again, Dr. Woodhead. It was just an example." Annika tapped her chin. "But this isn't like messing with the research of a competitor, or even arranging plans with a hired killer. Whatever the encryption key is for takes a unique set of skills. Hacking at this level is far different from social engineering for corporate espionage."

Bernadette stood and paced in a circle. "But surely this has changed. You were hired to kill Leopold Montclair, and someone beat you to it, using an almost-untraceable poison. You've used nearly-untraceable poisons before."

"I thought I might be getting set up," Annika said. "But the police never showed up. And that means a communication breakdown at Parr Medical."

"So—you think someone who actually works at Parr Medical—and not a hired killer—murdered Leopold Montclair?"

Annika shrugged. "Looks professional to me. Until now, though, everyone I met at Parr Medical had plausible deniability for all the murders. No one ever directly told me to kill someone. I always got untraceable messages—I only figured out Leopold Montclair sent a few of the messages because he got sloppy."

"But you went through plastic surgery. You had your identity changed."

"And Leopold coordinated all of that," Annika said. "He picked me up from the hotel and drove me to the hospital. Even visited me in recovery and drove me back. Gave me a card to order food when I was recovering."

"And placed you at Kilbourn Tech as a research assistant under a fake name? That's fraud."

Annika pressed her lips together. "A few days before I was sent to Milwaukee, Leopold gave me a burner phone, it's true. But the instructions were delivered on the phone —and they were anonymous. I mean, Leopold could have sent those messages, and sometimes I assumed he had. But I could never be sure. Now that we found this phone in his safe-deposit box? Made it pretty clear that he gave the orders. At least some of them."

"Speaking of burner phones..." Bernadette took out the evidence baggie from her purse. "You ready to see if there's a number on the burner phone?"

Annika nodded.

"What is our course of action if there is nothing on the burner phone?" Kep asked. He had his back to the conference room door.

"I guess we wait for it to ring," Bernadette said.

"And then what happens?" Annika said. "You think whoever calls you will simply accept that *you're* the one who answered?"

"Are you suggesting you need to answer it?" Bernadette retorted. "None of us are supposed to have this phone on us. It's supposed to be locked up in the safe-deposit box." She looked at Kep. "In fact, if only Marnie Synskey and Leopold Montclair are supposed to have access to this phone, don't you think they'll expect *Marnie* to call?"

Annika shook her head. "Marnie doesn't make calls. She doesn't receive calls. She just makes sure the right person gets the phone."

"Then how come Leopold Montclair had a key?"

Annika rolled her eyes. "Because he gave some of the orders," Annika said. "To be my contact for the plastic surgery, he must have known who I was. Maybe he even gave me the order for the carjacking in Jacksonville."

"So why did you get an order to kill Leopold Montclair?"

Annika tilted her head.

"Oh." Bernadette rested her elbow on the table and put her chin in her hand. "Because he screwed up."

"If you want my opinion—or my conjecture," Annika said, glancing at Kep, "he screwed up with *you*. Not only did you get away from the prison riot, but Dr. Woodhead wasn't even at Taycheedah. And then the containment didn't work."

"The containment?"

"The car bomb."

Ah, right.

"Montclair brought more and more attention to Parr Medical with everything he tried to do to kill the two of you." Annika reached her arms above her head and stretched. "And then Parr Medical's mole in the FBI was compromised. Years of work down the drain. Someone had to pay."

"And it was him." Bernadette cocked her head. "Why did they pick you?"

A wistful look appeared in Annika's eye. "Leopold trusted me. With our history, he probably thought I'd be on his side."

"But you're only on your own side. Your side—and your sister's."

"And she disappeared on me." Annika gave Bernadette a wry smile. "I'd like to think she's loyal to me the way I am to her, but who knows? When I find Marguerite, I might discover she's the one who put everything in motion to put me in jail in the first place. But I don't think so. I think she's just as much of a pawn in this game as I am." She stood and clapped her hands. "Now, let's see if there's a number on that phone."

Bernadette nodded and picked up the evidence baggie from the table. She unsealed the bag at the top, shook the phone out into her hand, opened the clamshell phone, and pushed the red power button. After a moment, the screen flickered on. She pushed the button with a five-pronged star on it—that was probably the Favorites button.

"They'll know the phone is at the police station now," Kep said.

One number: a 216 area code. Bernadette glanced up; Annika was looking over her shoulder.

"Recognize the number?"

Annika shook her head. "I assume it's another burner."

"Shall we try it?"

Annika pressed her lips together. "All it will do is tell the person at the other end of the phone they've been compromised."

"Or the person on the other end of the phone might think you're Marnie Synskey and reveal some information." Bernadette tapped the phone lightly on the table. "Like it or not, this is the only lead we have right now. We might as well see where it goes."

Annika slumped her shoulders, but she nodded.

Bernadette pulled her small notebook out of her purse and opened it to a blank page, taking her pen out, ready to take notes. Using the arrow keys, Bernadette scrolled to the number, then pressed *Call* and turned on the speakerphone.

It rang: once, twice, three times.

Then the sound of the phone being picked up.

"Mr. Belgrade?" asked a woman on the other end.

Bernadette flinched. Mr. Belgrade? As in Andy Belgrade—the person who had signed the purchase order for the FBI recording devices found in Leopold Montclair's boat? Why did the woman expect Andy Belgrade to call in?

But Leopold had mentioned Andy Belgrade when he'd tried to reach Yates Raphael. Maybe Leopold was holding this phone for him.

Annika's hand swooped forward, catching Bernadette's attention.

Bernadette stood from her seat, narrowing her eyes at Annika.

Annika pointed to Kep, then moved her hand as if miming talking.

If they expected a man speaking, it would explain why Annika wasn't the one talking.

Kep leaned forward. Bernadette pictured the wheels turning in his head. How was he supposed to sound? What was he supposed to say?

"I won't have the status report for you until this evening," the woman said.

"That's fine." Kep's voice was more confident than Bernadette expected. He pulled out a conference table chair and sat.

"Have you seen any movement on the Becker woman attempting to get the agent's encryption key?"

Kep looked up, searching Bernadette's face, then Annika's. Annika nodded.

"I've been tracking her," Kep said. "She's reached out to Ms. Quimby's co-workers."

"No," the woman said. "She'll get too close."

"We can—" Kep said, then stopped, his forehead creasing.

"We agreed to accelerate the plan if this happened," the woman said. "But if I set the acceleration in motion, you'll need to use the Platinum Prime information."

Platinum Prime? What was that—code for something or someone? Bernadette's mind raced. If this woman wanted to deliver a report to Andy Belgrade in a few hours, it would only take the initial conversation before she would figure out that she hadn't been talking with him earlier. Bernadette pointed at Kep and mouthed, "Say yes."

"Of course," Kep said, and Annika's head snapped up.

"We've received information on the location," the woman said. "I'll leave as soon as possible. Half dog tomorrow."

The call ended.

"Did she say 'half dog tomorrow'?" Bernadette asked.

Kep slumped in his chair, a sheen of sweat on his forehead.

"Seven-thirty," Annika said. "Possibly in the morning."

Bernadette glanced up at Annika. "Care to tell me what that was about?"

"It was code," Kep said.

"I know it was code," Bernadette said. "What I want to know is, why didn't you pretend to be Marnie Synskey? You know this organization much better than Kep or I do. Why give it to him?"

"Because—" Annika began. "Because the woman expected a man. Mr. Belgrade."

"That's not why," Bernadette said. Annika was a good liar, and most of the time, Bernadette couldn't tell. But somehow, she knew this was a lie. She folded her arms and waited.

Annika cleared her throat and looked down at the table.

"Because," Kep said, taking out a handkerchief from his inside sportcoat pocket, "the woman on the other end of the phone would have recognized Annika's voice."

"Even if she'd disguised it?"

"Even if she'd disguised it." Kep patted his brow with the handkerchief, then turned to Annika. "Sisters often know you better than you know yourself."

Bernadette blinked, and she took a deep breath. "Hold on. That was *Marguerite?*"

Annika bit her lip and said nothing. She glanced at Kep, who fixed her with a stare. Annika looked away.

Yep. Marguerite.

Chapter Twelve

Annika folded her hands in front of her and stared down at the conference table.

Bernadette sat back down in the chair across from Annika. "And what does it mean, accelerate the plan? What are they going to do if they think I'm getting too close to another FBI mole?"

Annika rubbed her chin, but said nothing.

"Well?"

"I don't know," Annika said. "These plans—they take care to make sure everyone is on a need-to-know basis, and I wasn't told what the plan was. The only way I know that they even want Joanna Quimby's encryption key is because I saw that email when I wasn't supposed to."

"Can you find out? Are they going to get an FBI agent to feed me some misinformation? Maybe point me in the *right* direction so I can get information about where the encryption key might actually be?"

"I can try," Annika muttered.

"Or," Kep said, "might they attempt to create a more credible threat to your daughter?"

Bernadette stared at Annika. Annika's shoulders were hunched. Yes. That's exactly what they would do.

Her breaths came short and fast as the tips of her fingertips felt numb. Pins and needles. First in her fingertips, then traveling through her fingers, into her palms—

A hand on her shoulder. "Sophie's in a safehouse," Kep said, reaching over the chair between them. "We don't even know where—that's how safe she is."

Bernadette couldn't remember him *ever* touching her before. She stared up at him; he was looking across the table at Annika.

"And we clearly have our next move," he continued.

"Tell me," Annika said simply.

"We find Marguerite," he said.

Annika laughed, biting and derisive. "I've been looking for her for years. Exactly how do you propose to find my sister if I couldn't?"

"We have a phone number now," Kep said. "From a prepaid cellular phone that we can be confident Marguerite will have powered on." He turned to Bernadette. "How do you think Joanna Quimby tracked you?"

"Because I spoke to her on my burner phone when she told me I wasn't in danger anymore," Bernadette said.

"And how did she use that phone number to discover your location? A software tool?"

"I assume so. The FBI has a lot of tools like that."

"Do you have any present contacts in the FBI who could potentially access—" Kep began.

"I'm *not* putting Marguerite in their crosshairs," Annika interrupted.

"I don't trust anyone at the FBI," Bernadette said. "Let's talk to Maura and see if we can get Lesley access to software tools that can track cell phones by their number."

Kep held up his phone. "I can make the call right now." He pulled his phone out of his pocket.

Bernadette made eye contact with Kep, then inclined her head slightly toward the door of the conference room.

Kep furrowed his brow, and Bernadette repeated her head motion.

"She wants you to make the call somewhere I can't hear," Annika said. "It's fine. I wouldn't trust me either."

A light burst of color rose to Kep's cheeks. He stepped around the edge of the conference table and walked out the door.

For a moment, the conference room was silent. Annika continued to stare at her folded hands. Bernadette tapped her fingers on the table, then leaned forward slightly.

"Marguerite mentioned we'd need to get information from Platinum Prime," Bernadette said. "What does that mean? More code?"

Annika looked up. "Platinum Prime is the most expensive steakhouse in downtown Cleveland. If I were you, I'd go there and start asking questions about Parr Medical."

"And about Andy Belgrade, too?"

Annika folded her arms.

"Who's Andy Belgrade, Annika? Is he behind all this?"

"All I know is that I got Leopold Montclair treating me well, shuttling me to the hospital, paying my hotel bill, and then getting instructions on a burner phone. All *after* my sister disappeared. I just want her to be safe. I've heard the name *Andy Belgrade* in passing, but I don't know who he is or how he's connected."

"You never talked to anyone else at Parr Medical?" Bernadette narrowed her eyes. "You had plastic surgery for that corporate espionage job at Kilbourn Tech. You didn't just kill a researcher. You didn't just kill a member of my team—someone I considered a friend. You changed your looks, you changed your name. You changed your whole life."

Annika hesitated for a moment. "I don't know what you want me to say. I did what I was told to keep my sister safe. But I've had enough. I need my life back. *She* needs her life back."

Another long silence settled over the table.

The door opened, and Kep came in. "Your lieutenant submitted the software tool requisition," Kep said. "And she did not want to involve the FBI."

A thought struck Bernadette. "Why not just call the burner phone and tell Marguerite the truth? Have Annika explain everything—if Marguerite wants to be out of that life, we can see if she can meet us somewhere. Put you both in witness protection."

"Witness protection?" Annika scoffed. "Parr Medical has people *everywhere*. Both of us would be dead in a week."

Bernadette furrowed her brow. "Why—why didn't you tell her who you were when she answered the phone?"

"Because I don't know who's with her." She paused. "And I suppose I was in shock. I hadn't thought of what I would say to her if I called a random phone number and she picked up."

Kep pointed at Bernadette. "You must know of safe-houses we can use that are outside the purview of the FBI or the police departments that employ Parr Medical insiders."

Bernadette nodded. "We can talk to Maura."

Kep rubbed his bearded chin. "Without calling the

prepaid mobile phone, however, I am at a loss how we coordinate with Marguerite. And I am uncomfortable pretending to be Andy Belgrade again." He directed a sharp look at Annika.

"Annika won't tell us who he is," Bernadette said.

Annika leaned forward in her seat. "Because I don't know."

"Then our only option is to track Marguerite's phone," Bernadette said.

"Glad to be of assistance." Annika rose from the chair.

"Wait," Kep said.

Annika and Bernadette both looked at Kep. He stared at the floor for a moment, then crossed his arms and leaned against the wall.

"Kep?" Bernadette asked.

He took a deep, shuddering breath, then clapped his hands on his upper thighs. "I need to know what happened to Jack."

Annika blinked. "Who?"

"Jack Woodhead," Bernadette said softly. "Kep's son. An investigative reporter for *The Boston Chronicle*."

Annika shook her head. "I don't know anything about that."

"The hell you don't," Kep murmured, and the menace in his voice shocked Bernadette.

Bernadette raised her head to look Annika in the eyes. "The SD card," she said. "Hidden in a gusle I bought from Pike Place Music. You know that, of course."

Annika said nothing.

"A spreadsheet encrypted in a folder called 'Marguerite.' Every single person entered in that spreadsheet is now dead. They all died within the last five years. Some of those people's deaths are *solved* murders—thought to be domestic disputes or home invasions. Some of those people died in automobile accidents, or of sudden heart attacks. And a few of them—like Jack Woodhead—are still open, unsolved cases."

Annika pressed her lips together tightly.

"You know the police considered Kep a suspect for a while. Maybe Parr Medical even wanted him to be the prime suspect. You must know Kep spent a small fortune hiring investigators to look into his son's death, but they came up with nothing." Bernadette cocked her head. "Now that I hear those words coming out of my mouth, I wonder if Parr Medical paid off those investigators, too."

Annika shifted in her seat.

Kep pushed off the wall and put his hands flat on the table, leaning inches from Annika's face. "You let me—"

Bernadette was up, blocking his body and guiding him back. "Hold on," she said. "Hold *on*, Kep."

His breaths came short and fast. "If you'd—"

"Let's take a minute."

Kep took one more deep breath, then took a small step back and straightened his sportcoat. Bernadette still stood between him and the conference table. Kep averted his eyes. "I suppose you're correct."

Bernadette put a hand between his shoulder blades and steered him toward the conference room door, keeping her hand on his back as she opened the door and guided him out into the hall, closing the door behind her.

"We just left her in there with the pay-as-you-go mobile—"

"Hey," Bernadette murmured. "Annika is the only person who's given us a lead—not just to how we can find who killed Leopold Montclair, but just maybe how I can protect Sophie and how you can find out what happened to Jack."

Kep exhaled.

"I don't have to tell you," Bernadette said, "that it will be much easier for Annika to give us information if you keep your cool."

Kep stared daggers at Bernadette. "You are truly one to talk. You've—"

"Yes, I'm usually the one who can't control my temper, and you're usually the one to calm me down. Now I can return the favor." She turned Kep to face her and gripped him by both shoulders. "You have every right to be pissed off, but you can't show it in front of Annika. If you want her to tell you anything about Jack, you'll have to wait. She's not ready to say anything."

"She can be protective of her sister, but I can't be—"

"No," Bernadette murmured, as gently as she could. "You can't. Because even though Jack's name was in that spreadsheet, I don't think Annika killed him."

"Then who—"

"That spreadsheet was in a folder labeled *Marguerite*. That spreadsheet is Marguerite's hit list, not Annika's. Since Annika had no proof Marguerite was alive when she hid that SD card in the gusle a year ago, I don't think she had anything to do with Jack's death."

The sides of Kep's mouth raised slightly, then turned back down. "I do not feel particularly good about working so closely with a convicted murderer."

"But putting her back in jail—assuming Parr Medical doesn't do something even more heinous to get her out— won't help anything," Bernadette said, dropping her arms to her side and taking a step back. "The people who hired Annika to perform corporate espionage, steal company secrets? They'll still be there. If not Annika, it'll be Marguerite—or the guy in the Kansas State sweatshirt who put the bomb under our rental car. They already had you and me in their crosshairs once. You don't think they'll jump at the chance to kill us when our guard is down?"

Kep blinked, once, twice, three times. "After—" His voice cracked, but he cleared his throat and tried again. "After Jack was killed, I failed to discern what was important to me anymore. I became obsessed with finding who killed my son." He hung his head. "My wife left because I was so angry all the time. The television production company bought out my contract because my attention became erratic. Yates Raphael—he's the one who made that decision." Kep took off his glasses and rubbed his eyes. "I only took this consulting job because CSAB paid for my expertise without a significant time commitment. I could continue to focus on the investigation into Jack's— into Jack's murder."

Bernadette nodded slowly. "I'm sorry, Kep. I've never lost a child, but Sophie is in danger, and I'm losing my mind. If anything happened to her, you better believe I'd be a mess."

Just then, Detective Herrera came around the corner. His brows were knotted in frustration. "You two left Marnie Synskey in the conference room?"

Bernadette raised herself to her full height. "Dr. Woodhead and I were discussing strategy."

"Well, next time, use your brain. You left a civilian in the front conference room earlier—"

"A civilian? You mean Fred Montclair?"

Herrera set his jaw. "Maybe you've been in the feds so long you forgot some relatives don't process grief so well. I found him wandering the halls. Said he was looking for the bathroom, but he was halfway to our evidence room. He probably didn't even realize where he was."

"I *told* you he was—" Then Bernadette heard the defensiveness in her voice. "I told him someone would see him out, and I relayed that message to you."

Herrera exhaled loudly. "And in my world, that means you're taking care of it." He leaned forward. "I'm serious when I say don't talk to Synskey too long. She's well-connected. And to the wrong people. Finish up her statement and get her the hell out of here."

❧

Bernadette and Kep sat back down at the conference table. The burner phone still sat in the middle of the table and Annika still sat in her chair in the same position she was when they'd left the room.

The phone rang in Bernadette's purse. It was Lesley. Bernadette got up from the table and answered it.

"Lesley—any news?" Bernadette opened the door and stepped out into the hallway.

"I don't know what Dr. Woodhead said to Lieu, but I've already gotten a link to that software tech to track the burner phone."

"Oh—wow. Well, Maura moves fast when she's motivated."

"If only Dr. Woodhead could convince her we need a decent espresso machine." Lesley cleared her throat. "The first thing I need is the number of the burner phone to track."

Bernadette nodded. "I'll text that over to you right away."

"The second thing: I need to know if you want me to wait for a warrant."

"Oh." Bernadette blinked. "No. I need to know where that phone is as soon as humanly possible."

"You know the repercussions—"

"Yes, yes, I got it. No fruit from the poisonous tree. But lives are at stake."

Lesley fell silent. She didn't point out that Maura was bending the rules because the lives in questions were Bernadette's daughter and ex-husband, but the unspoken accusation hung thickly over the phone call. Lesley must have known that Maura set the wheels in motion for Bernadette to talk to Sophie through Agent Reese earlier —in itself, highly unusual.

"Of course, apply for the warrant as soon as you can." Bernadette tapped her fingers against her thumb. "I don't know who we can trust, though. Can you keep the warrant application under wraps?"

"I'll do what I can. A little more paperwork, maybe an extra day or two. I'll send you the warrant application form, then you fill it out."

"I'll have it to you within the hour." Bernadette's voice lowered. "Anything on Andy Belgrade yet?"

"His name isn't showing up in a cursory search of the employee listings," Lesley said. "For anything more than it, I need to get my cone of silence."

"Thanks, Lesley. Oh, while I've got you on the phone, one more thing."

An overworked sigh. "Sure."

"Leopold Montclair left everything to charity. Fred was saying Leopold's money was all over the place, so I wonder if he had secret accounts where he stored money from any illegal activities. Can you see if any large amounts of cash are squirreled away somewhere? In a Swiss bank account or in a holding company or something?"

"What are you looking for?"

"A possible financial motive."

"Gotcha."

They said their goodbyes and Bernadette ended the call.

Bernadette stepped back into the conference room, and almost immediately, Annika tutted. "So, was that your contact at the FBI?"

Bernadette shook her head. "Like I said, I don't trust the FBI. I trust the person I was on the phone with. Keeping this under wraps is a priority."

Annika looked down at the table, then leaned back and crossed her arms. "What else do you need?"

Bernadette glanced at Kep. "We'll keep the burner phone here at the station. If anyone tracks the location, it'll be here."

Annika paused, then turned to Kep. "Don't you think it would be wise to return the phone to the safe-deposit box?"

Kep paused and looked at Bernadette. "Possibly," he said.

"It really depends if we think Marnie Synskey will go to the bank again," Bernadette said. "If she does, won't the bank personnel say, 'Oh, Ms. Synskey, so nice to see you again after last week'? That'll give it away that something's up."

Annika rubbed her chin. "And what good can come out of leaving the phone here?"

"We could give it to the cybercrimes unit, see if they can—"

"Not until *after* we make that phone call to Marguerite," Kep said.

"Right." Bernadette turned back to Annika. "So it's settled, we'll keep it. And you'll get Marnie her driver's license back."

Annika brought her hand up. Marnie Synskey's ID was in her palm.

"You can do this in your sleep, right? Just like being a pickpocket, but in reverse." Bernadette rubbed her chin. "Same coffee place every day, right?"

"But she'll be watching for strange things at the coffee shop." Annika glanced at Bernadette. "Marnie is an easy mark. You could do it when she visits Guardian Fitness— the one on Euclid and Thirteenth."

Bernadette shook her head. "We agreed you'd do this, Annika. Not one of us. That was the plan. You're the master of disguises and sleight-of-hand. But you'll need to do it soon, before Marnie notices it's gone."

"She works out every day at four thirty," Annika said. "She's at Guardian Fitness for about an hour, then either goes back to work or heads home."

"If you're worried about Parr Medical catching you, go in disguise. Slip the ID back into Marnie's purse at four thirty, then go underground."

"You're right," Annika said. "I agreed to do it."

"Let us walk you out," Kep said. "We want appearances to be kept up, after all." He rose and opened the door, and Annika stood, closed her eyes for a moment, then affected Marnie Synskey's walk as she strode out of the interview room. Kep and Bernadette followed closely behind. They walked through the police department's chilly, air-conditioned lobby, and Kep held the door open for both Annika and Bernadette.

Bernadette felt the warm July sun hit her face, then turned to Annika. "So let us know when you've put the ID back—"

An Asian woman in a business suit stared at her. "Are you talking to me?"

"No," Bernadette said, "I was talking to—" She pointed to the space next to the woman. No one was there. She spun around and almost bumped into Kep.

The woman walked away.

"Did you see where she went?"

"Annika?"

Bernadette narrowed her eyes. "Marnie Synskey, yes."

Kep blinked. "Weren't you walking right behind her?"

"I was, but..." She put her hand in her purse to grab her phone—

And her hand found a hard, rectangular card.

Bernadette groaned, bringing the card out. Marnie Synskey's driver's license.

Annika had vanished.

Chapter Thirteen

BERNADETTE BROUGHT her laptop into the conference room. Lesley had sent her the form for the application for the federal warrant. She had to get a little creative for a couple of the answers, but everything was straightforward: they were searching specifically for location information of the burner phone. Kep had little to add, and sat in the corner, resting his head against the wall behind him, his spectacles in his hand, his eyes closed.

Bernadette added her digital signature and sent it off to Lesley. Then she opened the Pike Place Music forum and sent a message to Alaska Afternoon.

Bernadette hit *Enter*, then stared at the screen for a moment. She didn't really expect an answer; Annika was probably on her way to a bar. Or her next hit.

A ping from the laptop. It was a reply from Alaska Afternoon.

> Sorry but after getting my sister on the phone I can't risk it
>
> You and Doc are smart
>
> You'll figure something out

"Great," Bernadette said.

"Annika is in the wind?" Kep asked.

"She is. And we still need to get the driver's license back to Marnie Synskey. Hopefully before she signs in at Guardian Fitness at four thirty." She looked at Kep. "Any ideas how we do that?"

"As Miss Nakrivo suggested, we meet Marnie Synskey in front of Guardian Fitness. I can tell her the poison test returned a false positive. I can apologize profusely. While I'm conversing with her, you replace the driver's license."

"We can't do a pratfall this time," Bernadette said. "Any physical bump will get Marnie suspicious."

Kep was silent, creases of thought in his forehead.

Bernadette rose from her chair and paced around the table. "Maybe we can tell Marnie that our tests have ruled out murder."

"What would that accomplish?"

"I'd look for tells. If Marnie knows something, it might show on her face."

"I do not believe that will be conducive to us obtaining a swab under false pretenses." Kep sat up straight and put his glasses on.

"We blame the bureaucracy. We get her to trust us—at least a little—by saying Montclair's death is no longer treated as a homicide, but that the order came in from CSAB and we have to execute a swab test, anyway. Makes it seem like she's helping us out without putting her under suspicion."

Kep scratched his beard. "You would have to do the talking. I am unsure I could thread the needle of that nuance."

"No problem."

"Your plan *would* allow us an excuse to handle her purse."

"Do we know what we could we use for the swab?"

"I believe a simple alcohol pad would suffice," Kep said.

A corner of Bernadette's mouth turned up. "I'm a little surprised at you, Kep. I'd have thought you'd be of the opinion that an alcohol pad wouldn't be believable."

"On the contrary," Kep said. "Specialized surface swabs exist to detect the presence of many recreational drugs. If our Ms. Synskey has flown a commercial airline in the last decade, she will be familiar with the Transportation Safety Administration testing the surface of passengers' hands for nitrates and glycerin. Even if Ms. Synskey is familiar with the latest technologies from government agencies for many controlled substances, she doesn't know the specific type of poison we're looking for and therefore won't know how we test for it."

"If you think you can pull it off, be my guest. The only trick I know is how to magically make my husband appear in my co-worker's bed." She smiled at her joke, a bit surprised by the stab of pain that accompanied it.

Kep glanced at Bernadette. "I dabbled a bit with amateur magic when Jack was in third grade. He became fascinated with sleight-of-hand for several months, though I'm not sure how much I remember."

Bernadette checked the time on her phone: 12:48. "We can talk more about this over some food. I'm starving."

She stood up too quickly and got slightly lightheaded. Her vision swam for a moment, and the swirl of color reminded her of—

Oh.

"Hang on, Kep, give me a minute." She pushed herself forward to the conference room door, opened it, and made it down the hallway to the women's room. She flung the door open and found herself in front of the mirror, leaning on the sink, trying to catch her breath.

The swirl of colors she'd seen when she got up reminded her of a dress she'd bought for Sophie for a spring concert years before: a bunch of first-graders adorably singing off-key. She'd gone with Barlow. The concert had been one of only a few of Sophie's extracurricular activities she'd attended that year. Barlow had been snarky with her, even though she'd caught an earlier flight from her assignment in Dallas, had to rush to the airport, which had pissed off Declan—and having an angry partner at the beginning of a CSAB assignment was not a good thing. Now she wondered: was Barlow so short with her because she'd messed up his plans, maybe a plan to see another woman?

But no; how would Barlow have managed that? When Bernadette was out of town—and increasingly, even when she wasn't—Barlow was Sophie's primary caregiver. He would have been busy with dinners, bedtimes, cleanup. He wouldn't have had time to start an affair.

And besides, he wasn't a disconnected dad like Bernadette's own father had been. Barlow knew how Sophie liked her lunches. He took her to soccer practices, signed permission slips, ran lines with her for her school play.

And now Sophie was in hiding with Barlow, and it was Bernadette's fault.

If she didn't have this job at CSAB, if she had taken a normal job like a policy analyst, none of this would be happening.

Maybe a new career as a policy analyst would be boring, but she could take Sophie to a music festival halfway across the country and not worry about having her daughter and ex-husband whisked away to a safehouse.

Bernadette hung her head, staring into the empty sink. Her brain spun at a million miles an hour—

A thudding noise in her ears.

Her pulse was racing. She closed her eyes, took a deep breath, then let it out slowly, counting to twenty, but only reached twelve. Another deep breath, this time inhaling to the count of fifteen, exhaling to seventeen, then inhaling again. This time, she went all the way to twenty. On the exhale, she couldn't hear the thudding anymore.

Bernadette pushed off the counter and drew herself to her full height. She sized herself up in the mirror. She'd lost a little muscle since—what? Since the demotion? Since she'd started being Kep's handler—"case analyst," as she insisted on framing it? Since the separation? Her blazer was loose around the shoulders. She wasn't working out as much, she wasn't eating the protein-rich diet she'd been on as an agent.

She was losing her edge.

And she felt a twist in her stomach that she wasn't with Sophie—and couldn't even contact her.

Maybe she'd get another call from Agent Xavier Reese again.

She had to fix this. She had to find the person—or

people—behind the murders. It didn't matter how powerful Parr Medical was. Her family depended on it.

A knock on the door. "My apologies," Kep's voice said from the other side, "but if Bernadette Becker is in there—"

"I'm fine, Kep. Give me a minute."

"I'll wait."

Bernadette turned back to the mirror. Creases in her forehead, no color in her cheeks, shoulders slumped.

But still the same spark in her eyes she had before, when she was an agent. A pep talk. She needed to tell herself it was all going to be all right, that she knew what she had to do, that she'd see her daughter in just a few days.

Bernadette opened her mouth, but nothing came out.

She stared at the mirror for another fifteen seconds, then turned and walked out of the restroom.

❧

The faux-Gothic building on Euclid Avenue had an octet of royal blue doors, with three steps in front of each and small, hand-painted signs on five of them. One of them, almost illegibly, read *Las Perihuanas*.

"It's hard to read," Kep said, squinting through his glasses, "but this is the place."

"Good eye." Bernadette hesitated. "Or, more probably—"

Kep touched his nose. "Aji chiles." He climbed the three steps and opened the door.

The smell of aji chiles and garlic was stronger as she walked through the threshold, then up a staircase. At the top landing, the hallway turned left and an open room greeted them. A host stand stood directly in front of them with the same illegible logo, a small bar on the back wall, and about twenty small tables with walnut veneer and four mismatched chairs at each. Three booths with high backs sat next to the wall on the right, parallel to Bernadette's line of sight at the entrance.

The room was empty except for the two of them and a dark-haired woman behind the bar, who set her bar towel down.

The woman straightened her posture behind the bar, and with a broad smile on her face, extended her arm and motioned to the entire room. "Anywhere you like."

Bernadette walked to a seat near the window, taking a seat in a short-backed wooden chair bathed in a sunbeam.

Kep cleared his throat and pointed to the booths. "We should sit in a location where no one can see us from the entrance."

"If not for your superschnozz, we'd never have found this place. I think we have enough privacy." But she looked at the server, striding toward them with two menus in her hand. The booth tables couldn't be seen from the bar, either. Slower service, but yes, privacy. She followed Kep to the booths, and they sat in the rear booth furthest from the door.

The server dropped off two menus. "Can I get you anything to drink?"

Kep pushed his glasses up on his nose and grinned. "Leche de Tigre?"

The woman shook her head. "Not on the lunch menu."

"Chicha morada?"

The woman smiled. "We have Inca Kola."

Kep clapped his hands together. "Perfect. We will have two."

Bernadette opened her mouth. "I don't—"

"No, no," Kep said. "After our adventure with the Wisconsin Old Fashioneds in Milwaukee, I am permitted to order you a beverage."

"Coming right up," the server said.

"I've never had Peruvian."

"A word of warning: don't expect Mexican cuisine," Kep said. "Much different flavor profiles." He leaned forward. "The aji chiles are fresh, which are difficult to find in the Midwest. They must know an importer."

"Inca Kola?"

"Not as good as my other choices."

"The best bad option, huh?" Bernadette forced a smile. "Now let's hurry up and decide on our order. We have work to do—*you*, especially." Bernadette pulled her purse up onto the table and took out Marnie Synskey's driver's license. She slid it across the walnut veneer to Kep.

"I found three video tutorials online," Kep said. "I may not even need a sleeve if I can do this properly."

"No sleeve required?"

"Apparently, the trick is to hide the card in the palm of your hand." He took the driver's license. "I suppose it helps that the playing card is larger, with a higher degree of flexibility, but I'm not trying for misdirection or swapping the card out with an ace of spades. I'm simply hiding the card in my hand until such time as I can drop it in the purse without being noticed." He wedged the license in the palm of his hand. "The fold of my hand just above my thumb joint can hold the bottom corner, then if I curl my pinkie slightly, like this..." He turned his wrist so the back of his hand was facing Bernadette, then tilted his head.

She peered at Kep's hand, then squinted. "That's good. I can't even tell you're holding anything."

"You, of course," Kep said, "will create a diversion to distract Ms. Synskey."

The server appeared with two Inca Kolas, setting down the chilled glass bottles with blue and yellow labels. The yellow liquid inside looked like antifreeze. "Are you ready to order?"

"Will you permit me to suggest a dish," Kep asked, "given your history of restaurant orders when we have dined together, and knowing what I do about the spices you favor?"

Bernadette sat back. "Go ahead."

Kep ordered for them both: a beef dish called lomo saltado for her, a chicken dish for him.

After the server left, Bernadette raised her eyebrows at the yellow liquid bubbling inside the glass. "I thought this was a Peruvian version of Coke."

Kep reached for the bottle and took a swig, setting it down with a satisfied smacking of his lips. "The taste is similar to a flowering plant in South America called lemon verbena." He indicated her bottle. "I find it delightful."

Bernadette took a drink, then set it down. "Bub-blegum." Not her thing; she pushed the bottle aside. "Dry run?" She pulled her purse toward herself, reached in, and pulled out an alcohol wipe in a packet. She tossed it to Kep, who dropped the license on the table as he attempted to catch the wipe.

"I shall endeavor to prepare myself for the unexpect-ed," Kep muttered, as he replaced the identification in his hand.

"Can you do that with one hand?" Bernadette said.

"I can certainly make the attempt." Kep laid the iden-tification on the table, then tore open the packet with the alcohol wipe and pulled a corner out. Taking a deep breath, he placed the palm of his right hand on top of the driver's license. His brow furrowed in concentration as his hand tightened and loosened. If Bernadette hadn't known what Kep was doing, she wouldn't have suspected a thing.

His eyes brightened, and he lifted his hand from the table. Nothing underneath.

"Nice," Bernadette said.

With his left hand, he grabbed the corner of the alcohol wipe and jerked his hand so the wipe came out completely in his hand. He reached for Bernadette's purse with both hands and pulled it an inch or two toward himself.

"Hold on, let me—" Bernadette started.

"Of course," Kep said. He pulled his hands back.

"Okay, now hold it like this." Bernadette grabbed the purse and put it at a ninety-degree angle to the table. "See, it'll be easier to—" She glanced up at Kep, whose eyes twinkled.

She leaned forward, looked in her purse, and Marnie Synskey's driver's license stared up at her.

"Not bad for my first attempt," Kep said.

Chapter Fourteen

THE LOMO SALTADO WAS GOOD, though Bernadette expected it to be spicier. Kep oohed and aahed over his chicken between additional attempts to palm the driver's license and drop it in Bernadette's purse.

After the server took their plates, Bernadette glanced at the clock on her phone. Still three hours before Marnie Synskey would be at her gym, although they should probably leave in an hour in case Marnie showed up early— she'd been late to the coffee shop that morning, after all.

She gazed across the table at Kep, her eyes unfocused, as he brought his right hand from under the table, sponged Bernadette's purse with the alcohol wipe, then took his hands away. He waited a couple of seconds, reached into the purse and removed the driver's license, brought it under the table with his right hand.

Then he repeated the whole procedure. The lines in his face relaxed and his eyes seemed less strained.

"You're getting the hang of it," Bernadette said.

"I may not even require a diversion tactic," Kep said, the corners of his mouth turning up. "I was unaware of the sense of accomplishment I'd feel learning a skill that has nothing to do with my olfactory sense."

"Don't get a big head there, Houdini," Bernadette said, grinning.

⚜

The sky had clouded over when Kep and Bernadette exited the Peruvian restaurant. Kep had a spring in his step from not only the food and the Inka Kola but also from getting the last few dry runs perfectly executed.

Even with the cloud cover, the heat rose from the sidewalks.

"I'll be all sweaty when we get back to the police station."

"Then," Kep said, "you'll be pleased to know we can stop in an air-conditioned establishment on our way."

Bernadette gave him a quizzical glance.

"I selected Las Perihuanas for its proximity to Platinum Prime." He motioned his chin across the street; down a block was a black onyx sign with two elegant interlocked P's.

Bernadette blinked. "But—we're nowhere near ready to go forward with an interview. We don't have any background on Platinum Prime yet. We don't even know what we're looking for."

"If you'll recall," Kep said, a touch of irritation in his voice, "Annika instructed us to simply go to Platinum Prime and ask about Parr Medical. While she denied knowing specifics, she clearly made the implication that we could shed more light on the situation with that simple request."

"We don't even know *who* to ask."

Kep pressed his lips together. "I am loath to lead this interview," he said, "but as you know, time is of the essence."

Bernadette opened her mouth in protest, but then snapped it shut and stopped walking. Entering the restaurant and asking questions without preparation? Far from ideal. But given their time constraints and the threat on Sophie, Kep's suggestion wasn't terrible. "Give me a minute," Bernadette mumbled, closing her eyes.

How had Marguerite phrased it on the phone?

We agreed to accelerate the plan... you'll need to use the Platinum Prime information.

But who did she need to talk to? Running a background check on the staff or the owners of Platinum Prime might have revealed a connection. Bernadette sighed. At worst, she'd ask the host, the maître-d', the owner— someone—about Parr Medical, and she'd get a blank stare. Possibly someone would know that she and Kep were asking questions. But on the phone call with Marguerite, she had called Bernadette "that Becker woman." She was already on their radar. The risk was worth the reward.

"Okay," Bernadette said, opening her eyes. "I'm ready."

❧

The air in Platinum Prime felt cool against Bernadette's skin. Dark wood columns framed the host stand, rich and warm. The hostess, studiously examining something on the stand, wore a royal blue sheath dress. The fabric looked expensive, and her long hair was piled on top of her head in an elegant up-do, more suited to an evening at a gala event than a midday lunch rush. Bernadette gave the woman a smile, though she didn't look up from the stand as Bernadette approached, Kep trailing a step behind.

"Good afternoon," Bernadette said.

"We're no longer seating for lunch," the woman said, not looking up. "We open again at five, but I suggest reservations."

Bernadette held out her identification. "Federal investigators."

The woman looked up in surprise. But instead of deference, she narrowed her eyes. "We've cooperated fully."

"I'm sorry?"

"We are, of course, willing to help. But this is harassment. And it disrupts our business."

"Federal investigators have already been here asking about Parr Medical?" She should have foreseen this; since Marguerite thought she was talking to Andy Belgrade, and since Belgrade worked for the FBI, it only made sense that he'd gotten the information from Platinum Prime through interrogation.

The woman held up a finger. "I'll get Kim."

Kim. Huh. Maybe the owner. And the hostess said they'd already cooperated fully. Bernadette's mind whirled. The hostess's reaction was after Bernadette had said "Federal investigators," so had someone from the FBI been there? Joanna Quimby, perhaps?

Bernadette took a step back, next to Kep. "What do you think?"

"I think we've struck a nerve." Kep scratched his beard. "Did you notice she said they'd already cooperated fully?"

Bernadette nodded. "I'm thinking FBI. Belgrade sent people to conduct interviews. Maybe Joanna was here."

"Joanna Quimby was on the same side as the Parr

Medical people who threatened your daughter. Therefore, interviewing the employees here shouldn't alert the FBI. We could find valuable information."

Bernadette sighed. The best bad option.

A different woman appeared at the host stand, dressed in a black blouse, a nametag reading *Kim,* black trousers, and a short bob haircut, light brown with streaks of gray. "Is there a problem?"

"No problem, ma'am," Bernadette said, raising her identification. "I just need to speak with a staff member about the Parr Medical employees who've eaten—"

"You," Kim said, smiling despite the tight lines in her forehead, "have already been over this with us. For hours. I'm fine cooperating—"

"Hold on," Bernadette said. "*I* haven't questioned you."

"Well, no," Kim admitted, "not you. But a team of federal investigators. Had three of my people off the floor during dinner rush. It was a disaster. Then they came back and took *more* of my servers off the floor the next night. We can't afford to deliver subpar service, no matter the excuse."

Bernadette pulled out her phone. "Bear with me for just a moment." She tapped her photos app and scrolled quickly. Sophie's softball games, a bunch of receipts she submitted for reimbursement—ah, there it was. A photo of Joanna Quimby and Bernadette together. They were on a hike. Must have been two or three years ago. Bernadette showed Kim the screen. "This woman? On the right side, here?"

Kim shook her head. "No, it was a man. On the short side. Aviator sunglasses."

A man—not Joanna. Maybe it was Andy Belgrade himself. "When was this?"

"Two or three weeks ago."

Bernadette flinched. Two weeks ago—that would be *after* Joanna had been killed. But three weeks? That would be before Bernadette's trip to the Upper Peninsula; about the time that Bernadette was getting the SD card from Joanna at the gun range. Something had set the plan in motion for the FBI to ask about Parr Medical. "Do you have the exact dates?"

Kim frowned. "Shouldn't you already know when you were here?" She rolled her eyes. "My tax dollars at work."

"Different agencies," Bernadette said. "If you have an exact date, that would be helpful."

Kim sighed melodramatically, then lowered her head to the top of the host stand. The clicking of a keyboard; the monitor must have been hidden from view. "Two weeks ago. Uh—let's see. That was when we had the birthday party in here. Yes, there it is." She looked up at Bernadette. "June twenty-first and twenty-second. That's when the FBI almost put us out of business."

That had been *after* Joanna's death; maybe that was the catalyst. "Did they leave a card? Any way for you to contact them?"

Kim shook her head. "There were three of them. Black suits, stiff white shirts, sunglasses. Right out of a movie."

"And when you say they were federal investigators, you said they were from the FBI?"

"I think so, anyway." Kim scratched her head.

"Did you get a name?"

"I'm sure he said a name, but I don't remember it."

Bernadette took a stab at a name. "Andy Belgrade?"

A flicker of recognition in Kim's eyes. "Yes, that's it. So you *do* work with him."

Bernadette tightened her jaw. "No."

Kim crossed her arms. "I appreciate that you didn't come during the evening rush this time, but we've got to prep for dinner service. I can't give you any of my people's time."

"What did Belgrade want?"

"Those three suits interviewed the servers who had the tables of that one guy from Parvo Medical."

Ha. Parvo Medical. Bernadette didn't bother correcting her. "Which one guy? Was it Leopold Montclair?"

Kim furrowed her brow. "I don't think that was it."

Kep pulled out his phone. "Would you recognize a photograph of—"

"I wouldn't recognize anyone—I don't work on the floor. I just pulled the credit card receipts."

Bernadette raised her eyebrows. "Oh, could we see which ones you pulled?"

"I gave all the hard copies—with the Parvo guy's signature—to that FBI guy."

"Andy Belgrade."

"Right. But I know we have the digitized copies."

"That'll work." If she could figure out what Belgrade took, maybe she could figure out how it connected to Joanna's death.

Another sigh from Kim. "It'll take me a couple hours to pull the records."

"I don't need it right now. But I would appreciate it."

"Anything for the feds." Kim put her hands on her hips. "End of tomorrow okay?"

"Of course." Bernadette paused. "Were those receipts from Jeremy Niehaus, by any chance?"

A smile quirked at the corner of Kim's mouth. "And

here I thought government agencies didn't talk to each other."

"Maybe it was a lucky guess," Bernadette said, then hesitated. Why would Joanna Quimby request hidden microphones to be placed in Leopold Montclair's yacht? Why would Belgrade sign off on the requisition? Why would Marguerite Kerovic expect a call from Belgrade? And why would Belgrade then ask for Niehaus's credit card receipts from a top-shelf steak restaurant? She realized Kim was staring at her. "I apologize for Mr. Belgrade's zeal. We'll let you get back to running your restaurant."

"Perhaps we can speak with—" Kep began.

"No," Bernadette interrupted, turning to Kim. "The FBI did enough damage here. If we don't get the information we need from the credit card data, we'll call you and schedule something when it's convenient."

Kim grunted but looked a little mollified.

Bernadette took a business card out of her purse and handed it to Kim. "My email address is on there. So's my phone number. If you have any questions, or if you can think of anything else, please give me a call."

"You'll have the credit card data by this time tomorrow," Kim said, the tone in her voice assuring Bernadette that she'd get nothing else.

◈

Back outside, the sun had disappeared behind a cloud. Still warm and muggy, but a light breeze had kicked up, and Kep and Bernadette barely broke a sweat walking back to the police station. But when they entered the lobby, Detective Herrera was sitting in a plastic guest chair.

"Afternoon, Detective," Bernadette said.

"Can I talk to you two a minute?"

"Uh—" Bernadette glanced at Kep, who tightened his jaw. "Sure. What do you need?"

"Not here." Herrera glanced around the lobby of the police station. Ten or twelve people walked through, sat in chairs, or stood in line in front of the receptionist's desk. What did Herrera think he was looking for?

He turned and crossed in front of the receptionist desk —a different way than Bernadette was used to—and opened an ash-colored door at the side. He motioned toward Kep and Bernadette with his head, and they followed.

Herrera led them down a corridor without windows, lit only by bright fluorescents in the ceiling. At a door marked "A643," Herrera stopped and opened it with a key. The room was dark, and Herrera turned and flipped on a light.

Bernadette peered around Herrera's shoulder. File boxes. Not a small room, either. Several metal shelving units, full of plain brown file boxes. Three boxes were white or powder blue, in the middle of the stacks.

Bernadette glanced through the boxes. Most had a "Property of Cleveland P.D." label and listed a range of file numbers on the side, plus the year. Bernadette didn't see any file boxes from the last three years—everything was older.

"We're going in there?" Bernadette asked.

"That's right," Herrera said.

"Computerized files haven't gotten to Cleveland yet?"

"Very funny—you, of all people, making fun of this. You work for the Feds. You know how long it takes for the rules and regulations to catch up to technology. All this paperwork was legally mandated. And you know we've got to keep it all for twelve years." He looked at Bernadette out of the corner of his eye. "CSAB probably has twenty rooms just like this. We need to have a conversation, and we can go in here without anyone interrupting us."

"What kind of conversation?" Bernadette stepped into the room, Kep at her heels. Herrera pushed the door closed behind them, then turned to Bernadette.

His eyes were wide and the frown on his face dug into his chin. "Are you crazy?" he hissed.

"Probably," Bernadette said. "My ex told me so all the time. But I assume you're not calling me crazy because I want my towels folded in thirds."

Herrera glared at Bernadette. "Marnie Synskey. I didn't want to say anything when she was within hearing range, but you may have seriously compromised your safety. *My* safety, too."

"I don't understand, Detective. Marnie Synskey worked closely with our murder victim. Any half-decent investigation would interview her."

"You shouldn't have brought her *here*," Herrera hissed.

Bernadette furrowed her brow. "What do you mean?"

"Come on, don't pretend you're ignorant," Herrera said. "I've researched Marnie's background. She's the Head of Executive Services; she knows how everything in that company works. I think the only reason she isn't in the C-suite is because she doesn't have an MBA. Everything you asked her is going right to Jeremy Niehaus and the board of directors."

"I'm not sure you're right about that." Bernadette wondered if she should tell Herrera that it wasn't really Marnie Synskey. But how would she explain it?

Herrera tapped his foot in frustration. "These are dangerous people, and if you make a big deal about bringing them into the station, it makes Parr Medical look bad to the public and they'll take it as a direct threat."

Bernadette was quiet.

"I can help you," Herrera said.

Bernadette glanced out of the corner of her eye at Kep. His mouth was set in a line, his eyes revealing nothing.

Herrera leaned forward. "I know Parr Medical has cops on the take here."

"We know that, too."

Detective Herrera took a step back. "I see. You're not sharing information with me because you're worried I'm one of them."

Bernadette looked at Kep, then back to Herrera. "We'd be fools not to consider the possibility."

The detective turned and paced slowly; not a lot of room between the stacks of file boxes. "Okay, well, maybe I can't convince you I'm clean—"

"You're cheating on your wife," Kep said. "Your infidelity provides an organization like Parr Medical leverage. I expect you would go to some lengths for your wife not to become aware of your affair."

The detective stopped pacing and tapped his chin. "Yeah. You're right. You shouldn't trust me. And that makes it hard for me to share the information with you, too, because you'll probably think I'm misdirecting you. Leading you into an ambush or some such."

Kep nodded.

"But look," Herrera said, "if I were working for Parr Medical, and they wanted you dead, don't you think I already had ample opportunity to do so?"

Kep and Bernadette were silent.

"Ah," Herrera said. "I take it from your silence there's a reason they haven't killed you yet."

"They tried last month," Bernadette said, "because they thought our deaths couldn't be traced back to Parr Medical. But now, with the FBI—" She paused. How much should she say? All the names on the list on that first SD card. Most of the investigation into those deaths were closed as accidents or suicides. A couple of them were homicides where others had been arrested. Maybe those arrested were patsies or hired killers who'd run afoul of Parr Medical. And now Joanna's encryption key— Parr Medical thought Bernadette could get what they wanted.

She thought hard, back to her first case with Kep back in March in Milwaukee. Kymer Thompson's death was staged to look like a suicide—the historical chapel, the religious positioning of the body. If she and Kep hadn't been assigned to the case, the authorities would never have found the toxin that killed Kymer Thompson. Annika Nakrivo would never have gone to prison.

Sophie wouldn't be in danger.

"You work for the Cleveland Police any time in the last few years," Herrera said, "you know about Parr Medical. You hear things. Parr Medical does what they want."

Bernadette and Kep were quiet for a moment.

"What are your reasons for staying?" Kep asked quietly.

"In Cleveland?" Herrera asked. "My family's here. Plus, it's not like it would be better anywhere else. Someone always has undue pull over the chief or the sheriff or someone."

"Private security pays better," Bernadette said.

Herrera nodded, a hint of a smile in his eyes. "Who knows? Maybe I've already got some interviews lined up."

Silence for a few moments. Bernadette stared at the

ground, turning everything over in her mind. Then she lifted her head. "We'll think about sharing what we know."

"Just stay away from Marnie Synskey," Herrera said. "Don't bring *anyone* from Parr Medical back to the station."

"We'll keep a low profile," Bernadette said, "but they know CSAB assigned us to the case. So we need to at least *appear* like we're investigating them." Even so, they'd have to figure out why the FBI—and in particular Andy Belgrade—was investigating Jeremy Niehaus. She tilted her head at Herrera. "You have any suspects yet?"

He shook his head. "Nothing yet. Not many clues. No witnesses. No suspects. No motive, either."

"Maybe Leopold just got out of line." Bernadette tapped her chin. "If he put Kep and me on the hit list, maybe Leopold got the blame for the Feds putting the spotlight on Parr Medical. If they'd succeeded in killing us and making it look like a prison riot or a faulty gas tank, Parr would still have their mole in the FBI and the hit list would still be under wraps."

"I suppose that's possible," Herrera said. "But in my experience, a guy in a criminal organization gets out of line, the organization wants to make an example out of him. Something very public, very painful, and very symbolic. They don't hide the murder in a heart attack."

"But Parr Medical obfuscates all their homicides," Kep said. "They remove the problematic person without calling attention to their methods. The public cannot perceive that a publicly traded company completes their transactions in blood."

"Then why—" Bernadette began, then snapped her mouth shut.

Kep arched an eyebrow. "Then why was Jack

murdered? Why is his death one of the few murder cases that are still open?"

Bernadette dropped her eyes to the floor.

"Jack is your son, Dr. Woodhead," Herrera said.

"That's correct," Kep said evenly. "He was an investigative reporter. Found dead in his apartment, shot in the forehead."

Herrera knitted his eyebrows. "And you think Parr Medical killed him?"

"His name was on a list," Bernadette murmured.

"A list?"

"A list. Everyone on the list was dead. Most of them worked for Parr's competitors or for government regulators. Pretty clear it was Parr's hit list."

Herrera folded his arms. "I'm sorry."

"Me too," Kep said.

"If you need me to help with the investigation, just let me know."

Bernadette nodded.

Herrera stepped between them and opened the door into the hallway, then strode out. His footsteps went down the hall, getting quieter.

"Shut the door," Kep whispered.

"Sure, let's debrief," Bernadette closed the door. "It seems like Herrera didn't realize that Annika disguised herself as Marnie—"

"Not a debrief," Kep said sharply.

"Then what?"

Kep pointed behind Bernadette. "The blue file box," Kep said, "is from Boston."

She turned. Several stacks of file boxes were on the floor in front of one of the shelving units. The powder blue box was second from the top. Instead of the Cleveland Police Department stamp, these boxes were pre-printed with "Property of Boston Police Department," with a simple logo on the top right of the side of the box: a silhouette of a police badge with a short thick red line underneath. All the elements were in a white circle with a black outline.

Like the Cleveland boxes, a year and a range of case numbers were written on the side.

"Five years ago," Bernadette murmured.

"And Jack's case number is in that range," Kep said. "Herrera knew about Jack. That's why he brought us in here."

"You know Jack's case number?"

"Of course I know Jack's case number. It's burned into my brain." Kep folded his arms. "I hired three private investigators who couldn't get me a copy of the police file. While I saw the original police report, I never saw the file or a single piece of evidence."

"Weren't you a suspect?"

"True," Kep said. "Detective Albrecht told me several times that I couldn't see the files precisely because of my status as a suspect."

"But after they stopped considering you as a suspect?"

Kep turned his eyes down. "I don't believe the police officially removed me from the suspect list."

"Not even after we found the SD card with the hit list?"

"No one has informed me either way."

Bernadette turned toward the stack. "How did the box end up here?"

Kep put his hands on his hips. "I continually tell you not to jump to conclusions, but I fear I cannot prevent myself from jumping to my own at this moment."

"Which is?"

"Someone at Parr Medical bribed someone at the Boston Police Department to transfer this box of files here."

"Or one of the Cleveland police officers who's on the take asked the Boston police to send this file box here."

"Whichever it is," Kep said, "I suspect there is something in the file that whoever ordered my son's murder wanted me to see. Or, perhaps, did *not* want me to see."

"Maybe they didn't want the investigators to put two and two together."

Kep dropped his arms and strode toward the stack of boxes, picking up the box above the blue box and setting it on the floor behind him.

"The Boston box hasn't been here very long," Bernadette said. "It's not dusty."

Kep stood and took the powder blue box down carefully, set it on another box at waist height, and opened it.

"Hah," he said. "Physocarpus opulifolius."

"What does that—oh, the smell?"

"Pollen from vineyard ninebark," Kep said. "It flowers in late June. The Southwest Community Garden is across the street from the parking lot of the Boston Police Headquarters."

"You can smell the pollen?"

"That's correct. Vineyard ninebark is not as invasive as the common varietal. Its range is limited to the greater Boston area and Cape Cod."

"How did it get in the box?"

"I'm familiar with the building where the Boston Police housed their evidence. If the breeze was blowing in the right direction, at the right time of year, the cars in the parking lot would often get covered in ninebark pollen. Employees would often complain; the odor is rather unpleasant, and the pollen is quite sticky. For two weeks in June, employees would track the pollen into the headquarters building. Quite problematic for those with allergies. It often stuck to employees' clothing, hands, even eyelashes. And those employees would transfer the pollen to their papers, their desks—"

"And file boxes?"

"Not much, of course, but more than enough for my nose to detect. Based on its pungency, the pollen is two to three weeks old."

"Which means it was in Boston right about the time everything came out about Parr Medical and the FBI mole."

"Correct. Perhaps that changed the minds of the Parr Medical personnel who oversaw the 'hit list,' as you call it," Kep said. "Perhaps something exists in Joanna Quimby's files—on her laptop, in her apartment—that might point investigators toward Jack's file. It's likely that Parr Medical people did not want it getting out."

"Or," Bernadette said, then rubbed her chin.

"Or what?"

"Detective Herrera requested the box when he found out you'd be coming."

Kep blinked. "For what purpose?"

"To get us on his side. Look, he's the one who's said he uses this room when he doesn't want anyone following him. He might have requested the box, then brought us in here. He obviously put the box in plain sight so you'd notice it. Then talking to us specifically about trusting him."

Kep raised his eyebrows.

"It's too coincidental to be a coincidence," Bernadette said.

"It should be straightforward enough to track who requested the box transfer. If Detective Herrera did it, we shall be aware of it soon enough." Kep pulled a thick manila folder out. "What do you suppose the chances are that the information in question is still contained within this box?"

"I don't know," Bernadette said. "If Herrera is on the take, you won't find anything in the box for sure. It'll be nothing but a ruse to get us to trust him."

"And if the detective isn't corrupt?"

Bernadette shrugged. "We might find it, or we might not. There are a lot of papers to go through."

"Talking isn't doing. It is a kind of good deed to say well; and yet words are not deeds."

"Does that mean we need to go through the box right now?"

Kep gave Bernadette a determined smile. "Precisely."

Chapter Fifteen

Kep handed Bernadette a folder. "You can go through this one."

"I don't know what I'm looking for."

Kep pulled out his phone. "Take pictures of each of the files. We can upload them to an online file storage system and analyze them later." He bobbed his head at the door. "See if there's a good overhead light in here."

Bernadette took the folder from Kep and stepped over to the door. A bank of four light switches; she turned them all on. Harsh fluorescents flickered on in the ceiling, and Bernadette squeezed her eyes shut at the sudden brightness.

"Excellent," Kep muttered, holding his phone steady above the open manila folder resting on top of the open box. He tapped the screen; the distinct sound of a shutter click. He turned the page, tapped the screen with another click.

Bernadette turned to the stack of boxes next to her and took the top two boxes and set them on the floor. She opened the manila folder Kep had handed her, took out her phone, and began taking pictures of each page as well. This folder seemed to contain the paperwork from Jack's files: credit card bills, mostly; Jack paid the cards on time. Every so often, another paper bill would be in there, but Jack probably paid his bills online and went paperless. Perhaps the credit card bills were still sent via paper for a reason. Possible that a charge on Jack's credit card would reveal something important.

They worked in silence.

After Bernadette finished with her first folder, she glanced up at Kep.

"Have you had any thoughts about where Joanna's encryption key could be? Do you think it might have something to do with the story Jack was working on?"

Kep furrowed his brow. "I think it's obvious that Parr Medical believes you are in possession of something of Joanna's. Either something she gave you, or something of hers that you're holding."

"I thought of that, too." Bernadette frowned. "I even called Barlow's girlfriend. Had her eviscerate a teddy bear Joanna gave to Sophie on her last birthday."

"What did you discover?"

"Nothing."

Kep paused. "How much more time do you have?"

"Before I need to find the encryption key? I started with four days. And that was three days ago. So—tomorrow's the deadline. I mean, they're in the safehouse, but I'm still nervous."

"So we either catch the killer by tomorrow—"

"Or I figure out what the encryption key is."

Kep set the file folder down on the box and stared at the ceiling in thought. "Have you made a list of everything Joanna gave you in the last two years?"

"The teddy bear and the SD card with the hit list on it. That's it."

Kep stroked his salt-and-pepper beard. "I suggest the existence of something else that perhaps you are not aware you have. Perhaps it did not register as being a gift from Joanna when you received it."

"Like what?"

Kep blinked. "I apologize; I do not have a reasonable example. A plant or housewarming gift? Or did she return something of yours that she borrowed?"

"No, and no. Not that I can think of, anyway."

"I suggest you continue to let your subconscious work on it."

They continued to work for another ten minutes. Kep stretched his arms above his head, then moved to a new folder. He opened the folder and immediately drew in his breath sharply.

"What is it?" Bernadette asked.

"Jack was working on an exposé on Parr Medical," Kep said. "He kept detailed records of his call logs. Fifteen calls to Jeremy Niehaus, fifteen to Leopold Montclair. Other board members as well, but Niehaus and Montclair are the only ones with more than five calls each. No other notes."

"Maybe they wouldn't talk to Jack."

"I can't imagine that any of the board members would have responded to an investigative reporter," Kep mused. "Yet he kept calling both Niehaus and Montclair."

"So you think he discovered something he could put their names to?" Bernadette took a picture of the last bill and closed the folder.

Kep opened his mouth, then closed it again, his shoulders slumping. "Speculation."

Bernadette walked over to Kep, putting the folder

back in the box, and studied the call log. Handwritten on graph paper. Jack's handwriting was remarkably similar to Kep's—they both made their capital M's the same way, with sharp angles, and the middle of the M dipping all the way to the baseline of the letter. She tapped the date next to one of the calls.

"He called them both on the same day. Every time. First Niehaus, then Montclair."

"That's true," Kep said, rubbing his beard. "I wonder what it means."

"If I were to speculate," Bernadette said, "maybe he discovered something with both of their names attached, and he wanted comments from both of them." She scanned the page. "I don't see his level of tenacity for any of the others."

Kep pointed to the checkmark next to a few of the names. "If *I* were to speculate," Kep said, "I would suggest that Jack spoke with those with checkmarks next to their names."

"Did you take a picture of this?"

"Of course." He turned the page. "More call log pages." He raised his phone and took a picture.

"There." Bernadette pointed to the middle of the page. Marnie Synskey. With a check mark next to her name.

"She talked to Jack," Kep murmured.

"Seems like it," Bernadette said. "Then—look at the time Jack wrote next to Marnie's name, then who he called right after."

Kep nodded. "Jeremy Niehaus."

"And no check mark."

"But unlike all the calls on the first page, Jack didn't follow the Niehaus phone call with a call to Leopold Montclair this time."

"Right. Even though he didn't get through to Niehaus. So—whatever he was searching for, did Marnie say something that put him onto Niehaus instead of Montclair?"

"Or perhaps Jack only had time to make one phone call. Or a delivery at the door interrupted him, or another call came in. There are hundreds of reasons Jack may not have called Montclair after calling Niehaus."

"But he kept such good notes on his calls," Bernadette insisted. "If he came back to his call log after getting interrupted, surely he would have called Leopold next, if he'd intended to do so."

"Jack could have made the call after five o'clock," Kep said. "Perhaps when he *did* come back to it, the reason he'd called Niehaus had gone stale, or he uncovered other information suggesting alternate areas of concern."

"I guess," Bernadette said. "But even though I know it's conjecture, with all this information—with his name showing up on the hit list, with this evidence box disappearing from Boston and showing up in the evidence room in Cleveland—you've got to think that *something* in this box is the reason Jack was killed."

"But perhaps that information is no longer here," Kep said, turning the page and taking another picture. "If this box has been in Cleveland for any length of time, Parr Medical may have already searched this box and removed —perhaps even destroyed—the evidence." He continued turning pages and taking pictures. "But if Parr hasn't gotten to this box yet, the evidence is somewhere in this box. I will take a picture of every piece of paper in this file and perhaps I can unravel exactly what Jack uncovered that got him..." Kep pushed his glasses up on his nose and cleared his throat.

"I bet there's no record of this box being transferred to

Cleveland, either." Bernadette tapped her chin. "I wonder if the computer files have been wiped, too."

Kep's jaw tightened as he continued to turn pages and take pictures. "If we suppose Parr Medical is trying to hide this case file from me, I fail to grasp why someone would delete the entire file; that would raise too much suspicion. They would simply remove *parts* of it. There would be no record of the electronic information except perhaps in backup copies or snapshots."

Bernadette paced back and forth in the narrow corridor between the boxes, then tapped the screen on her phone.

"What are you doing?"

Bernadette tapped the screen of her phone, then tapped the speakerphone.

"Hi, Bernadette," said Lesley Gill, on the other end of the line. "I don't have any information on the burner phone yet. We're working on it—the judge signed the warrant—and we got the request over to the telecom. Just waiting for a response. Hopefully not too much longer."

"I know I've asked for a lot," Bernadette said, "but we've found something else. Kep is here with me."

"Hi, Dr. Woodhead."

"Hello, Miss Gill," Kep responded, continuing to take pictures of the papers in the file folders.

"Three weeks ago, on June nineteenth or twentieth, just after Joanna—" Bernadette suddenly felt a tightness in her throat. She'd been able to talk about the incident for weeks; why was this any different? "On either of those dates, can you see if there were any calls between Parr Medical's offices and the Boston Police Department? Particularly the records unit."

"Um, sure."

"We found the box with Jack Woodhead's case file here in a file room at the police headquarters here in Cleveland."

A pause. "And you'd like to know how it got there?"

"Yes."

"Might be better if I ran a query on the requests for a transfer. What's the box number?"

Kep read out the box number.

"I'll get right on that—" Lesley began.

"Hold on," Bernadette interrupted. "The transfer should be the first order of business, but I don't think you'll find any request for a box transfer to Cleveland. If my gut is right on this, the box was supposed to disappear."

"We postulate," Kep said, "that Parr Medical was convinced something in Joanna Quimby's effects would lead me—or some other investigator—to something in Jack's file that would expose vital information. Perhaps about who ordered Jack's murder, or perhaps about what Jack was working on. Perhaps something else entirely."

Lesley had a tone of amusement in her voice. "Bernadette told me you don't like to participate in conjecture, Dr. Woodhead."

"We are in a race against time, Ms. Gill," Kep said. "As we're still waiting for the telecom company to give us vital information, perhaps theorizing who wanted the file box from my son's murder will give us a clue to the identity of the Parr Medical personnel who authorized not only the murder of my son, but threatened my colleague's daughter."

"Right," Lesley said, her voice sobering. "But, Bernadette, if you don't think there will be any record—"

"That's why I want you to check calls between the Parr

office and the Boston Police Department. If we get a date…"

"Gotcha," Lesley said. "Then you can look for clues *after* the date it might have arrived."

"That's right," Bernadette said. "Someone from Parr Medical may have come to the building to take those papers or whatever out of this file box."

The sound of a keyboard clacking. "The FBI gave the order to search Joanna's office two weeks and four days ago. Can you narrow down the time window?"

Kep took out his phone and began to tap.

"We know it was in the last couple of weeks," Bernadette said.

"How?" Lesley asked.

Bernadette glanced at Kep, who was studying his phone screen intently. "Vineyard ninebark pollen in the box. The plants only bloom—"

"Never mind," Lesley said.

Kep's head snapped up. "In precisely the last eleven days."

Bernadette blinked. "You said two to three weeks."

"Based on the scent, yes," Kep replied. "However, the Southwest Community Garden has a video feed." He held up his phone. "Any website visitor can view footage from the last year. Physocarpus opulifolius was not in bloom twelve days ago. It did, however, bloom one day later."

Bernadette shook her head. "That's only when we know someone opened the box, not when the request came through. Expand the search to the last two weeks."

"Will do," Lesley said.

"Thanks, Lesley."

"Oh, Bernadette, one final thing. Did you know

Leopold Montclair had less than a hundred grand in his bank account?"

"Lots of people live beyond their means."

"But I don't have any record of what he spent his money on—nothing that would explain where his millions went."

"Offshore accounts," Bernadette said. "That's what makes sense to me. Lowering tax liability; the assets could probably be made liquid at a moment's notice."

The sound of a keyboard tapping. "Which we can't get to without a routing number and an account number. The information I've found doesn't match any known ABA number. We're wondering if the account transfer information was faked. I *have* been able to determine that the order for both those transfers didn't come from the MAC or IP addresses normally associated with Niehaus or Montclair. Either they were trying to hide those transactions, or someone else moved their money."

"Who? An assistant, or maybe a stockbroker?"

"Whoever it was, they didn't want to be tracked. I suppose it *could* have been Niehaus and Montclair, especially if they're thinking about leaving the country." She sighed. "Anyway, I'll look into it and ping you when I find anything."

Bernadette ended the call. "Let's go see if we can get the visitors' logs from the last two weeks. Maybe that'll give us a clue."

"I suspect that course of action may alert certain corrupt police officers. Doing so would signal that we know my son's case file is here."

Bernadette shrugged. "We can't play it safe anymore, Kep. We either get the information, or we don't. Either Herrera is on the take, or he isn't." She jerked her thumb over her shoulder toward the hallway. "And he just pointed us to a connection leading us to the visitors' logs. Come on."

❦

"Visitor logs from the last two weeks?" the officer at the front desk said. About thirty years old, with freckled porcelain skin, he wore his bright orange-red hair in a crew cut. He rubbed his clean-shaven skin. "I suppose I can give you a login to the system. Everything is on the network." He stuck his hand forward and tapped on the terminal in front of him.

Bernadette shot a look at Kep. He frowned under his mustache and beard.

"Every visitor signs in, Officer...?" Bernadette asked.

"O'Donnell—but please, call me Tim." He stood from his stool behind the counter and pointed at the monitor. "Everyone. ID gets scanned, name, and the reason for the visit."

Bernadette remembered when Herrera had first signed them in: driver's license scanned, signatures, purpose of visit. And they'd just gone through it with Annika-disguised-as-Marnie.

"But surely not everyone," Kep said. "The precinct captain's spouse?"

"Even him," Tim said.

"The mayor? City councilmembers?"

"Even police officers from other precincts," Tim said. "The officers don't like it much, but it's the new protocol. No one gets an exception."

"Then," Bernadette continued, "we'd be very interested in who's visited the last two weeks."

"It's a matter of public record," Tim said. "Couldn't stop you if I wanted to."

Bernadette looked at the monitor, with its badge-shaped *Cleveland Division of Police* logo and a bright blue *Sign In* button. "So anyone who goes to see the homicide detectives, the evidence lockers, the file rooms—they all go through here?"

"That's correct. If they don't want to scan their ID, they don't come in." Tim smiled. "Just yesterday, there was a man who tried to throw his weight around here. You probably know the type. Had one of his lackeys with him—a short guy in a bad suit with his hair sticking up."

"You said he threw his weight around?"

"Sure. He came in wearing one of those fancy Italian suits that cost more than I make in a month and thinks his shit don't stink." Tim folded his arms. "Asked for Captain Markham—"

"Captain Markham—he's not in homicide, is he?"

"No, no—he's in charge of evidence and he runs our master files. But Markham was out in the field. I told Mr. Expensive Suit to scan his ID and we could get someone else, but he said he'd wait. Then when I insisted on scanning his driver's license, he just turned and left."

Kep pulled his phone out of his pocket and tapped on his screen, scrolling, then turned the screen toward Tim. "This him?"

"Mr. Expensive Suit himself," Tim said.

Kep turned the screen to Bernadette.

Above a caption stating "Chief Executive Officer of Parr Medical" was a photo of Jeremy Niehaus.

Chapter Sixteen

SIX BLOCKS SOUTHWEST of the homicide division building, Settler's Landing Park stretched along the riverfront. Few people were around despite the sunny mid-afternoon. Bernadette and Kep sat on a concrete separator next to the Cuyahoga River.

"You think Niehaus was trying to get at your son's files, right?" Bernadette asked.

"It certainly is a possibility," Kep said. "But I want to point out he wasn't alone."

Bernadette nodded. "Which means he wasn't worried about hiding what he was doing there."

Kep stroked his beard thoughtfully. "Who would he bring with him?"

"Any number of Parr Medical employees who are trying to get in the CEO's good graces." Bernadette stared out across the river, watching a sandhill crane take flight from the shoreline. "Or it could have been a distraction—get the lackey to ask an officer to do some real work while Niehaus sneaks off to the file room with Markham."

"We lack evidence to know for sure."

Bernadette glanced at her watch. "We've got about fifteen minutes before we need to head over to Marnie Synskey's gym."

A buzzing of a phone. Kep pulled his phone out of his pocket, frowned, tapped the screen, then put the phone back in his pocket. Bernadette looked at him quizzically.

"Yates Raphael," Kep said.

Ah, the executive producer.

"Texted to ask if I wanted to have dinner before he goes back to Hollywood tomorrow." Kep held up the phone. "He made sure to mention his private jet."

"Compensating for something?" Bernadette asked.

Kep ignored her. "It's likely the purpose of the dinner would be to continue making me feel bad about the way my time on the show ended. His timing was always rather poor." He looked over his shoulder. "I don't believe anyone followed us from the precinct."

"Considering that Niehaus was there to see the person in charge of the evidence and files, I'd say the chances were good that the walls in the station have ears," Bernadette said. "So I get why you're cautious." She leaned forward, her elbows on her knees.

Kep looked out over the riverfront at the Detroit Superior Bridge, set at a forty-five-degree angle to the river. Bernadette stared at the arch on the far side, trying to keep calm.

"My question is," Kep said, "where do we go from here? If this were a typical investigation, I would suggest we interview Niehaus. But I'm wary we would alert him unnecessarily."

"He might be onto us already," Bernadette said. "And the problem with someone who commits a murder for hire is getting evidence of the trail between the hired killer and the employer. Remember, we couldn't track any of the payments made to Annika a few months ago. If Lesley hadn't found the flights that Annika took between Cleveland and Milwaukee, we wouldn't have figured out her role in that first murder in Milwaukee."

Kep scratched his beard. "That seems like a mistake on Parr Medical's part," he said. "Annika made it clear that Leopold Montclair arranged those flights. And she said he arranged the plastic surgery as well. Yet every other communication with Annika was done anonymously."

Bernadette blinked. "Could be that's why Montclair was killed. Because he wasn't careful enough."

Kep nodded slowly. "A possibility. Additionally, we cannot ignore that Niehaus attempted to gain admittance to the police station without providing identification. At the very least, it strongly suggests that Niehaus is involved."

"So you want to interview him?"

Kep motioned to Bernadette's purse, sitting beside her on the concrete bench. "I humbly request you contact his office and arrange a time for us to visit him tomorrow."

"And let him know we're working on the case?"

Kep waved his hand. "He saw us at Montclair's house. And if he agrees to an interview, we can tailor our questions to get the information we need."

"He'll just deny everything if he's involved."

"Ah, but if you've taught me anything, the information will be in the manner of his denial." Kep waved his hand. "At any rate, the plan, such as it is, will never be put in motion unless we meet with him."

Bernadette opened her purse and pulled out her phone. She searched for the Parr Medical number, tapped on the number, then held the phone to her ear.

"Parr Medical, how may I direct your call?"

"Jeremy Niehaus's office, please."

"Who may I say is calling?"

"This is Bernadette Becker with the Controlled Substance Analysis Bureau. I believe he knows who I am. We have some routine questions to ask him."

"Regarding?"

Bernadette arched an eyebrow. "The death of his colleague, Leopold Montclair."

"Please hold."

The strains of instrumental electronica filtered through the phone for a moment, then lowered in volume while a steady male voice began extolling the praises of Parr Medical's research, asking listeners to visit Parr's website. After the voice stopped, the music swelled in volume again.

"Jeremy Niehaus's office. This is Victoria."

"Hi, Victoria. This is Bernadette Becker with the Controlled Substance Analysis Bureau. We're the lead investigators in the death of Leopold Montclair."

A sharp intake of breath on the other end. "Yes?" Victoria's voice wavered.

"We have some routine questions to ask Mr. Niehaus, and I hoped to arrange a meeting in his office for tomorrow."

"Oh—well, of course, Mr. Niehaus would be more than happy to help a federal investigation, but unfortunately, he's out of the office this week."

Bernadette furrowed her brow. Niehaus had just come by Montclair's house the day before.

"Where is he?"

"A pharmaceutical leadership conference in San Francisco."

"Ah."

"He should return next week. I can put something on the calendar."

"Monday morning?"

"He has a nine-thirty available."

"Perfect."

After saying goodbye, Bernadette ended the call, tapping her chin with the edge of her smartphone.

"Monday morning?" Kep asked. "Isn't that going to be too late?"

"He's not in town," Bernadette replied. "He left for a conference in San Francisco."

Kep arched an eyebrow. Ah—perhaps the assistant was lying.

Bernadette raised her phone and tapped on the Messages app, then began a message to Lesley.

> Can you check if Jeremy Niehaus checked into any flights in the last day or two? Parr Medical says he's in SF for conference

Kep put his hands on his hips. "Quite odd for Niehaus to leave so suddenly. Didn't our favorite detective ask him to stay in town?"

"Some rich people never think they have to follow the same rules as everyone else."

Kep dropped his hands to his sides. "I believe our time is up. We must head to the local gym or risk missing our chance to return Marnie Synskey's driver's license."

"Yep, let's go," Bernadette said, standing. She took a step, licked her dry lips, then paused. "Do you think we should ask Marnie any questions? Like if she knew that Jeremy Niehaus was leaving for that conference?"

"It does seem odd, with Niehaus choosing to fly off to a conference when his colleague has been killed." Kep took a few steps up the grassy hill toward Superior Avenue and the train station on the far side of the park. "I would think that someone who did not want to be seen as a suspect in Mr. Montclair's death would take a day or two of mourning."

"And as the head of executive services, shouldn't she be aware of his calendar?"

"It's a possibility." Kep pushed his glasses back up onto the bridge of his nose. "But she is under no obligation to make our jobs easier."

❦

Ten minutes later, Bernadette and Kep walked down Euclid Avenue toward Thirteenth Street. The afternoon had heated considerably, and the pedestrian traffic had picked up at the Public Square.

Bernadette gave a sidelong glance at the Parr Medical building as they passed it on Euclid Avenue. "Doesn't look like the headquarters of an evil corporation," she mumbled.

"They never do," Kep said.

Three blocks later, they stopped next to the curb in the shade of a building, the sign for Guardian Fitness a half a block farther up.

"Do you believe Ms. Synskey is walking here from her office?" Kep asked.

"I'd be surprised if she didn't. Parking is a nightmare in this neighborhood, and it's only three blocks. There's a reason we left our car at the hotel."

Kep nodded and looked southwest down Euclid, over

Bernadette's shoulder. She followed his lead and looked over his shoulder northeast.

"We're early," Kep noted.

"I didn't want to miss her."

They stood in silence for a moment, then Bernadette's phone buzzed. A text from Lesley.

LESLEY

Finally an easy request

Jeremy Niehaus checked in for flight 2336 from Cleveland Hopkins to San Francisco International at 9:32 AM

Assigned seat 4A in first-class

The flight arrived at 11:09 AM Pacific Time

Niehaus picked up his rental car from Royalty Rentals at 11:51 AM Pacific Time

BERNADETTE

Have you heard about the tracking information on the burner phone?

LESLEY

Not yet

Should be within the hour

Bernadette held up her phone. "Niehaus left this morning. Picked up his rental at SFO"—Bernadette quickly calculated the three-hour time zone difference in her head —"uh, about an hour ago."

"So he's well and truly out of the state."

"Right."

Bernadette tapped her screen, calling Lesley and putting the speakerphone on.

"Hey—what's up?" Lesley answered.

Bernadette let her eyes lose focus, organizing her thoughts. "Lesley, Niehaus was helping Leopold's brother with some of the logistics of, you know, managing the death."

"Because the brother was the executor of Leopold's estate?"

"I assume so." Bernadette's eyes snapped back into focus as she crossed the street with the light. "Now that Niehaus is out of the state, and since we couldn't give Fred Montclair any information regarding our investigation, can you check if Fred's gone too? I assume he was staying in one of the local hotels."

Kep inclined his head. "What are you thinking?"

"If we're lucky, and Fred's still in town, he might talk to us. See if Niehaus let anything slip, or if he knew more about his brother's extracurricular business dealings than he originally let on." Bernadette looked down at her feet as she walked. "Niehaus might have tried to keep Fred away from us deliberately—"

"Which probably means Mr. Niehaus didn't board the airplane to San Francisco until he was confident Ferdinand Montclair had departed for home."

"Might be worth a phone call, even if Fred's left town," Bernadette said. "Who knows what Fred will say now that Jeremy Niehaus isn't hovering over him?"

"Okay," Lesley said. "I'll check the hotels and see if I can get a phone number."

A small crack of inspiration. "Niehaus told me Fred lost his daughter a couple of years ago." Bernadette sucked in air through her teeth. "Can you find out details? Maybe it'll help establish some rapport with Fred if we talk to him."

"Sure. I'm on..."

Bernadette paused. "Lesley, you there?"

"I'm an idiot," Lesley said under her breath.

"What?"

"The routing number and the account number. From the stock cashouts."

"Right, the account numbers that don't exist. And the transactions where we don't know who initiated them."

"You were told you needed to get an encryption key. But it's *not* an encryption key."

"What do you mean?"

"Have you heard of *tokenization?*"

"Uh... no."

"So when you have a spreadsheet or a database, the data must be formatted in a certain way. An ABA routing number is nine digits, for example. If you put ten digits, include nonstandard characters, anything that doesn't conform to the rules, the database throws an error. So if you run an ABA routing number through encryption, you get a long string of characters, and you can use the key to decrypt it back into an accurate ABA routing number. But you can't store the encrypted result in the database. The database will reject the format."

"I'm guessing this is where tokenization comes in."

"Right. The banking information was tokenized, not encrypted. I told you that Niehaus and Montclair didn't initiate those sales or the money transfers. If they're after the routing number and an account number where the stolen money is hidden, they're not after an encryption key—it doesn't exist."

"Well, then a tokenization key."

"There's no such thing. Tokenization is different. I'm oversimplifying the explanation, but tokenization creates a random number—a token—that substitutes for the accurate data, which gets stored in a secure database. If the real number is 1-2-3-4-5-6, the token could be 7-4-5-2-9-0. And the tokenized number isn't related to the original data at all; you can't get a key and translate it back to the original ABA number."

"So… what they're asking me for is impossible," Bernadette said. "Why would they say encryption when they meant something else?"

"Because the average person doesn't know the difference. They see a number they can't crack, and they assume they can break it. But that's not how tokenization works."

"How certain are you that they're looking for this banking information?"

"An educated guess. But you don't need to find the encryption key—it doesn't exist. You need to get the financial information."

"How were they able to deposit the money with only the—what did you call it? The tokenized number?"

"Deposits versus withdrawals," Lesley said. "The rules are different. You want to put money into accounts, banks will happily do it, especially offshore banks."

"Without full information of the account?"

"You need to have some of the right information, or prove your identity. But no, generally speaking, you don't need the full account information."

"It's not the same for withdrawals?"

"Nope. Getting that money out? You need to prove who you are *and* that you have authorized access to the account."

Bernadette closed her eyes. "Great. And we think Joanna had that information?"

"Like I said, it's an educated guess. But I bet fifty bucks I'm right."

"Not a bet I'm gonna take."

"Let me do more research. I'll get back to you."

"Talk to you later, then."

Bernadette ended the call.

A cool breeze blew down Euclid, from the direction of the lake, and Bernadette took a deep breath. She could tell her blood pressure was up—and she was getting antsy about there being no answer from the telecom about where Marguerite Kerovic might be—and this tokenization issue with the ABA routing number complicated things.

"I see Ms. Synskey," Kep said quietly.

"You do?"

"Yes. Coming this way from the Parr Medical office building."

"Does she see us?"

"Not yet. She's still in her business suit. Looking at her phone."

"But she'll pass us."

"Correct. Do we want to meet her here on the sidewalk, or by the front doors to Guardian Fitness?"

"Here should work. It's a little less crowded."

Kep took a deep breath and exhaled, forming an O with his mouth.

Bernadette shut her eyes. "Okay, here we go." She waited until Marnie Synskey was about ten feet away, then stepped to the middle of the sidewalk.

"Ms. Synskey?"

Marnie looked up from her phone and stopped in her tracks. "Not you two again."

Bernadette held her hands palms-out in front of her. "It's not what you think—it's actually good news."

"What?"

"The tox screen our experts ran on Mr. Montclair? Turns out it was a false positive."

"I'm sorry. I'm afraid I'm not following."

Kep took a step forward, standing next to Bernadette. "The first toxicology screen strongly suggested the possibility of an anomalous toxin that Mr. Montclair had ingested. However, the second screen—a more thorough test, but one that takes several days to get through our system—did not find any traces of the toxin."

"That's right," Bernadette said, nodding. "So we're looking at the possibility that this might not be foul play after all."

"Not foul—" Marnie frowned. "I don't understand. You were conducting yourselves like Mr. Montclair had been murdered."

"That's what we thought, too." Bernadette continued to nod. "But that should be good news for you and the rest of the Parr Medical team."

"Oh—yes, it is."

Bernadette looked carefully at Marnie. Was she really taken aback? Did she believe them? Marnie's face was a mixture of surprise and relief, and Bernadette cleared her throat. "Now that I've given you the good news, I have a small request to make of you."

"You've done quite enough, haven't you?" Marnie said.

Bernadette glanced at Kep, whose right hand was in his pocket. "You see, the judge had already signed the order for skin surface testing for Leopold Montclair's co-workers."

"Skin surface testing?"

"Have you been through TSA at the airport, where they pull you out of line and run a swab over your hands? It's like that." Bernadette motioned with her head to Kep. "We can conduct the test. Just your hands and the outside of your purse." Bernadette pulled two single packets of alcohol wipes out of her purse and held them in front of her.

"Didn't you just say you had a false positive?"

"I did—but unfortunately, the court order was given *before* the false positive was discovered."

Kep took one of the two alcohol wipe packets with his left hand. "I assure you, it will take fifteen seconds."

Marnie narrowed her eyes. "So this is all for show? I don't like it."

"Believe me, I don't like it either." Bernadette had to think fast; she took a deep breath. "We can take you back to the station and show you the court order. We might have to wait a couple of hours, and if you got a lawyer involved, I'm sure you wouldn't have to undergo the swab. I wish we didn't have to come all the way down here and do this, but a court order is a court order."

"Two hours at the station?" Marnie asked.

"Or fifteen seconds now," Kep responded.

Marnie sighed, rolled her eyes melodramatically, and held out her purse to Kep. Kep hesitated for a moment, then grabbed it with the same hand holding the alcohol wipe. Bernadette grimaced. Not very smooth.

Bernadette ripped the paper packaging of the alcohol wipe she was holding and grabbed Marnie's hand—and Marnie, surprised, swiveled her head from her purse in Kep's hand to Bernadette.

"Sorry, I'm not used to doing this." She managed a smile. "I'd make a terrible phlebotomist!" She wiped

Marnie's right hand, attempting at least a modicum of professionalism, praying that keeping Marnie's attention on her would give Kep enough time to put the driver's license back in Marnie's purse.

Time crawled as Marnie's frown deepened.

Finally—although it was likely only a second or two—Kep held up the alcohol wipe. "It appears your purse has passed the test. As you can see, there's no color alteration."

Bernadette was impressed—she'd only seen Kep take his right hand out of his pocket. She caught his eye, and he gave a barely imperceptible nod.

Marnie jerked her hand out of Bernadette's. "Color alteration? That's a two-thousand-dollar Enzetti."

Whew. She didn't suspect a thing. Bernadette gave Marnie a sympathetic look. "We appreciate—"

The screech of tires.

From the corner of Bernadette's eye, a black SUV—hard to tell the make—had pulled up next to the curb.

A honk behind the SUV.

"Marnie?" A voice from the rear seat—window was down—

A man. Black ski mask.

Bernadette planted her feet and turned toward Marnie just as the man brought a pistol up with his hands, out the open back-seat window—

Bernadette jumped toward Marnie—could she shield her from the gunman?

Bang. Bang. Bang.

Chapter Seventeen

BERNADETTE'S ARMS wrapped around Marnie Synskey's torso, knocking them both off their feet. Marnie's purse skittered on the sidewalk.

Bernadette waited for the burn. Where would it be? Her shoulder or leg if she was lucky, her back, her spine, her neck, her head if she wasn't.

Bernadette and Marnie crashed in a heap onto the sidewalk.

Tires screeched—the SUV was getting away.

Kep—had Kep gotten hit? Had Marnie?

Maybe Bernadette hadn't jumped in time.

No burn. She could move her fingers, her toes.

She closed her eyes. A flash of Declan's dead, sightless eyes from that night outside Wichita.

A screech—not of tires, of a woman's voice. Marnie Synskey was underneath her, and she was sobbing.

Bernadette rolled off her and pushed herself to her feet. As if she'd just removed a pair of earplugs, she suddenly became aware of the screaming all around her. A drive-by shooting, but instead of the target being a drug dealer, the bullets had been intended for a rich white woman in a business suit. Two muscled men in tank tops and gym shorts ran from person to person—are you hurt? are you hurt?

"Kep?" Bernadette called.

She saw him at the edge of the sidewalk, a slightly dazed look in his eyes but upright and unhurt.

Had Marnie been hit? Had Bernadette been too late tackling her? "You all right?"

"I—I scraped my knee. And I think I tore my suit."

"Were you hit by a bullet?" Bernadette said through clenched teeth.

"I, uh," Marnie pushed herself into a sitting position, the trousers of her pantsuit ripped at the knee, and yes, an angry red scrape on her kneecap. Looked like it couldn't decide whether it wanted to bleed. She pressed her hands gingerly to her abdomen. "My button," she said. The button holding her suit jacket closed had popped off.

But no other blood.

"I wasn't hit," she mumbled.

"Doesn't look like I was either," Bernadette said.

One of the muscular men—she assumed he'd been in the gym, maybe even an employee or manager—crouched next to Bernadette and Marnie. "Are you okay?"

"We're both okay."

"I'm calling the police."

Bernadette grabbed for her purse. Miraculously, it had stayed over her shoulder during the tackle. She pulled out her identification and showed it to the man. He narrowed his eyes. "Federal?"

She nodded. "Call the Homicide Division. Ask for Detective Bobby Herrera."

The man had his phone out, stood, and dialed—probably 9-1-1.

She turned her head to Kep. He stood on the sidewalk near where Marnie's purse had scooted across the sidewalk. He held Marnie's purse in his hand. Kep stood stockstill, his glasses slipped down his nose. Shock, probably. Kep had been through a few dangerous situations in their previous investigations, but he'd never been shot at.

She pulled herself to her feet and shuffled over to Kep.

"You all right?"

"The shooter didn't hit me, if that's what you mean." Kep handed the purse to Bernadette. "I believe this belongs to Ms. Synskey." She took it from him and noticed his hands shook slightly.

"You all right?"

"I have not been shot at before." He cleared his throat. "I've been to shooting ranges, but not in the open air like this. And certainly not when I've considered myself in danger."

"You need to sit?"

"Perhaps." He took a deep breath. "In the shooting ranges, I've always smelled significantly more nitrocellulose and nitroglycerine. Strange how one's perceptions change with a burst of adrenaline."

Bernadette nodded. "Gun ranges have limited stimuli. No one screaming, no SUVs driving up and away."

Bernadette studied Kep carefully. If he'd never been shot at before—or even if he had—he might be in shock. Kep took another deep breath, then motioned to Marnie Synskey with his phone. "I suggest you return to Ms. Synskey's side. I suspect the Cleveland police will want to bring her to the police station to get her statement."

Bernadette glanced at Marnie, who still sat on the sidewalk, head bowed. Bernadette went to Marnie, crouched, and put a comforting hand on her shoulder.

"You didn't get hit," Bernadette said. "Neither did I. It doesn't look like anyone was hurt."

"He's trying to kill me." Marnie's breaths hitched as she tried to get herself back under control. "I knew I shouldn't have gotten so close to Leo."

Bernadette paused. "Who's trying to kill you?"

"I know Leo wasn't a good guy," Marnie murmured.

Bernadette grunted. "Marnie, tell me who's trying to kill you."

Marnie raised her head and looked Bernadette in the eye. "I won't be saying anything. I'm in enough trouble with them already."

Bernadette tried again. "Who else at Parr Medical planned the corporate espionage and the murders?"

Marnie's head jerked like she'd just had an electric shock. "You—you *know* about that?"

"Of course I do," Bernadette said. "Dr. Woodhead and I put one of the hired killers behind bars a few months ago." She didn't mention that Annika had escaped.

"I don't care what your lab tests concluded about the poison," Marnie said. "Leo's death was a warning. That's why I wanted to get away from you two so quickly this morning. I didn't want to be seen cooperating with the Feds."

Bernadette pressed her lips together. This wasn't good, especially as she suspected some Cleveland officers were on the take from Parr Medical. The odd scenario that ran through Bernadette's head: a dirty police officer had seen Annika-as-Marnie in the police station, they'd contacted Parr Medical to tell them, and Marnie got put on the hit list.

A large black sedan pulled up next to the curb and braked hard. Detective Bobby Herrera got out, his eyebrows knotted in frustration. He locked eyes with Bernadette and shook his head, shutting the car door. He stepped up onto the curb and crouched next to Synskey.

"Ms. Synskey, I'm Detective Bobby Herrera. I heard what happened here."

"I don't want to press charges." Marnie looked down and pressed her lips together.

Herrera smiled sadly. "Pressing charges—that's not up to you. Someone fires a gun in a downtown thoroughfare at rush hour? That becomes the public's business. We'll need you to come back to the station again and make a statement."

Marnie's brow furrowed. Oh no—she was about to question the detective's "back to the station again" remark—Herrera didn't know he'd seen Annika in disguise, not Marnie.

Bernadette stepped forward. "I understand you're frightened, Ms. Synskey, but the people who want you dead are already targeting you. You can't make things any worse by giving a statement."

Marnie blinked a few times in rapid succession. "Can I have a minute?"

"Of course." Herrera stood, then motioned with his head to Bernadette and stepped about twenty feet away, out of earshot. Bernadette followed. Herrera motioned to Kep, too, and he walked toward Herrera.

Next to the curb, in front of Guardian Fitness, Herrera looked from Bernadette to Kep and back again. He opened his mouth, shut it, then rubbed his forehead.

"This is a complete disaster," Herrera said.

"I wasn't aware that our interview with Ms. Synskey

would put her in danger," Bernadette said. "And you didn't warn us about that either. You just said Parr Medical would be pissed off about it. You warned us we were endangering *ourselves*, not her."

"You should have seen this coming," Herrera said through gritted teeth.

Kep took a step forward. "With all due respect, Detective, no one could have seen this coming. Gun violence is not how Parr Medical addresses their issues. Their modus operandi has been to make deaths look like accidents. The researcher at Kilbourn Technical wasn't shot. His death was staged to look like a suicide. Leopold Montclair's death was staged to look like a heart attack—death by natural causes."

"Escalation is—" Herrera began.

"I'm not talking about the carjacking death of that witness in Jacksonville or the murder of my son," Kep said, his voice rising. "Which I'm assuming you knew about."

Herrera blinked. "Now, look, I just saw a blue evidence box from Boston P.D. in that evidence room, which is weird, okay? We don't store files for other police departments. And after I found out I'd be working with you, I put two and two together."

"Then I suggest you start adding two and two again, Detective." Kep bristled. "This shooting looks like Ms. Synskey was targeted specifically for her role in providing information to the investigators of the Montclair death."

Herrera scoffed. "The reason someone wants her dead is because of *you* two." He jerked his thumb over his shoulder at Synskey. "I know she's scared out of her mind, and she thinks if she comes down to the station again, that'll put her more in danger—"

Oh no. "Sorry," Bernadette interrupted. Oof—should

she say this? She didn't think she could trust Herrera, but this situation was forcing her hand. She took a deep breath. "That wasn't Synskey we interviewed earlier today."

Herrera paused. "What are you talking about? We've got her on video. She signed in as Synskey. Everyone who saw her in the halls recognized her as the Parr Medical executive assistant."

"Head of Executive Services," Bernadette mumbled.

"Whatever. Now you're saying it wasn't her? What'd you do—mess with the video footage? Hire an actor?" He blinked, then dropped his hands to his side. "Oh, great. That's exactly what you did." Herrera ran a hand over his face and sighed melodramatically. "Do you know how many rules you broke? You've heard judges talk about 'fruit of the poisonous tree,' haven't you?"

Bernadette rubbed her forehead. Yes, Bernadette was operating way outside the lines on this case. But Sophie was in danger, and Bernadette didn't much care if she was following the rules or not. "Yes, you're right. We arranged for a—a lookalike."

Herrera's brow furrowed. "Why?"

"To get—well, look, there was a key."

Herrera folded his arms. "You better start at the beginning."

Kep shot Bernadette a glance.

"I don't think we have a choice," Bernadette said.

Kep pursed his lips.

"Otherwise, he's going to ask Marnie what she told us in the interview today, and Marnie will have no idea what he's talking about."

"Perhaps the detective can trust that we're acting on

information we can't disclose in order to best protect those involved with the investigation."

Bernadette looked the detective in the eyes. "You brought us into that file room so we'd find Jack Woodhead's evidence box."

"Of course I did."

"But someone had to put Jack's file box in that room." Bernadette ran her hands through her hair. "Do you know who did that?"

Herrera hesitated.

"You believe it was Captain Markham," Kep said. "But you are reticent to accuse your direct supervisor.

Herrera crossed his arms. "Walter Markham's been with the force for over thirty years. We're taking bets on when he'll retire." He smoothed his mustache. "But if he's getting paid by Parr Medical to screw around with our evidence and files, he won't be leaving anytime soon." He kicked at a loose brick in the sidewalk with his foot. "Look, you haven't told anyone about my affair yet."

"Who would we tell?"

"My captain. Your lieutenant. Or you could just talk too loudly in the break room. We didn't exactly get off on the right foot."

"I haven't told anyone because it's none of my business," Kep said quickly. "However, it is something that our enemies—or, really, any enemies of the police—could hold over your head. Even if we were to trust you on a personal level, we don't know if Parr Medical has found out about your affair and is using that information to blackmail you."

Herrera nodded. "It's a concern. I'll tell you, if anyone *does* know about me and Larissa, I haven't heard about it yet. And as far as I know, neither has my wife."

"You can understand, however, that we don't wish to trust you with our lives."

Herrera smoothed his mustache. "Well, for now, I'll keep it to myself that a Synskey lookalike was in the police building yesterday."

"I appreciate it." Bernadette looked over her shoulder at Marnie, still sitting on the brick sidewalk.

"If her gym is unsafe," Kep said, "it stands to reason that her office and her home are both unsafe. Is there a safehouse for her?"

"Cleveland P.D. might provide one." Herrera chuckled. "But I'm sure they're not the ritzy accommodations she's used to."

"She might prefer staying alive," Bernadette said. "Maybe we can pull some strings at CSAB."

"I'm sorry," Herrera said, "but I've got to follow protocol here. We've had a shooting in a public place. I've heard my officers on the radio on the way down here— several witnesses heard the shooter shout Ms. Synskey's name. We *have* to take her down to the station to get her statement."

"Can you guarantee her safety?"

"There are a few guys I trust. Between the three or four of us, we can."

Bernadette turned to Herrera. "Tell you what—all three of us will walk Synskey back to the homicide division. It's what, a ten-minute walk? Give her some time to get her bearings. Calm down."

"Nice try, Ms. Becker," Herrera said. "She's just been the target of a shooting, and you want her out on the street? I'll drive her back to the station, thank you."

"You want everyone to see Synskey getting in your car?

Then everyone will know she's talking to the cops. That'll put a target on her back for sure."

"In case you hadn't noticed, she's already got a target on her back." Herrera shook his head. "No, she goes with me. If you want to complain about it, go to my captain."

Bernadette glanced at Kep. No choice seemed ideal. Every path forward was fraught with the possibility of losing control of the investigation, or worse, putting Marnie in danger.

Herrera was right. They couldn't risk Synskey walking on the street back to the police station, even if a phalanx of police and federal investigators surrounded her.

Bernadette's shoulders slumped. "All right, Detective Marnie goes to the station in your vehicle. I'll get her."

Chapter Eighteen

"I DON'T WANT to go to the police station," Marnie Synskey said. Bernadette had threaded her arm around Marnie's elbow and walked with her down the sidewalk toward the detective's police car.

"It's for the best," Bernadette said. "We'll be there to meet you—"

"Haven't you been listening to me?" Marnie said. "I stayed out of it as much as I could, but he thinks I know too much."

"Who?"

"That's why he wants me dead," Marnie said, as if she hadn't even heard Bernadette's question.

"Who wants you dead?" Bernadette asked.

"You think I'm going to tell you, out here in the open?" Marnie shot Bernadette a look. "I know your team has been investigating us for months now. Surely you know as well as—"

A loud honk across the street. Bernadette turned to look—was that the black SUV? But no, it was a silver sedan with rust on its rear fender, attempting to drive around the traffic cones the police had put up.

"To the station," Bernadette said, quickening her pace with her hand on Marnie's elbow. They arrived at Herrera's car and Bernadette opened the back door.

Marnie blanched. "In the back seat, like a common criminal?"

"Just procedure, I assure you, Ms. Synskey."

Herrera appeared at Bernadette's side. "Thanks. You want a ride back too?"

Bernadette shook her head. "We'll walk to the station." She needed to regroup with Kep, and wanted to do that out of earshot of Detective Herrera and Marnie. "With this traffic, we might even beat you there." A wave of exhaustion suddenly came over Bernadette. Hopefully, she could get her second wind before she walked back to the station.

"They've assigned interview rooms three, four, and five for witnesses in this shooting," Herrera said. "I'll be waiting for you and Dr. Woodhead in room five. I'll do the whole 'coffee or soda' thing with Ms. Synskey before you get there. Hopefully, we can get right to some questions."

"The interview room has eyes and ears, though. How are you planning on keeping Marnie safe? If she gives up any information on who's behind the killings—"

"I will not argue about this here. Middle of the sidewalk with the target of the attempted homicide standing in front of an open car door. We'll talk at the precinct." Herrera took a few steps back toward the car and leaned forward to talk to Marnie, now sitting in the backseat. "I apologize for what you must be going through, Ms. Synskey, but unfortunately, I must follow procedure. We have a five-minute ride, then we'll get you a cup of coffee, we'll talk, and we'll try to get you back to your life as fast as possible."

Marnie opened her mouth to speak, took a breath, then thought better of it. "Thank you," she mumbled, and let Herrera gently close the car door.

Then Herrera hurried around the other side of the sedan, got in, and with a flash of his left-hand turn signal, pulled out into the street and around the corner.

Kep walked to the edge of the sidewalk next to Bernadette. "Now what do we do?"

Bernadette drooped her shoulders. "We go back to the precinct, just like we told the detective." She took a deep breath; it would only be fifteen minutes of walking; she'd run further than this in Milwaukee. Bernadette willed her second wind to come.

She turned to walk west on Euclid Avenue, toward the Public Square and the Homicide Division building. One foot in front of the other.

Kep rushed to catch up, stepping beside her and matching her pace.

Nothing about this investigation made sense. The FBI ordering surveillance on Leopold Montclair. Jeremy Niehaus flying to San Francisco in the middle of the investigation. Someone shooting at Parr Medical's Head of Executive Services in broad daylight. She tried to fit the puzzle pieces together, but her head spun.

They walked several more blocks in silence. Bernadette focused on putting one foot in front of the other, trying not to think about Sophie. But nagging questions crept into her head anyway. Was she scared? Was she lonely? Was she being treated well?

Other questions, too: was Sophie still angry at Bernadette? Probably. Bernadette could hear Barlow's voice in her head talking to Sophie: this is your mother's fault; if she weren't so stubborn about this job, we'd never be in this position; your mother cares more about becoming a federal agent than she cares about you—

That last one stung, almost like Bernadette had been slapped across the face. She glanced at Kep; if he'd noticed a change in her gait or demeanor, he hadn't shown it. He, like Bernadette had been, was staring glassy-eyed at the inlaid-brick sidewalk in front of him, his scuffed brown oxfords going one after the other.

From Bernadette's purse, a buzzing.

She unzipped the top and pulled her phone out. It was Lesley.

"Any news?" she asked.

"Yes. I heard back from the telecom company."

"I've got Dr. Woodhead with me," Bernadette said. Up ahead on the left, maybe ten yards away, a gap—an alleyway, maybe—just after the Halle Building. They'd get out of the noise of the traffic. "I'm putting this on speaker." She tapped the button on the screen and made a beeline for the corner of the Halle Building, Kep on her heels.

"Location information on the burner phone you asked me to track," Lesley said. "We have it in Philadelphia day before yesterday, then it pinged in the Philadelphia International Airport before it disappeared for a few hours. Showed up again in Phoenix for about two hours, then off again before coming back on in Sacramento a couple of hours after that."

Bernadette stopped in the alcove. A little shelter from the street noise and the wind. "A cross-country plane flight." Philadelphia to Sacramento, with a change of planes in Phoenix. "You getting the passenger manifest?"

"That'll take some time, but I suspect whoever it is traveled under an alias."

"Narrow it down by people who purchased the ticket in the last two days." But Bernadette's heart sank. Did that mean that Marguerite was on her way to kill Sophie? And did that mean that CSAB hid Sophie and Barlow in a safehouse in central California? She knew CSAB had a few apartments—even a couple of small houses an hour or two drive from the Sacramento airport. Methamphetamines were a big issue in the northern part of the valley, from Sacramento County all the way to the Oregon border.

"We're on it," Lesley said.

Kep took a step outside the alcove, standing in a square of sun on the sidewalk and staring over Euclid Avenue.

"Anything else?" Bernadette said, a chill running down her back. "Did Maura—or anyone—have any ideas about why the phone is headed to Sacramento?"

Lesley was silent.

"Come on, Lesley," Bernadette said. "Tell me. Does Maura know where the safehouse is?"

"After she heard the burner phone was traveling out west, she went into her office to make some calls."

The safehouse was probably in Northern California, somewhere near Sacramento. And Marguerite knew. That's where she was going. Bernadette swore under her breath. "Can you get me on the next plane to Sacramento?"

"I don't know if CSAB will reimburse you—"

"Lesley, I don't care if they reimburse me. I don't even care if they fire me. Get me on a plane."

"Okay, I'm on it." The tapping of a keyboard. "One more thing."

"Yes?"

"Ferdinand Montclair—that's Fred, right?"

"Correct."

"Checked out of his hotel this morning. He was staying at the Kepler Grand Suites."

Bernadette pressed her lips together. "Parr Medical must have been paying for that insanely expensive hotel. Probably to keep Fred quiet—and on their side."

"Want me to check flights?"

"He was driving back to Columbus," Bernadette replied. "Said he needed to get back to work."

"Should I confirm his story?"

"Might as well." Hmm—maybe more. "Find out where Fred works. I'd like to call him, ask him if Niehaus let slip anything that might be suspicious. Maybe they were together when Niehaus got a call from a hired killer, for instance, and Fred could give us Niehaus's half of the conversation."

"That's a long shot, Bernadette."

"We get enough long shots, one of them is bound to hit." Bernadette exhaled loudly, puffing her cheeks out as she did so. Then a thought came into her head. "You know," she said, "one of our theories about why Leopold Montclair was killed is that he knew too much about the murders Jeremy Niehaus ordered, and Niehaus had him killed."

"Right..."

"What if Freddy Montclair found out about the killings too? Niehaus kept him on a pretty tight leash whenever I saw him. What if Niehaus had Freddy killed, too?" She'd read reports of organized crime families dumping their victims in the Cuyahoga River, in ditches off the side of the highway—

"There's absolutely no evidence to support that," Lesley said.

"And there definitely won't be once we *find* Freddy." Bernadette crinkled her nose. "I'm sure I'm being paranoid. Text me when I need to be at the airport." She waved to get Kep's attention, and he turned in his square of sunlight to face her. "How long will it take to drive to Sacramento? If I can't get on a plane today, I need to know my options."

Kep paled. "I don't know. At least a day, and that's if we drive straight through. We could drive in shifts."

For a moment, Bernadette was touched. He just assumed he'd be going with her, helping her out along the way. Driving all night.

"Jeremy Niehaus," Lesley said, snapping Bernadette back to the present.

"Right—we were told he went to San Francisco for a conference."

"He flew into SFO, true. And he picked up his rental car."

"I sense a 'but' coming."

"But he never showed up at the conference. They gave his keynote address slot to someone else."

"So where is he?"

"The electronic toll pass issued to his rental car shows he crossed the Bay Bridge toward Oakland about an hour ago, and the Carquinez Bridge about forty-five minutes after that."

"The Carquinez Bridge?"

"It's on Interstate 80 on the way to Sacramento. Another hour, hour and a half, and he should be in Sacramento."

Bernadette stopped in her tracks. "Lesley, why would the FBI be investigating Parr Medical?"

Lesley was quiet for a moment. "Is this about Andy Belgrade?"

"It might be. Belgrade went to a fancy steakhouse a couple weeks ago, after Joanna died, and had the staff give him all of Jeremy Niehaus's credit card receipts. Interviewed a few of them for hours."

"Belgrade," Lesley said, chewing the word. "Yeah. About Andy Belgrade. I think he's a ghost agent."

"A what?"

"Every time I put in a request for information? Classified. Redacted. I can't even get a hire date on the guy. Whoever he is, he's involved with pharma somehow. I suspect he's deep undercover, working on the pharma industry and the opioid epidemic. They call those FBI employees *ghost agents*. Just a guess, but from the companies where his signature shows up, I'll bet fifty bucks that I'm right."

"We figured the name was probably a pseudonym."

"I asked around. Five years ago, Belgrade was apparently the leader of an FBI team called Orion's Wolfpack."

"Oh."

"You know it?"

"Declan, my, uh, former partner. He knew a guy in Orion's Wolfpack. They were like a gang. Took care of a lot of stuff that no one knew about. Assassinations of cartel leaders that looked like accidents, that kind of thing. The guy was finally kicked out of the FBI. Substance abuse, I think."

"Yeah, well, when Vargas took over the FBI, he dismantled a lot of that secret stuff. I guess he had a use for Belgrade, though, if he's still around."

Bernadette rubbed her left temple. "Then what is Joanna doing with an FBI requisition for listening devices that Belgrade signed off on?"

"I wish I could get an answer for you." A small sigh, then Lesley's tone brightened. "And it looks like Belgrade paid Joanna all those almost-ten-thousand-dollar payments."

"How did you figure that out?"

"The bank numbers match an account in his name. And I found a mailbox, based in a GlobalSend store in Cleveland. He covered his tracks pretty well—all the documents I've gotten from my information requests are pages with every single word redacted. But if you think Belgrade's investigating Jeremy Niehaus..."

"Then maybe Jeremy Niehaus is the one who put out the hit on Leopold Montclair." She ran her tongue over her teeth. "And I think he put out a hit on Marnie Synskey, too."

"Marnie..." Lesley stopped typing. "The head of executive services?"

"I think she was setting up meetings between the executive staff and, for lack of a better term, hired killers—but she's playing dumb. I know Synskey met Annika a few months ago—right when Annika was going through her plastic surgery. She knows a lot more than she's letting on, but how much more?"

"That's the question," Lesley muttered to herself.

"No matter how much she knows, though," Bernadette said, "it's too much. That's why I think Jeremy Niehaus wants to eliminate her."

"Why do you say that?"

"Because Marnie Synskey just got shot at in broad daylight."

A gasp on the other end of the line. "Is she okay?"

"No one was injured."

"No one—that sounds like you were with her when she was shot at!"

"We're okay, too."

"We're—you and Kep were both there?"

"And now we're walking to the police station to take her witness statement."

"Okay." Another tapping of the keyboard. "Okay, unfortunately, I can't get you on the last flight that can get you to Sacramento tonight—it's leaving Hopkins in twenty minutes. You'll never make it. They're not even letting me buy the ticket." Another click. "First flight out tomorrow is at five forty-five. You change planes in Denver, an hour layover, then arrive in Sacramento at nine thirty A.M. local time. It's twelve hundred dollars."

"We'll take it," Kep said.

Bernadette looked at Kep, one eyebrow raised.

"I shall cover the cost."

"No." Bernadette clicked her tongue. "I mean, I appreciate it, and it's faster than driving, but we'd still be too late. Jeremy Niehaus and Marguerite Kerovic look to me like they're both on their way to wherever the safehouse is, and tomorrow at nine thirty will put us at least twelve hours behind them." Bernadette ran her hand through her hair, the feeling of powerlessness washing over her. She'd pay ten times that to get back to her daughter, but there was no way she'd make it in time.

Kep sucked in air through his teeth, his eyes bright.

"What?"

"Let's leave it as a last resort," Kep said. "Thanks, Lesley. We'll call you back." He reached out and ended the call.

"Hey!"

Kep pulled his phone out of his pocket, tapped and scrolled on the screen, then lifted the phone to his ear. After a moment, he spoke.

"I know, Yates, I surprised *myself* calling you."

He listened for a moment.

"I'm afraid I'll have to take a rain check on dinner. However, yesterday in the Public Square, you said if there was anything you could do to help—"

He was quiet again, listening.

"I'm afraid it's a rather large request," he said, "but—" Kep closed his eyes and took a deep breath. "It is literally a matter of life and death."

He listened again.

"You're taking a chartered plane back to Los Angeles, correct?"

Silence.

"I humbly request that you find another way to get back to Los Angeles. My co-worker and I need to be in the Sacramento area as soon as humanly possible."

He paused. "If you could, I would be most grateful."

More silence.

"We're not sure of the exact location. Do we need to decide now?"

Another pause.

"Yes, that should work. I am appreciative—" Another pause, this one longer. Kep took his glasses off and rubbed his eyes with the back of his hand. "Of course. Pick my brain. Yes, that true crime series sounds compelling. And though I hate to ask again, I need confirmation of the flight. Will you arrange the jet for us?"

Kep replaced his spectacles. "Yes, I am aware that

chartered planes are expensive. I realize this is a sizable favor."

A longer period of silence this time.

"Ready to go in three hours? Then we shall be at the Burke Lakefront Airport." Kep closed his eyes. "And yes, you shall have first right of refusal on the story, should we come back alive." A shorter pause. "Yes. Quite exciting, indeed. The adrenaline is fairly coursing through my body." He hesitated and cleared his throat. "I cannot tell you how grateful I am, Yates," he said gruffly. "This kindness shall not go unnoticed."

He ended the call, then turned to Bernadette.

"Yates assures me his chartered jet will be prepared and ready to go in less than three hours," he said. "It shall arrive at any commercial airport of our choosing. The journey will take roughly five hours to arrive at any airport in Northern California, including Sacramento International." He paused. "They may still be ahead of us, Bernadette, but if there's any way we can get to your daughter before Marguerite Kerovic and Jeremy Niehaus, we shall do so."

Bernadette let that sit with her for a minute.

She and Maura had each other's backs when they were both agents, and while the two of them still went out for the occasional dinner or drinks, their friendship was considerably more strained since Maura had become Bernadette's boss.

Was Kep the first true friend she'd made since her demotion?

Was he the first true friend she'd made in *years*?

She blinked. She shuffled her feet and looked down. "So what's the plan, then? Back to the hotel to pack?"

Kep shook his head and started walking down the sidewalk again. "We have three hours before the plane is ready. We need to go to the precinct, as Detective Herrera expects us to, and question Ms. Synskey."

"I don't want to miss—"

"We shall miss nothing," Kep said. "If you have never taken a chartered flight before, let me assure you: the crew waits until the passengers are ready. Otherwise, there's no point to the flight."

"Oh. Right. That makes sense." Bernadette paused. "You know, we shouldn't have wiped Marnie's leather purse with an alcohol swab. That will damage the purse. I might be paying her to replace an Enzetti. I'm not sure my budget allows for that."

Kep tilted his head. "You do not honestly believe I wiped an alcohol swab on an expensive Italian leather purse, do you?"

Bernadette blinked. "But you held up the swab."

"Did you see me make contact with the swab and the purse?"

"You had it in the same hand—"

Kep wiggled his fingers. "I can be fairly dexterous. I thought I proved that at the Peruvian restaurant."

Bernadette gave Kep a slight smile.

"We also need to await Lesley's call about exactly where we are going," Kep said.

"We *do* know. Sacramento."

"The safehouse might be a hundred fifty kilometers south—or two hundred kilometers north—of the Sacramento airport, and in that case, we would want to refile our flight plan to a closer airport." Kep sped up his pace as they passed a circular theater on the left; the light crossing Ninth Street turned green. "One advantage to the use of a chartered jet is that we have additional options. If Lesley returns information on where the safehouse is, we can make up time."

"Assuming they're far away from a commercial airport. If their safehouse is an apartment complex near Sacramento International, Niehaus and Kerovic will definitely get there before us."

"Another reason we should return to the precinct," Kep said, "is that we may get some actionable information out of Ms. Synskey."

"Why? Don't we have plenty of evidence to place both Jeremy Niehaus and Marguerite Kerovic under arrest?"

"Do we? I'm uncertain that the evidence we have connects either of them to the murders we've uncovered."

"You've heard the old saying that a grand jury will indict a ham sandwich," Bernadette said.

"But the ham sandwich, to extend the analogy, will get dumped in the cafeteria trash by any judge who's familiar with the rule of law," Kep said. "I would suggest that Niehaus may focus on keeping us from getting certain information. Safeguarding this information may be why Niehaus is so committed to keeping us away from this case. If we can find out what that information is—"

"What could be worse than the spreadsheet outlining all the hits Parr Medical has ordered over the last five years?"

Kep stroked his beard. "We have yet to tie any names at Parr Medical specifically to that spreadsheet. We strongly suspect two people had access to that sheet: Leopold Montclair and Jeremy Niehaus. But surely there were others."

"I bet Marnie Synskey knows."

Kep squinted. "If she served as a facilitator, yes."

"Which she totally did. She was the second name on the safe-deposit box."

"Note, too, that Synskey, despite being assigned the role of head of executive services, did not accompany Jeremy Niehaus to Montclair's house."

"Right. Leopold's brother was with Niehaus. The executor of his estate."

"And what purpose did they serve in being there?" Kep pushed his glasses up onto the bridge of his nose.

"You remember Niehaus said that Freddy Montclair pushed to release the crime scene?" Bernadette asked. "Maybe that was at Niehaus's urging."

"You suspect he wanted to obfuscate possible clues?"

"Maybe. Niehaus could have been there to make sure the killer he'd hired left no clues. He could have encouraged Freddy Montclair touched a bunch of stuff in the house. That way, if CSI had to go back, they'd be processing a compromised crime scene."

"A theory, but one with no evidence."

"Or maybe he was there to find the safe-deposit box key."

"If your postulations are correct," Kep said, "Annika Nakrivo threw a wrench into all that." He turned suddenly to cross Euclid Avenue at Fourth Street. "If not for her, we may not have ever known Montclair's death was foul play. That is a fact not in dispute."

Bernadette almost bumped into another pedestrian as she changed direction to follow Kep.

"And I'm confident," Kep continued, "there is a mole at the Cleveland Police Department who let Niehaus know that Montclair's death was popping up as a possible homicide." Kep turned left, down the sunny side of Euclid Avenue.

"Captain Walter Markham."

"He is one possibility."

Bernadette thought for a moment as they walked in silence. Two blocks later, they arrived on the other side of Rodeway from the Public Square, now crowded with people, many of them taking pictures in front of the Sailors and Soldiers Monument. Kep looked up and frowned.

Bernadette pointed to the right. "We can walk north, along this side of the street, and then take—"

"It's not that," Kep said, motioning with his chin to a black sedan parked at the bus stop on Superior Avenue, half a block away.

"Is that—"

"Detective Herrera, yes."

Bernadette stopped for a moment and watched. The sedan didn't move. "It's just sitting there, idling."

"I would propose that he is waiting for us."

"What's he doing—"

Just then, the black sedan turned right onto Rodeway, heading south toward them.

"Is he—" Bernadette squeaked.

The sedan made a U-turn at the Euclid Avenue intersection, eliciting an angry honk from a small SUV turning left. The car slammed on its brakes right in front of Kep and Bernadette. Its rear window rolled down. Marnie Synskey peered out. Her lower lip trembled, and her eyes were wide with fright.

"Please get in," she said.

Chapter Nineteen

BERNADETTE BENT over and looked through the passenger window at Herrera. "Detective?"

"One of Niehaus's bodyguards at the police station," he said. "I'm not putting Ms. Synskey in danger. We need to regroup."

She swallowed hard; she'd have to trust the detective. "Go around the other side, Kep."

Kep looked at her and blinked, but Bernadette took a few steps toward the sedan, as if in a daze, and opened the passenger side door. Kep hesitated for a moment, then hurried around the back of the car—another honk, this time from a small coupe that swooped around the sedan.

They were both in the car, Bernadette in the passenger seat next to Herrera, Kep in the back seat behind Herrera and next to Synskey. Bernadette turned around three-quarters of the way, with both Synskey and Herrera in her sight. "Tell me what happened."

Herrera looked over his left shoulder and pulled out into traffic. Bernadette turned a little farther and looked at Synskey.

"I saw one of Jeremy's bodyguards," she said. "Standing at the entrance to the station. I didn't think I could walk past him without—" She swallowed hard.

"So Jeremy Niehaus is trying to kill you?"

Synskey hesitated, then closed her eyes and nodded.

"Where are we going?" Kep asked.

"I don't know yet," Herrera said through gritted teeth. "Let me get to the freeway."

"At this time of day?" Kep folded his arms. "We will be stuck in traffic for thirty minutes. 'Sitting ducks,' I believe, is the phrase."

"What do you suggest? Can you smell your way through the streets to avoid rush-hour traffic?"

Kep sank down in his seat.

"I have an idea," Synskey said tentatively.

"What?" Bernadette asked.

"Well—I have access to Mr. Montclair's helicopter service profile. I would often make reservations for him to fly to the airport, so he'd be sure to reach his flight at rush hour." She cleared her throat. "I know the helicopters can travel two or three hundred miles. That would be enough to get out of Cleveland. We could be in Detroit or Indianapolis in a few hours. Or even Toronto, if leaving the country would be safer."

"We already—" Kep began, but a look from Bernadette silenced him.

"Where is the helicopter service based?"

"Cuyahoga County Airport," Synskey said. "I know it'll take about an hour to get to in traffic, but it's the closest airport to Montclair's home, so that's where his service is." She hesitated. "I doubt his executor has closed his account, and I have full access to it."

Bernadette nodded. "You still have your cellphone?"

"Uh—yes."

"Make the reservation from your phone," Bernadette said.

"Now?" Kep asked.

"That's right." Bernadette said. She turned to Herrera. "Know how to get to Cuyahoga County Airport?"

Herrera nodded. "We're heading toward the interstate. We just take it east for fifteen miles or so."

"Great. And how about the, uh, other airport?"

"Hopkins? That's the other direction."

"No, no." Bernadette looked at Kep. "The *other* airport."

"Burke Lakefront," Kep said.

"Oh—that's before we get on the freeway. Well, I guess depending on which way we go, but it's literally at the end of Ninth Street."

Bernadette turned to look out the window. "We're on Superior?"

"Right. Just passed Thirteenth."

"Okay, okay, that's good."

Kep blinked and looked at Bernadette with a question in his eyes, but Bernadette just returned his look. *Trust me, Kep.*

"Hi, this is Marnie Synskey," Synskey said into her phone, "calling on behalf of Leopold Montclair, account number three-six-eight-zero. I need to reserve a helicopter for a flight as soon as possible." She paused. "Of course. Destination." She looked up at Bernadette.

"Toronto," Bernadette said.

"Toronto," Synskey repeated, then paused. "Oh— which airport in Toronto?"

"Pearson."

Kep shook his head. "Too busy. We won't be able to get a flight plan filed in time."

"If we want to get to Toronto as quickly as possible, where would you—" Synskey said into the phone, then waited. "Yes. I see. That makes sense. Let's do that." She took the phone away from her face. "Brampton has a heliport."

"Perfect," Bernadette said.

"Passengers? Uh—four." Another pause. "Yes, we all have identification, and we're all authorized to travel to Canada."

"I don't have my passport on me," Herrera said.

"That's okay," Bernadette said.

Kep shifted his weight. "I'm afraid my passport is back in Boston."

"It's fine," Bernadette murmured.

"Ninety minutes?" Synskey said, raising her eyes to Bernadette's.

"Perfect," Bernadette responded.

"See you then." Synskey ended the call.

"Now remove the SIM card from your phone," Bernadette said.

"What?"

"Niehaus's people are probably tracking you right now," Bernadette said. "Phone tracking. That's how Parr Medical found me in the middle of a national forest in Michigan a few weeks ago." She pointed to Synskey's phone. "Turn off your phone and take out the SIM card."

Marnie held the side buttons of the phone down, and the screen flashed, then the phone powered off. "Okay, I turned it off, but I, uh, don't really know how to remove the card."

Bernadette stuck her hand out and Marnie reluctantly

placed the phone in her hand. She reached into her purse, dug around, then pulled out a paper clip. She straightened it, then found a small hole in the top of the phone. A few moments later, the drawer of the SIM card popped out, and Bernadette shook the card out into her hand. "There. That should do it."

Marnie held her hand out, and Bernadette gave her phone back. "What happens if the helicopter company needs to contact me?"

"They'll get your voice mail." Bernadette dropped the SIM card into the side of the car's center console.

"But we won't be able to—"

"We're not going to Toronto."

Marnie blinked.

"You should contact Lieutenant Stevenson," Kep said to Bernadette. "You are operating quite far out of protocol."

"As soon as I can, yes."

"I understand you don't believe contacting the lieutenant is urgent, but Ms. Synskey needs a safe haven. It's well within reason for the lieutenant to provide a safehouse for Ms. Synskey when we land." He stared at Bernadette from the back seat. "And she could provide additional protection for Sophie before we land."

"Before we land?" Marnie asked. She looked from Kep to Bernadette.

"Yeah," Herrera said, "I gotta admit, I'm lost, too."

"Jeremy Niehaus and a hired killer are converging on a safehouse in California where I believe my daughter is in protective custody," Bernadette said. "Kep arranged for a private jet to take us there." She pointed at Synskey. "I can have my boss arrange for protective custody for you, too."

Synskey paled. "But—but how will I be safe *closer* to Niehaus?"

"We'll—" Bernadette paused. An excellent point. Obviously, Parr Medical was able to find a mole within the FBI or within CSAB who provided both Niehaus and Marguerite Kerovic with the location of the safehouse. Even if Maura could get Sophie and Barlow to a different safehouse, there was no telling whether their new location would be safe. "Okay, we can figure that out. We've got three hours before the jet will be ready—"

"Closer to two, now," said Kep.

Bernadette nodded. "And we've got five hours in the air to get to Sacramento. I'll get the location information from CSAB on where the compromised safehouse is—and ask Maura to move Sophie to a different location. When we get to Sacramento—"

"Or another airport in the area," Kep added quickly.

"—then we'll get you under protective custody." And Bernadette would go protect Sophie herself, if she needed to. "If we can stop Jeremy Niehaus and Marguerite Kerovic, then you'll be safe."

Marnie nodded. Bernadette saw Marnie's eyes relax, too. Maybe Marnie really believed that she'd be safe.

Herrera's phone rang, and he grabbed it, pressing it to his ear. "Herrera."

He listened for a moment. "Yes, sir. Unfortunately, someone the witness recognized as a threat was waiting at the entrance of—"

Herrera stopped talking, then listened for a moment. "I understand, sir, but putting the victim in danger isn't—"

Again, he stopped talking and listened. Bernadette heard the low male voice on the other end, loud and impatient.

Finally: "Understood, sir." Herrera ended the call and placed the phone in the center console.

"What was that about?"

"Captain Markham," he said. "Said if I don't come to the station right now, I'm fired."

"You can't put Marnie in danger like that."

"He didn't technically specify she had to be with me."

Marnie folded her arms. "Well, I'm not going back to the police station. I'm sorry if it will cost you your job, but I refuse to give Jeremy Niehaus's thugs another chance to shoot me."

Bernadette screwed up her mouth. "We'll need someone to keep Marnie safe while Kep and I head into the belly of the beast."

"You know," Herrera said, "I got an offer earlier this week for a private security job. Wasn't planning to take it, but I guess the decision's been made for me." He shot a smile back at Bernadette. "Plus, I haven't been to California for years. Looks like you're stuck with me for a while longer. My first freelance security job."

Bernadette turned back to Marnie. "Okay, Ms. Synskey. We've got about seven hours before we hit Sacramento. Start talking."

Synskey's eyes darted down toward the floor of the car. "I—I need to have a lawyer present."

"What?" Bernadette asked, her voice sharp. "Jeremy Niehaus's hired killers have put a target on your back! Talk to a lawyer—are you kidding me? Bobby, pull over."

"Pull over?" Detective Herrera asked incredulously.

"Ms. Synskey can get out on the side of the road and take a FlashRide back to her office. She can take her chances."

"Hey," Herrera said, "you can't—"

"I'm done with the rules," Bernadette snapped, pointing a finger at Synskey. "Her boss threatened to kill my daughter. I don't care if I get fired—my daughter's life is more important." She turned to Marnie. "Decide now. You want to walk, or you want to talk?"

Marnie looked up at Bernadette, her chin thrust forward, a hard look in her eyes. Had Marnie Synskey ever been told no?

Then the harsh light in Marnie's eyes extinguished, and her shoulders slumped. "I swear, all I was doing was setting up meetings."

"In return for what?"

Marnie sighed. "Stock options. Lots and lots of stock options."

Bernadette nodded. That made sense.

Kep pulled out his phone and started scrolling and typing.

Marnie pointed to Kep. "How come he gets to have a phone and not me?"

Bernadette gritted her teeth. "Because we've taken precautionary measures with our phones, but we haven't with yours."

"What kind of precautionary measures?"

Bernadette glared at Marnie. "Focus, Marnie. Talk about your role in Parr Medical's corporate espionage."

"I just told you—I only set up meetings."

"How about why Parr Medical is targeting Dr. Woodhead and me?" Bernadette asked. "And my daughter."

"Your daughter wasn't supposed to be part of this," Marnie said. "That's not how this was supposed to work."

So she *did* know that people were getting hurt—and killed. But Bernadette shelved that thought for the time being.

Marnie set her jaw. "After our primary contact at the FBI was exposed, Montclair wanted to push pause on the whole thing."

"Primary contact—that was Joanna Quimby?"

"I never got a name."

"Did the team stop?"

Marnie pursed her lips. "They argued whether to stop."

"Let me guess. Jeremy Niehaus wanted to keep going."

"That's right," Marnie said. "Leo wanted to lie low. Jeremy wanted to keep going. We had a few competitors he wanted to, uh, dissuade."

"And did they fight about it?"

"Yes. Made a scene in a restaurant a week or two ago."

Bernadette glanced at Kep. "Platinum Prime?"

Marnie snapped her head up. "Yes."

"So you think Jeremy had Leopold murdered?"

Marnie pressed her lips together. "For the record, I said if people were getting hurt, it would make sense to take time. Figure out where we were."

Bernadette opened her mouth—*I thought you just set up the meetings.* But catching Marnie in a lie would just have her shut down. Bernadette needed Marnie to keep talking.

"Did you hear Jeremy threaten Leopold?"

"Jeremy told Leo he'd regret acting like a coward," Marnie said quietly. "But Leo was adamant, and so was I. The two of us had Jeremy outnumbered."

Bernadette really should have read Marnie her Miranda rights before this conversation, but she didn't care. She didn't care about her pension or going back to becoming an agent. She just wanted Sophie at home, safe.

"I didn't understand it at first." Marnie tapped her chin. "I thought Jeremy was threatening Leo's board of directors position. I didn't think he meant..."

"Murder?" Detective Herrera suggested.

Marnie looked out the window.

"And you didn't say anything after Leo was killed," Bernadette said.

Marnie raised her eyes, pleading. "I didn't know what they were doing, I swear. I just set up the meetings."

"But you had your suspicions."

Marnie looked from Kep's face to Bernadette's face, then nodded. "I didn't want to end up on the list with all the dead scientists."

Ah—Marnie had slipped up. She'd seen the list that Annika had put on that SD card—maybe even a newer version of it. Bernadette tried not to let her glee show in her face. "Plus, the stock options were making you rich. That must've made you feel a little better. You could justify sticking it out another month. And another, and another."

Marnie was quiet.

Bernadette turned around farther in the front seat, her eyes boring into Marnie. "How many murders did Niehaus and Montclair order?"

"I'm telling you, I only—"

"How many did you *suspect* they ordered?"

Marnie sank into the rear seat. "Well, I know about the grad student at Kilbourn Technical in Milwaukee. There were the two researchers at that biotech startup in Kansas City. I know there was a company accused of falsifying data about four years ago, and their CEO was killed in a boating accident. But I never found out if that was Jeremy or not."

"A CSAB analyst was also murdered during the Kilbourn Tech investigation."

"Oh. I'm sorry. I didn't know about that."

Bernadette studied Marnie's face. Her mouth and forehead looked sympathetic, but those emotions didn't reach her eyes.

Marnie was probably too caught up in the massive piles of money she was making. She'd have to get Lesley to go through Marnie's financials.

"So let me get this straight," Bernadette said. "Leopold and Jeremy—acting together—decided who stood in the way of their massive profits, and killed everyone in their way."

"Not everyone," Marnie said lamely.

"And when Leopold got cold feet about continuing..."

"Correct. After Jeremy's FBI mole had been found out."

"And killed."

Marnie startled. "I didn't know she'd been killed."

Bernadette nodded, a lump in her throat. Joanna was supposed to have been her friend. "Why us, Marnie? Why did your company try to kill me and Kep? Why are you after my daughter?"

Marnie hunched over farther, folding herself forward as if she wanted the back seat to swallow her whole.

Chapter Twenty

❧

BERNADETTE'S SHOULDERS hurt from twisting in the passenger seat, but she didn't care. "You know more than you're letting on, Marnie. Your people have threatened my daughter."

Marnie swallowed hard. "The FBI mole who got killed? She isn't Jeremy's only insider at a federal agency."

"Andrew Belgrade."

"Andy?" Marnie's head snapped up. "You know about him, too?"

"I do. But I need to know what *you* know about him."

Marnie pressed her lips together and said nothing.

Bernadette sat back in the passenger seat. She needed to calm down; her pulse was racing. Marnie knew things. She might only have set up meetings, but Bernadette was sure Marnie knew more than Jeremy Niehaus and Leopold Montclair assumed.

But she needed a break from Marnie; her entitlement, her smugness, and her attitude of acting above the law really got on Bernadette's nerves.

A ping on her phone. Lesley.

No update on the plane flights but I've been researching Fred Montclair

Looks like he's a business consultant

Several clients in the Columbus area

Still working on his whereabouts

Bernadette felt a chill run down her spine. She'd thought that Fred had heard something useful—half a conversation between Jeremy and Marguerite Kerovic, for instance. But what if he had and Jeremy Niehaus had *him* killed, too?

Niehaus's words echoed in her head: *Fred hasn't been the same since his daughter died. And now his brother, too.* Yes, grief could make someone do out-of-character things. But if one of those things was reacting in anger about his brother's death?

Another ping from Lesley.

Fred's daughter died from complications from an appendectomy three years ago

Cause of death was a reaction to fenezamil

Alarm bells went off in Bernadette's head. The way Jeremy Niehaus had handled Fred—essentially using a grieving father and brother as a weapon to delay and frustrate the murder investigation? There was a special place in hell for him.

She wanted to ask Lesley to find additional connections between Fred and Jeremy Niehaus. How long had Niehaus been using Fred?

But no, that wasn't relevant to the investigation. Still, if she didn't catch Niehaus, she was afraid Fred would wind up in the Columbus medical examiner's refrigerated drawer in the near future. She shuddered.

In the rear seat, Marnie folded her hands in her lap.

Bernadette stared out the window.

Leopold Montclair had wanted to hit pause. He didn't want more deaths piling up when the FBI was putting Parr Medical under scrutiny, especially when their biggest mole had just been rooted out and killed. But Jeremy Niehaus kept wanting to play the corporate espionage game—and wouldn't take no for an answer. Not from Leopold, and—if the failed attempt on Marnie's life was any indication—not from Marnie, either.

And perhaps this was too much.

"Marnie," Bernadette said, "did Jeremy Niehaus do something to Fred Montclair?"

Marnie sank further into the rear seat. "What?"

"Jeremy Niehaus. Did he do something to Leopold's brother? Did you set up a meeting with Fred as the target?"

Silence for a moment. Marnie opened her mouth, closed it, then said carefully, "Do you think something happened to Fred?"

Bernadette shrugged. "We can't locate him. Last I saw, he was with Jeremy Niehaus. If you think Jeremy ordered Leopold's death, and if Fred is asking too many questions—"

Marnie shook her head. "No. I'm sure Fred is fine."

"If Jeremy is trying to cover his tracks..."

Marnie clasped her hands together in her lap and bowed her head.

Bernadette turned back around to the front. She couldn't look at Marnie right now. Denial—at a time like this? When Marnie had just been shot at? Wouldn't she acknowledge Fred being in danger as a possibility?

Then it hit her: Marnie could be in shock. She wasn't used to being shot at. She wasn't used to her professional life falling apart because the CEO's corporate espionage project had a body count.

After a moment, Marnie spoke. "He's gotten paranoid in the last few weeks."

Bernadette let the silence settle for a moment, hoping she'd say more. But Detective Herrera broke the silence. "Paranoid how?"

"I know the Parr Medical headquarters building is supposed to be a weapons-free zone, but he's been carrying his gun with him everywhere. I don't know what he thinks is going to happen or who he thinks he pissed off, but he's always got his gun in his shoulder holster."

Herrera frowned and smoothed his mustache, keeping one hand on the steering wheel. "What kind of gun?"

"A handgun, of course. Not one of those small purse-sized guns, either."

"Revolver? Semi-automatic?"

"I don't know." She raised her head.

"Make? Model?"

But Marnie just sank into her seat.

Maybe it was finally getting through to her. Marnie Synksey might have to testify. Prison was a very real possibility. Right now, Marnie was worth more to them talking, giving them information. But she wasn't that naïve. She'd figure out that she could be charged soon enough—and that testifying was possibly her only way to avoid a lengthy jail sentence. She could almost see Marnie's shoulders sag under the weight of the realization.

The car slowed as Herrera turned the steering wheel. A control tower was visible through the side window.

"We're already here?" Bernadette said. "I thought it'd be further away."

"Yeah—it's just north of downtown, on Lake Erie."

"We arrived early," Kep said.

The parking lot was only half full, and they found a spot close to the entrance. The roofline of the airport was something out of a 1950s futuristic model: sharp angles that resembled inverted airplane wings. Round patio tables with neon green umbrellas sat on the well-manicured lawn areas between the three sets of automatic doors.

They all got out of the car, and Bernadette walked around the car until she stood next to Kep. "It's great to get witness testimony from Marnie," she whispered, "but we could use irrefutable proof that Jeremy ordered at least *some* of the murders."

"And how," Kep whispered back, "would you prove that?"

"Lesley's tracking Marguerite's burner phone." Bernadette glanced at Marnie; she started walking next to Detective Herrera, toward the airport entrance. "If we can figure out the calls made to Jeremy Niehaus..."

"Unless Marguerite Kerovic testifies, I fail to see how the United States Attorney would be willing to take the case."

"We must think of *something*," Bernadette said.

Kep scratched his beard. "We have five hours on the airplane between here and Northern California. Ms. Synskey cannot physically get up and walk away from you. If you were to extract some information out of her that she took part in illegal activities, perhaps you could leverage it into her testifying against Jeremy Niehaus."

Bernadette gave a slight nod and began walking. "If you can learn sleight of hand over lunch, I suppose I can get Marnie to implicate herself."

Kep fell into step with Bernadette. "The charter company is called Cross Continent Solutions. I think Yates said we could find them behind the terminal to the left."

"We look weird without suitcases," Bernadette said.

"It is far from uncommon when flying a chartered plane." Kep said.

"Fine—then *I* feel weird without a suitcase."

The four of them walked across the parking lot. Marnie's shoulders were slumped, her feet dragging on the ground. Bernadette changed her angle to walk alongside her. "You might not have a sense of urgency around this, Marnie. But remember, it's my daughter that your boss has threatened. We've got a long flight ahead of us, and I want you to think about how unpleasant that flight will be if I think you're delaying us."

Marnie said nothing but quickened her pace.

Kep sped up, passed in front of the other three. and walked into the glass-encased chamber of the terminal.

Bernadette slowed to a stop, letting Herrera and Synskey follow Kep into the terminal.

Bernadette shook her head. There was no way the plane would be ready for them yet. And time was ticking away. Yes, they'd be in California a good twelve hours before a commercial flight would get them there, but both Marguerite Kerovic and Jeremy Niehaus would be in Sacramento by now—or at least, Jeremy would be close. And if the safehouse were anywhere near Sacramento, Sophie could already be...

No. Bernadette shut her eyes tight. She couldn't allow herself to think like that.

Her phone rang in her purse.

She pulled her phone out. Maura. "I have to take this," she said, turning her back on the detective and Marnie, and walking away out of earshot. She tapped *Answer*.

"Maura—hi. Any news?"

"Yes. Most importantly, was Agent Reese able to get in touch with you?"

"A couple days ago, yes. Thank you." A pause. "I bet you had to cash in a lot of favors to make that happen."

"Yeah, well, drinks are on you next time," Maura joked, then her tone became serious. "You didn't get another call from him?"

"Well—no, but I've been busy. I don't think I've missed any calls."

"Okay—it's possible they had other priorities for the secure line. National security will beat a request for a protocol exception every time."

"Sophie said Agent Reese and his team were treating them well."

"Good." Maura paused. "I want to talk about the case."

"Lesley said that the Parr Medical CEO and Annika's sister were both heading to Sacramento. Probably already there."

"Yes, that's why I called. Obviously, we have a leak somewhere." An edge of anger crept into Maura's voice. "And I'm evaluating options."

"To keep Sophie safe?" Bernadette asked. She hated how weak her voice sounded.

"That's correct. I expect to be implementing a plan within the hour."

"Who, though?" Bernadette asked. "Is it one of our agents?"

"I'd be shocked. We fully vetted all our agents. But Parr Medical seems to have their fingers everywhere."

"Joanna was compromised. She might not be the only one in the FBI who is."

"True." Maura was silent for a moment. "What about local law enforcement?"

"We suspect the homicide precinct captain, Walter Markham. His behavior suggests he may be giving information to Parr Medical, and possibly coordinating some activity with them."

"What kind of activity?"

Bernadette lowered her voice. "We found Jack Woodhead's case files in the evidence room in Cleveland."

Maura paused. "And you think this captain had something to do with it?"

"Yes, based on some of the logs we found. At first, I wasn't sure we could trust the detective assigned to the case—"

"Bobby Herrera?"

"Right. He's having an extramarital affair, so that means he's got something Parr Medical could use against him. But he seems like he's successfully kept it under wraps. He's the one who led us to a file room and pretty much pointed out Kep's son's file box."

"Why would Parr Medical want Jack Woodhead's files shipped from Boston to Cleveland?"

"Excellent question."

"You have a working theory?"

"Possibly so that Jeremy Niehaus, the CEO of Parr Medical, could remove something from the file box. Niehaus came to the homicide division building a couple of days ago and asked for Captain Markham, but he wasn't in. Niehaus left without seeing anyone. And according to the logs, he hasn't been back."

"So you think whatever was in the records is still there?"

"And Kep and I took pictures of every single piece of paper in the file. We haven't had time to review."

"You know you can send all those file pictures to Lesley?"

"Right. Of course." Bernadette cleared her throat. "Are you moving Sophie?"

"Their safehouse has been compromised. Of course we're going to move them."

Bernadette's heart sank. "We're at an airport. We were about to take off for Sacramento. I was hoping you could narrow down where Sophie's safehouse is. And I was hoping it was a few hours' drive from Sacramento."

Maura clicked her tongue. "I didn't want you to know where she is. I'm worried you're being followed."

Bernadette was silent. She'd gone off the script quite a bit: first, contacting Annika, not just once, but several times. Then by dragging Marnie Synskey into this. Yes, she was a conspirator, and they could probably arrest her for felony murder with the evidence they had. But she was likely the key to solving this case. If they could stop Jeremy Niehaus, they could put a stop to all the danger that Kep and Bernadette and Sophie and Barlow were in.

Things could go back to normal.

"Parr Medical hired Annika Nakrivo to kill Leopold Montclair," Bernadette blurted.

Maura exhaled. "Not a surprise. When Parr Medical goes through the trouble of breaking out a hired killer from prison, I expect it's because they had a job for her."

"Right. But Annika didn't do it. Instead, she's been leading us to some clues—and it looks like those clues are pointing to Niehaus."

"She turned informant? You didn't promise her immunity, did you?"

"No. She was hoping our investigation would lead her to her sister—and it did. We found a safe-deposit box that held the burner phone, and we called it—Marguerite was on the other end."

"So she's alive?"

"Yes. Lesley's been tracking the phone for us."

Maura was quiet for a moment. "You know, I've been able to piece a lot of this together, but I couldn't figure out how you knew the voice on the other end belonged to Marguerite Kerovic. I find it hard to believe that she just introduced herself. Did she pick up the phone—'Hi, this is Parr Medical's hired killer Marguerite Kerovic. How may I direct your call?' I can't think of a single scenario in which she would reveal her identity to you."

Bernadette was silent.

"The only possibility I can think of," Maura continued, "is that Annika Nakrivo was with you. I can't think of anyone else who would recognize Marguerite's voice. Annika Nakrivo isn't just an informant—you're working *with* her. You're showing her evidence that she shouldn't see."

"I can explain."

"No, I don't want to know," Maura said. "Because if I know what really went on, I'll have no choice but to fire you. No explanation will make it okay with CSAB brass that you're working with an escaped murderer." Maura cleared her throat. "So when you file your report, make sure no one comes to the same conclusion I did."

"I don't think anyone would conclude I had Annika Nakrivo with me," Bernadette said. "If there's recorded footage from the bank, or from outside the bank, you'll conclude that Kep and I were with the head of Parr Medical's executive assistant staff. Her name is Marnie Synskey. Look at the footage from the police station, too, after we visited the bank. The name on the visitor log is *Marnie Synskey*."

"We both know Annika Nakrivo is excellent at disguises."

Bernadette took a breath. A fine line—she could just lie to Maura, but that felt wrong. Still, Maura needed plausible deniability. And frankly, so did Bernadette. "The evidence we've gathered—and yes, some of it is anecdotal—is that Synskey set up meetings between Marguerite Kerovic and others at Parr Medical. Synskey's admitted it, though I'm not sure we can use that admission in court."

"Do I want to know why not?"

Bernadette bulldozed on. "We don't think it's unreasonable to think that Synskey would recognize Kerovic's voice."

Maura was silent. The moment stretched out awkwardly. Finally, a sigh on the other end of the phone. "If this comes back to bite me—"

"Besides," Bernadette interrupted, "even if we work with Annika Nakrivo, she would help us get information so we can get enough evidence to arrest the person who hired her. We do this all the time. We always work with lower-level cogs in the machine so we can get the big boss."

"Let me remind you, Case Analyst Becker, that we do not allow hired killers to escape, even if they turn informant. We give them lighter sentences, we put them in less

uncomfortable prisons. We don't let them go. How did—"
Maura took a deep breath, then exhaled. "No, no, I don't
want to know."

Ouch. Maura had called her *Case Analyst Becker*.
Reminding Bernadette of her recent demotion from *Agent*
—and the thin ice on which she was skating.

Bernadette rubbed the center of her forehead in a
small circle. She had to ask Maura anyway. "I need a favor."

"A favor? Bernadette, have you not—"

"Not for me," Bernadette said. "I mentioned the head
of Parr Medical's Head of Executive Services."

"Marnie Synskey."

"This is the real Marnie Synskey, not someone in
disguise. Like I said, she set up meetings between Parr's
CEO and Marguerite Kerovic. But something happened,
and it seems the CEO is now targeting her."

"The CEO—that's Jeremy Niehaus?"

"Yes."

"Does this have anything to do with the shooting in
downtown Cleveland today?"

"Yes. She was the target."

"Are *you* the reason she never showed up at the homicide division to give her statement? And now a homicide
detective has gone missing."

"Synskey recognized a member of Niehaus's security
staff in front of the entrance to the station. She thought
she'd be in danger."

"So what's the favor?"

"She needs to go into hiding. A safehouse, I guess,
although I'm not sure how we can guarantee her safety,
since we have a leak."

Maura paused. "Does she have any evidence? Would
she be willing to testify?"

"I'm working on it."

Silence on the other end of the line. Then Maura let out a sigh. "You said earlier that 'we' are about to take off for Sacramento. Who's 'we'? You and Kep and this Marnie Synskey?"

Bernadette saw her career flash in front of her eyes, but she didn't care. She just had to make sure Sophie was safe. "And Detective Herrera."

"Ah. The rogue detective." Maura clicked her tongue. "And you want me to put Synskey in hiding? Without a deal to testify against Parr Medical?"

"I don't know what other choices I have. I can't leave her in Cleveland. Not when she's been shot at today. Not when people are waiting for her at the police station to kill her. And not when she might testify against Jeremy Niehaus. She's got to get on the plane with us."

Maura was silent for a moment. "Okay—but you're going to use the time on the plane to get her to testify."

"Understood," Bernadette said automatically. "So maybe we should know which of the twenty or thirty municipal airports in Northern California is closest to the safehouse—or wherever you're moving her to."

Maura was silent.

"You kept her location from me so that no one would find out where she was," Bernadette said. "But that doesn't seem to have worked out."

"No," Maura admitted. "We've got a leak—and there are only a few people who knew where she is—or even *who* she is."

"What do you mean, '*who* she is'?"

Bernadette could almost hear the gears turning in Maura's head, debating whether to let Bernadette in on the need-to-know information. Finally, Maura spoke.

"We've given them other identities. We told the agents they were witnesses to a cartel shooting, not that Parr Medical threatened their lives." Maura sniffed. "So there are six people, including me, Agent Reese, and the other agents who were assigned to the safehouse, who know where Sophie and Barlow are. We're swapping the teams out right now, and I just spent the last three hours giving the other four agents different stories. We'll see if I can root out the mole."

"Really?"

"Yes. I've told everyone we're moving the safehouse. You familiar with Northern California?"

"I've been to San Francisco a couple of times. But other than that, not really."

"Well, it's not all San Francisco, that's for sure. You get about a hundred, a hundred and fifty miles north of Sacramento, around Mount Shasta, and you get a rural area that's just as spread-out and individualistic as anything in West Texas. There's a town about eight miles east of Interstate 5, about two hours north of the Sacramento airport, called Las Moredades. We've got two safehouses there, one on the west side of state route 99, and one on the east. The one on the west is closer to the stuff in the town—it's not big enough for any of the big fast-food chains, but there's a family restaurant and a Burgeropolis."

"Sounds like Sophie would be bored out of her mind."

"That's not where we put her and Barlow. For our higher-security witnesses and families—and Sophie and Barlow certainly qualify—we've got a five-acre parcel off Las Viñas Road. That's about two miles east of state route 99. The DEA seized it about fifteen years ago—it was a whole compound owned by a big-time drug lieutenant in the Orozco cartel. The cartel is no more, but this compound is solid. No one's getting in or out. There's a back road that's not on the online maps. There are tunnels from the wine cellar that go under the creek. They mostly open up near roads, but a couple of them open up on the banks of the Sacramento River. If the compound gets attacked, we'll be able to get Sophie and Barlow out of there about ten different ways. And Parr Medical can't cover all the exits. Not with just two people."

Bernadette knotted her brows. "We don't know that it's only two people. Look, Maura, the reason Sophie was threatened is that Parr Medical thinks I know how to access Joanna's encryption key. Lesley just told me the encryption key probably doesn't even exist."

"Lesley told me. Probably looking for banking information." A brief pause. "Maybe Joanna gave you the banking information and you don't realize it. What do you have of Joanna's that no one else has access to? Did she give you anything in the last few months?"

"Besides the SD card she tried to trick us with?" Bernadette smiled wistfully. "She gave me a paper target from the shooting range. She was a perfect shot, of course."

"Did she lend you a book? Or maybe a piece of jewelry, or a gift for Sophie?"

"I already had Lisa destroy a stuffed bear Joanna gave Sophie last year. Nothing inside."

"Oh—I'm sorry."

"Don't worry about it. Sophie never really liked it, and she's too old for it anyway."

"No—I meant you had to talk to Lisa."

Bernadette sighed. "The worst part of it? Lisa was *nice.*" Bernadette thought for a moment, then cleared her throat. "But I can't think of anything else Joanna gave me. She picked up the tab for drinks once, but we'd barely seen each other in the last year. Always kept making plans and breaking them."

"Maybe you'll remember something. Whatever it is, it's the reason you and Kep are off their..." Silence.

"Maura? Did I lose you?"

"No," Maura said distantly. "I've just gotten an email. Looks like we have evidence that Jeremy Niehaus hired killers for at least four people who were on the hit list from that SD card."

"What? How did they find that?"

"There's a restaurant in Cleveland—"

"Platinum Prime," Bernadette said.

"Ah, so you're a little ahead of me. Evidence just came to light that Niehaus would meet with the hired killer there, and then a few days later, the target would be dead." The sound of a mouse clicking. "Dates, photographs—it's all here. Eyewitness testimony from one of the servers, too."

"All coordinated by the FBI?"

Maura clicked her tongue. "Yes. How did you know?"

"We went to Platinum Prime, too. The FBI had already been there, disrupting their business. Created hostility with the staff." Bernadette hesitated. "Who sent the email? Was it Andrew Belgrade?"

"Lesley's already got that name on her radar. And no, it's not him."

"Have *you* ever heard of Belgrade?"

"Well—funnily enough, yes. I had a colleague over at the EPA who asked me if I'd heard of him. Apparently, his name was associated with a hazardous waste company—I guess he was trying to root out corruption there or something. Hard to tell, since everything was redacted."

An itch in Bernadette's head. "You remember the name of the company?"

"Something generic, I know that. That makes sense, if Belgrade is as undercover as Lesley says he is. Everything with him is an agency-only, need-to-know-basis kind of thing."

Bernadette paused. "Well, if you've got enough to arrest Niehaus, maybe Marnie Synskey doesn't have to testify?"

"You're not getting out of it that easily," Maura said. "We can't convince the U.S. Attorney to rely on a single piece of evidence. We need corroboration. And right now, Marnie Synskey is our best chance at getting that corroboration."

"I thought you had an eyewitness from the restaurant."

"To say that Niehaus was having dinner with someone we believe to be a hired killer. But only Marnie can connect the dots for us."

"Do you have any photos with Jeremy Niehaus, Marnie Synskey, *and* one of the hired killers at the restaurant?" Bernadette asked. "That would be the easiest way to persuade her to testify."

"I'll see what I can find," Maura replied. "Hold on a second—let me arrange for Synskey's safehouse."

Chapter Twenty-One

THE AFTERNOON WAS GROWING WARM, and Bernadette entered the terminal, still on the phone, though Maura had put her on hold. In the small food court, Marnie Synskey and Detective Herrera stood in front of a kiosk selling snacks and drinks. They were both regarding the other warily, but looked like they were making small talk. Kep was nowhere to be seen, but he was probably checking on the readiness of their plane.

She felt her heart beat faster. They were on their way to get Sophie out of danger, and Bernadette had to spend five hours on a plane with a woman who'd facilitated many of the killings that got Sophie into this mess.

Not only that, she and Kep were no closer to finding out who Andy Belgrade was, and whose side he was on. Was he working to catch Jeremy Niehaus, or was he part of the cover-up? True, he had signed the approval for Joanna's requisition of the recording equipment, but had he known Joanna was dirty, or had he been just as fooled as Bernadette?

And what was the issue with Joanna's banking information? Was Lesley even correct? Maybe there was still an encryption key for something entirely different. She'd had Lisa tear the bear to pieces, and the only other thing Joanna had given her was that SD card—which Joanna hadn't even provided successfully. Just a spreadsheet.

Bernadette blinked.

Was it just a spreadsheet?

Maybe that hit list wasn't a murder list. Or, rather, maybe it wasn't *just* a murder list.

Could there be something hidden in the spreadsheet?

It was a long shot—probably an even longer shot than thinking Joanna hid something in Sophie's teddy bear—but it was all she had to go on.

A click on the phone. Maura was back. "Okay—Bernadette, you still there?"

"Yes."

"We're getting Marnie to a safehouse. One near—" Then she paused.

"What?"

"It's near Sophie and Barlow's safehouse."

"The new one, or the old one?"

Maura was silent.

"You said you were going to move her," Bernadette said.

"I said nothing of the sort. I said I was telling the other five people who know that I was moving her."

"And giving them all different locations."

"None of which is where she's going to be."

"Then where—"

"Right where she is." Maura clicked her tongue. "I'm changing everyone out, but Sophie and Barlow are getting different names when I bring the other team in."

"I thought you trusted Xavier Reese."

"I do. He's the only one staying put. And I figure you won't endanger your own daughter."

"But you don't know if I can be tracked."

"I know I just said I can't make any assumptions, but I've seen the tech in your phone. I'm not assuming you and Kep won't be tracked—I know it." The sound of a pencil tapping on a desk. "But that means when you land, you get Detective Herrera and Marnie Synskey to their safehouse—the *other* safehouse in Las Moredades. Tell them there was a mix-up and CSAB moved Sophie and Barlow to a different safehouse—but don't tell them where it is. Then say that you and Kep are going back to the airport, so you can fly to your daughter's new location and join her."

"That way, if Detective Herrera is compromised—"

"Right. He won't be able to get any information to Niehaus."

"Won't Jeremy Niehaus and Marguerite Kerovic—and whatever army they've got with them—go to the compound in Las Moredades?"

"If everything goes according to plan, the mole will contact them to go to another one of those five locations. And since Lesley can track both Marguerite's burner phone and Jeremy Niehaus's rental car, we'll have every law enforcement officer and SWAT team in a thirty-mile radius converge on them."

Bernadette nodded. Impressive. No wonder Maura had been promoted over her. She thought about all the moving pieces, and she had a plan to address all the potential problems. Bernadette doubted that any of Maura's predecessors had had to deal with internal compromise at this level before.

"And where will Kep and I go?"

A pause. "You haven't seen your daughter in several days. If this information about Niehaus pans out, you might be able to go see her."

"You—you think the investigation is that close to wrapping up?"

"I wasn't planning on it at the beginning of this call, but after everything you've told me in this conversation? You found a witness who may testify that Jeremy Niehaus ordered the murder. And you got us the information to track both Niehaus and at least one of his hired killers to Sacramento. Lesley might find something in their financial records to arrest them. Even if we don't, they won't get far."

Bernadette kept her mouth shut. Was Maura talking herself into letting her see Sophie?

"The compound at Las Moredades," continued Maura, "is the safest place for you and Kep to be. And Sophie, too. All the fake addresses we're giving out are at least fifty miles away from Las Moredades." Maura cleared her throat. "Now, go get on that plane, try to convince Marnie Synskey to turn on Jeremy Niehaus and testify, and then go reunite with your daughter."

Maura gave Bernadette the information of the closest airport to Las Moredades: Farolillo Municipal Airfield, about fifteen miles northwest of both the compound and Marnie's safehouse. They said their goodbyes. Bernadette ended the call and put the phone back in her purse.

Kep entered the terminal from the tarmac entrance, spied Bernadette, and raised his hand. She hurried over to join him, as did Synskey and Detective Herrera.

"The crew was waiting for a replacement flight attendant," Kep said. "Apparently, one of them has been delayed in St. Louis."

"How much longer?" Bernadette asked.

"They're ready now."

"We've got a new destination."

"Not Sacramento International?"

"No. Farolillo Airfield. Closest airport to the safehouse."

Kep nodded. "I'll tell the pilot as soon as we board. May take a bit to re-file the flight plan, however."

"But it'll save us about a three-hour drive." Bernadette didn't mention the possibility that Niehaus might be arrested before they landed in California. She'd feel a lot better about things once Maura or Lesley told her that Jeremy Niehaus's GPS was on track to one of the fake safehouse locations. And that Marguerite Kerovic's phone was headed there too.

They walked out the back set of glass double doors onto the tarmac, the way Kep had come. Kep led them all down a painted path on the left, about ten feet from the building. A Gulfstream jet, white with a classic red stripe from the nose to the tail down the side of the plane, waited for them, its staircase door down. A brunette woman in a long-sleeved red button-down collared blouse stood just inside the jet, hunched slightly, and motioned to them. The four of them rushed to the airplane.

"No luggage?" the woman asked, her Georgia drawl thick. "Then you can come in and have a seat. The captain's just about ready." As the four of them climbed into the cabin, she smiled warmly. Standing about five foot six, the woman's teeth looked big for her mouth, and she had an almost witchlike pointedness to her chin and nose. "Y'all have to forgive me—I'm Eleanor, a replacement flight attendant for Ashley. I'll figure out where everything is eventually, but until then, I hope y'all will bear with me."

"Quite all right," Kep said. "We're much more concerned with getting to our destination quickly." Then he sneezed.

"You okay?" Bernadette said.

Kep nodded.

Herrera pushed past them in the aisle. "You trying to convince me that your nose turning off is real?" He smiled, his teeth showing, then put his sunglasses on. "I believe you, Doc. You don't need to be dramatic." He made his way to the back of the plane.

The layout of the cabin differed from a commercial jet. Two sets of single seats were in short rows on either side of the aircraft, with the first seat facing backward, toward the second seat. Marnie Synskey took a few steps toward the back of the aircraft, but Bernadette stopped her.

"We should talk," Bernadette said, then indicated the two seats facing each other on her right, a table between them. She'd seen the layout on trains, but never on an airplane. "Let's sit here."

"I'd rather sit farther back in the plane. And I don't have my laptop with me, so I don't need the table."

Bernadette gave Marnie a tight smile. "I'm sure you'd like to sit farther back, but you and I have some things to discuss. Much easier to have a conversation when we're facing each other rather than trying to talk across the aisle, don't you think?" She tapped the tabletop—wow, was that real mahogany?—and inclined her head. "And I have my laptop with me, so I can take notes."

Marnie narrowed her eyes, but exhaled resignedly and sat in the forward-facing seat. Bernadette took the rear-facing seat in front of her. No overhead bins—must be a private jet thing. She put her purse and laptop bag behind the seat.

Kep came out of the cabin. "The captain was more than amenable to change the flight plan."

"We're changing the flight plan?"

"Closer to your safehouse," Bernadette said.

Kep sneezed again.

Bernadette inclined her head. "Something bugging your superschnozz?"

"Our flight attendant is wearing Hibiscus Heaven."

Bernadette winced. "Is that inexpensive? I didn't know you were allergic to cheap perfume."

"I am decidedly *not* allergic to inexpensive scents. But the issue is not the cost of Hibiscus Heaven. It happens to contain a strain of Botryosphaeria fungus."

"Botryo—what?"

"It causes a disease called *canker* in several species of trees. This particular fungus is problematic to spruces and eucalyptus."

Bernadette furrowed her brow. "Is that what Detective Herrera—"

"Yes, Detective Herrera poked fun at me for the episode in which the blighted eucalyptus tree interfered with my olfactory abilities. The team visited a park full of eucalyptus trees, where the victim had been buried. I couldn't recognize any scents because the trees had been infected with Botryosphaeria the year before."

"Ah." Bernadette pushed her laptop bag with her foot, and it slid another two inches under the seat. "Well, fortunately, there shouldn't be any scents on this flight that you'll have to identify."

Eleanor went through the safety features in her gentle Southern drawl.

The private jet experience was a little more relaxed, but Eleanor still gave them the lecture about seat belts, just before the instructions on connecting to the wi-fi. Once Eleanor sat in her seat near the rear of the ten-passenger jet and the captain had closed the plane door and returned to the cockpit, Marnie raised her eyes to Bernadette across the table as the plane taxied out onto the runway.

"Farolillo?" she whispered, though the annoyance was clear in her voice. "Is that where your daughter is?"

"It's a safehouse for you. Detective Herrera will stay with you until we can get federal agents assigned."

"You're not staying with me?"

"I'm in the middle of an investigation, Ms. Synskey," Bernadette said. "I've been assigned other duties." Maybe the appropriate thing to do was to pat Synskey's hand reassuringly, but Bernadette couldn't get past her annoyance. "I'll miss our talks."

❦

Once they were up in the air, Bernadette turned to Marnie, who was staring out the window.

"Ms. Synskey?"

"I've never taken off from this airport," she said. "I bet it's beautiful to go over Lake Erie."

"When you're landing in Milwaukee, someone put a sign on their roof that says 'Welcome to Cleveland.' I was kind of hoping someone in Cleveland who lives near the airport would put a 'Welcome to Milwaukee' sign to return the favor."

Marnie's eyes went to her lap, and she folded her hands. "I suppose you have some questions for me."

"Yes, I do," Bernadette said.

"I'm not sure I should answer without my lawyer."

"This is an offer that expires when we land."

"Then I should definitely have my lawyer here."

"There are no questions, Ms. Synskey. Just an offer."

Marnie stared at Bernadette.

"You'll need to testify against Jeremy Niehaus. What you saw and heard when you interacted with him. Who you set meetings up with. Whether you were present for the meetings you set up between him and those third parties."

Marnie sat back in the seat and said nothing.

Bernadette studied Marnie's face. She seemed resigned. Maybe her conscience had finally gotten the better of her. And, of course, she was probably terrified that her boss was trying to kill her.

"Has anyone been added to the list in the last two months?" Bernadette asked.

"The list?"

"The hit list. A spreadsheet with names of people who ended up dead."

"I don't know about any hit list."

Bernadette pulled her laptop out of the bag behind her seat. "I've got the list right here." She opened the laptop and pushed the power button, the screen coming to life. "I bet you'd recognize some of these names." She opened the spreadsheet and it appeared before her, then she scrolled down and tapped the screen with her fingernail. "There's the witness set to testify against Parr Medical, who was killed in a hit-and-run the week before she was to take the stand." She scrolled down another screen. "Kymer Thompson, the researcher from Kilbourn Tech. An investigative reporter who was looking into Parr Medical. Dozens and dozens of names. I'm sure all their deaths preceded an activity where Parr Medical found itself in an advantageous business or financial position. I can see if our CSAB team can—"

"Where did you get this list?" Marnie said sharply.

Oh. Bernadette had struck a nerve. How did she want to play this?

She certainly wouldn't tell Marnie about Annika storing the encrypted spreadsheets on an SD card in the gusles. "I'm a federal investigator, Ms. Synskey. Finding things out is part of my job." She inclined her head. "I know you've seen this list."

Marnie stared at Bernadette for a moment, then looked out the window.

Bernadette was getting through to her—Marnie was starting to crack, she could feel it. "Lots of names in this spreadsheet," Bernadette said. "Names, contact information, addresses." Columns T and U were fine, but column W was a little too wide to see as much as she wanted to on the monitor. She clicked on the header line—and paused.

Columns T, U, and W. Where was column V?

It couldn't be this easy, could it? Did the human brain see the U and W and leap automatically over V? Or if not every human brain, then everyone at CSAB who'd seen this spreadsheet?

Cursing under her breath, Bernadette selected the entire spreadsheet and right clicked, then selected *Unhide All Columns* from the pop-up menu.

Like magic, column V appeared, right between the home address and work address.

The column had no header row value. But in the next row, a single character: "6."

What was that "6" supposed to mean? She scrolled down. That column just had a single numeral in each row.

Bernadette counted the rows with numerals in that

column. There were more names than characters. The first nine rows had numerals, then a blank row 10. Then fifteen rows with numbers.

Bernadette closed her eyes and rested her forehead in her hands, her elbows propped on the table.

"Are you okay?" Marnie asked.

"Fine," Bernadette said. "Hold on a moment." She grabbed her laptop, unbuckled her seat belt, and walked two rows behind to Kep's seat. "Take a look at column V," she said.

Kep frowned. "Random numbers."

"But they aren't random, Kep."

He looked. "A blank in row 10."

"Nine rows before, fifteen after. This is the spreadsheet Joanna gave me. It was on Annika's SD card—the one hidden in the gusle I bought in Seattle. I don't know when this column was added, but I know Joanna never thought I'd crack the encryption. Anyway, Column V was hidden. I've shared this spreadsheet with Lesley and Maura, but no one else."

"Twenty-five rows with a blank row 10?"

"That's right."

Kep sat back in his chair. "There are nine digits in an ABA routing number, and there are often fifteen digits in a banking account number."

Bernadette nodded. "That's what I think, too. Joanna was hiding the account info in plain sight. In a hit list she got from me."

Kep cocked his head.

"Yeah," Bernadette said. "That doesn't make a lot of sense. Why would she hide it in this spreadsheet—on *this* SD card?"

"Perhaps she never thought you would think to look

there. Or perhaps she forgot she'd hidden the column before she sent it to you."

"Maybe." It still didn't make sense.

Bernadette tapped on the keyboard, copying and pasting the characters in each of the cells until all twenty-five characters were laid out on the screen in front of her.

"That's it," Bernadette whispered. "This is why they threatened my daughter."

After sending the routing information and account number to Lesley, Bernadette carried her laptop back to her seat across from Marnie, sat down, and put her seat belt on.

Marnie pulled her gaze from the window and looked Bernadette up and down. "You look almost happy."

"Headway in the case."

Marnie nodded slowly.

Hold on—was that a glint of worry in her eyes? Bernadette reached down to put her laptop bag behind her seat and surreptitiously glanced behind her to gauge the distance between her seat and Kep's. Herrera was back there, too; sunglasses over his eyes, his seat reclined. Probably asleep.

Bernadette had kept her voice low, and the engine noise was high. Marnie probably hadn't heard their conversation.

But how much did Marnie know? Did she know the "encryption key" was why Sophie was threatened? Did she have something to do with it? And if so, was she aware that figuring out the banking information meant that

Bernadette didn't need to do Jeremy Niehaus's bidding anymore?

Not that she was planning to give Niehaus the account info. But Marnie didn't know that.

Bernadette opened and closed her laptop bag for dramatic effect, then straightened up. "My boss wanted me to convince you to testify."

"You're crazy," Marnie said. "No way. I already have a target on my back."

"Exactly," Bernadette replied. "Nothing will change except the amount of protection we give you."

"And the number of people trying to kill me."

Bernadette shrugged. "Have it your way. With some of the information we just figured out, it looks like we might not need your testimony. That'll save us some cash. And once this—"

"What do you mean, it'll save you cash?"

"We don't have to put you under the same rigorous protection that we'd have to if you agreed to testify," Bernadette said. "That kind of protection really eats into our operation budget."

Marnie paused, then leaned forward. "I only got on this plane because you agreed to put me in a safehouse. I don't believe you. You're going to protect me, whether I testify or not."

Bernadette nodded. "Okay, then. Suit yourself."

Eleanor walked from the back of the plane and stopped at their table. "Can I get y'all anything?"

"Just a diet cola, thanks," Bernadette said. She opened her laptop.

"White wine?" Marnie asked.

Eleanor nodded and went to the row behind Bernadette.

Bernadette pulled out her laptop and opened it on the table between them. "You know about the list, Marnie. A list of dead people. You called them 'dead scientists' earlier today."

Marnie flinched slightly.

"Some of them are unsolved murders, some of them were considered accidental deaths, some of them were called natural causes. But they were all murders." Bernadette leaned forward. "Knowing who these victims are, and that Parr Medical was behind those deaths? We can move lots of investigations forward." She steepled her fingers and studied Marnie's face. "You've already told us you set many of the meetings up between these hired killers and Parr Medical personnel. Maybe Leopold Montclair, maybe Jeremy Niehaus. Whoever you contacted, you're looking at over forty counts of felony murder."

"But I did nothing! I just facilitated meetings."

"The getaway driver doesn't do anything but keep the rental car running in front of the bank," Bernadette replied. "But if the security guard gets killed in the robbery, that driver goes down for murder, too. It's no different here."

"I'm not the getaway driver," Marnie said. "I'm the worker at the rental car counter. You don't charge them, do you?"

Bernadette shrugged. "You can make that argument in front of the judge."

Marnie opened her mouth, but seemed to realize her position. She slumped a bit, then furrowed her brow. "If I testify against Jeremy Niehaus, you'll drop the charges?"

"We'll see what the U.S. Attorney says. Not up to me. But I'll tell you one thing: you're going to prison for the rest of your life if you *don't* testify."

Marnie slumped in her seat. "This is bullshit," she said under her breath. "I didn't do anything wrong. I was just doing my job."

"And if you can convince the U.S. Attorney of that, you'll get a sweet deal."

"When did you get that list of names?" Marnie said. Hmm—she'd said that quicker than usual.

"The eighteenth," Bernadette said. Maybe she'd received it a couple of days before that—although the SD card had been at least a year old when she'd retrieved it from the gusle in Seattle. But on the eighteenth of June, Joanna had slid the SD card into her paper target, then into her hand.

Marnie tapped her chin thoughtfully. "Then there's one name you don't have."

Bernadette raised her eyebrows. "What name is that?"

Marnie shook her head. "You can connect to the internet up here, right? Get me a deal with no jail time, and not only will I testify, I'll get you the name of Jeremy Niehaus's next planned victim."

Chapter Twenty-Two

ANOTHER VICTIM.

"It better not be my daughter," Bernadette snapped. "Because I already know about her."

"I assume Jeremy threatened your daughter to make sure he gets what he needs," Marnie said. "This is someone different."

Bernadette leaned forward. "Unless you want to be arrested as soon as this plane lands in California, you'll tell me now."

"But I—"

Bernadette slammed her hand on the table. "Tell me *now.*"

Of course, Marnie knew more than she let on. She had access to the safe-deposit box—and Jeremy Niehaus didn't. What did *that* mean?

And Marnie didn't know that Bernadette had used the phone in the safe-deposit box to contact Marguerite Kerovic. Marnie didn't even know that CSAB *knew* about the safe-deposit box, never mind the phone—and never mind Marguerite Kerovic.

Synskey averted her eyes, staring down at the table. Her breaths came fast and short—Bernadette had unnerved her. Good.

"There's—" Synskey began, then her voice cracked, and she cleared her throat to start again. "The chief science officer of the FDA."

"What about him?"

"Her. Dr. Janelle Cardiff. She was supposed to be a guest speaker at the American Association of Pharmaceutical Leaders conference this week."

"The one in San Francisco? The one that Jeremy Niehaus went to attend?"

"Right." Still not meeting Bernadette's eyes, Synskey ran her hands flat across the table between them. "Have you heard of vezuflozin?"

Bernadette blinked. "Vezu—what? Vezuflozin?" She *had* heard of it. But where? Oh, that's right: Annika had mentioned it. "A medication for chronic heart and kidney disease, right?"

"That's right. And has the potential to be lucrative."

"How does Dr. Cardiff come into play?"

Marnie pulled her hands back into her lap, staring at the table. "I've seen the testing results. I don't have a medical degree, but I can read charts."

"Bad news?"

"Vezuflozin has some unacceptable side effects."

"I've heard. It triggers autoimmune disease. You could lose millions of dollars—in lawsuits or in lost research investments. Or both."

Marnie frowned; was she annoyed that Bernadette had heard this already? "We made some tweaks, and now our tests show rates as acceptable. Still borderline, but acceptable."

Maybe Annika *didn't* have all the latest info. "So, what's the problem?" Bernadette asked.

Synskey gritted her teeth. "Parr Medical was mentioned in a conversation that Dr. Cardiff had with some of the other FDA leaders. She's pushing to lower the acceptable limit of these liver test results."

"And, let me guess: the recommended limit is below what vezuflozin's current results are."

"That's what Niehaus believes, anyway. Just when we want to get this product on the market—we'd be unable to sell it. And for Jeremy Niehaus, that was unacceptable. He talked about winning the Nobel Prize."

"And you think Dr. Cardiff is next on Jeremy Niehaus's hit list?"

Marnie flinched. "Well—in a way."

Bernadette narrowed her eyes.

"Dr. Cardiff is a high-risk target," Marnie continued. "Our—our normal stable of contractors—"

Hired killers, thought Bernadette.

"—weren't willing to accept the proposal."

Bernadette tilted her head. "Then who?"

Marnie set her mouth in a line. "Niehaus himself. I think he's been training for this moment."

"Training with what? YouTube videos? It's not like learning magic tricks."

"I'm not sure where he learned how to, uh, *do it*. But this is supposed to be his last hurrah, riding off into the sunset."

A tingle up Bernadette's spine: Lesley was right—and Bernadette was glad she hadn't bet fifty bucks on it. Jeremy *was* looking for the banking information. Riding off into the sunset. It clicked in Bernadette's head: Niehaus and Joanna had been planning this together, and

Joanna had the information they needed to go into a well-funded retirement—and kept the account information so Niehaus couldn't screw her over. And Niehaus probably had a way to access the millions coming his way from vezuflozin—a Caribbean bank account, for instance.

"You have confirmation that Niehaus is targeting her?" Bernadette asked.

"Well," Marnie said carefully, "I'm certainly not privy to every email and communication the FDA sends. But my understanding is that Dr. Cardiff hasn't yet put her recommendation down in writing."

"And Niehaus wants to get to her before she can recommend changing the policy."

Marnie looked down at the table again.

Bernadette unlocked her phone. She'd rather have a voice conversation with Lesley, but on the plane, texting would have to do.

I have an urgent request

She had to stop Jeremy Niehaus from having Dr. Cardiff killed.

Bernadette breathed a sigh of relief as three dots immediately appeared on her screen.

LESLEY

What do you need?

BERNADETTE

Dr. Janelle Cardiff – FDA bigwig

Supposed to speak at a conference in SF

Need her located

LESLEY

This could take a while

BERNADETTE

She's the Chief Scientist of the FDA – she might have her calendar publicly available

LESLEY

Let me check

Bernadette looked up from her phone; Synskey was looking right at her.

Bernadette lifted the phone from the table. "My colleague." She cleared her throat. "Niehaus didn't show up at the conference in San Francisco."

Synskey frowned. "That's news to me."

Bernadette ran her hand over her face. Synskey had been in the loop—well, perhaps not quite the inner circle, but awfully close. And then something had happened. Not only had Synskey been removed from the loop, but Niehaus wanted her dead.

But Niehaus's trip to California was odd. As far as she could tell, he was always miles away from all the murders he likely ordered. Much easier to deny you're involved when you're hundreds of miles away. But Niehaus had specifically gone to the same conference where his target was—and if he wanted her dead, wouldn't that put him closer to the potential crime scene?

Was Synskey right on both counts? Did Niehaus want to meet with Dr. Cardiff to convince her to see things his way, then brought in a hired killer as a backup plan? Perhaps Cardiff's change of plans threw a wrench into everything. This didn't make sense—but then, when killers got desperate, sense often went out the window.

Her phone buzzed. A text from Lesley.

> Dr Cardiff gave the keynote address and has already left the conference

> Scheduled to be at a teaching hospital in Sacramento today

> Dinner reservation 8pm at The Walking Duck for 2 – I'm contacting her staff to see who else will be at the dinner

> She's booked in a suite at the Signature Collection Hotel tonight

Bernadette blinked.

Was Jeremy Niehaus scheduled to have dinner with his intended murder victim tonight? It wouldn't take much to slip something poisonous into her wine or a cocktail. Bernadette had been joking that murder wasn't like a magic trick, but if a YouTube video could teach Kep how to slip a driver's license into Marnie Synskey's purse with no one noticing, maybe Jeremy Niehaus could learn how to dump arsenic into Dr. Cardiff's diet cola.

And Marguerite Kerovic was on her way to Sophie's safehouse to make sure Bernadette knew the threat was real. To ensure that she'd get the account information to Niehaus on time.

She picked up her phone again and texted Lesley back.

> Get police protection to that teaching hospital now

> Dr Cardiff is a possible target of Parr Medical's next hit

> If Dr Cardiff is having dinner with Jeremy Niehaus at The Walking Duck, have him detained so he isn't in the same room with her

Bernadette scowled. She thought she'd gotten ahead of this. That the safehouse had stayed safe, that with the evidence the FBI had gathered and the potential testimony from Marnie, they'd arrest Jeremy Niehaus and put an end to all of this.

There was still time to capture Jeremy Niehaus before Sophie was endangered any further. Bernadette felt a mix of nervousness and relief at having the account information, though. If the Niehaus plan got screwed up, she could give him what he wanted.

Bernadette sat back and slouched, staring at Marnie Synskey. Marnie had pieced together almost everything Jeremy Niehaus and Leopold Montclair had done. They both had underestimated Synskey's intelligence and her ability to connect the dots. But something had made Jeremy Niehaus stop trusting both his partners in crime. He'd already eliminated one of them, and was intent on eliminating Marnie, too.

Bernadette lifted her head. "Why are you a target?"

Marnie flinched. "What do you mean?"

Bernadette picked up a pen and pointed it at Marnie. "I mean, the obvious answer is that you know something that Jeremy Niehaus wants to stay hidden."

"He got to Leo first."

Bernadette nodded. "I suspect that, until recently, you all were on the same side. Maximize profits at Parr Medical. First, maybe it was just corporate espionage. But then, you all had to do something dramatic to cover your tracks. And that's when one of you decided to hire people to remove the people who were most problematic."

"I don't know if that was Jeremy's idea or Leopold's."

"No matter whose idea it was," Bernadette said, "killing off the people in your way worked for a few years.

But then something changed. What was it? Did Leo get cold feet? Or did Leo try to kill someone, and it wound up going sideways?"

A brief flicker of recognition in Marnie Synskey's eyes.

"That was it," Bernadette mumbled. "Leopold Montclair ordered a hit, it didn't work, and you all thought you'd be exposed. And that's when everyone turned on each other."

"I don't know anything."

A light bulb in Bernadette's head. "It was us."

Marnie tightened her jaw.

"A few weeks ago, Kep and I left Taycheedah before Parr Medical could kill us."

"Like I said, I don't know—"

"And then Jeremy's insider at the FBI was killed. And all her information got exposed."

Marnie slunk in her seat.

"Niehaus got nervous. He thought one of you might rat him out." Bernadette grinned at Marnie—and Marnie recoiled. "What is it that Ben Franklin said? Oh, right: 'three can keep a secret if two are dead.' And he's making sure the two of you are dead."

Marnie Synskey grimaced.

"Your only move," Bernadette said, "is for us to put you in a safehouse so you can testify against him. You'll testify whether or not you do prison time. Because this is your only choice if you want to live."

Marnie sat still for a long time, then finally nodded her head.

Bernadette left Marnie sitting at the table and went to the back of the plane. First, she texted Lesley.

> **Bernadette**
>
> Jeremy Niehaus may be planning to leave the country after killing Dr Cardiff
>
> Can you see if there are any signs to support this theory
>
> **Lesley**
>
> Give me a few minutes

She opened her laptop and emailed Maura. The lieutenant replied almost immediately with directions to the safehouse and a promise to contact the U.S. Attorney in Sacramento.

A ding on Bernadette's phone: Lesley had texted back.

> Looks like several financial accounts belonging to Jeremy Niehaus were cleaned out
>
> Transferred to that same mystery account
>
> From the IP address it looks like this was actually Jeremy Niehaus making the transaction
>
> Still working on where it is

Bernadette felt her pulse race. Maybe Niehaus had gotten careless and hadn't covered his tracks well. Everything was in place for him to leave the country with millions—and get away with murder.

Eleanor appeared in the aisle. "We'll be landing in

about forty-five minutes," she said. "Can I get y'all anything before we land?"

"I'm fine," Bernadette said.

Herrera appeared behind her. "Could I get some water?"

"Yes, sir," Eleanor said.

"Oh." Bernadette raised her hand toward Eleanor. "Do you know if there's a car rental facility at the airport?"

Eleanor shook her head. "I'm not too familiar with this airfield." She walked toward the back of the plane.

"Local sheriff could meet us and take us," Herrera said. "I don't know them, but if we've got forty-five minutes till we land, I imagine we could get access to one of their spare vehicles. Or at least a ride."

Bernadette nodded. "You've got email access, Detective. Can you make that happen?"

"I can try," Herrera replied.

Eleanor appeared behind him, handing Herrera a bottle of water. "Here you are."

"Thanks." Herrera looked Eleanor up and down—ugh, was a wife and a mistress not enough for him?

Kep sneezed.

"You okay?"

"It's simply the perfume." Kep removed a handkerchief from the inside pocket of his sportcoat and covered his nose.

"Detective Herrera, we need to get Ms. Synskey"— Bernadette nodded in Marnie's direction—"to a safehouse in the area. I've already coordinated with my lieutenant."

Herrera leaned against the empty seat across the aisle. "I can email the local sheriff and ask for a second car. Farolillo, right? With three Ls?"

Bernadette nodded. "Would you accompany Ms. Synskey?"

"Sure. Not like I have a police detective job to go back to, anyway." He smiled. "I accepted the private security job two hours ago. It starts in a couple weeks." Herrera pulled his phone out of his pocket and went back to his seat.

Bernadette turned to Kep. "As for keeping the FDA chief scientist safe, I've contacted Lesley."

Bernadette picked up her phone and texted Lesley again, this time asking for an update on Dr. Cardiff's protection. When she looked up, she felt the plane tilt forward slightly. The private jet was beginning its descent.

Her phone dinged with a response from Lesley.

> The burner phone is now on Interstate 5

> Traveling north from the Sacramento airport

Bernadette set the phone down on the table and took a deep breath. She wasn't sure if Maura's ruse had worked. Was Marguerite Kerovic still on her way to Sophie's safehouse?

Chapter Twenty-Three

THE AIRPORT in Farolillo was even smaller than the executive airport in Cleveland. The asphalt runway provided a bumpy landing, but soon enough, they were taxiing to the terminal. Bernadette tapped her fingers distractedly on the table in front of her as the plane came to a stop. She unbuckled her seat belt, grabbed her purse and laptop bag, and then stood, stepping to the front of the plane. Eleanor stood behind the plane door, the steps that were part of the door upside down.

"Thanks, Eleanor."

"My pleasure," the flight attendant said.

"What now?" Bernadette asked. "When you got up this morning, I bet you didn't think you'd end up two thousand miles away."

Eleanor laughed—a friendly laugh as her blue eyes twinkled. "Oh hon, this isn't the first time I've landed in an airfield in the middle of nowhere. I'll see where the captain has us going next." Eleanor gripped a handle in the middle of the second stair, then stood in front of the closed door, smiling. The co-pilot stood from his seat and stepped to the area behind Eleanor.

Behind Bernadette, Kep stood, Marnie behind him, and Detective Herrera bringing up the rear.

The co-pilot tilted his head. "Anything needed before we let the passengers disembark? I understand they're in a hurry."

"No, no. I just—" She studied the door for a moment, then moved her hand to a metal lever on the right side. She pushed it—nothing. "My apologies—I'm used to flying on other models of jet. It's an adventure every day."

"You pull it," the co-pilot said.

"Of course." Eleanor pulled the lever, and the door, with the stairway attached, lowered. A burst of dry, hot air entered the cabin.

The co-pilot winced but said nothing.

"Hope you had a pleasant flight," Eleanor said, taking a step back so the passengers could get past her.

Bernadette was out the door first. Even though the sun had set, the heat was oppressive.

As she stepped onto the tarmac, she looked up. *Welcome to Farolillo.* A faded, poorly lit sign in a dated cursive script. The beige concrete of the building's walls did nothing to inspire confidence.

Bernadette was in a hurry. She hadn't talked to her daughter in days, and the constant threat on Sophie's life had aged Bernadette a year in the last week. She rushed across the asphalt toward the welcome sign. Reaching a half-height chain-link fence, she went through a gate, then went into the terminal.

The interior looked like a dentist's waiting room from the 1970s. Fake wood paneling. A teal faux-leather sofa sat behind a coffee table with rounded edges. A restaurant sign at the end of the short hall: *Valley Airpark Diner, 7 AM–3 PM.* It was far past closing time; Bernadette's stomach rumbled, but she didn't want to eat until she was reunited with her daughter.

The whole terminal was roughly twenty feet from front to back, and she strode through the room. Detective Herrera and Marnie Synskey were right behind her.

"Man, that pilot was reading our flight attendant the riot act," Herrera said.

"Really? For what?"

"Apparently, she didn't check through the window of the airplane door before opening it. Safety protocol violation. You'd've thought the flight attendant had just slept with his wife."

Bernadette looked out of the corner of her eye at Herrera, but he seemed oblivious to his hypocritical use of the metaphor.

Bernadette pushed the front door open to the parking lot, another blast of hot, dry air hitting her face.

A police cruiser—*Farolillo Police* on the door—sat next to two midsize, nondescript American sedans, one a newer silver model and one decade-old black car with a dent in the right front fender. Herrera nodded. "My contact did good," he said. "Two Eureka sedans. We're supposed to get the keys from one of the officers."

Bernadette pulled her phone out. She'd missed the text from Lesley, but she read it now. The addresses of two safehouses: one for Marnie, and one where Sophie and Barlow were staying. She forwarded the first address to Detective Herrera, hearing the ping on his phone a few seconds later.

The cruiser door opened, and a uniformed officer, gray temples and a weathered face, got out.

"You've got the keys, Officer?" Herrera asked.

"Sure do. Welcome to Farolillo." He handed Herrera two sets of keys. "You know where you're going?"

"GPS will figure it out," Herrera said, tossing one of the keychains to Bernadette.

Bernadette caught the keys with one hand. "Good luck, Detective. Stay safe."

Herrera nodded, then took Synskey by the elbow, gently but firmly, toward the silver sedan.

Bernadette hurried to the driver's side of the older black sedan. "Thank you, officer," she called over her shoulder, as Kep rushed to get in the passenger side.

She put her purse on the center console and tossed her laptop bag into the back seat. Bernadette started the engine and shifted into reverse before Kep had fully gotten into the car. "Should have had you smell for plastic explosive first." She pushed her purse toward Kep. "Get the address from Lesley's text and put it into your map on your phone."

"Of course."

Bernadette put the car into *Drive* and drove toward a sign that read *Airport Exit*. Then, a few minutes later, she turned off Airport Boulevard toward another sign for Interstate 5.

"I have the directions," Kep said.

Bernadette pushed the accelerator down, ignoring the speed limit. The road was lined with houses and apartment buildings, several with dead lawns. At the stop light, a Marks-the-Spot stood on the left. The road ended at a divided highway. A large sign below the stoplight: *South Main St.* On the corner, a sign that said *Freeway* with an arrow to the right.

"Toward the freeway?"

Kep nodded.

"I can't see you that well in the dark, Kep."

"My apologies. Yes, turn right here."

After a quarter mile, a pair of signs above the road: I-5 to Portland toward the left, Sacramento to the right.

"Which way?" Bernadette asked.

"Straight," Kep said. "Las Moredades isn't off the interstate."

"Great," Bernadette mumbled.

"Makes it harder for our adversaries to find," Kep said.

"See if Lesley has the whereabouts of Marguerite's cell phone."

Kep began tapping the screen and inhaled loudly through his nose. "I can't tell you how relieved I am to be away from the woman wearing the Hibiscus Heaven."

Bernadette flew past the two lights for the interstate, passed a car in the right lane. A gas station. *Friendly Acres RV Park*. A sign: U.S. Historic Route 99 West. Then the streetlights stopped lining the sides of the road, and only the car headlights illuminated the asphalt ahead. Bernadette pushed the accelerator down farther as the speedometer went past eighty.

"How long till we get there?"

"At this rate of speed, perhaps fifteen minutes."

Bernadette gritted her teeth.

Kep's phone rang, and Bernadette jumped in her seat.

"It's Lesley. I shall answer on speakerphone." He tapped the screen. "Greetings, Miss Gill."

"A lot has happened. Figured I'd call."

"Did that banking information check out?"

"Yes. A financial institution in the Caymans. Almost a billion dollars in the account—we're trying to get more information around it, but the bank doesn't want to cooperate with us."

"How about the burner phone?"

"Well—it disappeared."

"Disappeared?"

"We're working on finding it. Maybe the battery died."

A chill ran down Bernadette's spine—she no longer trusted that the Marguerite Kerovic was safely far away. Maybe Marguerite was already there.

Kep and Bernadette would be at the safehouse in another fifteen minutes. Could Agent Xavier Reese and his team protect Sophie in the meantime?

"But there's more news."

"What?"

"We believe we've located Jeremy Niehaus's rental car."

"That's—that's great! Is he in it?"

"Unclear. His car is parked in front of the restaurant in downtown Sacramento where he was scheduled to have dinner with Dr. Cardiff. We have a team moving in."

Bernadette furrowed her brow. "You're considering him armed and dangerous?"

Lesley gave a soft grunt. "We're exercising caution. If your information is correct, he may have a fast-acting poison in his possession. It may be unlikely to be deadly when airborne, but we're not taking any chances."

Bernadette rubbed her forehead. "What about Dr. Cardiff?"

"We're holding her at the teaching hospital until we have Jeremy Niehaus in custody. So far, we've seen no suspicious activity. The police did a sweep of the blocks surrounding the Signature Hotel, just in case Niehaus had a backup plan. Dr. Cardiff is changing her hotel tonight to be on the safe side. The police are collecting her things and will move them to a different hotel. Undisclosed location."

"So everyone is safe so far?"

"Well, mostly."

"Mostly?"

"Bernadette, I haven't located Ferdinand Montclair yet."

"He hasn't shown up in Columbus?"

"No. He lives in a *very* pricey neighborhood. No sign of his car, and his house alarm hasn't been turned off since Sunday."

"Airports? Train stations?"

"I've been busy with other things, but locating him is next on my list."

Bernadette sighed in frustration. She pushed the accelerator down more, but the engine whined and the speedometer stayed stubbornly below ninety. "So even if we have Niehaus, he might have killed Leopold's brother?"

"I can't answer that," Lesley said.

"And Marguerite Kerovic might still be on her way to the safehouse if Niehaus doesn't get Joanna's banking information. Even if he's under arrest."

"I can't answer that, either."

Bernadette gripped the steering wheel tighter as the dark scenery flew past.

Chapter Twenty-Four

❧

"I CAN'T BELIEVE IT," Bernadette mumbled, after ending the call with Lesley. "We've got Jeremy Niehaus cornered in a fancy restaurant in Sacramento, and Sophie *still* might be in danger."

Kep scratched his beard. "Is there any possible way you could get the banking information to Jeremy Niehaus before he gets arrested?"

"I don't—" Bernadette paused, then dug in her purse, pulled out her phone and thrust it at Kep. "Look in my email. Get the latest messages from Joanna's address."

Kep took the phone, held the screen in front of Bernadette's face briefly to unlock it, then tapped on the screen several times.

"'Get the encryption key or Sophie dies,'" Kep read. "'Send within four days.'"

"That's it?" Bernadette asked. "I just send the encryption key—or the bank account information—to that email address and everything is over?"

Kep tapped the screen a few more times. "I'm compelled to point out that we've begun day four."

"Yeah, I get it. And I know he's serious, since we were tracking a hired killer's cellphone and it's disappeared."

"So you can simply reply?"

"I'm surprised at you, Kep. I'd have thought you'd want me to be stronger than this."

Kep sucked in a breath. "Perhaps I might have felt that at one point in my life. But I would do anything for my son to still be alive. If that meant letting a killer escape to a country without an extradition agreement with the United States, then so be it. I wouldn't stand in your way."

Bernadette nodded. "Kep—can you call Lesley back and see if she can find Jeremy Niehaus's personal cell number? I need to buy a little time until I can use my laptop. I need to have Niehaus call off the killer—or at least hit pause for an hour."

Kep hesitated.

"What is it?"

"Do you want to put Miss Gill in that position?" Kep asked. "I don't know that she will provide you the number if she suspects you will give Niehaus the encryption key."

"Why wouldn't she? It'll save Sophie's life, and they've got Niehaus surrounded. Or they should soon, anyway."

"I suppose we can try." Kep pulled the handkerchief out of his pocket and dabbed his nose.

"You okay?"

"Yes," he said. "That perfume—it's similar to having blinders on, but for my nose. I cannot detect a tenth of what I usually can."

"Yeah, it was a good thing we got away from her—"

Bernadette stopped talking.

Kep looked at her. "We have a left turn in about six kilometers."

"No, it's not that," Bernadette said. "How many people know about your allergy?"

"Quite a few. As I mentioned, it was on an episode of *Cases That Won't Die.*"

"So—if someone wanted to disarm your nose—"

Kep furrowed his brow. "Yes. It would be possible to do so."

"Call Lesley, Kep."

A moment later, the phone rang through Bernadette's phone speaker.

"Hi, Bernadette." Lesley's voice cracked.

"Lesley, do you have the cellphone number for Jeremy Niehaus?"

A pause. "I do. Why do you want it?"

Bernadette's turn to pause, and she decided to stretch the truth. "If a CSAB team is on its way, the best thing I can do right now is distract him. Keep him focused on his goal. I'm planning to call him and tell him I need another forty-five minutes to get the information he's after."

"Oh—that's a good idea. And keep him on the phone as long as you can."

"Of course. And one more thing. Kep, didn't our flight attendant—Eleanor—say that the regularly scheduled person called in sick?"

"I'm unsure if those were her exact words, but I believe that was the implication."

"What if..."

A moment of silence, with only the whine of the engine and the road noise.

"What if Eleanor was a plant?"

Kep's eyebrows raised. "Do you mean to say that Parr Medical created a situation in which the regular flight attendant was indisposed, and they placed Eleanor on that flight instead?"

"That's exactly what I'm saying." Bernadette smacked the steering wheel. "Remember Eleanor got yelled at for not checking outside the window before she opened it?" Bernadette pursed her lips. "When I was standing next to her, it didn't even seem like she knew where the release lever was."

"Why would Parr Medical plant someone on your plane?"

Bernadette was stumped for a moment, then she smacked the steering wheel. "Not Parr Medical. That was Annika Nakrivo. I should have recognized her eyes. But her face was different. And her voice, too. She was wearing Hibiscus Heaven so you wouldn't be able to smell her."

"If you had Annika Nakrivo on your plane," Lesley said, "I would assume she'd work with someone at Parr Medical to undermine you and Dr. Woodhead."

Bernadette turned everything over in her mind. "I don't think she's doing Parr Medical's bidding anymore," Bernadette said.

"Annika may have realized that following us was the best way to locate her sister," Kep said. "She might attempt to contact her. Or possibly get Marguerite to disappear with her."

Bernadette tapped the steering wheel. "Niehaus doesn't think he's cornered yet, right?"

"Not as far as we know," Lesley said. "He thinks Dr. Cardiff has simply been delayed in traffic."

"How far away is the CSAB team?"

"Twenty minutes."

"And you've got Dr. Cardiff safe?"

"On her way to another hotel."

"And still no sign of Marguerite Kerovic's phone?"

Lesley paused. "No."

"All right. I'm going to call Jeremy Niehaus as soon as you send me the number. And could you inform the agents at the safehouse that we'll be there in the next, uh, ten minutes?" She glanced over at Kep.

"Seven minutes," Kep said.

"Of course," Lesley said. "Sending you Niehaus's number as we speak." A ding from Bernadette's phone.

"Hopefully, we'll beat Marguerite Kerovic there."

"Here's the turn," Kep said.

Bernadette spun the wheel.

"I apologize, Miss Gill," Kep said, "but we are close to our destination, and I will need to assist in navigation."

"Talk to you later." The call dropped.

"A bridge is coming up," Kep said.

"I'll deal with driving, Kep. You call Niehaus."

Kep tapped the phone. The phone speaker clicked, then one ring, two, three, four. "You've reached Jeremy Niehaus, CEO of Parr Medical."

"Call again," Bernadette said.

Kep ended the call and redialed. Again, four rings and voicemail.

"Again," Bernadette said.

As the phone rang again, houses flew by on both sides of the street. Then a building appeared on the left with a lit sign: *County Museum*.

"Is this Las Moredades?" Bernadette asked over the voicemail message.

Kep shook his head. "The next town over. Across the river."

"Keep calling until that bastard picks up."

A sign for farm equipment on the right. Then the

street narrowed as it crossed a bridge. A green sign with white lettering: *Sacramento River*. Bernadette looked to her left; a railroad bridge, likely a continuation of the tracks they had just crossed. Another voicemail. Kep called again.

Orchards and farmland surrounded the road on the other side of the bridge. Even though they'd just driven through a small town, Bernadette felt like she was in the middle of nowhere. She looked down at the speedometer: it hovered just under seventy.

And Niehaus picked up. "Who is this?"

"I thought for sure you'd want to take a call from Bernadette Becker from CSAB," Bernadette said. "You've asked me for something. Made me an offer I couldn't refuse, as they say."

A pause. "What are you talking about?"

"We don't have to play that game," Bernadette said. "Just know that I accede to your demands. I've got the encryption key—well, I've got the ABA number and account information. That's what you wanted, isn't it? I just need to get somewhere I can get wi-fi, and I'm on the highway in the middle of nowhere right now. But call off your dogs for another hour. You'll have what you need."

Silence. "ABA number? What the hell are you talking about?"

Bernadette gritted her teeth. "Mr. Niehaus, neither of us has time to pretend we don't know what the other is referring to. This call isn't being recorded. California is a two-party consent state anyway, so I couldn't use what you say on this call against you."

"What exactly do you think I've done? I know you wanted to interview me, but I had a business trip."

"I understand," Bernadette said. "Just tell me you'll give me another hour."

"I still don't know what you're talking about."

"Call Marguerite Kerovic and tell her to wait for an hour. You'll get what you need."

"Call *who?*"

Bernadette tapped *End Call.*

Kep stroked his beard and took a breath.

"You want to say something, Kep?"

"Mr. Niehaus is a talented actor. I bought into his disbelief."

"You heard the evidence against him."

"I certainly see that the current evidence shows he is the prime mover behind everything," Kep said. "But I must say, his reaction to your call has sprouted a seed of doubt in my mind."

Bernadette shook her head. "If not him, then who? We've been over the other members of the board—none of them have the skills or the money to make this happen. Marnie was shot at. Leopold Montclair is dead. Freddy Montclair is probably dead too."

"What about Andy Belgrade?"

Bernadette sighed. "A ghost FBI agent who signed off on Joanna's purchase req? I suppose it's a possibility."

A sharp intake of breath from Kep.

"Even Lesley calls him a ghost—"

"No, no, stop, stop—" Kep said, grabbing the handle above the passenger window.

The car crested a hill—and a large, white concrete building loomed in front of them. A stop sign appeared on the right. It was the end of the road. Bernadette slammed on the brakes and spun the steering wheel. The car swung onto the two-lane road, tires squealing as she blew through the intersection. She passed a sign that read *Welcome to Las Moredades* and a *Speed Limit 25 MPH* sign.

Kep wiped his brow. "Almond Avenue, coming up on your right."

"I didn't keep Niehaus on the phone nearly long enough," Bernadette grumbled. "I should have let him string me along. He was willing to play dumb. I could have gone for a few more minutes. I could have told him I found the encryption key, or given him that whole tokenization-versus-encryption explanation that Lesley gave me. Maybe I could have asked what all the money was for."

"If we're wrong about Annika, perhaps she heard you had discovered the bank account information." Kep braced himself for the next turn. "And perhaps she contacted Niehaus to let him know."

"So Niehaus would know I was just trying to buy time."

"Perhaps." Kep pushed his glasses up on his nose. "Take your next left."

A moment of silence passed between them before Bernadette piped up. "I never told you thank you."

"For what?"

"For calling in a favor with that producer friend of yours. He must think he owes you big."

Kep nodded. "*Cases That Won't Die* made him tens of millions of dollars. But he will ask me to return the favor soon enough." He pointed. "You'll make another left at the next street, then it's the property at the end. Gated—we'll need to talk to the agent guarding the gate."

Bernadette exhaled in relief. "Did I mention what Maura's plan is?"

"No, I don't believe so."

"She reassigned all the agents out except one—Xavier Reese. He's the agent who met me and Sophie at the Milwaukee airport."

"For what purpose?"

"Trying to find the leak," Bernadette said. "She said there's only five people she told about the safehouse, and she told all of them she was moving Sophie and Barlow."

Kep inclined his head. "But Sophie and Barlow are still here?"

"Right. Maura gave different location information to each of the people she told before. Only Maura, Lesley, and I—and Agent Reese—know that Sophie and Barlow are still here."

"And now me." Kep sat back in his seat. "How are we supposed to get past the agent? The one who I assume will provide security at the gate?"

"What do you mean?"

"I assumed we would show the guard our CSAB identification, and that you would be let through on the basis of your familial relationship with Sophie. But if these guards all believe that Sophie isn't Sophie, we'll need another story to provide the agent guarding the safehouse."

Bernadette blinked. "Yes, I suppose that's true."

"Lieutenant Stevenson may be able to enlighten us."

"She might not have thought of that either." Bernadette pulled to the side of the road. She was in a hurry, but they had to know how to get past the gate. Kep was already tapping on his phone. He put the speakerphone on, and the line rang on the other side.

"Dr. Woodhead?" Maura's voice sounded tired. Of course it did—it was past midnight on the east coast. "What is it? Have you arrived at the safehouse yet?"

"We are perhaps three hundred yards away," Kep said. "However, I've just been informed that the people in the safehouse no longer have the same identities."

"You said you gave the new CSAB agents a story about

them being cartel witnesses," Bernadette said. "So how will they know to let us in?"

"Agent Xavier Reese will meet you at the gate," Maura said. "He will recognize you both."

"I'll be happy to meet Agent Reese again," Bernadette said, and paused. "And thank you for keeping me on this case. I'm—I need to see Sophie."

Maura was quiet for a moment, then muttered, "You're welcome."

Ugh. Maura was going way out on a limb for Bernadette. Going against protocol. Bernadette pressed her lips together. That "you're welcome" carried foreboding. Someone would get disciplined for Bernadette's behavior. But she'd take the heat for Maura, even if it spelled the end of her CSAB career.

Maybe that was okay. Sophie and Barlow didn't want Bernadette to keep her job, anyway.

"I can't let Dr. Woodhead stay with you, however," Maura continued. "The official word is that you're replacing Agent Thomas Delancey at the safehouse. Delancey will be relieved of this assignment and will take Dr. Woodhead to the restaurant where law enforcement will take Jeremy Niehaus into custody. We need someone familiar with the Parr Medical case to ask the right questions."

Kep and Bernadette shot a look at each other.

"So Agent Delancey must get Dr. Woodhead on the road as quickly as possible," Maura said. "You think I would leave the interrogation of Jeremy Niehaus up to Puckett or Durango?"

"Puckett and Durango are leading the Niehaus team?"

"Who else am I going to use?"

But—but *I'm* Kep's case analyst, thought Bernadette, glancing at Kep.

Kep folded his arms. He'd been sitting on a plane for five hours, then sitting in a car for twenty minutes, and now another two-hour drive ahead of him. At least CSAB paid him well.

"Thanks, Maura."

"Call with an update after Dr. Woodhead leaves, Bernadette."

"Will do."

Kep tapped the screen, and the call ended.

A minute later, the road ended at a tall chain-link fence, surrounded by a few tall gnarled oaks. Bernadette's headlights cast eerie shadows on the ground, gentle hills sloping up on either side of the driveway past the fence.

The chain-link fence had two large gates: one aligned with the driveway, supposedly for cars to come in, and a smaller pedestrian gate at the side of the car gate.

Bernadette saw no one, either standing in front of or behind the fence.

"How do we proceed?" asked Kep.

"I'm not sure," Bernadette said. "I don't see Agent Reese. Maybe he didn't get Maura's message yet."

"Perhaps it takes longer than seven minutes for Agent Reese to get from the safehouse to the gate."

"Even if that were true, I thought the gate was under guard twenty-four-seven. *Someone* should be at the gate."

"It's conceivable that the guard is walking the perimeter of the property. Or perhaps is investigating a secondary issue."

Bernadette caught movement out of the corner of her eye and pointed to the other side of the fence. "Behind the tree."

"Or perhaps he is relieving himself."

A man dressed in black stepped out from behind one of the gnarled oaks and walked toward their car. He lifted the heavy metal latch of the pedestrian gate and with a little effort, pulled it open and stepped through.

Bernadette rolled down her window.

"Can I help you?" the man said. As he came closer, the headlights illuminated him better. Wiry. Light skin—probably white, though in this light, it was hard to tell. Short hair—possibly a buzz cut—under a black baseball cap. Five foot four, perhaps. Dressed in a black long-sleeve tee shirt and black trousers, almost like combat gear. Black boots. A shoulder holster worn to show off his gun—not strictly recommended for agents, but in an informal setting like this, Reese might have okayed it. A small communications radio on his belt. Again, unusual, but not out of the realm of approved wear for FBI or CSAB agents.

But he wasn't anyone Bernadette had seen before—and he certainly wasn't Xavier Reese. Maybe Kep was right, and it was taking Reese longer to get to the front gate.

Bernadette pulled her CSAB identification out of her purse and held it up so the guard could see the badge, but hopefully not be able to make out Bernadette's name. "I was told to meet Agent Xavier Reese here."

"And you are?"

"Swapping places with Agent—" Bernadette reached for the name. "Agent Thomas Delancey," she said. "He's supposed to drive my colleague here to Sacramento."

The guard frowned. "Hold on just a moment, please." He stepped away from the vehicle, taking his radio off his belt. On his forearm, a tattoo of three stars and a wolf silhouette.

The click of the radio going on, the crackle of static,

but Bernadette couldn't hear any of the conversation. The voice was low—probably a man. Made sense. He was probably communicating with Reese. Any moment now, Reese would come down the driveway from the safehouse and let them in.

Kep reached out and placed a hand on Bernadette's arm. "I don't like this," he said.

"Yeah, it's unexpected."

"Our friend has the distinct odor of a Mexican-style lager called Soledad de Reloj. A fairly popular brand locally, I believe."

"He's drunk?"

"He was drunk last night," Kep said. "I can detect the scent on his skin."

"But that's preposterous," Bernadette said. "No agent would let—"

Kep's grip tightened on her arm. "I know."

Then it hit her.

Only one person could pull a team together with someone who had that tattoo: three stars—like the belt in the Orion constellation—and a wolf silhouette.

Only one person could pull a team together with someone who had that tattoo: three stars—like the belt in the Orion constellation—and a wolf silhouette.

Jeremy Niehaus wasn't behind the threat to Sophie. It was Andy Belgrade—the leader of the Orion Wolfpack.

Bernadette had it all wrong: Jeremy Niehaus hadn't been using Freddy Montclair as an excuse to do his bidding—it was the other way around. Niehaus had puffed out his chest and pontificated and been noisy, and Freddy had flown under the radar. He wasn't dead in the Cuyahoga River or on the side of Interstate 71. The pieces slid together. Fred was *running the whole operation.*

Fred Montclair was Andy Belgrade.

Everything fell into place in Bernadette's head.

Fred could have easily convinced his brother to use his millions to advance the cause of the FBI. Access to chemicals, access to hospitals. Bernadette wondered if Leopold had set up Annika's plastic surgery under the ruse that he'd been helping his country so that an undercover agent couldn't be traced. Had Leopold simply been duped, thinking he was helping the FBI when he was really helping his brother kill people, making it look like Parr Medical was behind the murders?

Because even if Parr Medical hadn't murdered all those scientists or Kep's son, they still had been responsible for hundreds, maybe even thousands, of deaths. Including Fred's own daughter, dead from a drug that should never have been on the market in the first place: fenezamil. And one of the first people Fred—or Belgrade—had killed was the FDA inspector who took the bribes to get fenezamil on the market.

Another click in Bernadette's head. Belgrade had been the owner of the hazardous disposal company who had taken the bromeladine from the suede company. But he knew bromeladine was a byproduct of the ED medication manufacturing process, so he could easily shift the blame to Parr Medical. He'd known he would kill Leopold for a long time.

And working as Andy Belgrade, Fred had spearheaded the raid at Platinum Prime, bribing witnesses and planting evidence that Jeremy Niehaus was responsible for many of the murdered people CSAB had found on that SD card.

Oh—the SD card. The hit list on Annika's SD card had been copied from somewhere before it landed on Annika's SD card inside that gusle. The hit list *wasn't* from Parr

Medical. It was a list of Andy Belgrade's targets. And Belgrade was working with Joanna.

That's why Joanna's banking information had been in the spreadsheet—because *Joanna* had created the spreadsheet.

With that realization, more puzzle pieces slipped into place: the purchase requisition for the recording equipment, the money siphoned out of Leopold's account—it was all a long con by an FBI ghost agent, one who only existed on the margins. Part revenge for his daughter's death, and part billion-dollar embezzlement. And Bernadette and Kep had screwed up all of Freddy Montclair's carefully laid plans.

"It's Fred," Bernadette whispered. It felt like she'd been thinking for an hour, but it was only a second or two.

"Fred?"

"Andy Belgrade. It's not Jeremy Niehaus—Andy Belgrade is Ferdinand Montclair. And he killed Leopold."

Kep's jaw fell open.

"And we have more immediate concerns." Bernadette motioned with her head to the guard in conversation on the walkie-talkie. "This man isn't part of Agent Reese's crew. He's a member of Orion's Wolfpack. And when that guard is done chattering, I suspect he's going to shoot both of us."

Chapter Twenty-Five

KEP BLINKED. Neither of them had weapons. They were sitting ducks.

Bernadette took a deep breath. "The Orion's Wolfpack team must have overpowered the CSAB agents."

"Perhaps." The veins in Kep's neck tightened.

"Sophie and Barlow are still in danger."

"As are we."

Bernadette looked up toward the guard. He was still deep in conversation on his walkie-talkie, talking in hushed but aggravated tones. They didn't have much time.

Bernadette reached up to the dome light and clicked it off.

"What are you doing?" Kep hissed.

"The best bad option." Bernadette grabbed the door handle and gently pulled it. The door mechanism clicked loudly, and she sucked in a breath, glancing at the guard, still with his back to her. He didn't turn, but now his voice raised in volume, and he gestured with his arms.

"If the feds know where these two are, they'll expect them to check in," the guard said.

Bernadette pushed the door wider. No creaking noise. No light from the car.

"And if they don't check in, how long do you think it will take before someone else comes looking for them?"

The radio crackled on the other end, but Bernadette couldn't hear the response.

She looked at the ground between the car and the dead end. Mostly asphalt. No sidewalks out here, but there was a concrete footpath from the dead end to the gate, and the guard stood on the footpath in front of the wide-open pedestrian gate.

Bernadette swung her feet out of the car, her flats clicking softly on the asphalt.

That wouldn't do. She wouldn't be able to sneak up on him.

Dammit.

She pushed the sleeves of her blazer up to her elbows. She could run like this. Then she slipped her flats off and placed them softly in the wheel well. She took a deep breath: pebbles, some of them sharp. And her bare feet weren't rough; she'd definitely feel every poke and pinch.

But this was her only shot to save her life. And Kep's life.

And Sophie.

She narrowed her eyes at the guard as she rose from the driver's seat. Immediately, a small rock cut into the instep of her foot, sending a bolt of pain up her calf. She gritted her teeth. She'd worked through the emotional pain in Wichita, seeing her partner get blown apart right in front of her. Surely she could stand running in bare feet across the asphalt for five or ten seconds.

She put her left foot in front, tested her weight on her

right foot. Good thing she'd worn a pantsuit and not a skirt.

"Just like my eight-minute mile on the Riverwalk," she muttered.

She burst into a sprint.

Pebbles on the asphalt. Shooting pain from her feet up her calves. But she pushed through it. She raced toward the guard.

Another crackle on the radio and the guard spoke again. "Yeah, okay. I'll let you know when it's done." He released the button on the radio and turned around—

And Bernadette turned her shoulder and launched herself into the guard at full speed.

Her shoulder crashed into his chest. Sharp intake of breath. Bernadette's knee came up and found his groin.

He left his feet for a split second and his body fell straight, no arms or legs splayed to break his fall.

Bernadette landed on top of him, her right elbow at his throat, her right hand reaching for the gun in his holster.

The guard's head bounced on the concrete walkway with a sickening *crack*.

Then, nothing. The bottoms of Bernadette's feet prickled. A few pebbles stuck there, maybe, but it didn't feel like she'd broken the skin.

The guard didn't move.

Bernadette pushed herself up, sliding her legs onto his arms, and rose into a sitting position. His eyes were closed, and he was motionless.

She'd knocked him out for sure. He hadn't been expecting it and the slamming of his head on the sidewalk had been fortuitous. And Kep was right: she could detect the faint scent of stale beer. She reached for his throat to feel for a pulse.

Nothing.

Good.

Bernadette recoiled slightly at her reaction. She'd made a split-second decision based on Kep's warning. Now the man under her was dead.

What if Kep had been wrong? What if he was an FBI agent? What if he had been on the radio with Xavier Reese?

Bernadette rolled off the body onto her hands and knees and vomited into the dry bushes next to the walkway.

After a moment, she caught her breath, then spat. She took a deep breath, her breath making her gag again, but she got herself under control and pulled the guard's gun from the shoulder holster. A Winterfield 300S. Not an agency-issued gun. Whatever this guy had been, it wasn't an FBI or CSAB agent.

She checked the magazine. It was full—nine bullets.

She searched his pockets. No identification. She hadn't expected any. Another magazine, though, also with nine bullets. She dropped the magazine into the inside pocket of her blazer.

Footsteps running toward her from behind. She stood quickly, gun in hand—

Kep.

He held her flats in his left hand. "Do you need—"

"He's dead," Bernadette said, taking her shoes from Kep and putting them back on. "It's starting to make sense."

"What is?"

Bernadette lowered her voice. "The message from Joanna's email address threatening Sophie."

"Professional hackers," Kep murmured.

Bernadette shook her head. "Wouldn't have needed to come from Joanna's email to make me pay attention to a death threat to Sophie. But think about it: if you already *had* access to Joanna's email, then sending the threat from her would seem obvious."

"I see. You believe that Andy Belgrade—Fred—had access to Joanna's email?"

"A ghost agent working with a rogue agent," Bernadette said. "Just one of them might not get away with everything they got away with, but if they were working closely together, they could have covered for each other."

"I don't believe that anyone in the FBI would allow another agent to have access to their email."

"I don't know," Bernadette said. "If Joanna held the bank account info, I've got to assume Joanna and Fred must have been close. Business partners, lovers, maybe both. Close enough to have access to each other's money means close enough to have access to each other's email."

Kep swallowed hard, closed his eyes, and clenched his fists. "What is our course of action now?"

"Call Lesley. Tell her the safehouse has been compromised." Bernadette brushed off the bottoms of her feet with her hands, then put her shoes back on. "And we don't know if the CSAB agents inside are dead or alive—"

"But we can tell Lesley the identity of Andy Belgrade," Kep said, opening his eyes again. "I shall return as soon as possible. I left the phone in the center console of the car."

He turned—

Bang.

Bernadette grabbed Kep and pulled him down.

"What was that?"

"Someone shot at us," Bernadette whispered. "We need to move."

The echo of the gunshot through the trees—Bernadette didn't know where the shot had come from. But Sophie was inside the gate. She had to be.

She pushed Kep to a half-standing position and grabbed his elbow, pushing him through the open pedestrian gate.

"Are you crazy?" Kep hissed. "The gunshot came from—"

"I know," Bernadette said. "But Sophie's in the house."

Another shot. This time, a ping on the fence only inches above their heads. They both dropped to their knees and scooted farther away from the bright headlights of the car.

"Over there," Kep said, pointing to a dark glen of trees. Bernadette could barely make it out in the darkness.

Bernadette looked to her left. She hadn't been able to see it in the shadows, but the shrubs and bushes next to the fence were three or four feet high. Seemed to go on for the length of the fence, as well.

"Stay low," Bernadette said. "Stay between the bushes and the fence. Crawl if you have to."

"How far should I go?"

"As far as you can without making a lot of noise," Bernadette said. "Don't look back. Don't check on me. Keep yourself safe. If you can get to a phone without making yourself known, do it."

"But I—"

"Just go, Kep."

"What will you—"

"*Just go.*"

Kep nodded and crawled between the bushes and the fence. No shots. That was good.

A rustling sound from the glen of trees. The shooter might be trying to get a better look.

She'd have to help him out.

Bernadette felt along the ground. A handful of acorns. All right, that would do. She closed her hand, getting four, maybe five acorns, and keeping as still and quiet as she could, threw them in the opposite direction of the fence, over the cast of the headlights. Fifty or sixty feet. Not too loud, but it sounded like a couple of people snapping twigs and branches as they scuttled through the underbrush.

The best part: it was on the other side of the car. If the shooter wanted to investigate, Bernadette might see him illuminated by the headlights.

And the shooter might not know Bernadette was armed.

Her eyes were slowly adjusting to the surrounding darkness, and straight ahead, down the driveway, perhaps two hundred yards, was a house.

Dark—no outside lights on, no windows—perhaps blackout curtains. Keeping secret from the outside world.

Bernadette felt it in her bones; that's where Sophie was. Whether she was now being held hostage or hiding from the attackers. Whether Agent Reese was with her or if he'd been killed or injured trying to protect her. Barlow, too.

But what if Sophie had been...

No. Bernadette wouldn't allow herself to think like that.

She waited and listened.

A snap of a twig in the glen. Then a glint of light, about four feet off the ground. A gun? She stared at where the glint was, then some motion several feet to the right. Yes, the shooter was trying to figure out where that noise had come from, thinking the acorns were Bernadette and Kep.

She placed one knee on the ground. Despite the dryness of the day, the ground here was damp, and Bernadette's knee sank slightly into the wet earth. She braced herself with the other leg, in an L shape, her foot in front of her. Then rested her right hand, holding the Winterfield handgun on her left arm which rested on her leg. Solid. Just like they'd taught her at the CSAB training academy. Just like she'd done the last time she'd taken target practice at the range.

She tried to keep her eyes in focus, but with the darkness, she wasn't sure what she was looking at. Then she saw him.

He was dressed in all black, an overshirt and tactical trousers, with a black beanie pulled down over his ears. Much too hot for this summer night. The man was white, his face covered in stubble. He was much larger than the guard, maybe six-three or six-four. The man faced Bernadette's right, bobbing his head to locate the noise. He'd taken cover behind a tree—effective cover if Bernadette had been in the location where the acorns had landed.

She took aim.

The shooter continued to bob his head, trying to get a better look.

Even though she'd killed both Joanna and the guard in the last few weeks, she wasn't sure she'd ever get used to it. She blinked, steadied her hand, lined up the shot.

Bernadette squeezed the trigger.

The shooter's head popped to the side, then he sank down into the brush, out of sight.

Bernadette closed her eyes. The sound of gunshots would attract other people, and it might even force the hand of the people who'd compromised the safehouse. Bernadette had to move, and she had to move now. She stayed as still as possible, listening. Were the two men she had just killed the only two guards outside? But nothing— no rustling of leaves, no footsteps.

She hesitated for a moment, then rushed forward toward the glen of trees, where she had seen the shooter fall. Bernadette tried to be quiet, but her flats crunched twigs under her feet. She almost tripped over the body, but stopped just in time. Bernadette looked down; the man's arms and legs were angled awkwardly. She crouched, looking for the gun the man had been holding, and found it several feet farther away—it must have flown out of his hand with the force of the gunshot. Picking it up— another Winterfield 300S—Bernadette put the safety on. She tried to put the gun in her left blazer pocket, but it was too big; the gun wouldn't stay put.

Then a crackle. "Bravo-three, come in."

Which one of them had been bravo-three? And could she pretend to be one of them? Probably not. Her voice was too high—not high for a woman's voice, but definitely too high for a man's. She probably couldn't alter her register enough, either.

But she could buy herself some time. Maybe.

Bernadette turned the man on his back—and recoiled at his face. It was the man who'd worn the Kansas State sweatshirt she'd seen weeks before, first in the parking lot at Taycheedah Correctional, then in the photos that Joanna had told her was Darko Divjac. He was certainly the same man who had rigged her rental car with C4. She exhaled through her mouth, steadied herself, then unhooked the radio from the dead man's belt and pushed the button and let it go in rapid succession. A bunch of static, hopefully. They might wait a minute or two to get back in touch. And that might give her enough time to figure out what was going on at the safehouse. A moment went by. Bernadette checked the gun. Seven bullets left in the nine-bullet magazine. She checked his body for any more guns—oh, not a gun, but a hunting knife in a sheath. Even in the low light, she could tell it was of excellent quality. Good heft.

"We didn't get that, Theo. Come again?"

Bernadette nodded. More confident, less whiny. But once she heard it, it was unmistakable: that was the voice of Freddy Montclair—or, perhaps, that confident, less whiny voice belonged to the alter ego of Andy Belgrade.

She repeated the push-and-release on the radio. Where to put the gun? Bernadette didn't have pockets in these trousers, but she could stick it in her waistband until she found Kep.

She had time—at least a little. She debated for a moment—should she keep the radio? Would it give away her location? Then she figured it would be better to have the option. She could always ditch it later.

Then a crackle from the radio.

"Bravo-three. The car took off."

Bernadette blinked. Who was that? Then it clicked in her head. Kep. *He* had modulated his voice. He'd heard the guard's voice and, between the crackling radio and his mimicry, he'd gotten away with it so far.

A pause on the line before another click.

"I thought you were taking care of it." Despite the crackling on the radio, Freddy's voice was clear and loud.

"When I was talking with you, they turned around and left."

"And you didn't go after them?"

"Woulda been more suspicious if I had."

Another moment between clicks. "When I tell you to do something, Theo," the second voice said, "you do it. You don't think about how suspicious it looks, or how you're too chickenshit to kidnap a federal investigator. You said it was a woman and an old guy with a beard?"

"Yeah."

"That's just about the worst situation we could have had." Disdain dripped from the second voice—and Bernadette had a flash of recognition.

But from where? It had been in the last few days.

"Want me to go after them now?" Kep said. Footsteps on concrete in the background. Where was he?

"No, it's too late. And we need her alive, anyway. We can still do what we need with her out there."

A moment passed.

Then the lights, shining their harsh beams on the trees, went dark.

Bernadette's head snapped up. Was that the car's headlights turning off?

Of course. Kep. After hearing the gunshots, he didn't follow Bernadette's instructions to stay between the fence and the bushes. He'd gone back to the car. Where at least there was a phone. Hopefully, he'd picked up the radio after he'd called Maura or Lesley for reinforcements. Though how far away those reinforcements were, Bernadette didn't know.

"Come back to the house, Theo," the second voice said. "Andrei, you too. We've got to move."

Another crackle, followed by Fred's voice. "Delta-two, how much time do you need?"

"They're not going anywhere," a third voice said. "If we need to leave, I'll need twenty minutes and a couple more sets of hands."

Bernadette's jaw dropped open.

The third voice belonged to Agent Xavier Reese.

Chapter Twenty-Six

"Everyone, return to the house," Fred Montclair said. "We need to figure out our next move."

Bernadette crouched next to the dead man's body and checked his pockets. No identification, and just like the dead guard, no keys, either.

Return to the house.

Either Fred had people guarding the entries and exits of the house, or he'd left the doors uncovered. And Reese saying "They're not going anywhere"—obviously referring to Sophie and Barlow. Maybe other agents held against their will. Fred Montclair obviously expected Bernadette and Kep to be traveling together, and he wanted her alive. Kidnapped, perhaps, but if Sophie wasn't alive, he had no leverage against her. She couldn't figure out what he wanted her to do.

Sophie and Barlow were still alive, anyway. That was something, a glimmer of hope.

In the distance, a soft whine of metal hinges. Bernadette stood above the dead body and looked toward the car. The darkness was near complete; a hot, moonless night. Bernadette wiped the sweat from her forehead.

But the sound was unmistakable. Someone was opening the gate in front of the driveway entrance.

She hoped it was Kep. They might be outnumbered. They might have to go into a house they didn't know, find the room with Sophie and Barlow, free them—were they tied up?—and escape.

When Bernadette and Kep had arrived at the safe-house, they'd had no weapons. Now Bernadette had two Winterfield handguns and—she did the math in her head—twenty-five bullets. And they had the car and a couple of phones to call for backup. And they had the radios. That would keep them in touch with Fred.

But they didn't have much time. In five minutes, or ten at the most, Fred would realize that the two men Bernadette had killed wouldn't be returning.

Bernadette had a choice to make: move closer to the house, or go back to the car with Kep? Her feet froze with indecision. There was safety in numbers, even just having Kep, who couldn't shoot or drive. They'd also have the car, and that meant they could get away. But Fred's team would move Sophie and Barlow to another location.

However, Fred only needed *Bernadette* alive, not Kep—at least until he got Joanna's banking information. In fact, reading between the lines, she suspected that the guard's orders were to kill Kep. Bernadette gritted her teeth. She at least had enough time to go back to the car and tell Kep to leave for help. At the very least, Fred would move Sophie and Barlow to a second location, which meant he'd have to leave the house with them. Fred would be the most vulnerable—but he'd also be the most on guard. Especially if Bravo-Two and Bravo-Three weren't back.

Still, she had a little time. And she could save Kep.

She turned toward the gate and began walking as fast as she could. The darkness inhibited her ability to run safely, especially in her flats, with a gun in her waistband and a magazine of bullets in her inside jacket pocket. Nor could she risk being seen by turning her flashlight on.

She tripped over an exposed root and scraped the top of her foot. The barrel of the handgun dug into her upper thigh.

She was at the car a minute later, shrouded in darkness.

"Kep!" A stage whisper.

He stood from behind the car's rear bumper, a long, thick piece of tree branch held in his hand like a baseball bat. "Oh, thank God. I thought it was another guard."

"Are you all right?"

Kep nodded, dropping the branch. "I contacted both Miss Gill and Lieutenant Stevenson. Unfortunately, backup will not be arriving for at least twenty to thirty minutes."

"Is my phone inside the car?"

Kep pulled it out of his pocket and held it out for her. "I did not believe it was prudent to leave it in—"

Bernadette had already tapped Maura's number.

"Bernadette? Are you okay?"

"Reese," Bernadette said. "He's turned."

A slight pause. "No. If—if Xavier's turned, it must be under duress."

"I don't know what to tell you, Maura. I heard his voice myself. He's the one holding Sophie and Barlow. In a room in the safehouse. Reese is working with Fred Montclair."

"Hang on—the victim's *brother*?"

"He's a ghost agent at the FBI who goes by Andy

Belgrade. A few agents who used to be on the Orion Wolf-pack team inside the bureau."

"The Orion Wolfpack?" Maura was incredulous. "They were disbanded years ago."

"And yet."

"You're sure Andy Belgrade's real identity is Fred Montclair? And he's behind this?"

"Not a mild-mannered accountant from Columbus," Bernadette said. "I don't know what else he's responsible for besides kidnapping Sophie and Barlow. Maybe his brother's murder. And maybe everything."

"Everything?"

"All the hired killings we thought Parr Medical did? It might be Andy Bel—it might be Freddy Montclair."

Maura was silent.

"And they'll be moving Sophie and Barlow soon," Bernadette continued. "I've got another few hours to get the banking information to Fred before time runs out."

"Or before we capture him," Maura said.

"So let's get him." Bernadette wiped the sweat from her forehead. "When they move Sophie, they'll be at their most vulnerable. I can wait for them. I might be able to take a couple of them out and get Sophie and Barlow to safety."

"I can assist," Kep said.

"Absolutely not, Kep," Bernadette said. "Fred needs me alive. Sure, it's dangerous, but you can't—" She stopped. There was no easy way to say it, and their safety was more important than his feelings. "You can't shoot, and you can't drive. You're more of a liability if you go in with me."

A buzz on the radio. Reese's voice. "Andrei, you copy? I need some help with the kid."

The kid. That was Sophie.

"Get out of here, Kep." Bernadette clicked the button on the radio on and off a couple of times again. Hopefully, they'd think Andrei's radio needed new batteries.

"I'm not leaving," he said. "I will stay out of your way, but you need the car. You are unarmed."

"I took two guns off the guards," Bernadette said.

"You're not going in," Maura said.

Bernadette turned to Kep. "See?"

"Not him," Maura said. "You."

"Me?"

"The safehouse has multiple exits and a tunnel that goes under the Sacramento River. Agent Reese knows where they are. If he's working for Fred Montclair, he'll most certainly use the tunnel and one of the six exit points. We simply don't have the resources to cover all of them."

"When was the last time you talked to Agent Reese?"

"An hour ago," Maura answered. "After Dr. Woodhead told us of the combatants on the property, we thought Agent Reese had been captured or killed."

"Aha," Kep said. "'We can play such fantastic tricks before high heaven.'"

Bernadette closed her eyes. Not the time for another Shakespeare quote.

"Agent Reese does not know we are aware he has turned," Kep said. "Perhaps you can contact him and feed him false information."

"I see," Maura replied. "And do you have an idea of what we can—"

Kep pushed his glasses up on his nose. "As you said, you would have considered sneaking Ms. Becker into the safehouse and getting her family to safety through the tunnel. Do the same with Agent Reese."

"Tell him to send Sophie and Barlow through the tunnel?"

"Yes." Kep scratched his beard. "Does he know of your resource constraints?"

"Of course."

"Then state that you could get local sheriffs' offices involved. Perhaps S.W.A.T. teams. Say that it doesn't matter which exit they take—dozens of law enforcement personnel will be at each exit."

"The nearest S.W.A.T. team is over an hour away."

"But Agent Reese doesn't know that, does he?"

Maura was silent for a moment. "And that will force them out of the house through the front door?"

"Backup will be here in roughly twenty minutes, correct?"

"As far as I know." Maura hesitated. "But I don't want to get into a shootout with two hostages' lives at stake."

"I don't either, Maura," Bernadette said. "They don't want to kill me—not until I give Fred the banking information, anyway. Tell Reese he's safe because he's surrounded by police, and then let me get Sophie and Barlow out of there."

"How do you propose to do that?"

"I can get them to the car," Bernadette said. "Or if that's not available, back into the house and out through the tunnel."

Silence for a moment. "There's another way, too," Maura said. "There's a barn behind the property. In the northwest corner, there's a trapdoor. That leads down into a different tunnel, but one that comes up on this side of the river by the Veterans Hall. It's not a great option—too exposed. There aren't any other options, either, if they've blocked the exit."

"So you think Reese knows about that tunnel, too?"

"No. We only told the agents about the secret exits in the house, not in the barn."

"If you're feeding Agent Reese misinformation," Kep said, "tell him you had an agent who took out two of his guards but was killed in the exchange of gunfire. That will buy a little more time, and it'll explain why two of Fred's men aren't arriving back at the safehouse."

"This is assuming Agent Reese will even pick up his phone," Maura said.

"It's worth trying," Bernadette said.

"Are there cameras around the house?" Kep asked.

"Of course."

"Is the footage visible to those inside?"

"Yes."

"Do you have remote access to the cameras?"

"Hold on," Maura said. A tapping of the keyboard. Maura swore under her breath. More tapping. "They disabled the cameras a little over an hour ago."

"Probably so the agents inside couldn't see the attack coming," Bernadette said.

"But no one's turned the cameras back on," Maura said. "Could be they physically damaged them."

"The absence of cameras," Kep said. "That's how we were able to infiltrate the perimeter without alerting anyone in the house."

"I'll text you back," Maura said. "Five minutes. Keep your ringers off. Totally silent—no vibration mode either."

"Of course," Bernadette replied.

Maura ended the call.

"Okay," Bernadette said to Kep. "I can take it from here. You're right, I need the car, but you can get out of here. Probably only a ten or twenty-minute walk to the highway and to the town itself. Take your phone. Make a call when you're out there and you can get picked up."

"I'm not leaving, Bernadette." He pointed to his nose. "I can sense danger. I can be valuable."

"You're more likely to get yourself killed."

"Let me worry about that."

"I'm your case analyst, Kep—it's *my* job to worry about that."

Kep folded his arms. "You'll need a second person when Fred Montclair and Reese—and whoever else is in there—comes out with Sophie and Barlow. Someone to create a distraction. Someone to lead Sophie and Barlow to safety while you fight the others. Assuming, of course, you don't get captured yourself."

Bernadette opened her mouth to argue, but decided she didn't have time. She pointed toward the house. "I'll push the car up the driveway toward the house, turn it around. When Fred and Reese open the door, I'll—I'll shoot them, I guess. Tell Sophie and Barlow to duck. Tell them to get to the car. Then I'll drive like hell until we're out of range of their guns."

"Maura said to use the tunnel."

"The tunnel is within range of their guns. I'll have better luck in a car."

Kep shook his head. "You can't do that all by yourself."

"You have a better idea?" But as soon as the words were out of Bernadette's mouth, she knew: yes, he *did* have a better idea.

And as Bernadette reached to silence her phone, it buzzed in her hand.

MAURA

> Reese bought it all. Hook, line, and
> sinker.

❧

A black SUV stood at the top of the driveway, backed in. Bernadette crept around the back bumper of the vehicle. No one was behind the wheel.

The safehouse was still shrouded in darkness. No porch lights or patio lights. No lights visible through the windows, either—they'd put up all the safehouse blackout curtains. Perhaps a shrewd move—they certainly made sure that no one could see into the house. But with the cameras disabled, those inside couldn't see out, either.

Voices from inside, but everything was muffled. Sounded angry, disagreeing. Trouble in paradise. Agent Reese had likely given Fred Montclair all the misinformation that Maura had fed him. And in the absence of real-time feedback because of the broken cameras, they were arguing about what to do.

The front porch was only a few yards away from the black SUV. Bernadette took the sheathed knife from her other blazer pocket, pulled it from its covering, and sank it into the left front tire. She had to work to pull the knife out, and when she did, the hiss of the air seemed so loud it would wake any slumbering wild animals in the area. But no—nothing, and after a minute, the hissing volume lowered. She crept around the front and did the same with the other front tire, a strong initial burst of air joining the rapidly weakening hiss of the first tire.

Bernadette walked slowly toward the front porch, heel first, then arch, then ball of her foot, then toe. It was awkward, but she minimized the sound of her flats on the rough asphalt driveway. Her eyes had adjusted to the darkness, but the stars were out, lending at least a modicum of light to the area around the house.

She'd have an advantage here: her eyes had adjusted to the darkness; Fred and Reese and whoever else was inside: they were likely standing in a brightly lit kitchen or living room, arguing over how they should get out of the safehouse.

Oh—and Reese had asked specifically for Andrei—that was the shooter Bernadette had shot in the head. Reese had said earlier that he needed two or three extra hands to deal with Sophie and Barlow. If there had been another two or three people inside, maybe he wouldn't have called for Andrei. That meant only one or two more bad guys in the house besides Fred and Reese.

Assumes facts not in evidence. She could hear Kep in her head. But she had to be smart. Play the odds. She couldn't afford to wait to have every scenario dealt with, every base covered. She had one handgun and two full magazines. Bernadette gripped the hunting knife tighter in her left hand.

The corner of the house provided suitable cover, and there was no railing on the porch, so she could get to it fast.

The arguing voices got louder. They were coming toward the front door.

The doorknob jostled, a rattle inside—maybe a chain lock being disengaged. A deadbolt, then another deadbolt sliding open.

Bernadette inhaled and held her breath.

The front door swung open.

The six-foot-eight hulking form of Agent Xavier Reese appeared in the doorway, then took a step onto the porch.

Behind him a girl, a black canvas bag over her head, her wrists zip-tied together.

Bernadette's chest caught. Sophie.

From the other side of the trees, gunshots.

Bang.

Bang.

Bang.

Sophie screamed—and the door slammed shut, catching Reese outside. He flinched and pulled a pistol out, then turned on the porch to face the sound of the gunshots. Showing his back to Bernadette.

She lunged forward and drove the hunting knife hard into the left side of his back. Reese gasped, dropped his gun, and tried to reach behind him to grab the knife, grab his assailant, grab whatever he could.

Even though Bernadette was strong, Agent Reese was stronger. But Bernadette grunted and dug in, holding fast to the knife, and Reese couldn't turn his body. He opened his mouth, but only a squeak came out—and his flailing got weaker and weaker with each passing second.

Sophie kept screaming.

"Shut up! Shut up!" Fred Montclair appeared in the doorway, hair sticking up on the crown of his head. He raised his hand, holding a handgun, and caught Sophie with a blow to the head—hard to see where under the canvas bag.

Sophie's shoulder banged against the door frame with the blow. Bernadette saw red.

She took a step forward, biceps and quads screaming with the exertion of pushing Agent Reese forward.

Fred Montclair turned and saw Reese, opening and

closing his mouth like a fish—and began to laugh, a cruel, harsh sound.

Until the realization dawned on his face.

Bernadette raised her gun and fired.

And missed.

Fred jumped back into the house, scuttling down the hall.

Then another body came flying at Bernadette—another person with his head encased in a black canvas bag.

Barlow.

He fell into Bernadette with his entire weight—and she tumbled onto the porch. From the lighted hall inside, she saw Fred escape into the reaches of the house. Dammit.

Then a blur of motion as another man stepped between the hall light and Bernadette. And was holding a shotgun. The second voice.

Bernadette shut her eyes. How appropriate that she'd go out the same way as Declan. A shotgun blast tearing her body apart. Not as a hero, but as a case analyst who went off book, off the beaten path. She hoped Barlow and Sophie would live. That backup would get here soon.

A gunshot.

Bernadette waited for the searing pain—but nothing came.

Oh—that was a handgun, not a shotgun.

Flat on her back, Bernadette opened her eyes. Barlow still lying on top of her. Still breathing. Shuddering breaths, fear wracking his body, but still alive. She raised her head.

The man wasn't there anymore.

Bernadette pushed herself up a little more, her abdominals straining with the weight of her ex-husband. The man with the shotgun was sitting in an awkward position on the floor, a red bullet-sized hole in his forehead that was dripping blood down his face. His eyes, open and unseeing, stared above Bernadette's head.

She tilted her head back to look at the front of the porch.

An upside-down Kep. Still holding the Winterfield 300S at arm's length. Even Bernadette could smell the tang of glycerine in the air.

"Dammit, Kep. I told you to stay next to the fence. Out of sight. Three shots into the ground. I didn't want you playing hero."

Kep dropped his arms. "You're welcome."

"Where'd you learn to shoot like that?" Bernadette said.

"You'll notice I shot from close range," Kep said, his voice wavering. "And, perhaps, I received a healthy dose of good luck."

Bernadette pushed Barlow off and scrambled to her feet. "Thank you." She pulled the bag off Barlow's head. His hair was crazily sticking out in all directions, and he smelled of stale sweat. Bernadette pushed him off as he blinked, and she pulled herself into a sitting position.

Kep grasped Bernadette's hand and helped her to her feet.

Bernadette rushed to Sophie's side and pulled the canvas bag off her head. Her eyes were puffy, and she had a lump below her right eye that had swollen.

"Quick," Bernadette said, "you two go with Dr. Wood-head to the barn. There's a path to safety in there."

"Mom?" Sophie said weakly.

"I love you, honey," Bernadette said, hugging her. "I missed you so much. I'm so sorry all this happened."

"I told you, Dad," Sophie said shakily. "I told you Mom would come."

Bernadette pulled Sophie closer. Fred Montclair was getting away—he was probably already in the tunnels. But she wanted just another five seconds with her daughter.

"Go," Bernadette said, urgency in your voice. "Get to the barn."

Barlow held up his hands; they were zip-tied together. The plastic had cut into his wrists, and his skin was raw and red.

Bernadette stepped toward the body of Xavier Reese, slumped forward on the porch, legs positioned awkwardly behind him. She pulled the knife; it stuck for a moment, but then Bernadette got it out. Blood on her blazer.

She turned to Barlow, slightly green. He recoiled from the bloody knife.

Bernadette rolled her eyes. "Do you want the zip ties off or not?"

He nodded and held his hands out, and Bernadette carefully stuck the knife between Barlow's wrists.

"Hold still."

He shut his eyes.

Bernadette pulled up and the zip tie sliced neatly apart.

"Now you," Bernadette said to Sophie, who obediently put her wrists out. She was out of her bonds seconds later.

"Okay," Bernadette said. "Now go."

"You're not coming with us?" asked Sophie.

"I've got to catch one more bad guy," Bernadette said.

"Let him go," Kep said. "You don't know if there's anyone still in the house. Or in the tunnels."

"I can't, Kep," Bernadette said. "If Fred Montclair gets away—"

"He doesn't have access to the resources at Parr Medical."

"You don't know that. And even without access to Joanna's Cayman Islands bank accounts, he could have millions of dollars, and he'll move to a country without an extradition treaty, and he'll hire killers for you and me until he gets us." Bernadette checked the magazine in the gun. Still full. "That's no way to live. And we *won't* live."

Sophie's eyes crinkled, on the verge of tears.

"I'll be back as soon as I can, sweetie."

"You just got here!" Sophie's eyes were wide, brimming with tears.

Then from inside, a shotgun blast.

Bernadette pulled Sophie down as the window next to the front door exploded.

Bernadette dropped to a crouch, out of the way of the broken glass. "Everyone okay?"

Sophie turned and nodded, tears streaking her cheeks. Barlow grunted.

"Go!" Bernadette pushed Sophie off the porch, and she landed on her feet on the asphalt driveway. "Get them around the corner!" she shouted at Kep.

He nodded, the color drained from his face.

Kep led Sophie and Barlow around the corner of the house, glass crunching under their first few steps. Toward the barn—and toward the tunnel that would take them to safety.

Bernadette listened closely for footsteps. A handgun versus a shotgun. Fred might have gotten away and someone else might be in the house. She scuttled over next to the door frame and peered inside. The dead man who lay slumped against the wall of the hallway no longer held his shotgun. Someone had taken it—and Bernadette was positive that person was Fred Montclair.

A creak of a floorboard directly on the other side of the wall.

Shit.

Fred sat right next to the doorframe as well, but inside the house instead of outside. Bernadette closed her eyes for a moment and went right back to the cartel house in Wichita, both her and Declan crouched on either side of the front door, and then the blast of the shotgun, Declan's body—

Bernadette opened her eyes. That wouldn't happen to her. She had a life. She had Sophie. And she would get the man who had ordered the death of Kep's son.

Fred was right there, just a few feet away. If he were rich like his brother had been, he probably wouldn't be the kind of person who wanted to get his hands dirty. He wouldn't be trained like the people he hired.

"Bernadette Becker," Fred said, the whininess in his voice gone. "I should have known you'd figure this out."

"You never told me how to get in touch with you for Joanna's encryption key," Bernadette called back. "Figured I had to come deliver it myself."

"Kind of you," Fred said. Then a rustling sound. What was he doing?

"Figured you'd get all of Jeremy and Leopold's money, I guess?"

A smothered laugh. She was right.

"You got your revenge for your daughter, too, didn't you?"

No laugh this time.

"I don't blame you. I'd do the same thing in your shoes.

If you had hurt my daughter, I wouldn't rest until you were dead, either. Since you just threatened her, I only want you arrested."

She thought back to when she was in training—and when other untrained newbies were around her. They all made the same mistake, pouncing on the first sign of trouble they saw.

Bernadette nodded and looked around on the porch. Window glass shards everywhere, though none under her feet—at least, she didn't think there were any under her feet. A big piece of glass, larger than her hand, stuck straight up about three feet to her left, wedged between two slats of the wooden porch.

If she could pick up the big shard of glass without making a sound, then toss it somewhere away from herself, could that distract Fred enough for her to overpower him? Get the shotgun away from him?

Of course, she had no handcuffs, no way to take him into custody. But she'd cross that bridge when she came to it. She gripped the gun tightly in her right hand.

Bernadette held her breath and reached to grab the big shard of glass with her left hand. She could touch the edge of the glass shard, but couldn't grab it, and certainly couldn't do it without cutting the hell out of her fingers.

She leaned over another inch.

Crunch.

It wasn't a big crunch—probably a piece of glass no larger than a pebble—but it was enough.

Bernadette was facing the wrong way, her back to the doorway. She immediately spun around, staying low, her legs pushing forward toward the doorframe.

A flash of color, a glint of metal.

Bernadette fired once, twice. The shotgun twisted in

Fred's hand as he came around the doorframe. Her left shoulder hit the edge of the doorframe and she grabbed the handle of the gun with both hands, firing into the dark mass getting larger and larger.

He screamed in pain, the shotgun falling from his hands, the handle thudding on the wood decking of the porch.

She'd hit him. He was still moving, and she kicked her foot out instinctively.

And caught his ankle.

Fred Montclair fell face-first onto the decking of the porch—right on top of the large glass shard Bernadette had been trying to reach.

A thud as his body landed on the porch. And a hard, sickening gasp.

Chapter Twenty-Seven

Bernadette steadied her gun and trained it on the prone body of Ferdinand Montclair. He was still breathing, but it was clear he needed medical attention. She pulled the phone out of her pocket and called 9-1-1.

"Nine one one, what's your emergency?"

"This is federal investigator Bernadette Becker with the Controlled Substance Analysis Bureau. We have a suspect in custody who's been shot and has lacerations from window glass." She hesitated. "Possibly life-threatening." She gave the address, staring at Fred, watching his back rise and fall with his labored breaths.

When the dispatcher confirmed they were on their way, Bernadette ended the call.

"Ferdinand Montclair, you are under arrest for—" She paused and thought. "For kidnapping and for assault of a federal officer." The murder charges could come later. "You have the right to remain silent—"

Shallow, labored breaths. "You and Dr. Woodhead wrecked everything." Fred tried to push himself up, and Bernadette saw the shard sticking out of his chest.

"How long, Freddy, or Belgrade, or whoever you are? How long did you have Joanna under your thumb?"

His arms shook. "A true partnership," he said. "And you killed her—" Then his arms gave out, and he slipped back down onto his front. He was still.

Bernadette crept around to the front of Fred's body. His eyes were open, but he was no longer breathing. Careful to avoid more glass shards, Bernadette watched where her feet were going. She'd wanted to take Fred alive so he could give her answers. Could he tell them the extent of the damage that Parr Medical had caused? He'd been after the files—could Fred give Kep closure about his son's death? How long had he been Andy Belgrade?

Bernadette pulled herself to her feet. She wanted to join Sophie—maybe she could still reach them before they went into the tunnel—but she couldn't. She entered the house; she had to make sure no one was still in there. Secure the exits into the tunnel. Make sure the house had no surprises, no booby traps.

She'd call 9-1-1 back to have them send the coroner instead of the paramedics.

※

The sheriff's office in Farolillo was stiflingly hot when she entered the building just past one in the morning. Her body clock was still on east coast time—four o'clock.

"Ms. Becker, you can step this way to give your statement."

Bernadette looked at the young sheriff's deputy. Redheaded and freckled, still with the young air of idealism. He couldn't be older than twenty-four. Huh. Closer to Sophie's age than hers.

"Can I see my daughter?"

"Yes, she's just finishing her statement. I'll go get her. Your husband—"

"Ex-husband."

He inclined his head in a slight bow. "Sorry, ma'am. Your *ex*-husband and your colleague should be done in about twenty minutes, then you can give your statement. I'll go fetch your daughter and she'll see you as soon as she can."

Bernadette nodded. She followed the deputy to a small conference room. Her feet hurt; so did her ribs. Bruising all over, probably.

The deputy opened the door, and she entered, taking her laptop bag off her shoulder and placing it on the round beige table.

"Wi-fi?"

The deputy nodded. "We've got an open connection. 'Farolillo'—both the network ID and the password."

Bernadette nodded. Ah, the lax security of rural sheriff's offices.

"I'll be back with your daughter in a few minutes."

The deputy closed the door behind him, and she looked around the room. No one-way mirror, so this wasn't an interrogation. This nightmare was almost over. A two-hour drive to the Sacramento airport and a flight back to Dulles with her daughter, and this would all be behind her. An uninterrupted five or six hours with Sophie, even if Barlow was on the plane next to them.

She called Lesley.

"Bernadette—are you okay?"

Bernadette pressed her lips together. "Sophie's safe. So yes."

"So you won't be surprised to hear that Fred Mont-clair's accountant business is a front."

"No, I'm not."

"And it looks like Fred *was* Andy Belgrade. We dug through Joanna's files again and found a journal. Looks like they'd been working together for at least three years."

"And the Cayman Islands account?"

"I'm still figuring things out, but I see Parr Medical stock being cashed out, then the money transferred into this account—but not from the real authorized users."

"Any hint that Andy Belgrade was the agent who initiated the transactions?"

"The FBI is dragging its feet getting Belgrade's files over to us. I don't think they want to start an interagency war." A flip of pages. "We've made a request for the team known as Orion's Wolfpack."

"Agent Reese was part of that, wasn't he?"

"The document came back to us. Just a sea of redacted paragraphs. But we'll get there."

Bernadette sighed.

"And in Joanna's files, we also uncovered—"

"A bribe to an inspector at the FDA," Bernadette finished. "James Chester, I bet."

"That's right."

"So Annika's spreadsheet *wasn't* Parr Medical's list. It was Andy Belgrade's hit list. And Joanna hid her routing number in the spreadsheet after I gave her the file." Bernadette frowned. "Belgrade had the FDA inspector killed, then set up everyone responsible for that bribe. Revenge for his daughter, and he set up Parr Medical to take the fall."

"They're all bad guys, Bernadette. Jeremy Niehaus might not have hired killers, but he's responsible for thousands of deaths. He still was behind all the corporate espionage. He kept life-saving medications off the market, or pushed through ones that never should have been approved. All to get more money."

"I guess."

"And Leopold Montclair *did* arrange for Annika's plastic surgery. Going through his PC, we discovered he gave access to his brother."

"If we ever find Annika again, we can ask her why he did it."

"Listen, I've got a lot more research to do, and I've told you everything I know so far. I'll see you when you get back?"

"Sure thing."

They said their goodbyes, and Bernadette sat at the table, staring at the blank wall, then blinked hard. Ugh. She was about to nod off.

The door opened and Sophie ran in. Bernadette was barely out of her chair before Sophie crashed into her in an embrace.

"Hey, Sophie." Bernadette held Sophie tight. When had she gotten so tall? It felt like Bernadette hadn't seen her in a year.

Sophie broke from the embrace first. "You're a little stinky, Mom."

Bernadette looked down. Yes, her clothes were filthy and had bloodstains, too; Freddy's blood, dried into several brown spots on her blouse. Sweaty, messy work. She looked up at her daughter and forced a grin onto her face. "Nothing that can't be fixed with a shower and a change of clothes."

And a margarita.

The shower and change of clothes might have to wait

until D.C. The margarita would be hers at the first airport bar they passed.

"I was worried," Sophie said.

"I was too."

"I don't—" Sophie began, then stopped.

Bernadette pursed her lips. What was Sophie stopping herself from saying? That she didn't want Bernadette to do this work anymore? Well, neither did Bernadette. She could find something in the private sector. Maybe a consulting firm or a think tank. Maybe a boring desk job running background checks on government contractors. She'd hate that, but it would be better than getting shot at.

They talked for a few minutes, but quickly ran out of things to say. And they were both exhausted—Sophie hadn't been out of the safehouse since arriving.

After a minute or two of awkward silence, the door opened, and the redheaded deputy appeared. "Ready to give your statement, Agent Becker?"

"Yes." Bernadette didn't bother to correct him.

"Okay." He cleared his throat. "Sophie, you can wait in the break room. I'll get you a snack."

"I'd love some coffee," Bernadette said.

"Sure, I'll see what I can do."

Sophie reached out for Bernadette's hand and gave it a quick but gentle squeeze. "See you out there?"

Bernadette nodded, and the door closed behind them.

She stretched as her shoulders complained. She'd have a bruise where she smacked into the doorframe. As she sat at the conference table, she reached for her laptop bag and got out her PC. She connected to the network, then brought up the incident form. Better get this out of the way while everything was still fresh in her mind.

A ding from her purse. Bernadette pulled her phone out. A text from—Marnie Synksey?

> Help please a woman came into the safehouse and killed Detective Herrera

Bernadette's eyes went wide.

BERNADETTE

> Are you safe?

MARNIE

> Hiding right now

BERNADETTE

> I'll send help

MARNIE

> Hurry

A moment of horror.

Bernadette told Sophie, and she ran out of the room and into the office bullpen, trying to find someone she could report this to. She stopped the redheaded deputy.

"How is every—"

"Help," Bernadette said, shoving the phone screen first toward him.

The deputy read the text, his eyes grew wide, and he sprang into action.

"I should go—" Bernadette said.

"Absolutely not," the deputy said, a surprising note of power in his voice.

A flurry of activity. They dispatched a sheriff's cruiser. Two other deputies hurried out of the bullpen. She argued she should go there, that it was her case, but the deputies wouldn't let her. And she soon found she was too tired to argue. She slumped in a chair in front of someone's desk. Bernadette closed her eyes for a moment and took a deep breath.

She walked into the break room—and back to Sophie. Yes, there were people who were handling it. She needed to be with her daughter. It was the right move.

"Mom?" Sophie said, rising from her seat, a bag of chips in front of her. "Is everything okay?"

Bernadette smiled, trying to force a calm look onto her face. "You're safe," she said. "And that's what matters."

"But something's going on."

"Yes," she said. "But the police are taking care of it."

Sophie studied Bernadette's face for a moment, then nodded and sat back in her seat.

But how had this happened?

They'd lost track of Marguerite's phone when it was traveling north from the Sacramento airport. Las Moredades was in that direction—and maybe it wasn't Sophie's safehouse Marguerite was headed for.

The redheaded officer stuck his head into the break room. "Ms. Becker?"

"Yes?"

"I thought you'd want to know—Detective Herrera is still alive. On his way to the hospital."

"How is he?"

"Touch and go, they said," the officer said. "Still, better than the alternative."

Lucky. Detective Herrera had probably been in Marguerite's sights and survived. So far, anyway. If she was targeting Marnie—if Marnie had some information Marguerite wanted...

Bernadette smacked the table and stood, pursing her lips.

Marguerite Kerovic was out there somewhere. And so was Annika Nakrivo. Bernadette was willing to bet that Annika had disappeared as soon as they'd landed.

Did Annika and Marguerite know that Fred Montclair —or Andy Belgrade—was dead? Were they working together? Were they extracting some revenge of their own?

Bernadette paced around the circular table. Was she still in danger? Was Sophie? Was Kep?

She crossed her arms and stared at the carpeted floor. She'd thought this entire episode was behind her. But she wasn't safe.

Not yet.

Cast of Characters

THE CORE TEAM

Dr. Kep Woodhead: *A forensic toxicologist in his early fifties, Dr. Woodhead is both an expert in poisons and a "supersmeller"—he can detect and specify scents far beyond the olfactory range of most humans. His brusque manner rubs many people the wrong way, including...*

Bernadette Becker: *A recently demoted case analyst who has been assigned to manage Dr. Woodhead in relevant cases. Becker is Woodhead's fifth "handler" in the last two years. Freshly separated from her husband of nearly fifteen years, Becker is trying to get back on her feet both personally and professionally.*

Lieutenant Maura Stevenson: *Becker's immediate supervisor runs the CSAB Homicide Unit and joins Woodhead and Becker on* *important cases, greasing the wheels with local law enforcement agencies, cutting through red tape, and getting the needed resources.*

Lesley Gill: *The technical analyst working for the CSAB Homicide Unit.*

FRIENDS & FAMILY

Barlow Finnegan*: Bernadette's estranged husband—soon to be ex, when the details of the divorce get ironed out.*

Sophie Finnegan*: Bernadette's twelve-year-old daughter.*

Rochelle and Jenna Van Eckle*: Jenna is Sophie's best friend from school, and Rochelle is Jenna's mother, newly divorced..*

Lisa Rothchild*: Barlow Finnegan's mistress, with whom he now lives.*

Agent Joanna Quimby: *An FBI agent who betrayed Bernadette.*

Officer Lamar Chesapeake: *A Milwaukee police officer, he and Bernadette have been in a long-distance relationship for a few months.*

THE CASE

Leopold Montclair*: A member of Parr Medical's board of directors, he is found dead in his home of a supposed heart attack.*

Detective Bobby Herrera*: The Cleveland*

homicide detective assigned to the Montclair murder case.

Jeremy Niehaus: *The CEO of Parr Medical and colleague of Leopold Montclair.*

Fred Montclair: *Leopold's brother and the executor of his estate.*

Gui Herrera: *A Coast Guard officer who assists in the Montclair murder case.*

Marnie Synskey: *The head of executive services at Parr Medical, and the de facto personal assistant to both Jeremy Niehaus and Leopold Montclair.*

Claude Tristan: *A bank manager at the branch where Leopold Montclair rented a safe-deposit box.*

Walter Markham: *The Cleveland Police Captain in charge of evidence.*

Yates Raphael: *A television producer who used to work with Kep.*

Tim O'Donnell: *A Cleveland police officer stationed at the front desk.*

Xavier Reese: *An FBI agent assigned to Bernadette's security detail.*

Matt Vermeil: *A correctional officer filling in for co-workers on holiday.*

Annika Nakrivo, aka Anja Kerovic: *Caught between a rock and a hard place, Nakrivo has said her sister Marguerite is in trouble—and Bernadette may be her only hope.*

More by Paul Austin Ardoin

The Woodhead & Becker Mysteries

Book One: The Winterstone Murder

Book Two: The Bridegroom Murder

Book Three: The Trailer Park Murder

Book Four: The Executive Murder

The Fenway Stevenson Mysteries

Book One: The Reluctant Coroner

Book Two: The Incumbent Coroner

Book Three: The Candidate Coroner

Book Four: The Upstaged Coroner

Book Five: The Courtroom Coroner

Novella: The Christmas Coroner

Book Six: The Watchful Coroner

Book Seven: The Accused Coroner

Novella: The Clandestine Coroner

Book Eight: The Offside Coroner

Book Nine: The Warehouse Coroner

Book Ten: The Digital Coroner

Collections

Books 1–3 of The Fenway Stevenson Mysteries

Books 4-6 of The Fenway Stevenson Mysteries

Dez Roubideaux

Bad Weather

Non-fiction

From Zero to Four Figures:

Making $1,000 a Month Self-Publishing Fiction

Sign up for *The Coroner's Report,*

Paul Austin Ardoin's fortnightly newsletter:

http://www.paulaustinardoin.com

I hope you enjoyed reading this book as much as I enjoyed
writing it. If you did, I'd sincerely appreciate a review on your
favorite book retailer's website, Goodreads, and BookBub.
Reviews are crucial for any author, and even just a line or two can
make a huge difference.

Acknowledgments

Many thanks to my cover designer, Ziad Ezzat of Feral Creative. I want to give a special shout-out to the Wordforge Novelists group in Sacramento, whose comments and guidance are always valuable, but whose members went above and beyond to help me after the first draft was finished. I also want to thank the Just Write Milwaukee and Shut Up and Write Milwaukee groups, who provide encouragement and lots of focused writing opportunities.

Thanks to my early readers, including Dana Luco, Charlie Lemoine, Beverly Ange, Dr. Christina Bellinger, and Nicole Prewitt. Every one of you helped make this book better.

I'd also like to thank Jamie Sanfelippo, who keeps my newsletter, social media, and other marketing activities sailing smoothly.

To my wife and my children: I'm deeply grateful for your continued encouragement and support.

To my mother: I'm sorry you weren't around to read this one. I bet you'd have started to like Bernadette a little more!